PRAISE FOR PAUL BLACK'S NOVELS

2-Time WINNER for science fiction
Independent Publisher's Book Award.

Multiple GOLD and SILVER medalist for science fiction,
ForeWord Magazine's Book of the Year.

WINNER for science and general fiction
London, New York and San Francisco Book Festivals.

WINNER for genre fiction
Writer's Digest Magazine's International Book Award

"Science can be a boon to humanity. *The Presence* is a science fiction thriller set in a future where reality is something manufactured by corporations. Sonny Chaco is charged with finding something that resembles law in this world. As he tails one billionaire CEO who may have made those billions with a bit of foul tactics, he finds that the reality-manufacture industry is more tumultuous than he could ever hope, and that throwing in some romance only complicates the complicated. An EXCITING READ that should prove HARD TO PUT DOWN."

~ Midwest Book Review

"*The Presence* is fast-paced thriller, full of smart, interesting characters and suspense. You'll think it's one thing, but it's something else entirely!"

~ Writer's Digest Magazine

"It was a FAST READ and I enjoyed the trip that it took me on. It's one of the better hard Sci-Fi books I've read in a long time, and Paul Black is an author I'm looking forward to seeing more from!"

~ Jordan Mason, themoviepool.com.

"An exciting read that should prove hard to put down."

"Author Paul Black brings a fresh look to the near-future fiction-writing genre."

~ PearlSnapDiscount.com

"*The Presence* is fast-paced and WELL WRITTEN. Paul Black pulls futuristic tech into a believable and seamless world."

~ Darcia Helle, author Quiet Furry Books

"Dallas writer Paul Black makes his first foray into the world of science fiction with *The Tels*. It's a HIGHLY ORIGINAL novel set in the near future and IT MOVES AT LIGHTNING SPEED. Mr. Black has quite an imagination and puts it to good use. The MIND-BENDING PLOT centers on Jonathan Kortel, who is approached by a shadowy group called the Tels, who covet his telekinetic gifts. The ENSUING ACTION IS BIZARRE enough to read like something straight out of The X-Files."

~ Steve Powers, Dallas Morning News

"(*The Tels*) is WRITTEN SO SPLENDIDLY, at times I forgot I was reading science fiction – with the emphasis on fiction. The characters are realistic, and the hero is someone you relate to, worry about and wonder if he's going to be able to cope with the reality that is set before him. This is definitely ONE OF THE BEST SCIENCE FICTION NOVELS I've ever read...the BOOK IS REMARKABLE."

~ Marilyn Meredith, Writer's Digest's 11th Annual Book Awards

"...*Soulware* was a BRILLIANTLY EMBROIDERED STORY, mixing science and fiction in a plausible and entertaining way...I absolutely LOVED THIS BOOK!"

~ Ismael Manzano, G-POP.net

"A riveting science fiction novel by a gifted author."

"This story by Paul Black is as STRONG AND WELL WRITTEN as any of the stories of my heroes: Robert Heinlein, Isaac Asimov, Andre Norton, or Anne McCaffrey. He is one of those writers that we who worship this genre look for every time we pick up the novel of an author who is new to us...The CHARACTERS COME ALIVE for you. You feel right along with them. You can believe the decisions they make. And best of all, nothing is clear-cut and simple. The story brings us to a strong ending while leaving us with the desire for more...I recommend *The Tels* to every lover of sci-fi. Good work, Paul! Welcome to my bookshelves!"

~ John Strange, thecityweb.com

"Paul Black's ENGAGING PROSE promises big things for the future...."

~ Writer's Notes Magazine

"...a GREAT READ, full of suspense and action...."

~ Dallas Entertainment Guide

"A RIVETING science fiction novel by a gifted author...*The Tels* would prove a popular addition to any community library Science Fiction collection and documents Paul Black as an IMAGINATIVELY SKILLED STORYTELLER of the first order. Also very highly recommended is the newly published second volume in the *Tels* series, *Soulware*, which continues the adventures of Jonathan Kortel in the world of tomorrow."

~ Midwest Book Review

"...there's a grittiness and sensuality that pours out of every word..."

"Black rises above the Trekkie laser tag spastics found in your typical sci-fi novels resting on the grocery store racks. His sensibilities broaden from machine gun testosterone to discreet fatherhood, from errant sexuality to wry humor. HE DELIVERS A CHARGE OF VENTURE RARELY FOUND IN FIRST-TIME WRITERS. And *THE TELS* HITS THE MARK as a solid adventure serial, leaving you hanging for the next publication."

~ Brian Adams, Collegian

"*The Tels* is an ADDICTIVE READ from first-time novelist Paul Black, a promising new storyteller on the sci-fi scene. He manages to capture the reader in the first ten pages. He introduces us to a set of intriguing characters in a totally believable possible future. There is a grittiness and sensuality to his writing that pours out of every word in the book. Whether it's his description of the preparation of a good meal, the seduction of a beautiful woman, or a fight to the death, *THE TELS* HAS IT ALL. Even people who don't read sci-fi will want to read this book. The action is great and would make one hell of a movie. Is Hollywood listening? Paul Black has a winner on his hands. I can hardly wait for the next installment."

~ Cynthia A., About Towne, ITCN

"*Soulware* doesn't miss a beat as it continues Jonathan's story, the story of his quest to find out exactly who he really is and why the Tels are so interested in him. The ending makes it clear that there's more to come, and readers who crave their science-fiction with a hint of weirdness can look forward to the next book in the series."

~ Steve Powers, Dallas Morning News

NOVEL INSTINCTS PUBLISHING
Dallas | Santa Fe
www.paulblackbooks.com

ISBN: 978-0-9726007-1-2
1. Fiction / Science Fiction / High Tech 2. Fiction / Romance 3. Thriller / Suspense

Library of Congress Control Number: 2023920978

Printed in the United States of America.
10 9 8 7 6 5 4 3 2 1

First trade paperback edition.

This book's text is typeset in Times New Roman, 10 point / 18 point. Page numbers and chapter heads are in Avalon, and some titles are in Trade Gothic Next Bold Condensed.

BEING HUMAN
HUMAN BEING

PAUL BLACK

NOVEL INSTINCTS

Publishers of fine genre fiction and non-fiction.

1

YOU'RE GOING TO BUY ME DINNER.

Dating sucks.

Seriously, it *really* sucks.

Being in my late 30s and out of the game for years just made it worse. Bars are definitely *not* the place to meet your soulmate. Believe me, I tried. You might get laid, but the aftermath is beyond sad. Apps? I called it swiping and hoping, but the final results were abysmal, so I did what most single (and verging on desperate) adults do … I joined an online dating site.

"I can help the next person!"

"Hi, I have two tickets to the seven-thirty show under Cameron Harrison. I bought 'em online."

The teenaged girl worked the touch screen as if she had a split personality, looking up my purchase with one black-nailed thumb while texting with the other.

"Cameron *William* Harrison?" she asked through a curtain of stringy electric blue and black bangs.

"That's me."

The tickets churned out and she handed them over. "Enjoy your movie. Next in line, please!"

FindMeAnybody.com was one of the most popular dating sites. Its tagline – *When You're Really Desperate* – was spot-on. It asked for more info than a mortgage banker and required a hefty monthly payment, but several of my friends had used it with better than average results. David, my best bro from high school, actually married a girl he met on FindMeAnybody.

I'd been on four dates so far, each uniquely tragic. The initial three barely got out of the gate. The first was gorgeous and about 10 years younger. It was going well until I asked a casual question about one of her tats. Her future plans included flames in the pubic region. Hard pass. The next was the opposite extreme – a professional about my age. Small talk somehow morphed into what amounted to a job interview, but the meal was nice. I tried to split the middle with my next two matches. One couldn't stop posting selfies and food vids long enough to talk, and the other couldn't stop talking about herself. Somehow that was preferable, so we had two more dates. On the last, she confessed she was still in love with her ex, yadda yadda.

Tonight was my fifth and most likely final at-bat. Bottom of the ninth, swing at any decent pitch. Toni Anne Morgan. Her profile was sparse, especially for FindMeAnybody. I think it was the fact she called herself an "entrepreneur" that caught my attention. Code for "I sold my app and now I'm independently wealthy" or "I'm a trust fund baby." That and the fact she was pretty damn cute (I'm a sucker for dimples and curly blonde hair) inspired me to message her. She replied suspiciously quickly.

We messaged for a couple of days. Typical fluff – where did you grow up, what do you like to do when you're not working, what's your favorite restaurant. Replies were the standard fare. She made the first move and asked if I wanted to meet. Typically, I do lunch on the first date, which works well because you can test the chemistry and if it's off, you have a built-in time limit. No hassles. But this time, I don't really know why, I just went for it. Tickets to a movie, drinks, maybe dinner. A high-risk game plan with no exit strategy.

The movie was showing at one of those theater-drinks-dinner multiplexes taking over empty big-box retail spaces in strip centers and malls. I have to admit, the concept was great, especially the faux leather recliners. Press a button, recline, sip a bourbon, watch a great flick. *Love* it. The theater's three levels unfortunately merged into a tangle of staircases that collided in front of the self-order drink stations. As I pushed through the crowd in the lobby, I started to have a bad feeling I might never find Ms. Morgan.

"Pardon me. Excuse me. Sorry. Hi, just want to squeeze by."

I edged along and a guy wearing a Cowboys jersey elbowed me just enough to send a message, as if slowing him one second from him getting his drink on was *that* critical. I'm not small, and the urge to respond boiled up.

I eventually made it to the land of hipsters, who have the discipline to arrive early, relax and sip the latest precious mixology. Here, scarves could be worn regardless of the weather, and the guys sported trendy brown loafers and black jeans. Socks? Blasphemy!

I set my sensors for dimples and curly blonde hair and scanned the booths and two-tops. Nothing.

"Where the hell *are* you?" I muttered.

A short, portly middle-aged man stood from a two-top littered with fast food debris and walked away. Past his empty chair I saw her sitting alone in a booth, hands folded formally on the table. I'm not one for judging a girl just on her looks, but something about Toni, especially in person, dazzled me. Then, as if she had sensed me staring, she looked up and regarded me quizzically. I thought I saw a look of disappointment, but it grew into a smile. She scooted out of the booth and stood.

"Toni Morgan?" I asked, walking up.

"Cameron William Harrison?" Her voice was delicate yet strong. She extended a hand. The tilt of her head and stance were welcoming.

"Please, call me Cam."

"It's nice to meet you."

"You as well."

"You're more handsome in person."

"Um, thanks, I think."

For an awkward second, we took each other in. This was typical of online first dates. A litany of first impressions run through your head. *You seem to take care of yourself. Why did you pick that to wear? Your hair was longer in your profile.* You also can't help imagining what the other person might look like under their clothes. Not in a creepy, perv way. More like, am I attracted to this person? It *is* an actual date. Luckily, Toni was delightfully random. She displayed the unique quality of a lot of European women – the ability to don whatever was handy and fashion it into a chic ensemble. Her scarf looked like it could have come from a thrift store on Lower Greenville, but the torn dark leggings stuffed into glossy black work boots said *I'm an independent thinker with a touch of bad girl.*

I glanced at my phone. "We've got a little time. Can I buy you a drink?"

"That would be great." Her smile showed a little more gum than most.

"Let's save this booth." I took off my jacket and placed it on the table.

Toni watched me as if she had never seen this done. "Won't someone steal your coat?" she asked, looking over her shoulder as we joined the nearest drink line.

"I doubt it. So, um ..." *Oh my God, this girl was making me tongue-tied.* I felt the blush rise in my face. Again, Toni studied me.

"Are you okay?" Her concern was refreshing. "Your skin is changing color."

"Sorry. I'm just getting back into the whole dating scene. And I am *waaay* out of practice."

Her smile returned. "Me too!" She rolled her eyes. Her hand went to my arm in a delightful invasion of my personal space. "I hate small talk."

"Good. That makes me feel a lot better. What would you like to drink?"

She craned to see over a guy in high-waisted khakis to study the huge blackboard and its intimidating, chalk-scribbled list of microbrews. "This menu is crazy big," she said.

"Well, do you like hoppy beers or lighter ones?" I asked.

"Lighter."

The guy scooped up his drinks and stepped aside.

"Hi, folks." The bartender sported the close-cropped beard and half-shaved head popular with the tat-and-pierced crowd. An elaborate dragon crawled out of his starched white shirt and halfway up his neck. "What can I get you?"

"Two Hill Country pilsners," I said.

"Sixteen or twenty?"

As I said 16, Toni answered 20. The bartender smiled, glancing at me, and grabbed two glasses off the counter.

I leaned against the bar. "So you like beer?"

She thought for a quick second. "Yes, I think so."

"You *think*?"

"No, I mean I do."

The bartender topped off the pulls and slid our drinks up. "What else folks?"

"You want anything else?" I asked her.

Toni shook her head.

I paid for the drinks and we settled back into the booth. "I didn't even ask if you'd seen this–"

The sight of Toni polishing off her entire 20 ounces stopped me mid-sentence. I think, though I can't swear to it, she just opened her throat and poured it down. She lowered the tall glass and demurely placed it between us.

I watched the remains of the beer's head slide down the sides of the empty glass. "Toni, um … do you *usually* polish off your beer that fast?" I couldn't hide my sarcasm. My FindMeAnybody dream girl was becoming a familiar nightmare.

Her brow knotted. "I don't know. I guess–" The belch that erupted from her mouth would have been the envy of any high-school kegger. Awkwardness filled the space between us. A guy at a nearby table shot me a serious *What the hell?* look.

"Wow!" Toni exclaimed through a nervous giggle. "That was *so* cool."

At this point in a date going sideways, I would've been formulating my exit strategy, but all I could do was lean back and take in this bizarrely engaging woman.

"Since your profile said you were born in Ireland, I'm going to give you a pass on the beer-chugging and monstrously inappropriate burp thing." I laughed.

Toni put her hand over her mouth. "I'm so sorry." Her sincerity seemed completely genuine. "It just," she shrugged, "came out."

"Yes," I said leaning into her quirky charm, "it certainly did."

"*The seven-thirty showing of* The Carriage Tale *is now available for seating in Theater One.*" The male voice from the P.A. sounded all of 13.

I motioned for us to get in the queue. "That's us."

The Carriage Tale had garnered tremendous social media buzz and was up for half a dozen Oscars, so the line was already long. As we walked in silence, I couldn't get a read on Toni. Maybe she was deeply embarrassed or naturally shy, but her body language suggested something different, because every few steps our shoulders bumped. I think she was making it happen in some playful *I kind of dig you* way.

"So, Toni, when did you come over … from Ireland?"

She was an inch shorter than me and when she looked over, her smile was infectious. We stopped at the back of the line.

"I was very young ... about five or so."

"Hence no accent."

"I was, um, adopted, and we moved to Chicago."

"Really? I was born and raised in the western suburbs. Where did you live?"

Her hesitation was odd. The smile fell away.

Shit. I broke my first date rule: never dig too deeply with the conversation. I put a polite hand to her shoulder. "Hey, look, if this is a sensitive subject, you don't have to talk about it."

"No, it's not." The smile returned. "I was just–"

A guy in a shabby army jacket with unkempt stubble and the stench to match pushed through the crowd and brushed past us. His gait and the look on his face suggested he was late for his movie. Toni was knocked off balance, and my hand to her shoulder steadied her.

I gave the guy a little shove as he hurried past. "Hey douche," I said to his back, "get some manners."

The intensity in the snarl the guy shot me over his shoulder was jarring. I threw it back at him. He angrily pulled his look away and kept pressing through the crowd.

"You okay?" I asked Toni.

She waved it off. "He's an asshole deluxe."

I hardly knew this girl, but I liked her. I patted her shoulder and she actually leaned into my little affection test. The line began to move.

"Come on," I said, "let's go see the movie–"

Suddenly, a commotion broke out behind us. I turned and saw the Asshole Deluxe climbing onto the condiment station's counter. People were quickly backing away.

He struck a defiant stance and threw open his army jacket. The C4 vest was frighteningly recognizable. To my left, a woman's scream cut the air.

"ALLAHU AKBAR!" he yelled.

The room erupted into chaos.

The detonation's light flash was blinding.

I've never been to war or experienced a real explosion, much less from 30 feet away. My world crawled to a terrifying slow motion. I dove to the floor and clenched my eyes expecting the eternal blackness.

A deafening crack accompanied the light flash but it seemed too short, as if stopped midstream. Most people had also gone to the floor, some covering their loved ones, others curled into tight, fetal positions.

From the corner of my eye, where Asshole Deluxe had stood, I saw a perfectly round, swirling cloud of white smoke about 10 feet in diameter. The cloud appeared held together by a rippling distortion of air that undulated across the entire surface. Patches of red and pink and what looked like chunks of raw beef circulated as if in a large food processor, occasionally rising to the surface only to be sucked back into the storm.

Farther away, people were crouched and cowering, but others, who had looked back, were straightening and staring. A few had turned toward the exits. Then it hit me.

Where was Toni?

I looked around and saw her standing behind me. She was facing the maelstrom with a far-away look.

I grabbed her leg. "*Toni?*"

She was oblivious. Her arms were extended about waist height, and her hands moved nonchalantly, as if she were calmly molding a meatball about the size of a melon. Her hand movements seemed to direct the distortion around the sphere.

She stopped and cupped her hands together. The swirling storm of smoke and blood and body parts stopped, and the cloud compressed to the size of a soccer ball. Everyone was mesmerized watching the scene unfold. Toni pivoted to her right and the sphere followed. It hovered over a service cart's large open trash bin. Toni opened her cupped hands and the sphere plopped into the bin. Scraps of what had been the Asshole Deluxe splashed up and some tiny chunks splatted onto the floor. Dense white smoke rose from the bin, which sent the already panic-stricken theater goers into a wave of screams and an all-out mad dash for the exits. As the hysterical mob scrambled around us, I stood.

Toni's far-away look quickly receded. She turned to me and smiled. My brain was in overdrive. Either I just hallucinated the whole scene, or I was looking at a real life superhero. I grabbed her by the shoulders. My hands were shaking.

"What the hell *are* you?!" I demanded.

Her grin got a little goofier and she shied at my question.

"Do you realize you're on camera?!" I pointed to the black bubbles embedded in the ceiling. "Not to mention cell phones. This is going viral worldwide in about a frickin' second."

Her grin vanished. She jerked to stare at one of the bubbles, then the others. She raised a hand between us and spread her fingers. The cameras exploded, showering black plastic into the room and sending the last of the few remaining staff and customers fleeing for their lives.

Through the dissipating smoke, my FindMeAnybody dream date slowly brought her attention around and planted it on me. I reflexively took a step back and almost fell over an overturned café chair. The terror on my face must have been apparent, because Toni's stern expression melted away.

"I won't hurt you," she said with intelligent calm.

I waved my hands in a gesture that said *Get the hell away from me.*

She tilted her head and a soft grin appeared. "Come on, Cam." She stepped to my side and slid her arm around mine.

Toni started walking me toward the exit. A wave of ice-cold panic shot through me. "W-what are you doing?"

"I'm not doing a thing."

"What's that mean?" I asked, stumbling through the litter of overturned chairs, spilled popcorn boxes, and discarded purses.

"Our date is just starting." She squeezed my arm affectionately. "*You're* going to buy me dinner."

2

THIS IS A GOOD MAN.

We hurried from the theater to the sea of cars in the parking lot. In the distance, the din of sirens indicated that Dallas's finest were descending on the scene. The all-out panic inside the theater had spilled out to the sidewalks and the mall's common areas. Some ran for their lives; others huddled together in small groups; a few stood alone, crying. All were on their cell phones.

Toni had been on hers since we'd exited the theater, but the phone I saw in the few rushed glances didn't look like anything I had *ever* seen. The screen had no text or icons, just bright undulating blobs of color.

"So," Toni asked, pocketing the device in her coat, "where are we going?"

As we walked through the parking lot, I pulled my arm away, gained a little distance and shot her a harsh look. "Really? *Dinner?*"

"Sure, why not?"

As I angled through the BMWs, Teslas and F-150s I clicked my car's fob and it chirped two rows over. Toni was trailing, trying to keep up. I turned and cautiously regarded her when I reached the car. While she was very cute, dimples and all, there was now an ominous aura about her. What *was* she? Part of me was scared shitless, while another part was intrigued. Lurking in the background was the part that found her desirable, although it was rapidly losing ground to the other two. By the time she made it to the passenger door, every conceivable type of emergency vehicle was arriving at the theater doors.

"I'm sorry, you just went all Jean Grey in there, and I'm supposed to buy you *dinner?* You're gonna be the opening segment on every major newscast on the planet. Not to mention every social media outlet. I can't deal with this shit. Get out of here."

"Cam*eron.*" She leaned across the roof. "Don't *leave* me. I might be in big trouble."

I yanked open the driver's side door. "*Not* my problem."

Around us, people were hastily jumping into their cars and pulling out. A few shot worried glances our way.

"Cameron, *please*. Listen to me." She pointed to the theater. "I just saved dozens of lives in there, hundreds, maybe. I saved *yours*. Don't you want to know?"

She had me. I *did* want to know. This was epic, and if I walked away, I'd probably regret it the rest of my life. "Alright, yes ... I *do.*"

Toni extended her hand across the roof, inviting me to hold it. "I know you're kind of confused right now."

"Freaked is a better word." I put my hands in my jacket pockets. She withdrew hers.

"Look ... what I did in there ... it was a violation–"

Violation?

"–and there might be consequences, for me."

I shot her a stern, questioning glare.

"There's something else," she said.

"*What?*"

Toni reprised the shy look from before. "There's something ... between us."

"You're playing me."

"No! No, I'm not. You felt it, I could tell. And I felt it, too."

She had me again. God, she was cute. Ever since my wife's death, I hadn't felt even the slightest attraction to *any* woman. *Shit.* This was either going to be the biggest mistake I had ever made or one hell of an adventure. Either way, I had a feeling my life was going to change for*ever.* "Screw it." I gestured to the passenger side door. "Get in."

*   *   *   *

On a Friday night Terilli's is usually rocking and this Friday was no exception. The drive was awkward and totally silent. Toni was back focused on her phone/tablet thing, interfacing with it like it was her firstborn. Lucky for us, my buddy Josh was bartending. I texted him and begged for two spots at the bar.

"Cam, my man!"

"Hey, Josh." We bumped fists over the bar. "Thanks for making this happen."

"No problema." Josh eyed Toni. "And who is this lovely creature?"

I bit back a wry laugh. "Creature" was an understatement. "Josh Taylor, this is Toni Morgan." I pulled out my phone and started swiping through the news feeds.

"Thank you so much, Josh," Toni said, climbing onto the bar chair.

"Y'all eating?"

"Yes!" she said.

Josh snapped out cloth placemats, then set down menus and silverware roll-ups.

"Let's start with some drinks," he said. "Cam, the usual?"

"Double, please." CNN was completely covered with a dam failure in Kentucky. WFAA had a small blurb in their time-feed about a "failed terrorist event" at a mall in Dallas, but no images. And the bar's two big screens had sports feeds, thank God.

"For the lady?"

"Same," Toni said.

I looked up. "You don't know what I'm having."

"I trust your taste." The giggle was back.

"Two double Eagle Rares, lots of ice, coming up," Josh said. "Oh, and our special tonight is a miso sea bass, with smashed potatoes and a small Caesar."

"What are you looking for?" Toni asked me.

"Checking the major news sites to see if there's anything posted."

"Is there?"

"Nothing national yet. Channel 8 had a snippet, but no details or images." I pocketed my phone.

"That's good, isn't it?" Toni glanced over her shoulder. She had done this before out on the street after I had given my car fob to the valet.

Usually, Terilli's featured a jazz combo, but tonight there was only the tumult of the crowd. I caught Josh's attention as he poured our drinks. He gave me a thumbs up and mouthed *Way to go, bro.*

"Something wrong?" I asked Toni.

"No, why?" Apprehension edged her words.

"You keep looking over your shoulder."

"It's just weird being on another planet."

Oh, Jesus. Planet? "Okay." The bizarreness of what I was getting myself into was settling in. "Let's hear it."

"Hear what?"

"Your backstory ... the *real* one, and not the crap you posted at *FindMeAnybody.*"

"Here you go." Josh delivered our drinks with a flourish.

Toni took hers and raised it to me. "To us." The look she flashed was damn sexy.

I reluctantly raised my glass. "Right."

Toni began to take a big drink, but I put a hand to her wrist.

"You sip this," I implored.

She grinned and nodded, then took a cautious sip. "Oh, this is *good*. What is this?"

"Bourbon."

She took another sip while I knocked back a gulp.

Toni faced me and scooted her chair closer. It was a bit of an encroachment, but at this point, what the hell?

"What's a backstory?" she asked.

"You know, your history, what you do for a living. Or are you some super mutant from a secret government project?" I let my sarcasm carry the words and took another long pull.

"Oh, I'm not *that*," Toni said, like it was the stupidest question she'd ever heard.

"Then what the hell *are* you?" I didn't hide my impatience.

She set her drink down and pivoted the sexy look again. "I'm an alien."

"Very funny. Texas is full of them."

Toni Morgan leaned in until she was a few inches away.

"No, Cam," she said. "I'm," her eyes went to the bar's ceiling and landed back on mine, "an *alien*."

She was close enough to see the detail in her beautiful blue eyes. I think something swam across her pupils. I flinched.

"So what are we having tonight?" Josh asked, walking up.

I swung my attention over. "Dude ... we need a minute." I looked back at Toni, who was smiling around the rim of her glass. "Maybe a long minute."

"Just wave me over when you're ready to order."

I tried to process what Toni had said and was seriously thinking I had made a *huge* mistake. This girl was probably batshit crazy, and I didn't need any part it. I gulped down half my drink.

Toni put a hand to my wrist. "Easy, Cam … you *sip* it."

This was getting really weird. "Look, an *alien* … are you shitting me?"

Horror washed over Toni. "We don't *eat* your species." She made a face. "That's disgusting."

"No, Toni. It's an expression. It means are you *fooling* me."

"Oh … no, I'm not fooling you."

"Then please tell me you're not going to experiment on me."

Toni brought back the sexy look. She leaned in again. "Well, that depends on your definition of experiment."

In any other situation, I would've dismissed Toni's declarations as the ramblings of a disturbed person. But given what I had just witnessed, I was willing to consider the possibility. Defying the laws of physics has a way of getting your attention. Still, I was more than a bit nervous.

"So what's this?" I gestured at her. "Some kind of disguise, or do y'all naturally look like us?"

Toni glanced down at herself. "What … my ride?"

"Ride? You mean your body? What is it, a clone or something?"

"That's the closest term in your language."

"Where do you get the … I don't know, DNA?"

"I believe you call them mortuaries. We operate several of them across your world in the largest population areas that support the four main race sectors. When one of your people dies, we use the DNA from the body to build," she gestured to herself, "one of these. We only use people who have chosen to be burned."

"Cremated."

"Yes, cremated. We also try and pick people who come from small or no families. It's better that way."

"What did you mean by race sectors?"

"We've divided your planet into four main racial sectors. White-Caucasion, Mongoloid-Asian, Negroid-Black and Australiod. Variety is important when vacationing. You see, when–"

I put a hand up. "Wait a minute … *vacationing*?"

"What did you think?" She sat up and grew serious. In a lame robot voice, she said, "We are here to take over your planet. Take me to your leader."

"The thought had occurred to me."

"You watch too much of your science fiction, which, by the way, is waaaaay off."

"Look, seriously, if you *are* from another planet, which I'm thinking you might be since I just saw you create a force field with your hands, why vacation here?"

Again, her look suggested this was the stupidest question in the history of the world. "This is the coolest planet in the known universe. There's so much to do here. It has warm water and biodiversity and–"

"Okay, so if Earth is the Ibiza of the galaxy, where are you from?"

"My world is in what you call the constellation Draco. It's a watery planet much bigger than Earth, but our star is a red dwarf that emits less heat and light than your Sun, so our planet orbits pretty close to it. By your measure of space, it's about a hundred light-years away."

"So you're really close to us," I said, "relatively speaking."

"Very."

"And you're on *vacation*?"

"Uh-huh," she said through another sip of bourbon.

"How does that work? I mean–"

Then it struck me. I was making small talk with an alien, a real god-damn *alien*. But at the same time, in front of me sat an awesomely attractive woman, by human standards. I couldn't help but be attracted to her. What did she look like without the skin suit? A giant spider from *Starship Troopers*?

Toni's hand to my forearm snapped me back.

"Where did you go?" she asked.

I focused on her eyes and let my gaze linger. She held my stare.

"You're wondering what I really am," she said after a long pause.

What the hell, could she also read minds? "Um, yeah."

"Does it matter?" she asked.

Fair question. "Well–"

"Right now, in this body, I'm as human as you are."

"Are you sure?"

She made a sweeping gesture with her hand to the bar area. "How are you experiencing the world around you?"

I knew where she was going. "Through my senses, processed by my brain."

"Then how do you know *you're* not from another planet, here on vacation, but just don't know it?"

Another fair question, and it did raise an interesting possibility. "Okay … I'll give you that."

The hint of a smile appeared. "I still feel this." She gestured back-and-forth between us. "Do you?"

"Yeah ... I guess."

"Even though I could be a green glob of goo on my world?"

"Are you?"

She shook her head. "No, I'm actually blue."

"Ha-ha. Is humor big on your world?"

"Your species has the lock on that." She took my hand in hers. Her skin was warm, almost hot. "Cam?"

"Yes?"

"Do you understand what I was saying?"

"That it's what's inside that counts?"

"Maybe."

I scooted my bar chair in closer and took her hands into mine. "I'm not going to lie to you, this is the most bizarre date I have *ever* been on, and I'm really wrestling with the idea that you're an alien on vacation. I mean, come on ... that is literally–"

"Out of this world?"

"I thought you didn't have humor on your planet."

"Cam, there are many constants in the universe. The laws you call physics kind of force that. Your species, at this point in your development, has only scratched the surface of what's possible. I know all this is hard to process." The delicate smile returned. "On my planet, this connection, it doesn't happen like it does here. We don't have ... *this*."

"What do you mean by *this*?"

She shrugged. "I don't know. I'm still adjusting. I just know that what I'm feeling is different."

"Different than what?"

"Friendship?"

"Look, Toni, or whatever your name is, we just met, and in a crazy way. Typically, on my planet, when two people meet, they don't instantly get this," I gestured to me and her, like she had. "You have to get to know a person, date them for a while, see if there *is* a connection."

"I *know*. We study all this before we arrive."

"Study? Come on, you can't possibly learn all our languages, much less the slang and idiosyncrasies. That would take years. And there's our cultural rituals and subtleties. You can't get that from a manual."

"Cam, we've been at this for a long time, and your world isn't the first that we've encountered. There are other universals beyond physics that your species hasn't discovered yet. Technologies that would make what you have today seem primitive. You're correct, we can't know all the unique subtleties of every culture, but that's part of the fun of vacationing here ... experiencing what a human body feels like."

I grabbed my drink and finished it off. An adorable pout formed on Toni's face. Jesus. Could there be more? "*What?*" I asked.

"Setting aside the social ritual, I don't know what I'm feeling right now."

I propped an elbow on the bar and rested my cheek on my hand. "You really *are* new to this, aren't you?"

She mimicked me and swirled the ice in her drink. "I am, Cam."

"Is that what your vacations are all about?"

"For some. For most it's just about getting away."

I pointed with my empty glass. "Why are *you* here?"

Toni straightened and thought for a moment.

"You okay?" I asked.

She hesitantly nodded and looked like she might cry.

"Hey, what's the matter?"

"I don't know. I'm feeling another different emotion."

"Describe it."

"Loneliness? Is that right?" She looked at me like I had the answer. "I don't have the words to describe it."

"Did I hit a nerve?" Did aliens even have nerves?

She turned her hands over. "You didn't hit anything."

"No, it's also an expression. It means I brought up a subject that triggered a raw emotion. It's usually an emotion that's been suppressed, and I'm going to go out on a limb here and say that this connection you're feeling, with me, well ... that's missing in your life wherever you come from ... right?"

"Cala," she said, under her breath.

"Excuse me?"

"We call it Cala. You may be right."

Loneliness is a weird thing. It can sneak up on you and really do a number. Since Karen had died three years ago, I had been in its grip. Maybe it was one of those universal constants Toni had mentioned earlier. I know I was tired of it. I hesitated, then put a hand to her shoulder and rubbed. Her muscles were tense. She closed her eyes and leaned into it. Even though I was still torn about whether to believe her or not, she was right ... there *was* a connection. And it was wonderful to feel it again.

"That's nice," she said.

"Don't you study human emotions to prep for your vacations?" I stopped rubbing and waited for an answer.

She slowly opened her eyes. "We do. We're warned about many of them."

"Warned?"

"It takes time to get accustomed to being human. Emotional states, when we arrive, are very ... unpracticed. Many of your emotions are hard to control without experience. Sometimes it can be dangerous."

Josh interrupted. "Um, guys?"

"Hey, bro," I said.

"The kitchen is closing in 30 minutes. You still want dinner?"

"What do you think, Toni?... You still hungry?"

"No. I think I just want to go home."

"Tab us out."

Josh wagged a finger. "No, sir. These are on me."

"What? No, dude, just tab us out."

Josh leaned onto the bar. "How long have I known you?"

"Since high school."

"Right. And I haven't seen you like this since ... well ... you know."

"No ... like what?" I knew where he was going.

He gestured between Toni and me. "*This*."

"Thanks, man, but–"

"Nope. Your money's no good tonight." He spoke to Toni. "I don't know what's going on here, but I can tell you one thing," he pointed to me, "this is a good man, right here."

Toni folder her arms and eyed me. "I'm beginning to sense that."

Josh straightened and slapped the bar. "Okay, now, you two be safe going home."

I bumped fists with him. "Thanks, Josh. I'll talk to you tomorrow."

As we walked through the club, Toni did her little shoulder bump thing. There was a chill in the late-night spring air. I handed the valet my ticket and he ran off. We stood on the sidewalk and silently let the energy flow between us.

"Where do you live?" I asked.

"West Village."

"Did you Uber to the theater?"

"Yeah."

The cool wind slapped the collar of my coat across my neck. Toni leaned against me. It caught me off guard, but after a second I put my arm around her. She went with it.

"Hey, Cameron Harrison?"

"Yes, Toni Morgan?"

"I don't think I want to go home."

3

LIKE WHAT YOU SEE?

I padded barefoot through my loft and sat in the chair next to the couch. In the morning light, Toni resembled a young Meg Ryan from that old rom-com my wife had made me watch years back. She was tucked up under my UT letter blanket, softly snoring. Roz-boz, my chubby, 10-year-old black-and-white knucklehead of a cat, was curled up in the crook of her waist.

When we got to my loft last night, the local newscasts were done. I switched to CNN, but it was still consumed with the dam failure. Since there had been no real damage or loss of life at the theater, the dam, along with a 767 that skidded off the runway at London Heathrow, should bury our little "theater incident." Toni and I passed the time with short-lived small talk.

Whatever she had done at the theater had left her exhausted. She did, however, go to the window and glance down to the street. When I questioned her, she just brushed it off again as the weirdness of being on a new planet. As far as I could tell, she was worried about the ramifications with "her people." I offered my bed and I would take the couch, but she insisted that the couch would be fine. Who was I to argue with someone from an alien master race?

Toni stirred. She opened her eyes.

"Good morning," I said.

"Good morning," she replied through a smile-yawn.

Roz-boz twisted on her back and stretched both her front paws toward Toni.

"Oh." Toni was clearly uncomfortable with an earthly house cat spooning with her. "Who do we have here?"

"That," I pointed with my coffee cup, "is the Rozinator, also called the Roz-boz, and to me often just No-Roz. Let me move her."

I picked up Roz and she squeaked and squirmed in protest.

"The concept of pets is very foreign on my world," Toni said, sitting up.

"Here, they're treated better than humans." I let Roz down and she scampered away.

Toni patted the cushion next to her. "Come here."

I sat, and she snuggled up. I didn't have anything in the way of female sleepwear, but my old workout sweats kind of fit her in a baggy-sexy-morning-after sort of way.

"Thank you," she said.

"For what?"

"Not running away."

I put my arm around her. "What kind of host would I be if I didn't help out an intergalactic guest? After all, this is the largest, most exclusive resort in the universe, and we aim to give our guests the perfect experience." I hugged her and kissed the top of her head.

Shit! I just broke my second dating rule: never kiss unless you positively know she wants you to.

I pulled out of our embrace. "Um, sorry. I don't know why I just did that."

Toni sat up and looked at me. It wasn't the delicate smile or the quizzical look, just her, taking me in.

"What are you thinking?" she asked.

"Well…"

"Be honest."

"I want to kiss you."

She leaned in. "Then kiss me."

I did, gently. She felt warm and wonderful against my lips.

"Wow," she whispered, pulling back, "what was *that?*"

"Let me show you." I took her into my arms and put my all into my kiss.

THWACK.

Toni yelped against my lips. We both looked in the direction of the noise. Roz had knocked over a picture on my bookshelf.

Toni put a hand to her chest. "My heart, it's …"

"Racing?"

"What a weird sensation."

"You were startled. It's natural. Don't worry, you're not damaged."

I pulled out of our embrace and walked over to the shelf. How can a little frame make such a loud noise? I righted it into position next to the last pic I took of my mom and dad.

"Who is she?" Toni asked. "Your sister?"

"No, she was someone very dear to me."

Toni's quizzical look appeared. Then her eyes went big with realization.

"Oh," she said, "that's your wife, right?"

" *Was* my wife."

She walked over and put a hand to my arm.

"Cam, I'm so sorry. You had mentioned you were a widower … in your profile."

"It's okay. It's in the past."

"Can I ask how she died?"

"A drunk ran a red light. T-boned her into oncoming traffic, then a semi plowed into her car. Poof. Gone." I looked at her pic, her smile frozen in time during our last vacation in Paris. The pain began to rise, but I pushed it down. "Well," I said, "I don't know about you, but I'm starving."

Toni's look said she wasn't buying my change in subject. "Your species is very complex."

"How's that?" I asked, leading her into the kitchen.

"For one, you hide from so many of your emotions in a desperate attempt to avoid pain." Toni climbed onto a bar stool and leaned onto the counter. "But all you do is actually create more pain."

"They teach you that in your classes?" I topped off my cup. "You want some?"

"Yes, please. Just sugar. And, no, it's something I've picked up on."

"Do you mourn on your planet?" I poured her cup and handed it over along with my sugar shaker.

She took them and proceeded to pour in about a pound.

"You want some coffee with that?" I asked.

"This stuff," she pointed to the shaker, "is *amazing*."

"You didn't answer my question." And I had about a million of them.

"Death is different for us," she said, then slurped.

"How so?"

"We live a lot longer than you do, and for the elites in our society, life can be extended almost indefinitely."

"Then death has no meaning?"

"I wouldn't say that. We do pass on, as you call it, which, I have to say, is such a wonderful way to express the concept."

"But for some, like the elites, it doesn't happen often, right?"

"Correct," she said.

"Do you still feel the pain of the loss?"

"Not really, because by the time someone dies, their life has been long and full and there's really no reason to mourn. … At least, not like you do … with all the sadness I mean."

"I'm envious." I leaned onto the counter and savored my coffee. "So how old are you, in our years? If you don't mind me asking."

Toni thought for a second. "One hundred and eighty-four, give or take two or three."

"So you're a cougar."

The puzzled look was back. "I'm a human, not an animal. Although, some on my planet do choose to vacation as one. But it's *really* expensive."

I glanced warily at Roz as she ambled through, headed toward her water bowl. "Really? That's crazy."

"No, Cam." She took another loud slurp. "That was a joke."

"We're going to have to work on your manners."

"Oh, yes, please. Local customs are one of the hardest aspects to learn."

"To start, no slurping and no more burping. People here don't like it, at least in America."

Toni straightened and saluted. "Yes-*sir.*"

"And don't do that."

"What?"

"Mock. It's not polite. Sends the wrong message."

She shied. "Yes sir," she whispered.

I shook my head. "Do you know how adorable you are?"

"Maybe. We get to pick out our ride. I thought this one was exceptionally cute."

"Tell me all about this vacationing thing. How does that work? Do you pick out the kind of human you want to be?"

Toni looked down at herself. She cupped her boobs and bounced them through the sweat top. "I really like my ride. It's pretty without being too pretentious, and it's strong, but not real muscled." She looked up. "What do you think?"

"Honestly?"

"Yes, please."

"I think you're hot."

Toni put a hand to her forehead. "I am? I don't feel warm."

I stifled a laugh. "It means you're sexy, and I'm attracted to you."

"You *are* ... to my ride?"

I felt myself getting aroused and wished I wasn't wearing my thin cool-fit running shorts.

"Very." I leaned against the counter in a desperate attempt to stem my growing bulge. "Now, last night you said these rides are clones." It wasn't quite *Invasion of the Body Snatchers*, but there was a creepiness to it. "Has someone vacationing ever, you know, run into someone who recognized the body they were in?"

"Not that I know of, but I guess the potential is always present. From what I understand, there's a long time-lag between when the DNA is harvested and development of the body."

"That's reassuring. So how do they get *you* into *that* body?"

Toni turned and lifted the hair off the back of her neck. "Cerebral particle implant." She passed her finger across a tiny scar at the base of her neck. "It's a technology beyond your civilization's current level."

I came around the counter and looked closer. The scar was a perfect line, about the size of an inch-long piece of thread.

"Go ahead," she said, "touch it."

I did, and a faint glow appeared under the skin. I recoiled. "It just glowed."

"White or green?"

I touched it again. "White."

She turned around and smiled. "Compatibility."

"Really?"

"Every living creature, no matter what planet they come from, has a unique energy signature."

"An aura."

"That *is* a word for it, although it's not that mystical. The implant allows me to project into this body. The technology where I reside recognizes the energy signature of this body and," she gestured to herself again, "here I am, literally in the flesh."

"Projected? From where? You're close by?"

"I believe you call it the dark side of the moon."

Brilliant. "Really? Why haven't we detected you?"

Toni shot me an *Are you kidding?* look. "Cam, we're about ten thousand years ahead of you. I think we can hide ourselves."

"So what's there ... on the dark side of the moon?"

"A whole complex. First, there's our portal. It's how we travel through space."

"How do you do that? Warp time?"

Toni thought for a second, then laughed. "*Star Trek!* Warp signature."

"Yes."

"No, *Dune* was closer. The only word that might apply in your language would be fold."

"You *fold* space?"

Her face scrunched with frustration. "That's not quite it either. Traversable time-tunnels represent a class of exact metric solutions of the general relativistic field–"

I put my hands up. "Whoa, easy, girl. Dumb this down a bit."

"Okay, yes ... we fold space."

"Let me see if I have this right – you're in a pod, in an alien complex, on the dark side of the moon, projecting into a very old cloned human body, all to go on vacation."

"It isn't a pod, really."

"I'm in fucking *Avatar*," I said to myself. "Do you study our pop culture before arriving?"

"We do study many of your popular trends, especially science-fiction. ... It gives us insight into how you might perceive us. There's really no better way to learn about a civilization than through its arts and culture."

"I wouldn't lump our pop culture into the classical arts. Tell me, though, how long are you here? I mean, how long are your vacations?"

"For the elites, as long as they want. I've heard of some who've lived out a whole human lifespan here. But that's an extreme commitment. For the rest of us, just for a few of your months ... maybe a year."

"So you could be here a long time?"

"In theory."

Toni had her full sultry on. She stepped into my open arms. I pulled her close and she flinched.

"Hel-*lo*," she said looking down at my crotch. "They warned us about humans like you."

I stepped back. "Sorry. Natural reaction. It's kind of hard to control, especially with someone you're attracted to."

"Your skin is changing color again," Toni pressed against me. "I kind of like what I'm feeling." She rose up on her toes. "Kiss me again."

I did, and after about two minutes of serious necking, she stepped back.

"What?" I asked. "Did I do something wrong?"

Toni reproduced the sexy look from Terilli's and began unbuttoning the sweat top. It fell off her shoulders and landed around her ankles. Then she wriggled the sweatpants down and stepped out of them. She put her hands on her hips. "Like what you see?" she purred.

Toni's body was, at least for me, perfect. Her curly blonde hair fell down over her shoulders beautifully and stopped just above a set of exquisite small breasts. Her tummy was flat, but not ripped which can be a bit of a turn off. A tiny patch of strawberry blonde pubic hair disappeared into the crook of her toned thighs.

"Very much," I said.

She pointed at my groin. "Who's *that?*" she asked, playfully.

I looked down. "I think this is one of those universal constants." I pulled my t-shirt over my head and tossed it into the corner. My running shorts followed.

Toni pressed all of herself against me. "I think, Mr. Harrison, it's time for this alien to do some experiments on you."

4

LA VIDA LOCA.

We made it to the bedroom, barely, and she seemed intent on trying every conceivable position in one night. Was she experimenting, or had she memorized a Top 10 list? Believe me, I am *not* complaining, but she had a bit of trouble understanding the male human need to recuperate after orgasm. They must've skipped that part in classes, but to be frank, I've never seen a woman react with such deep passion. Don't get me wrong. My wife and I had an amazing sex life, but this was something different.

In the morning I took Toni to her apartment in West Village to change clothes. I waited in the car. We grabbed lunch to go from one of my favorite ramen places and ate in the park near Turtle Creek. Driving back to my loft, the sheer size of Dallas seemed to fascinate her, which made me wonder what cities were like on her home world. Did they even have cities? We got to my apartment around three and she led me back into the bedroom again.

We fell asleep naked on top of the sheets. Toni moaned. I woke and twisted onto one elbow. In the soft early evening light, I could only make out the contour of her face. I wondered if sleep was normal to her species. And did they dream? Was she dreaming now about her earthly experiences or her Calaian ones?

She moaned again.

"Hey," I whispered as I touched her on the hip, "you okay?"

Toni felt warm, like she was running a fever. Maybe it was the tech inside of her. I stroked her head and she made a guttural growl, kind of the way Roz did when she spotted a squirrel out the window.

I kissed her forehead. Her eyes slowly opened.

"Hi," she whispered.

"Hi." I scooted my body next to hers.

"You feel good against me."

"You do, too."

"What time is it?"

I glanced at my phone. "About six-thirty."

"Morning or evening?"

"Evening."

"I'm hungry."

"I know a great place."

She turned face-to-face and snuggled into my arms. "Let's go back to Terilli's. I like your friend."

I grabbed my phone off the nightstand and texted Josh. He answered almost immediately.

"They're slow right now. He said come on in."

"Good." She squeezed me tight. "But not yet." Her hand moved south and went searching. "Oh, what happened to it? I want to continue with our experiments."

"Sorry, lady. You need to feed me."

She slapped my chest. "Not fair."

"That's the way it is. Say, can I ask you something?"

"You can ask me anything."

"What did you mean, outside the theater, when you said you violated something by doing that, you know, whatever it was that you did with Asshole Deluxe? And how *did* you do that?"

"Gravity."

"You can control gravitational force?"

"Uh-huh," she said, stifling a yawn.

"Just like that?"

Toni raised her hand and snapped her fingers. Roz, who had hopped up and was about to climb on our legs, lifted off the bed and hovered a foot off of the blanket. She tried to squirm, but something held her in position. I could barely make out the faint ripple of a distortion field around her. Roz, even though she had resting panic face, looked more panicked than usual. Toni gently lowered her and the distortion vanished. Roz sprang off the bed.

"That's amazing," I said. "How does it work?"

"The technology behind my implant allows us to control your planet's gravitational field, in limited ways at limited distances. We have a mental cue we trigger, and the field is created. All I have to do is think about what kind of field I want, and it happens. And I don't have to snap my fingers. I just did that for effect. More fun that way."

"Why do you have it ... the gravity thing?"

"Protection."

It made a lot of sense. Earth, no matter where you are, is a dangerous place.

"It's essentially undetectable and instantly deployable," she said.

"Can it stop a bullet or a missile?"

"Mine can't." She yawned, turned away and hugged one of the king pillows. "Besides, vacation isn't about stopping one of your stupid wars."

Fair enough. "What about money?"

This elicited a little chuckle. She twisted back around. "This obsession with currency is so funny. You're the only inhabited planet that still depends on this type of system to function."

"Yeah, but you're here, so how do you live?"

"Remember when I said we're ten thousand years ahead of you?"

"What, do you get unlimited funds?"

"If we want, but it's discouraged. It draws too much attention. In your civilization, people who are mega rich are celebrities or important business-people. None of your billionaires live under the radar, so one can't just sudden-ly appear out of thin air. We can have a lot of fun without going crazy-rich-human. And it isn't all about fun, Cam. Some of my kind come here as an anthropological quest. ... They don't want to be rich or live *la vida loca*. They want to experience the human condition."

I slid my arm under her head and pulled her close. "What do *you* want to do on your summer vacation, young lady?"

She grinned big and her eyes squinted into adorable slits. She raised her fists and punched the air. "I want to live *la vida loca!*"

*   *   *   *

"Do you still have the miso sea bass?" Toni asked.

"Yes, ma'am." Josh was on point.

While Toni showered, I had texted him that we would be there in about an hour, *and* that she had stayed the night. Big news in my small world. I also told him there might be something building between me and my Find-MeAnybody date. He replied with a string of emojis: crazy face, heart and a hand making the "OK" sign, which caught me because I wasn't sure what that meant beyond okay. I asked him, and he texted back three words. *Wild sex fun.* I loved Josh like the brother I never had, but sometimes he displayed his bachelorhood a little too much.

"I'll have the sea bass, please," Toni said.

"And for my man?"

"I'll do the filet," I said. "Medium-plus."

"All *right*, getting the protein. Worked up an appetite." He winked. "I'll be right back with your wines."

I shook my head. "You have to excuse Josh. He can be a little sophomoric."

"I think he's cute. Besides," Toni reached over and poked my side, "you *did* work up an appetite."

"Not just me, woman."

"Well, yes. But it was in the name of science."

"Okay, two KJs." Josh set down our Chardonnays.

On the two large screens behind the bar, CNN had a segment about the "attempted" terrorist act in Dallas. I nudged Toni. "Hey, check it out."

Josh turned and looked up. "Oh, dude, have you seen this? It's crazy. Happened last night."

The segment showed two shaky and mostly blurred cell phone vids of people scrambling to get out. Then it cut to a security vid from one of the black bubbles, which caught part of the cloud sphere, and a lot of the crowd running for their lives. But if you knew what you were looking for, in the lower left corner I could see Toni, with me crouching in front of her. At that angle and distance, she just looked like someone scared shitless and frozen in place.

Josh noticed where I was focused and did a double take. "Hey," he said turning around to Toni, "isn't that you in the corner?" He pointed to the screen.

"Shhh. Man, we were there," I said cautiously.

His eyes flared. "No *way*. Girl, you look freaked out. I would've already been running."

"I was too scared to run," she said smartly.

"And my man, on the ground. Next time, bro, you need to protect your lady." Josh jerked a thumb to Toni.

As the video looped, the whole scene looked unreal. Actually, it was. The talking head said all the security video had malfunctioned, and this few-second clip was all that had been captured. Even the cell phone videos were rough and hard to make out. Some eyewitness accounts told the story of the cloud shrinking and plopping into the trash bin, but as usual they couldn't agree on some key details. Bottom line, experts agreed it was a miracle the vest hadn't detonated correctly and so many lives were saved by that malfunction. The magical movement of the cloud was attributed to hysterical recall. More than likely, the terrorist had been standing next to the trash bin and the botched explosion had somehow blown what was left of him into it. Again, a miraculous event.

"Is that what y'all saw?" Josh asked us.

"Dude, I hit the ground," I said. "I didn't see jack."

"I only remember bits and pieces," Toni said. "He *was* standing next to the trash can. Could you please change the channel? I can't watch this." Toni looked genuinely upset.

"Oh, sure. Sorry." Josh grabbed the remote and switched to a spring training baseball game. I got off my bar chair and comforted Toni.

"I'll go check on your food," Josh offered.

"Are you really upset?" I asked her.

"No. I just wanted to get it off the screen."

"It looks like you really lucked out."

"Probably not with *my* people."

"Yeah, you never answered my question. What did you violate, some Prime Directive thing?"

"You like *Star Trek*, don't you?"

"It's my guilty pleasure. So, did you?"

"We have a lot of leeway on our vacations, you know, to protect ourselves from harm. But we are forbidden to take any action that can cause a change in the basic direction of a culture or society."

I climbed back onto my bar chair. "I don't see you broke that rule. From the news, it's being treated as a botched terrorist act. The rest is up for debate. Besides, you were, technically, protecting yourself. You just happened to protect a bunch of other people too."

"It *is* borderline." Toni eyed her wine, then threw back a big swig.

I grabbed her bar chair and pulled her over.

"Yeeees?" she asked, sliding.

"If it's any consolation," I pulled back her hair and whispered in her ear, "I'm happy you did what you did. I wouldn't be here, along with lots of other people. And you ... well, I guess you'd still be somewhere, but not with me."

"You want me to be with you?"

We had been together for less than 36 hours, so I hadn't really considered the idea of "wanting" her to be with me, but it also didn't sound wrong. "Yeah ... I think I do."

"You *think*?"

I leaned in and kissed her. "Yes," I said against her lips.

"Excuse me." Josh cleared his throat. "Got your dinners here."

We both pulled away, chuckling.

"Here we go. Miso sea bass for the lady, and a filet for my man. Enjoy."

"Thanks, Josh." I turned to Toni. "Excuse me, I'm going to go wash my hands. I'll be right back."

"Okay," she said poking at her seabass.

As I made my way to the Men's, I felt a hand at my shoulder.

"Hey, bro?"

"Josh, what's up?"

"Dude, I just wanted to say, I think it's so cool you're happy with this girl. You two look natural together. How long you been dating?"

I glanced at my watch. "About thirty hours."

"Are you kidding? Bro, that is out*standing*!" He slapped my arm. "Good for you. Hey, she got a sister?"

If he only knew. "I don't think so."

As I came out of the restroom I was still chuckling at Josh and his little pep talk. It was nice, yet totally out of character. We had grown up a block from each other in a suburb of Chicago, and after college we had moved to Dallas together. While my career took off, his didn't, but he was the kind of free spirit that wasn't into a career, so it never bothered him.

Rounding the corner of the kitchen area, I saw a guy sitting in my bar chair chatting it up with Toni. "Hey, Toni," I said walking up, "who's this?"

"Cameron, this is Daniel. Daniel is a personal trainer to the *stars*."

"Great. So, uh, Daniel … mind if I have my seat back?"

The guy turned. "Man, your food was getting cold, and your lady here was getting bored."

What the hell? I didn't need this. This guy was way deep into happy hour. "Look, dude, just let me sit down, okay?"

"What if I don't want to?" he slurred.

I put a heavy hand to his shoulder. "Don't make me ask you again."

The guy stood, knocking the chair into the woman next to us, and brushed my hand away in one motion. She shot an irritated look over her shoulder.

"You want a piece of–" The guy winced and grabbed his head. He groaned and stumbled past me. "Shit, my fucking head."

"Oh, what's the matter, Daniel?" Toni said playfully. "One too many drinks?"

The guy sank to one knee and groaned again.

Out of the corner of my eye I caught Josh coming around the bar with what looked like a black miniature baseball bat.

He stormed up. "You need help, bro?"

"This guy's being an asshole deluxe." I glanced at Toni who was doing a bad job at suppressing a laugh.

Josh was about equal in size to the trainer, maybe bigger. He'd played rugby in college and had a bit of a temper. He grabbed the guy by the ear and yanked him onto his wobbly feet. He jammed the bat under the guy's chin. "Time for you to tab out, my friend."

The guy nodded as best he could with the business end of the bat jamming his head back. Josh pulled on his ear and led the guy toward the back of the restaurant. The guy stumbled along, clutching his head and groaning.

I retrieved my bar chair back and apologized to the girl who was bumped. Toni was snickering. "What's so funny?" I asked.

"You're really cute when you're chivalrous. I'm kind of turned on."

"Thanks, but that could have easily gone sideways."

"I don't think so."

I took a long sip of my wine and faced her. "That was you, wasn't it?"

She put a finger under her chin and shrugged girlishly.

"How?" I asked.

She motioned me close. "Self-defense," she said. "We're taught to go for the brain. We can create a tiny gravitational field inside the brain and pinpoint it on a certain area, then compress the field.

"To induce a headache or stroke?"

"A stroke is for severe situations. We can also cause hemorrhaging, like a serious concussion. We receive extensive training in human anatomy, especially the brain."

"Can you kill?"

"Killing is forbidden. Disabling a person is usually enough."

Josh returned his bat to its place behind the bar and came over. "Sorry about that," he said. "This is a high-class place. We don't allow shit like that to happen. Y'all okay?"

"We're fine," Toni said. "It's nice to have men fighting over me." She smiled ironically. "Makes me feel special."

"Okay then. Eat up, and whatever you want to drink, it's on us. Hey," he pointed to my plate, "you want me to get you a new one?"

"That's okay, man, but thanks."

We watched Josh walk down to the other end of the bar and welcome a couple settling in.

"You're so lucky," Toni said.

"I know. He's a great guy." I cut into my steak. Perfect.

"I meant your species, but Josh is great."

"You don't have friendship on Cala?"

"I wouldn't call it friendship. More like strategic arrangements."

"How's that?" I asked.

"Our society is an interconnected collective. Each individual has a purpose, a responsibility to the whole."

"Like the Borg."

She rolled her eyes. "No, not like the *Borg*. Come on, I'm being serious."

"I'm sorry, please, continue." *Don't be a douche, douche.*

"It's hard to make close, personal relationships when you're so dependent on every other individual."

"What's your role?"

She hesitated.

"I'm sorry, Toni. Is that too personal?"

"No. I work in something like your medical industry … it hard to explain."

"Give it a try." I polished off more of my steak and took a sip of wine.

"Okay … I have a duty to–"

"Excuse me," said a large, middle-aged African-American man. Behind him stood an equally large, young Hispanic woman. Their muscular bulks were squeezed into dark grey suits like summer sausage. This didn't feel good.

"Yes?" I asked.

The guy flipped out a badge wallet. DHS. Department of Homeland Security. *Shit.*

"Cameron William Harrison? Toni Ann Morgan?" he asked, coolly.

My heart leapt into my throat. "Yes?"

"Can you come with us, please? We'd like to ask you a couple of questions … about the incident at the theater."

"I appreciate the invite, agents, but we're not finished with our–"

The guy leaned in. "This *isn't* a request."

5

I LOVE YOUR CUTENESS.

The man was Agent Davis and his partner Agent Robb. They shuffled us out of Terilli's (not exactly a perp-walk, but damn close) and put us in their cliché black Ford SUV. We hadn't been handcuffed or read our rights, and God help us if they knew what kind of illegal alien they *really* had in their back seat.

Toni gave me a questioning look as we drove away. I think she was considering going Grav Bitch on them. I flared my eyes and slightly shook my head "no." The agent glanced over his shoulder.

They took us to the Earle Cabell Federal Building in downtown Dallas. It was an excruciatingly quiet ride. I'd been there once for a jury summons but wasn't picked. It was mostly courtrooms as I recalled, but I guess DHS had an office there for, well, whatever they did.

We went through security, and as they passed the wand over Toni I freaked about her tech. She just stood there nonchalantly with her arms spread. She winked when the female guard reached the back of her neck. We walked briskly to the door marked DHS, and after taking our fingerprints, we were ushered into separate rooms. Mine was the size of a classroom that could accommodate roughly 30 people. It was after hours, so the place was quiet. The buzz from the overhead fluorescent cans was starting to give me a headache. Agent Davis entered.

"Am I under arrest?" I asked, pulling out one of the putty-colored plastic stacking chairs from the long, faux beach wood table.

"Have a seat," he said.

I did and asked the question again.

A forced smile appeared. Agent Davis's teeth looked almost fake against his dark skin. A few crow's feet appeared and vanished. "No, Mr. Harrison, you're not under arrest."

"Then why the fingerprinting?"

"Procedure." He opened a yellow file folder.

"I have Global Entry."

Davis glanced up over his half-rim reading glasses. "We *know*."

This was going to be painful. I noticed the black camera bubble in the corner of the room and thought of Toni opening her hand and exploding the same type of bubbles in the theater.

"Is your name Cameron William Harrison?" He hadn't looked up from the folder.

"Yes."

"Were you at the Prestonwood Draft Cinema two nights ago?"

"Yes."

"Was Toni Ann Morgan with you?"

"Yes. We met up on a FindMeAnybody date."

"Yes or no, Mr. Harrison."

"Yes."

"Did you see or have contact or talk to this man?" Davis produced an 8-by-10 color photo of the Asshole Deluxe and handed it to me.

"Yes."

"Which?"

"Yes, I saw him, touched him and talked to him."

This got a surprised look. "Explain."

I told the story as succinctly as I could.

"What was his reaction to you *shoving* him?" Davis asked.

"He looked pissed, like I had interrupted something important."

"You did," he muttered, taking the photo back. "Did he say anything to you after that?"

"No."

"Where did he go?"

"He walked up to the trash can."

"What happened next."

"He threw open his coat and screamed something in Arabic. I saw the bomb vest and went to the floor. I heard it go off–"

He removed another 8-by-10 from the file folder. This one wasn't an Interpol mugshot; it was a pixelated still from the security camera footage. "Can you describe this *cloud*?"

"Not really," I said. "I was on the ground. It all happened so fast. I've never been through something like that."

This drew a half-smirk. "What did you see when you finally looked up?"

"Smoke coming out of the trash can."

He pulled out another pixelated still from the security camera footage, but it was the same one we had seen in the CNN segment. It had been zoomed in and cropped on me and Toni.

"This suggests you were standing before the smoke rose up from the trash bin."

Shit. "Yeah, well, okay. I did stand, but I was looking at Toni. I was worried about her. When I finally turned, I saw the smoke."

Davis pulled out one more 8-by-10. "Are you *sure*?"

This image, blurry as it was, showed me facing the hovering cloud (barely visible in the corner of the frame).

Fuck. I leaned into his outstretched hand and inspected the image.

"Gosh," I said, sitting back. "I don't recall it that way. I mean, it all happened so fast."

My sarcasm earned a solid 10 seconds of staring down. Davis broke eye contact and asked about my relationship with Toni, how long we'd dated (my answer got a raised eyebrow), where we went after the "incident," what we did at my house (no details, he didn't press). He suddenly returned to the incident itself, zeroing in on Toni's actions. I repeated my story. I was crouched and cowering. He asked about her hand movement. I said I didn't recall any. After two questions out of left field about my parents (very weird), he settled back and regarded me like a father who caught his son sneaking in the window after curfew.

"Mr. Harrison, have you ever, before this incident, seen a terrorist blow themselves up?"

"Once, on the news. Pretty gross, really."

"Would you say that what happened at the theater was similar?"

"I guess, but I didn't really see him blow up. Like I said, there was a flash and I dropped to the floor."

"Do you think the small explosion could have blown the subject into the trash bin?"

I shrugged. "That's above my paygrade. I'm not a physicist. I design websites. If that's what the evidence says, I guess that's what happened."

Davis let out a long sigh and closed his folder. He removed his readers and tossed them across his laptop.

"Will you be leaving the country anytime soon?" he asked.

"Hadn't planned on it, but you never know. I like vacations."

The agent slid his business card across the table. "If you do, try to inform us, please."

*   *   *   *

Uber took 10 minutes to arrive at the Federal Building. After we climbed in, Toni wanted to talk about her interrogation, but I was pretty rattled and shushed her. I'd never been arrested or questioned by police, much less Homeland Security, and lying to Davis had unnerved me, especially faced with his video stills. The cloud wasn't clearly visible, thank God, and Davis had given the impression that our interview was just an item to check off on his investigation to-do list. Maybe they didn't have anything on us? After all, it was routine detective work to identify all the witnesses on video and ask them what they saw.

The ordeal took more than three hours. The driver dropped us back at the restaurant, which was still pretty quiet.

"Can we *please* talk now?" Toni asked, climbing onto the bar chair.

Josh came up from behind and put his arms around both our shoulders. "Dude," he said as I sat, "what the hell was *that?*"

"That," I said, "was your tax dollars at work."

"Feds?"

"Homeland Security."

"Did they take you into locked rooms with one-way mirrors?"

"Not exactly, I was in a classroom."

"Me, too," Toni said.

Josh wadded up his bar towel. "I thought I'd never see y'all again."

"They just wanted our statements," I said. "They have to track down witnesses. My session seemed pretty straightforward. How about yours, Toni?" I tried to be nonchalant, but my stomach was tied in knots again.

She shrugged like it was no big deal. "About the same."

"Dude, I would not mess with those people. I've heard stories. Hey, the kitchen's about to close, you want your meals again? You barely got a chance to eat."

"Sure," I said.

"And two Eagle Rares?"

"Yes, please," Toni said.

Josh went behind the bar, entered our orders and started on our drinks.

"Was yours really straightforward?" I asked Toni.

"I guess. I've never been in this kind of situation before on Earth."

"How can you be so calm?"

"I'm not worried about your people. I'm worried about *my* people. Besides, based on all the images they showed me, we were just standing there."

"You were standing. I was hitting the deck."

"Hitting the *deck?*"

"It's an old Navy term, when an enemy plane buzzes a ship–"

"Ship? Like a boat?"

"Yes, and ... never mind." My right leg was nervously bouncing on the bar stool footrest. Toni noticed it.

"Here you go." Josh set our drinks down and went to another couple.

I knocked back a swig, stared into the Scotch stacked behind the bar and considered what a huge mistake I'd made with this woman, alien, or whatever the hell she was.

"You're really upset, aren't you?" Toni hadn't touched her drink.

I took another swig. "Josh is right, you don't eff around with Homeland Security."

"Concierges can take care of them." She reached for her drink and took a long sip before joining me in staring straight ahead at the bar's high-end Scotch bottles.

"Concierges?"

"It's the only word that adequately describes their position. They handle pre-trip details and any issues that might arise on planet."

"A fixer."

"A what?"

"A person who can get you out of a jam. Fixes the mess you've gotten into."

"Like stopping a terrorist from killing hundreds of people?"

"More like revealing to the world that you're a being from another planet who, by the way, steals human DNA to create clones. But, hey, it's just a vacation, so humanity doesn't have *anything* to worry about."

We sat there, staring at the bar's impressive collection of exotic liquors, and sipped our drinks. My sarcastic derision loitered between us.

"I'm sorry, Cam."

I regarded the amber contents of my glass and let her apology die.

"I'm being a dick," I said, finally.

"Maybe a little."

"I just wanted to get out … you know, meet someone. I wasn't expecting miracles and federal agents and–" I bit off the thought before my anger rose to the surface.

Toni slowly set down her empty glass. "I can leave if you'd like."

I shook my head. "No. … Stay."

She tentatively reached for my hand. It was a tender gesture, and I could feel her "thank you" when I reciprocated her touch. We sat there quietly, staring into empty drinks.

"So, tell me," I said, "are you on the grid, as in do you have a digital trail established before you take a vacation?"

"We have a complete digital footprint implanted into your system about a year before we arrive." She swirled an ice cube around with her finger. "Credit cards, bank accounts, medical records. Because your internet, as you call it, is so fractured, it's relatively easy to embed information without drawing attention."

"The old ten-thousand-year advantage again?"

"You're catching on."

"I'm not as dumb as I look."

"I think you look awesome." She leaned over and kissed me on the cheek.

"What was that for?" I asked.

"I don't know, the urge just came up. Does that happen a lot … with people like us who have a connection?"

"It did for me and Karen."

"Karen is … I'm sorry, *was* your wife?"

"Yes."

"Tell me about her."

"I don't think–"

"Hey, I'm sorry. I shouldn't have asked."

"It's my past, it's just … well, I try not to dwell on it too much anymore."

"Were you not *past* it?"

"Not for a long time," I said. "Years. You know, she was a lot like you. Funny. Adorable. Quirky, in an endearing way."

"Quirky?" Toni asked.

I tilted a look. "Girl, you're an extraterrestrial being from a planet a hundred light-years from earth. Believe me ... you're more than quirky."

Toni abandoned her empty glass and looked at me in a curiously serious way.

"You okay?" I asked.

"What is this?"

"What's *what*?"

"When I look at you, I feel like I've known you a long time. But that's impossible. I just met you."

"Have you ever been on a date before ... A human date?"

"No."

I faced her. "What you're experiencing is what we call puppy love."

Her face screwed up into an adorable questioning expression. "I'm not an animal."

I sighed out a laugh. "Puppy love is typically felt by adolescent human children. It's intense but kind of shallow. They think it's love, but it's not."

Toni scooted close. "Love?"

Uh-oh. I used the L-word. Not smart. "It's not *true* love. It's just an infatuation."

Toni's questioning stare deepened.

"Look, there's a lot of different kinds of love," I said. "If someone says they love your cooking, or loves the way you did your hair, or even loves your quirkiness, they're not *in* love with you."

"You *love* my quirkiness?"

"Well yeah, I-I mean no, not like that – Toni, using the word love casually is a wonderful thing. It means someone really likes or cares for something about you."

"Oh, I understand," she said. "I'm not in *love* with your quirkiness either."

I thought about correcting her, but it probably would've been lost.

"I have an idea," she declared. "Let's take a vacation … a *human* one, like you would go on."

This was random. "Look, I'd love to, I-I mean I'd *like* to, but I run a business. I have clients and projects." With the economy stalling, my freelance business had actually slowed down, plus I had just lost my biggest account.

"I can take care of that," she said smugly.

"Unlimited intergalactic funds?"

"Maybe."

"Don't forget, the Agents in Grey may not let us."

"The who?"

"Homeland Security."

She pondered my pun. "Oh, I get it. A play on the movie *Men in Black*. That's cute." She smiled slyly. "I *love* your cuteness."

6

NO GOING BACK.

"I'm not getting on that ... that *thing*."

I hadn't experienced Toni's bad side yet. What if she got *really* mad at me? Would I collapse in a heap, clutching my head? Would I end up like the Asshole Deluxe?

"It's a plane, Toni. It's the safest way to travel."

"Maybe on *this* planet. How does it work?"

As a kid I wanted to be a pilot, so I had a rudimentary understanding of the physics of flight. I hit her with it.

"Lift, thrust, weight, drag. The wings," I pointed out the huge window to our waiting American Airlines Dreamliner, "create lift. The engines," I pointed again, "create thrust. The thrust exceeds the plane's drag at take-off. The lift of the wings overcomes the plane's weight. Result? Our trip to Rome … first-class, I might add."

"You've mentioned this before. Are we being taught something on this trip?"

"No, the word class, here, references quality. We're traveling in the best *quality* this airline can offer."

"Oh. Good … I think."

"Believe me, it's *really* good."

Toni stared at the plane with the same weird look she had when she went into Grav Bitch mode. My attention jumped between her and the plane. In the late afternoon light, I could barely make out the development of a distortion field forming around the fuselage.

I grabbed her arm. "Toni," I scolded, "stop!"

She blinked back. "What?"

"You can*not* lift that plane."

"I think you're right, it's extremely heavy–"

"Jesus. Come here." I hustled her away from the window and we sat in the only two open seats left in the gate area.

"You hurt my arm, Cam," she said, rubbing.

"I'm sorry. Really. But, Toni, you can't just go around warping our gravity whenever you want."

"I wasn't going to engage it fully."

I tried to explain the whole security thing and that we didn't want to be thrown in jail, not to mention how mechanical issues can really jack up a flight schedule and our trip. She seemed to understand, but I could tell my little manhandling didn't sit well with my girlfriend the alien.

"Do you understand?" I asked.

She nodded, still rubbing.

"Hey, Toni, I'm sorry about your arm. I just got frustrated. Let's not start our trip on a bad note. I want you to be happy and experience my world … with me."

She perked up. "You do?"

"Absolutely."

"Okay. I'll get on this plane thing. Does it have bourbon?"

"It has whatever you want."

Her sexy look formed. "It *does*?"

"Yeah, but–"

"I want *you*, on this plane thing." Her hand went to my thigh. I stopped its advance.

"Toni, um, while I would love to usher you into the mile-high club–"

"How do we join?"

"It's not a real club. It's just another expression. It's when a couple, you know, does it in flight, usually in one of the plane's lavatories."

"It?"

"Have sex," I whispered. The older woman sitting next to us looked up from her phone and threw me a dirty look.

"Experiments," Toni said.

"Look, you can't anymore. The rules are too strict, and the bathrooms are too tiny."

"We could make it work."

"*No*! No, we can't. Don't even think about it."

Toni folded her arms. "Okay. I'll be a good girlfriend."

"*Your attention, please. We will now begin boarding our first class and World Elite customers.*"

I stood and extended my hand. "That's us. Come on, Ms. Morgan. Let's get this Roman holiday started."

Toni took my hand, and it occurred to me that it was the first time we had ever walked hand-in-hand. As we made our way down the jet bridge, she squeezed my palm.

"This is nice," Toni said. "This is a custom, right?"

"It is."

"For people with a connection?"

"Usually. Friends can do it too, but that's more of a European thing."

"So we're friends, too?"

"So far."

*　　　*　　　*　　　*

"Mr. Harrison, would you like another drink?"

Kip, our personal flight attendant, was one of the best I'd ever had. He was older than most of the other attendants, but his boyish good looks made him seem younger.

"No, I'm good, Kip."

"And Ms. Morgan?"

Toni looked up from her alien phone/tablet. "Yes!"

"Um, no," I said.

"No?" she asked.

"Pace yourself. We have eight hours."

Kip was doing a bad job of hiding his amusement.

"Okay, I'm good too." Toni said.

Kip leaned down and smiled. "Honey, if you want another drink, just come see me. We won't tell," he gave a nod in my direction, "you know who."

"Guys," I said. "I'm right here?"

Toni nodded. "I will."

Kip chuckled and continued to another pod.

Toni downed the last of her drink and eyed her glass. "This bourbon doesn't taste like Josh's."

"Nope, he has the good stuff."

"You know my implant can nullify the effects of alcohol," Toni remarked.

"Actually, I didn't. But what fun would that be?"

Toni set her glass down and went back to her device.

"Does that mean you never get a hangover?"

"Uh-huh," she said.

"Tell me, what is that?"

She set the device down on the console between us. In the pod's spotlight, I could finally see a few details. It looked remarkably like a tricorder from the latest *Star Trek* reboot, but its interface graphics were blurry irregular patches of color and its surface resembled water, ripples and all. It had no human symbols or icons or letterforms.

"We use this to interface with the moon base and Cala, pretty much anything Calaian. It's also an omnipresent, long-range cortical particle path enhancer, at least that's the closest I can come in English."

"How does it work?"

"The short explanation is that it enhances the range and power of the cerebral particle energy signal, along with other things."

"Like your gravity protection plan?"

"No, for me that's a constant power level."

"What if you accidentally turned off your pad?"

"You mean like this?' Toni touched one of the pastel blue colored shapes, and immediately went limp. Her eyes were still open, but she was un-responsive. My heart jumped.

"Toni?" I nudged her. Nothing. "Very funny, now come on." Still nothing. A little bit of drool started collecting at one corner of her open mouth. *Shit.* "*Toni?*"

A big grin spread across her face. "Fooled you," she said through a laugh.

I didn't find it remotely funny. I turned away.

"Cam?"

My mind, for some reason, went to the night I had to identify Karen's body after the accident. Karen, unfortunately, had left without her wallet or cell phone. They found my name through the car's registration and address. Since we didn't share the same last name, I had to go down to the morgue. Contrary to the TV drama way of pulling back the white sheet, they took me to a private room and showed me a photo of her face. Her eyes were partially open, and her mouth was slack. Even through the bruises and cuts, her beauty remained. She was still my love. I threw up on the picture.

"Cam? What is it? I thought humans liked humor."

"It's nothing. I over-reacted. You were just goofing around."

"No, what? I've never seen you like this."

"Um … it's just …"

"Cam," she said softly, "you can tell me."

"When you went limp, just now, with your eyes open …"

Shit, this was harder than I thought. Just say the words. "It just re-minded me of … Karen. After the accident. In the morgue."

Toni covered her mouth. "Oh no, I'm so, *so* sorry. Please forgive me."

"It's okay, you didn't know. Hell, *I* didn't know it would trigger that kind of a reaction."

Kip walked by.

"Excuse me, Kip?" I asked.

He turned and smiled. "Two more bourbons?" He picked up on the energy. "Is everything okay?"

"Oh, yeah. Everything's fine." I turned to Toni. "Have you ever had ice cream?"

Her eyes brightened. "*Yes.* It's amazing."

"Two chocolate sundaes?" Kip asked.

"That would be great," I said.

"I'll bring a little Kahlua." He winked at Toni. "You'll love it." He headed to the galley.

"Aren't we supposed to eat dessert after dinner?" she asked.

"Technically yes, but we're on vacation. We can break the rules."

"Hey, are you okay? I'm sorry for what I did."

I patted her leg. "Yeah, just a tough moment there."

*   *   *   *

I had traveled first-class once, but the dinner on this flight was pretty damn amazing. I had the chicken. Toni the fish. Kip had been an excellent host, always ready with whatever we wanted. Toni was surprised at how smoothly the plane-thing moved through the air. The pod's ability to convert into a bed also fascinated her. I couldn't quite grasp if Cala was a nice place or a totalitarian hellhole. For a being 10,000 years ahead of us, Toni seemed too interested in the most mundane things. Take, for instance, my coffee maker … an endless source of fascination. And my shaver? Amazing. Even my washer and dryer were worthy of her intense Calaian scrutiny.

"So we sleep here?" she asked.

"You can. The seat folds flat," I said. "The bedding is in the cabinet behind you."

"This is *so* cool." Toni opened the cabinet and inspected the bedding bag. "Your species really has this luxury living concept down."

"And yours doesn't?"

"For a select few, life is better. But for the collective whole, life is, um, adequate."

"Are you a caste-based society, and I'm assuming your whole planet is one society?"

"Caste-based?"

"Like India. Did you study about India?"

"Just a little, and yes, it's similar, but on Cala, there are four major Houses–"

"Excuse me, Toni Anne Morgan?"

A bald, immaculately dressed, older man in an expensive black Prada sweater and close-cropped salt-and-pepper beard was standing in the aisle Toni's pod faced. My radar went up.

"Yes?" she asked cautiously.

"Your hair looks so pretty today."

I'd never seen Toni concerned or even frightened. Not even at the theater or with the Agents in Grey. But this man and the weird way he complimented her hair seemed to scare the shit out of her.

The guy leaned into her pod and looked at me. "You must be Cameron." He extended a hand.

I cautiously took it. It was too warm to the touch. *Oh shit. One of her own.*

"Cam," Toni said slowly. "I have to go to sleep now. Please don't be alarmed. I'll be asleep for–" she looked questioningly at the Prada man.

"About fifteen minutes," he said as if this was simple routine. "Cameron, it was a pleasure to finally meet you. I hope you and Toni have a wonderful time on your holiday." He walked down the aisle, through the drawn drapes, and disappeared into business class.

"Toni, what's going on?"

The fear hadn't faded from her face. "I'm so sorry. I'll be fine. Just a little nap. Don't try and wake me, you won't be able to."

"Are you in trouble?"

She hesitated, then nodded tightly.

"It's about the theater, right?"

Another tight nod.

"It'll be okay." I had no idea *what* I was talking about, but maybe a little encouragement would help. "Tell them the truth. You were just protecting yourself."

"I will," she said.

"Okay now, knockers up."

"*What?*"

"It's a riff on keep your chin-up, a British term. It means to be strong. Karen used to say it. I-I thought you'd find it funny."

Another nervous nod. Toni settled back into her seat. "Cam?" she said, sitting up.

I took her hand. "Yeah?"

"I–"

Her eyes closed, and she fell back against the seat. Her head lolled toward me.

"Toni?"

No reaction.

I leaned over her pod's center console and kissed her forehead. "Good luck," I whispered.

"Well, look who's had too much fun." Kip stepped into the spotlight of my pod. They had dimmed the cabin lights after dinner, and his form seemed to appear from the shadows. He knelt in the aisle next to me.

I mimicked taking a drink. "Yeah, my girl's a lightweight when it comes to the old bourbon."

Kip regarded Toni. "She reminds me so much of my partner's sister. I don't know why she just didn't use her cerebral particle implant to cancel out the effect."

A spikey cold shiver went through me. I looked into Kip's dark eyes.

"What?" he asked, a faint smirk playing. "Did you think all of us are here on vacation?"

"You're ... like *her*?"

He nodded.

"How did you know she was Calaian?" I whispered.

He pointed to her pad. "It's pretty obvious."

"Why are you working a job? And how did you know *I* knew?"

"I'll tell you a little secret ... this world of yours," Kip glanced furtively about us, "it's pretty addictive. After I met my partner, well ... I *had* to stay. I'm working because we only have an allotted amount of time. Go beyond that, and they cut you off. I didn't know you knew, but Toni seemed like the kind who would tell."

"She didn't tell me anything, she did something that kind of gave her away."

"Really?" Kip sat on the edge of the pod and folded his arms. "*This* I want to hear."

I thought about not telling Kip what Toni had done, but what the hell? I was already deep into the craziness, so what would it matter? I told him an abbreviated version of the theater incident. I also mentioned the Agents in Grey and our interrogations. The whole story didn't seem to faze him.

"What do you think?" I asked.

Kip looked at Toni. "I'll bet it's her first visit. This kind of thing happens occasionally, or so I've heard. Especially with the young ones."

"You know she's not, um, sleeping. Some guy in business class approached her ... about the incident. He knew my name."

Concern washed over Kip. He glanced at the business class curtain. "What did he look like?"

"Tall, older, bald with a salt-and-pepper beard. Wearing a black Prada collared sweater. Said she had beautiful hair today."

"That's one of the code phrases so you know you're talking with another Calaian. He's probably her Concierge. They handle all of your pre-trip aspects and assist you when you're on vacation. He probably handles over a hundred trips at once. Usually they're nice. How was he?"

"Matter-of-fact. He sure scared Toni."

Kip leaned past me and inspected her. "Hard to say what they're saying to her." He patted my shoulder. "I wouldn't be too worried. Sounds like she didn't change the course of anything major."

Even through Kip's casual attitude, I could tell he was worried. "Do a lot of you stay? I mean, longer than you're supposed to?" I asked.

"I don't know the numbers. If I had to guess, very few." He leaned down. "Our world is a *lot* different than yours," he whispered. "It takes a fair amount of courage and commitment to abandon it."

"Does your partner know ... about you?"

Kip straightened and shook his head.

"Will you ever tell him?"

"I don't want to ruin what we have."

"What about the glow from the implant?" I asked.

"They turn that off."

"So your *abilities* go away?"

"Partially. The implant is still working, so you can exist in your ride."

"So you become just a plain, ordinary human?"

"Pretty much."

"But what about where you're situated? You know, the installation on the dark side of the moon?"

Kip sucked in a long, thoughtful breath. "My Calaian body is still there, but once you commit to staying on Earth you get," he made quotation marks in the air, "*shifted.*" He leaned down again. "This is a one-way ticket."

"There's no going back?"

"No going back."

I let that sink in. "You must really love your partner."

Kip smiled. "I do." He stood. "So, Mr. *Harrison* … can I get you anything?"

"No, Kip, I'm good."

He smiled. "I'll come back when our princess wakes. She'll be *very* thirsty."

7

CHE CAZZO?

When Toni woke up, she *was* thirsty. Kip must have been discretely watching, because as soon as her eyes fluttered and opened, he appeared with a tall glass of water. He sat the drink down and whispered something into Toni's ear. Her eyes widened, then she slapped his arm and laughed and called him a little shit for not telling her sooner. The rest of our flight was a blast because Kip just kept serving whatever we wanted. We never saw the Prada man again, not at baggage claim or customs.

Having been so freaked, Toni now seemed nonchalant about what happened while she had been "napping." I asked about it, but she waved it off as routine and no big deal. Still, I could tell it affected her because her mood was more subdued. In the limo to the hotel I broached the subject again, which drew a pretty stern reaction. She emphasized that, as a human, some things I just couldn't be part of.

"*Damn,*" I said, stepping into our hotel suite, "this is amazing."

The room was awash in opulence. A 12-foot mirrored wall stood out from the other walls, which were thick with ornate white wainscoting. Black-and-white photography presented in oversized, elegant dark wood frames was neatly arranged in the large nooks that dominated each wall. A simple white art table greeted us in the entryway. Perched on its black marble top was a glass vase filled with two dozen white lilies.

Toni strolled to one of the tall windows and threw open its gold embroidered drapes. The room flooded with Rome's wonderful early-afternoon light.

"Look at this view!" She was in awe. "Isn't that St. John's?"

"It's called St. Peter's, but yes, that's the Vatican." I stepped behind her and wrapped my arms around her waist. "Come on, it's only one o'clock. Let's explore."

*   *   *   *

We spent the afternoon roaming the streets. We stopped in small cafes and sipped cappuccino, strolled the *Villa Borghese* Park and watched families play with their children. We even ran across an old-time organ grinder with a pet monkey near the *Tempio di Esculapio*, which delighted Toni. It was refreshing since her reaction to Roz had been less than accepting. Watching her interact with the animal, I mused about the possibility that she might choose to stay on Earth. But I quickly purged the thought. No need to set myself up for disappointment. More than likely Toni and I would have a great two or three months, her vacation would end, and I would have to say goodbye to my girlfriend the alien.

Around eight o'clock we stumbled into *Ristorante Vladimiro*, a charming classic Italian bistro where the old wood walls and racks of wine bottles complemented the plush red booths and white linen tablecloths. The staff was overly accommodating. They seemed to think we were newlyweds, and as one of the waiters put it, if we weren't, we should be. This got Toni going. She cut off a piece of rigatoni from our appetizer and slid it on her ring finger. All the female servers came and fawned over her gorgeous "wedding ring." I could only laugh. The girl had an irresistible charm that infected everyone within her magical radius. Was it a leftover trait from her host's DNA, or the Calaian tech inside her? Whatever it was, it worked.

Dinner was fabulous. I had the *spaghetti alla carbonara* and Toni tried the *risotto con pesto*. We paired the dishes with a delicious *Brunello* wine and finished our meals with a delicate lemon sorbet. After dinner, Toni's favorite waiter, Marco, stopped once again to flirt with the attractive American tourist. Placing his arm around her, Marco gestured in reverence at the rigatoni ring. Toni's eyes caught mine. Although clearly enthralled with Italy (and its men), she gave me a look that said *Are you okay with this?* I laughed and gestured for her to enjoy herself. Why not? She was a guest on our planet; she should get the royal treatment, Italian-style.

She shooed Marco and scooted over in the booth. "Is my man feeling neglected?"

"Not at all," I said. "You're having fun. That's why we're here."

"You need to be having fun too."

I put my arm around her. "I am. Just watching you enjoying yourself is a real treat."

Toni nuzzled close and kissed my neck. "I'm bored with all this," she cooed into my ear. "Let's go back to the hotel."

This girl was insatiable. "You aren't the least bit tired from the flight?"

"No, Mr. Harrison, I'm not."

I twisted in our embrace and kissed her. "Come on, let's get out of here."

Before I could ask for the check, Marco appeared at the table.

"Are we ready for the bill?" His accent was thick.

"We are," I said.

Marco pulled from behind his back a silver tray with the check. "I had a feeling you two were ready to go."

"What was your first clue?" I laid Toni's credit card down. It was a Dubai First Black card, and its rich matte surface seemed to absorb the light like a black hole.

"Ah, *Roma*," Marco said, inserting the card into his tablet reader, "the city of *love*."

"I do love your city," Toni said.

Marco eyed her as he handed the card back. "And it loves you, *signora*."

We said our goodbyes, and the staff replied with hugs and lots of faux cheek kisses. Marco was especially friendly, pecking Toni on each cheek, then holding her at arms-length and mimicking coming in for a kiss on the mouth, which got big laughs all around. He wagged his finger and said he had gone too far, and for us to leave before he asked Toni to marry him.

It was late, about 11:30, and the streets of Rome seemed unusually empty. Google Maps put the hotel a few blocks away, so we made our way down the sidewalk of a wide and quiet tree-lined boulevard.

"That was fun," I said to Toni as we strolled hand-in-hand.

A woman called to someone named Antonio, her voice echoing out of an adjacent alley.

Toni sighed. "Yes, it was. I could get used to this planet of yours."

Two men rounded the alley a half block up. They chuckled, and one sportively pushed the other into a trash can. They laughed and stumbled toward us. The red tips of their cigarettes glowed in the alley's darkness.

"*Buonasera*," the taller one said as he passed by. His buddy tipped his pork-pie hat and sucked in a long drag.

"*Buonasera*," Toni replied.

"Your Italian is good," I remarked.

Toni tapped the back of her neck. "The implant comes in handy."

The screech of tires pulled my attention around. A black van sped up the boulevard.

Toni hugged me as we walked. "I think we should make a bath in that big marble tub and–"

The van skidded to a halt next to us. Its side door slid open and locked into place with a menacing clunk.

"There's my sexy American girl," a familiar Italian voice said from the van's inky interior.

The waiter, Marco, emerged, arms spread. He flicked the last of his cigarette away and approached. My gut tightened. This did *not* feel right.

"Marco," I said. "What's going on?"

Marco's eyes cut to something behind us. I spun and saw the two drunk guys aggressively walking towards us. *Oh shit!*

"Run!" I yelled to Toni and shoved her into the alley.

The taller guy broke from the other one, ran past me and went into the alley after Toni. I turned just as Marco's fist was inches from my face. Something shiny across his knuckles caught the light from the streetlamp.

Jagged excruciating pain exploded across my jaw and into my skull, and I felt myself fall back. I hit the pavement on my left shoulder, and my head whiplashed against something metal. Toni's shriek reflected off the alley walls behind me.

After a long second of unconsciousness, I opened my eyes. A blurry Marco loomed over me. My head, jaw and shoulder throbbed in waves of violent pain. I could feel blood pouring from my nose. I had been dragged into the alley and was now lying in a shallow puddle.

Marco stepped over me and knelt, his features undulating in and out of focus. The pork-pie hat guy appeared behind him. Marco reached down, grabbed my shirt front and yanked me to a sitting position.

"I hate you *fucking* Americans," he snarled, "and your *fucking* big-shit attitude."

I tried to throw a wobbly punch, but Marco blocked it with his leg. He pressed his foot onto my arm and my shoulder screamed.

"We're going to take your *cunt* girlfriend and gang-fuck her." He skinned a steely smile across tar-stained teeth. "Then we'll sell her on the open market to the highest bidder." His eyes went to something behind me. I could hear Toni's muffled grunts as she struggled within the tall guy's grip. Why the hell wasn't she doing something?

Marco slid his attention back and his eyes narrowed. His other hand came into view. A loud click cut the air, and a long silver blade magically appeared. Cold adrenaline gushed through my nerves. Although he was a partial silhouette in the sidewalk's half-lit shadows, I could make out the grav field building around Marco's head. He looked at Toni and raised the switchblade.

"He said we can't have a witness," he hissed.

The knife plunged down and I felt the impact somewhere above my belt buckle. A fierce electric jolt shot up from my stomach. A scream erupted from my throat, then an intense heat burned its way up from my belly button.

As Toni's muffled shriek filled my ears, Marco's head exploded. I had a strange flashback to a childhood memory of Josh and I blowing up a watermelon with fireworks. Warm wet chunks of Marco's face, brains and skull splattered all over me and the legs of the pork-pie guy.

"*Che cazzo*?!" he yelled, stumbling back. The shock on his face said it all.

Marco's headless form flopped down to my right. A dark mass flew from behind me and into my field of vision. It was a body. The pork-pie guy tracked it as it went over us and was impaled on the broken edge of a fire escape. It was the taller guy. He retched blood as his hands flailed at the jagged rusted metal protruding from his chest.

"No!" the pork-pie guy yelled, his hands outstretched, palms forward. "No *senora*, please, *NO!*–"

He lifted off the ground in a blur, flew the forty feet to the van and slammed into its cabin. His hat landed next to my right foot. The van collapsed into itself, the distortion field folding it smaller and smaller until it was the size of a cigarette pack. The sound of the metal, glass and plastic breaking and compressing was sickening.

I struggled onto my good shoulder, my guts on fire, until I could see Toni. She was there, feet spread apart, arms out to her sides, fists clenched tight. Her eyes were partially rolled back. Then I realized she was floating a foot off the ground.

I reached for her with a bloody hand. "Toni," I tried, but her name puddled out.

She blinked a few times and focused on me. Horror etched her face. She dropped to the ground and ran over. I think she was yelling, "No, no, no!" She sank to her knees and held me in her arms. She was crying hysterically. I could feel my life seeping out between my fingers. I was shivering. God, it was getting cold.

"Oh no, *Cam*! Please, *please* don't die!" The second *please* came out as a tormented howl. She held my head and wailed a nonhuman sound into the air.

"Call ... the police." I could barely form the words.

She dug into her purse and pulled her Calaian tablet out.

"No ... the police ... *call* the police."

She didn't acknowledge me but tapped wildly on the multi-dimensional screen. Its dance of colors underlit her face. She set it down and cradled me again. Tears dripped from her cheeks and chin.

I looked into her beautiful blue eyes, now bloodshot and glistening. It felt like I had been kicked in the chest and my heart fluttered as it fought to pump what little life was left in my body. I coughed raggedly, which made my guts explode with hot pain. Blood splattered the front of Toni's cream-colored leather coat.

She wiped my mouth with her hand. "I'm so sorry."

"Why?" I barely got the word out.

"This is all my fault."

"It's ... not." It felt like the temperature had dropped 20 degrees, and I was shaking uncontrollably. My vision was tunneling.

She leaned down, kissed me and came away with a little blood on her lips. "Fight, Cam. Help is coming."

"Tell ... me."

"What?"

"Your ... real name ... on Cala." The words came out as a whisper.

"I-I can't say it." She sucked back more tears and motioned to her throat. "Not in this ride. I'm sorry."

The alley morphed into something else. I was dreaming, hanging from a cliff, a black abyss below me. My hands and arms ached from gripping the ledge.

Silence enveloped me.

And I let go.

8

RED.

I surfaced through a dark fog and opened my eyes to the semi-circular plaster patterns of a drab white ceiling. A sliver of muted light from a partially closed curtain bisected the room's blackness. I lay in a king-sized bed, naked, on cool white sheets. A light cotton blanket covered me to my waist. I reached for my stomach and touched a thick bandage just below my navel. Something was stuck in my arm, but in the semi-darkness I couldn't see an IV line or bag. My throat was raw and dry. A blurry figure stepped beside the bed.

"Welcome back."

A man's face came into focus. I tried to make sense of it.

"Kip?" His name scraped over my throat like sandpaper. "What are you doing here? ... Where is *here?*"

Kip smiled and put a hand to my arm. "Take it easy. You're alive, and that's what matters."

Toni appeared behind him and smiled.

"*Toni*," I said, the word catching.

She sat next to me, took my hand and pressed it to her cheek. "I thought I'd lost you."

Another figure emerged from the darkness. It took me a muddled second to recognize who it was. I pointed a limp finger. "You're the Prada guy," I said weakly. I tried to process what was going on. The room started to blur.

The man looked down. "He's going under again," he remarked in a husky baritone.

"You're all spinning." I coughed.

Toni kissed my forehead. "Close your eyes, Cam."

*   *   *   *

When I awoke, the room was filled with glorious light. I was dressed in a grey Nike Dry-Fit running warm-up. The cotton blanket was still on me, and when I felt for the dressing, I found a thin square bandage-pad stuck to my skin. The headache was gone, and my body didn't ache as much. Kip stood at the foot of the bed, arms folded, wearing a faded pink Polo and tan cargo shorts.

"Good morning," he said.

"Good morning." As I struggled into a sitting position, a sting shot up from my gut. I winced.

"Easy. Try not to move too much."

I leaned back against a mound of pillows and exhaled out the pain. "Man, that smarts."

"Not like it did when we first brought you here, I bet."

"Where is *here*?"

"This is where Paul and I live."

"Is he here?"

"Paul's doing an international flight. He'll be back in a few days."

"He's a flight attendant, too?"

"Nineteen years."

The room was well appointed with contemporary furniture in soft, dusty colors. A tortie cat sat in the window bay. It faced me and blinked.

"How long have I been out?" I asked.

"About three days." Kip said.

"Is that normal?" I tried not to sound too alarmed.

"We kept you under so you wouldn't be in pain. Human anatomy is very fragile–"

"There he is," Toni interrupted. She was carrying a tray of breakfast. She flicked out its legs and placed it carefully over my lap. "How's my guy doing this morning?" She leaned over and we kissed.

"Um, better … I guess." I nudged myself more upright and another jolt of pain stabbed me. I rubbed the bandage through the warm-up. "Why am I here? Why aren't I in a hospital?"

Toni moved an apprehensive look to Kip, then sat on the edge of the bed. "Cam ... please don't freak out."

"What the hell is going *on*?" I demanded.

"We had to, um, improvise–"

"Toni, what have you done?"

"There're robots in you," Kip said, "that are repairing the damage to the area where the knife penetrated."

Toni shot him a stern glare. "They're not *robots*."

"What would we call them?"

Toni shrugged. "I don't know, maybe–"

"Guys!" I blurted. "What the *hell* is in me?"

"It's a form of subnucleic hybridized therapy. They're kind of like nanobots," Toni said slowly, "but not that crude."

"They're microscopic," Kip added. "They'll flush out when they're through rebuilding your skin and organ tissues."

The thought of some alien microtech motoring around inside my intestines did freak me out. I yanked the warm-up top up, half expecting to see something crawling under the bandage-pad. "They're *alive*?"

"*No*," Toni implored, "they're harmless. They have no independent intelligence. They're designed specifically for repairing human anatomy."

"Jesus, guys, you could have at least *asked* me."

"You were in no shape to be asked anything," Kip said. "We had to make a judgment call."

"Cam, listen." Toni scooted closer. "It's my fault ... I made the decision."

Although the concern in Toni's and Kip's expressions seemed genuine, I was still anxious.

I lifted the warm-up top again and eyed the bandage. "They'll flush out?"

"In about three days," Toni said.

"Does it hurt?" I asked.

Toni's face filled with question. Kip suppressed a laugh.

"Um, no, Cameron," he said, "you won't feel a thing."

Toni perked up. "You'll just go to the bathroom and," she made a comical sweeping gesture with her hand, "out they go."

"Okay, then," I said reluctantly. "I don't really have a choice, now do I?"

"Not this time." Toni stood and spread the napkin onto my lap. "Besides, I wouldn't do anything to harm my guy." She slid the plate of scrambled eggs and toast closer to me. "Now, please eat. You need to build your strength."

I inspected the eggs with my fork. "Eating won't screw anything up?"

Toni walked over to a low-back cream-colored leather chair and grabbed a chiffon scarf out of its seat. She turned and considered me like a doting mother. "The tech will help you digest."

I took a sip of orange juice and cautiously swallowed.

"We'll be back in a couple of hours." She wrapped the scarf around her neck. "When you're done, try and go back to sleep. The tech works faster when the host is in a REM state."

The *host. Alien* micro-bots. Fuck *me.*

"Are we in trouble?" I asked.

"Trouble is the wrong word." Kip was obviously choosing his words carefully. "But yes, we're meeting with her Concierge."

Toni smiled as if she had picked up on my thoughts. "It'll be okay, Cam, really. ... You have to trust us."

Trust, I thought, *is the wrong word.*

I feigned an approving smile and watched them leave. The chink of a door locking spooked the cat off the windowsill. It sauntered into the swath of sunlight across the worn Persian rug and rolled onto its side. It twisted its head upside down and yawned.

I ate a slice of toast, poked at the eggs, and sipped half the juice. Eating seemed mechanical and nothing tasted good. I gingerly moved the tray off my lap and slid from the bed, trying not to flex too many stomach muscles, but that was almost impossible. Another punch of pain hit me about two inches behind my navel.

I shuffled to the bathroom and pissed. This must have been Kip and Paul's guest bedroom, because the bathroom was barely larger than the one in first-class. I studied the toilet's flush control and couldn't determine whether it was the left or the right of the two interlocking buttons that was for fluid waste. I gave up and pushed both.

The circular mirror was an elegant piece of design that had a swinging armature with an attached reversible mirror for close-up shaving and makeup. I splashed some warm water on my face and wiped off with a plush white towel. The water felt good, but when I pulled the towel away, there were dark red stains in the middle of it. I pulled the small mirror forward, flipped it to its greater magnification side and inspected my nose. Dark crusty patches of dried blood speckled the inside of my nostrils, and my nose appeared to be slightly bent. I pivoted my head and saw that the line of my jaw had a bruise running the length of it. Fragments of the abduction flashed through my mind. I tried to shake them away, but the motion sent the bathroom spinning. I grabbed the sides of the sink and tried to steady myself.

"Shit," I said to my reflection. The room slowed.

I rubbed the back of my neck and my fingers brushed an almost imperceptible inch-long raised line of skin. I could barely see it in the mirror. As my fingers searched the base of my neck, a faint patch of yellow light flared under my skin. I wasn't sure if it was real or a trick of the sunlight coming through the bathroom's narrow window. I hiked a hip onto the sink and craned for a better look. I felt around and the glow flared again. I gasped and staggered backward into the doorway. Another searing pain stabbed me in the gut. I doubled over.

"What the *fuck*!" I yelled at the black-and-white hexagon tiled floor.

My mind was racing. What were they making me into? Why had they lied? What else had they done?

I stumbled back into the bedroom, which was now fully spinning. The cat arched at my sudden entry. Its form blurred, then split into two. My stomach lurched. Breakfast hit the back of my throat. I went to one knee and retched across the dark wood floor. The cat hissed and scampered away.

I crawled to the bed and desperately tried to climb back in, but my guts were burning as if I had been stabbed all over again. The back of my neck near the scar was also on fire. I crumpled at the foot of the bed and puked again. The room swam in a maelstrom of colors and shapes. I curled into a fetal position and everything went black.

                    *   *   *   *

"Cam ... can you hear me?"

Toni's face came into focus. She was kneeling next to me and the late afternoon light backlit her, creating a shimmery halo around her curls. Kip was kneeling on the other side of me.

Toni helped me sit up and propped me against the mattress frame. The stench of vomit hung in the air. Then I remembered. I flinched and hit my head against the mattress. I jabbed a hand forward. "Get the hell *away* from me!"

"Cam, calm down."

I tried to scoot to the right, but Kip stopped me.

"Easy," he said. "Don't move."

I pointed to the back of my neck. "You fucking *lied* to me!"

Toni tucked her legs under herself and sat. "Don't panic–"

"Don't *panic*?!" I blurted. "You put a cerebral implant in me. What the hell, Toni? *Why*?" I fought to keep it together.

Toni regarded me for a long second, then her chin started to quiver. "Because." A tear slid down her cheek. "You were ... dead."

I swallowed hard. An instinctual fear shot through my nerves. " *W- what*?"

Her bottom lip trembled. Tears began to flow. "You *died* in my arms." She dropped her gaze to the floor and softly cried.

"By the time I got there," Kip said, "you were gone."

I tried to process what it all meant. "But, Jesus, why an *implant*?"

"It was the only way," Toni lifted her eyes, "to bring you back."

"I contacted her Concierge," Kip said. "He came with me."

"The Prada guy?" I asked.

"Yes."

"I pleaded with him," Toni said.

"More like begged," Kip added.

"You have to understand, Cam." Toni wiped her eyes with the sleeve of her sweater. "This has never been done. It's a huge breach of protocol."

"Only a Concierge has the authority to sanction what we did," Kip said. "Even so, there might be ramifications."

"Will this be in me," I swallowed again, "for the rest of my *life*?"

Toni hesitated, then nodded.

"Fuck *this*, I'm out of here!" I tried to stand but a knifing hot spasm ricocheted through my entire body. I slid down the side of the bed and crumpled back onto the floor. "Shiiiit!" I swallowed down the urge to puke again. Kip grabbed my shoulders.

"Cameron," he said gravely, "you need to pull it together."

"Fuck you!"

His fingers dug in and he pulled me close. "You were dead for *ten* minutes. ... We had no choice."

I had read somewhere that permanent brain damage happened within three minutes after death. I jerked out of his grip. "So this *shit* you put in me – the micro-fucking-bots – they're in my brain too?"

"Yes," he said coolly.

I leaned back against the mattress frame, wiped the sweat from my face and sucked in a ragged breath. My nerves retreated from redlining as I tried to process it all.

"So what the hell does the yellow glow mean?" I managed.

"The tech is still in the process of integrating with your nervous system," Toni said. "Once that's complete, the glow changes to green."

 "So what am I now, part of your fucking collective or something?"

"In a way you are," Kip said matter-of-factly.

"Just great." I leaned my head back again and sighed. "You can call me One of Three."

Toni leaned closer. "Cam?"

I tilted her a harsh scowl. "*What?*"

"You have to trust—"

I jerked a hand up. "I would *not* use that word right now."

She sat back and glanced at Kip. He gave an agreeing nod.

I tried to stand again. Toni reached out.

"I'll do this," I said rejecting her help.

I painfully clawed myself back onto the bed. Toni remained close. I gingerly moved under the blanket and turned away from them.

"Kip?" I said to the wall. "Can you give us a minute?"

"Sure, Cameron."

Kip walked from the room and quietly closed the bedroom door. Toni sat on the bed at a respectful distance.

"I assume the implant is directing the tech?" I asked finally.

"Yes," Toni said quietly.

"It'll take about three days?"

"Maybe four."

"Is there anything else you haven't *shared* with me?"

"No," she said just above a whisper.

I felt her hand at my shoulder. I twisted around. Tears rimmed her eyes.

"I-I'm so sorry, Cam."

I didn't hide my anger in the sigh I let out. "What's done is done, I guess."

"You're alive," she said. "That's what really matters."

She was right. I was alive, and it beat the alternative. I inched myself into a sitting position. Toni began to help, but quickly pulled back. I patted the bed next to me and she came over and sat. I took her hand.

"I guess I should thank you," I uttered.

A faint smile appeared, and she wiped her eyes.

"You have to understand," I said, "I took a chance – a *huge* chance – with you."

She dropped her attention to our hands. "I know."

"And now ... well ... I'm different, aren't I?"

Her nod was tentative.

"Look, Toni ... right now ... I'm not sure what I'm feeling ... about us. Hell, about anything."

Another nod.

"Look at me, please."

She lifted her head and our eyes met. The tears returned.

"I'm stuck with you guys, right?"

"For a while," she said, wiping her eyes.

"That's going to be a very *long* while." I rubbed the tops of her knuckles. "Toni, I have no idea what's in front of me ... in front of *us*. This is way uncharted territory."

"That's an understatement."

I let out a tired laugh. "No shit."

We sat there for a moment as the ramifications of what happened slowly settled around us. Part of me wanted to hug Toni. But a larger part was still freaked and raw and scared.

"Is there a manual?" I asked, breaking the moment.

It took her a second before another faint grin appeared. "No … there isn't."

"So what are all the colors about?" I was partly joking and partly not.

"The tech has two levels of color language. The first color displayed reflects the status of its host body. If you touch it longer, it displays a second color, which indicates the emotional state of the person. There're twenty-three different color levels. I can write them all down if you want."

"What color does it glow when someone has a connection … with another person?"

"It can't determine such a specific aspect of a general emotion."

"Can it determine attraction?"

"Yes."

"Okay then, so what color is it now?"

I leaned forward, and she awkwardly moved close and reached around and pulled the warm-up collar down.

"Well, what was it?" I asked.

"Red," she whispered.

9

DON'T BEAT YOURSELF UP.

For a brief moment of clarity during college, I was into Chinese religion. My favorite philosopher was *Lao-Tzu*. I liked a special passage associated with him: *Being deeply loved by someone gives you strength, while loving someone deeply gives you courage.* I'd had it inscribed on a simple silver bracelet for Karen. She'd been wearing it the day of the accident.

Toni and I were in bed back at our hotel, lying under the room's luxurious 1000 thread count linens and blanket. The hotel's website said the sheets had small amounts of gold carat and silk jacquard woven into them. I couldn't really tell a difference from the Crate and Barrel sheets I had at the loft. We would have stayed another day at Kip's, but Paul was coming home. At least I was feeling better, so the Calaian micro-bots must have been doing their job.

"Cameron?"

Ever since our little chat on the bed at Kip's, Toni had kept her distance. Not in a way that suggested she was mad; more like out of respect for the weird place I was in. Through the darkness, I felt her hand touch my arm.

"Yeah?" I answered.

"How's your tummy feel?"

"Better. Do you want to scan it again?"

Toni snatched her tablet off the nightstand. "Hold still," she said, looking intently at its screen. Its colors did their dance-thing and bathed her face in disco lights. "Do you feel any pain when you move?"

"Not anymore."

"How about when you go to the bathroom?"

"That's gone, too."

She nodded. "This is excellent progress, Cam. The tech is almost finished."

"Great. Hey, um, this heat thing." I pointed to the back of my neck. "Does that ever go away?"

"No," she said, still dealing with something on her screen. The glow on her face was green, now. "You'll get used to it."

She passed her hand across the screen and it winked out. We sat there in the darkness.

"Toni?" I asked finally.

"Yes?"

"Will I have powers?"

"Powers?"

"You know, the gravity thing."

"Yes," she said.

"Does it hurt … engaging the effect?"

"No, unless of course you engage too wide a field and get caught up in whatever it is you're having it do. Then you might get hurt."

"That's good to know. Well, good night."

"Good night, Cam. Sleep well."

We settled back into our respective positions, which were about as far away as we could get on a king-sized bed.

"Toni?"

"*Yes*?"

"Will you teach me how to use it?"

"I'm not that good with it."

"From what I saw the other night, you're a certified, bad-ass grav master."

She sucked in a long breath and sat up. "I didn't want to kill those men."

I twisted and faced her. "Why didn't you just disable them, like the trainer?"

"I couldn't see well enough in the light to make out Marco's head. I needed to see its exact shape and position in order to manifest the correct field inside his brain."

"I saw the field building around his head."

"I tried, but then he stabbed you and … I-I just *reacted*." She cupped her face with her hands. "What have I *done*, Cam? I've killed three humans!"

"Toni, you did what you had to do. Those bastards deserved it."

I hadn't told her what Marco had said about their plans. She thought they were just robbing us.

"Something happened inside me," she said, "when Marco drove the blade into you and you screamed. Something shifted, like a mental fracture, I guess, between my Calaian side and my human side."

"Sounds like your human side took over."

"You don't understand. Killing on Cala, even by accident or in self-defense, is *strictly* forbidden."

"Here on Earth, killing in self-defense is expected, and depending on the circumstances, it's even cheered."

"I can see their faces," she said. "They're stuck in my brain. Is that normal?"

"We call that haunting your mind, their faces, that is." I hesitated. "Toni?"

"Yes?"

"Don't be too haunted."

"You didn't kill–"

"They were evil, Toni ... *pure* evil."

I sat up and told her what Marco had planned for her. It was rough for me to recount. In the darkness, I couldn't tell how she was taking it.

"You all right with what I told you?" I asked.

"Yes," she said in a low tone.

"I'm sorry that you had to hear all that, but I wanted you to understand that the men you killed were what we call the scum of the Earth."

"Scum," she muttered.

"I was wondering something," I said. "How did you all clean up the aftermath and talk to the police?"

"I didn't call the police, I contacted Kip, via his implant's neural com. I used mine to connect with his."

"What do you mean … like he heard your voice in his mind?"

"And vice versa. I knew it would be the fastest way to communicate."

"Kind of like telepathy?"

"No, telepathy doesn't exist. What we do is driven by the tech. Anyway, he connected with my Concierge – they're trained in these matters."

"What did the Concierge do?"

Toni explained that when Kip and the Concierge arrived, the Concierge had dispensed with a guy who'd been comforting Toni with the flip of a fake badge and some stern Italian. After some Calaian tech magic to clean up the blood and nasty bits, he used his gravity trick to bring the tall guy down from his impalement. He and Kip positioned him in the alley next to Marco's headless body. While they were occupied, Toni had performed street surgery on my neck, inserting the cerebral particle implant the Concierge had brought and pumping blood back into me. A drunk couple had wandered into the alley, and after the Concierge shooed them away, they loaded me into Kip's car. Kip and Toni took me to Kip's apartment and continued to work on me. The Concierge had stayed behind and met with the police, acting as a witness and saying he had seen a black van pull up, dump the two bodies, and speed off.

"What about the man or that couple?" I asked.

Toni sighed. "We're just going to have to take our chances with them."

"Weren't there street cameras?"

"That alley doesn't have any, that's probably why Marco chose it."

"What about the van and the other guy?"

"It's still in the alley, and the man with the funny hat, well … he's *in* it. Even though it's the size of a bar of soap, it weighs as much as the van did, so no one can pick it up. I think the Concierge is getting a truck that lifts engines to take it away."

"That's crazy."

We sat in the darkness as the horror of the other night prowled around us.

"Do you regret meeting me?" she asked finally.

"I won't lie to you, Toni. … I'm still not really sure what I think right now."

"About us?"

It was my turn to let out a long sigh. "About everything."

"I realized something," she said, "as you died in my arms."

"What's that?"

"That the thought of you not being in my life was something I couldn't bear." Her voice cracked. "They teach us, in our classes, that if we fall in love, there may be no turning back."

"What do you mean?"

"Going home … to Cala. That the sheer power of human love's emotional pull is too much for some Calaians to handle."

"Like Kip?"

"I guess so."

"He seems happy."

"He's *very* happy. We've been talking about it over the last few days."

"And?"

"Staying on Earth was the hardest decision he's ever made. He didn't even get to say goodbye to anyone he knew on Cala. He just did it."

"You've never been in love before … have you?"

"It's different for us. It's not so life-consuming as it is here. I know this is going to sound corny, but when Marco stabbed you and you screamed, in that moment I felt my heart break in my chest. I had never experienced such an intense sense of loss. It felt like I, too, had been stabbed; that *I* would die next to you. The gravity fields formed instantly. It all happened before I knew what I was doing." She whimpered. "Oh, Cam, I feel so ashamed. Taking a life on Cala is-is just not *done*." She cupped her face again.

"Hey, it's okay. You acted on instinct."

Toni sucked back some tears. "That's what Kip said."

"You don't have instinct on Cala, do you?" I reached over, snagged a couple of tissues from the nightstand box and handed them to her.

"No," she said, wiping her eyes, "we lost that part of ourselves thousands of years ago."

"Come on, don't beat yourself up. You're human now. Instinct drives a lot of our actions."

You're a wonderful man, Cameron Harrison.

I sat up. "Hey. That was you … in my *head?*"

"Yes."

"Do it again."

Hey, you.

"Whoa, that's amazing. Are you constantly hearing my thoughts?"

"Oh, no. It doesn't work like that. You have to engage it with a certain mental cue."

"What's the cue?"

"You just think of the phrase *Engage with Toni's cerebral interface.*"

"That's too easy."

"It's meant to be."

I thought of the phrase, then the words *Thank you for saving my life.*

"You're welcome," Toni said.

10

WHAT ARE YOU?

"Just *think* it."

I did. Nothing.

"Try again," Kip urged, this time without the politeness of a moment ago.

I focused on the old beat-up metal trash can that sat in the field about 30 yards away and thought of lifting it a foot off the ground. It was a forty-galloner by the look of it.

Nothing. Again.

We had driven to a town on the outskirts of Rome, Monte-something, to a villa that belonged to someone Kip knew. He'd been insistent that we test my tech as soon as I felt ready, which was three days just as Toni had predict-ed. If the bots had flushed out, I never felt them. The home was more of a compound, straight out of a historical documentary, with a lot of land. The field where we stood looked over a beautiful valley speckled with old farm-houses. In the far distance, what looked like a medieval castle sat nestled among tall Tuscan cypresses. The bucolic setting was a stark contrast to the urban chaos of Rome. Cows grazed less than 150 yards away. One mooed on cue as if laughing at me.

Fuck you, cow.

"What are you thinking?" Toni asked.

I pointed. "Of lifting that … that *fricking* trash can."

The can glinted in the late morning light. It was mocking me, too.

Fuck you, can.

"Try thinking of it *being* where you want it," she suggested.

"As in don't think of it actually rising, just think of it already a couple feet off the ground?"

"Yeah."

I did. Nothing.

I turned at the sound of crunching grass behind us.

"*Gravitas* is Latin." The Prada man eyed me from under the brim of his straw fedora with a hint of arrogant amusement. "It means weight, Mr. Harrison. It is the natural phenomenon that brings all things with mass toward one another, even light."

"Is this your villa?" I asked.

"It is."

"Thanks for what you did the other night." I extended my hand.

He ignored it and looked at Toni. "It was the least I could do."

If every living being exuded an energy signature, as Toni had mentioned, then the Concierge gave off one that said *I am older than God.*

He stepped closer and put both hands on my shoulders. He was about six-two to my six foot, and there was a strength in his grip that felt otherworldly. He turned me towards the can.

"Weight, Mr. Harrison," he said calmly behind my right ear. "Gravity means *weight.*"

"And?" I asked, concentrating.

"Think that it doesn't have *any*," he whispered.

I did. The can shot into the air like a rocket. We watched it ascend into the blue cloudless sky.

"Toni," Kip asked, staring up, "*what* did you put in Cameron?"

"I don't know, now." Toni brought her gaze back to Earth and planted it on the Concierge. "What *did* I put in him?"

"Military grade bio-interlacement cortical neuralware," he said.

I turned to the group. "What does that—"

The can hit the ground with a startling clatter. We all flinched, except the Concierge.

"Are you insane?" Toni's shock was on full display. She took an angry step toward him.

"I thought it was necessary," he said calmly.

"What does that mean?" I asked.

Toni put her hands into the front pockets of her jeans and walked up. "That plane I tried to lift?" She shook her head. "That will be nothing for you."

She pivoted and looked harshly at the Concierge. "Are you *sure* this is the right thing to do?"

He eyed me again. There was no amusement in his look. "As a human, he'll need all the help he can get. Now." He pointed to the carcass of a flatbed truck that looked like it might have survived World War II. It sat abandoned and rusting about 10 yards away. "Crush that."

"Really?" I asked.

He nodded toward it.

I turned and thought of the van, back in Rome, and how it had compressed down. Nothing. "Wait ... let me try this again." I focused and thought of it *as* the size of a cigarette pack.

Nothing.

"CRUSH IT!" the Concierge yelled.

His voice startled the shit out of me. Adrenaline poured into my system. The truck compressed, and in a matter of seconds was gone.

The Concierge put a hand to my shoulder. "Fear," he said, "is a powerful catalyst."

"Like what Toni did to Marco and his men?"

"That was an anomaly. A rare influx burst in the cortical neuro-enhancer."

I pointed to where the truck had been. "Where did it go?"

"It's there, just too small for us to see."

Kip walked over and knelt in the middle of the indentation left in the grass by decades of the rusting hulk sitting in one spot. He felt around and looked back. The dismay on his face was unnerving.

"He compressed it to the molecular level," he shouted.

Toni gasped and turned to the Concierge. "What have you done?"

"I have given him a way to protect himself," he said calmly. "And in turn, he will protect you."

"He won't be able to control it."

The Concierge lowered his head in an odd show of submission. "I believe he will."

"Excuse me," I said.

Everyone turned.

"Look," I said, "I'm really new to all this *aliens walking among us* stuff, and I don't know dick about the Calaian culture, but … aren't you her superior?"

The Concierge hesitated.

"Kind of," Kip said, walking up.

"On Cala," Toni said, "your title ranks you in society, but your birthright is more important."

"Okay," I said, "so far, not so different from us. But I'm still not getting this. On the plane, you came across like you were going to, I don't know, reprimand her or something. Now you act like *she's* your boss. Which is it?"

The Concierge removed his hat and wiped his forehead with a white handkerchief. "Both." He returned the hat to his head and adjusted the brim down across his brow.

Toni's body language suggested she didn't like where the conversation was going, *at all*.

"Cameron," Kip said, "this is a little awkward to, ah, unpack."

"Awkward? *Really*? After all that you've done?" I folded my arms. "Try me."

"Toni is, on Cala, something a little like–" His eyes went to the Concierge.

"Okay, so she's a doctor or whatever. So what?" I turned to Toni. "What's going on? What *are* you?"

Toni shied.

"What would the word be in English?" Kip asked the Concierge. "Heiress?"

The Concierge sucked in a long breath. "No," he said, exhaling. "Royalty."

It took a second for the word to sink in. In the harshness of the midday light, Toni stood there looking as she always had: a little out of place, off beat in a quirky sort of way and pretty adorable. She produced her soft grin, but now I questioned its genuineness.

"Is this true?" I asked. "You're a princess or something?"

"I'm not a princess," she said. "On Cala I'm called a Sovereign's Descendant Legatee."

"She is the daughter of the High Sovereign of the Northern Governing House." There was a trace of pride in the Concierge's voice.

"So ... what ... do I bow?" I asked.

Toni brushed a wayward curl off her forehead. "No, you don't. I'm not like that."

"Yes, you are," the Concierge said.

Toni shot him a look. "No, I'm *not.*"

"With all due respect, you are, at least to millions on Cala."

"No one knows or cares who I am. I just work in a medical center."

There was clearly something more going on. The Concierge regarded Toni like a prideful uncle, whereas Kip seemed, I don't know, more protective. And Toni was not buying into any of it. She just saw herself as a plain-old Calaian, whatever *that* was. I, on the other hand, wasn't sure *where* I stood. Had our whole thing been an alien rich girl's romp? Was I just another plaything to be tossed on Toni's human boy-toy scrapheap? A weird sense of hurt pressed down.

"You okay?" Toni asked.

"Uh, yeah, sure." I turned to the Concierge. "You want me to go grav-ass on anything else?"

"We will continue your training after lunch," he said. "I can have Sofia prepare something for us."

The Concierge gestured to the villa's large patio, and he and Kip walked away.

I started to fall in behind, but Toni grabbed my arm.

"Hey," she said.

"What?"

"You're upset, aren't you?"

"What do you think?"

She stepped closer. "Look, Cam, I'm–"

"You lied to me, again. I asked you if there was anything else and you said no–"

Toni let out an exacerbated sigh. "Alright! I'm sorry. I should have told you from the beginning. It's just that … I don't see myself that way."

"*What* way?"

"Privileged."

"Are you?"

She shrugged.

"I want the truth, Toni."

"I do come from an old family of power and civic service."

"What are you, some rebellious daughter of a Calaian Rockefeller?"

Toni shrugged again. "I'm not *that* rebellious, and we're not royalty."

"So what am I ... one of your boy-toys?" My ego was bruised. Given all that had happened, I didn't hide it.

"*No*, Cam, you're not."

"Then why bullshit me?"

"To protect you."

"From what?"

"There are some in our society that fear change," the Concierge said walking up behind me.

His voice jarred me, and I felt something prickly at the base of my neck. I put a hand to the scar. My skin was very hot.

"Hmm, blue," he said.

"What's that mean?" I asked turning.

"That you've engaged the tech." He pointed to the field in front of us. "See?"

About 5 feet in front of the fallen trash can, I could barely make out the ten-foot spherical distortion field. Its edges shimmered in the sun as it hovered just off the ground. Its form distorted half the can.

"Think of it just being gone," the Concierge said.

I did and the sphere dissipated.

"After lunch, we will concentrate on your focus." He patted my shoulder. "We do not want you getting startled and leveling a city block, now *do* we?"

"What did you mean by *some in your society fear change?*" I felt the back of my neck again and it was normal.

"Toni's father had a vision for Cala," he said.

"What was he, your planet's president or something?"

"No, he was more of an ... industrialist."

I turned to Toni. "You *are* a Rockefeller."

"More like Steve Jobs," the Concierge said.

"What happened to your father?" I said to Toni.

"I believe the phrase is he *passed on*," the Concierge said.

Toni folded her arms tight against her chest. "He was murdered."

"I thought that was forbidden on Cala," I said.

The Concierge eyed me. "Precisely."

* * * *

I'm not sure why or how, but the Italians had elevated eating a meal to the level of high art. Lunch was delicious and consisted of everything I loved: pasta, fresh salads, stinky cheeses, olives and, yes, *vino*. Kip asked a lot of questions, mostly about my upbringing and family. I went into some detail, and the Concierge listened intently. About halfway through, Toni reached under the table and tried to take my hand. I was still a little pissed at her but took it anyway. Our fingers interlaced and her warmth felt good. After lunch, we returned to the field.

The Concierge pointed to the grazing cattle. "Form the largest spherical gravitational field you can."

The afternoon had heated up, and under my warmup little beads of sweat were rolling down my ribs.

I gave him a dubious look. "What if I build one the size of this town?"

"You won't."

"Are you sure?"

The Concierge didn't answer.

"That's what I thought." I started to think of a sphere, about the size of a small office building.

"And please, Mr. Harrison, make the field one that doesn't crush," he urged.

In the distance a massive sphere formed. It had to be at least a city block wide and equally tall. About a dozen cows slowly rose off the ground. A couple of them let out mournful moos as they ascended.

"Unbelievable," Kip said under his breath.

"Lower the cows," the Concierge urged. "We don't want to draw any attention."

I thought of them lowering and they did. After touching down, the last one bucked, then trotted off to join the others.

"How does he do it so effortlessly?" Toni asked the Concierge.

"His tech is extremely advanced and more powerful than yours or mine," he replied. "His interface is more integrated with his cerebral cortex."

"How powerful?" Toni asked.

"We do not know."

This brought all our attention around. The sphere collapsed.

Toni put her hands on her hips. "What do you mean, you don't *know?*"

"If he were a Calaian, we would know the capacity threshold. But since he is human, we cannot accurately ascertain that data."

"Then you also don't know what it's doing to his body?" she pressed.

"We know some of what is going on," he said. "He will adapt."

"You don't know that."

The Concierge approached Toni. "I swore an oath to your family's House that I would protect you." He pointed at me. "This man cares for you, and I would venture to say he might do anything to protect you." He threw me a look that said *you better or you'll have me to deal with.*

"I know your intent was good," Toni said. "But I don't think giving him–"

The Concierge's attention jerked to the sky out past the where the sphere had been. Kip cupped his hands to his forehead and squinted in the same direction.

Then I heard it. A high-pitched whine wafting in on the breeze, building volume.

"We have to go, *now!*" Kip said, panic edging his voice.

The Concierge and Kip hustled Toni towards the villa.

"Cam, come on!" she yelled over her shoulder.

A large drone appeared. Its winged metal fuselage caught the sun as it banked toward us.

"CAM!"

Toni turned back, but Kip and the Concierge grabbed her and picked her up under the arms. She kicked wildly as they carried her onto the patio.

Near the back of the drone's underbelly I saw a bright flash as a missile launched.

I thought of a grav field around the missile and visualized it nosediving into the ground.

It did.

The explosion and fireball sent the cows scurrying. The drone flew over us, banked away and circled for another run.

Cam, please. Toni's voice was bright and clear in my mind. *You'll be killed!*

Do not be a hero, the Concierge said. *Get in here, now!*

The drone skimmed the treetops, almost as if *it* was the missile. It disappeared behind the explosion's rising cloud of black and white smoke, only to pop through a second later. Its wings pitched left and right as it lined up for the attack.

I thought of a huge grav field, shaped like a dome, covering the area around the Concierge's villa. The skin on the back of my neck felt like it was sizzling.

The drone vectored in and approached at a high rate of speed, but about 40 yards out it exploded. The fireball defined the distortion field as it spread across its surface and rose into the air. Flaming parts slid down the field's curvature and rained onto the pasture.

I felt hands grab my waist. I was floating about a foot off the ground.

"Easy," Kip said, gently pulling me down.

My feet pressed into the grass and my knees buckled. Both Kip and the Concierge steadied me. I tasted blood on my lips and looked up at the fireball as it mushroomed above us. The last pieces of the drone fell to earth like tiny meteors.

"Well *done*, Mr. Harrison." The Concierge handed Toni his handkerchief. "Although just crushing it would have been the tidier solution."

Toni wiped under my nose. The handkerchief came away streaked with blood.

It felt like the wind had been knocked out of me. I bent over and took in a few deep breaths. I pointed to the still rising black cloud. "What the hell was *that* all about?"

"That was amazingly brave," Kip said.

"Or amazingly stupid." I straightened, my breath returning, and glared at the Concierge. "Answer my question."

"There is a war on Cala, Mr. Harrison," he said searching the sky. "It is, as you would say here, in the shadows, but it *is* a war nonetheless."

"What's it got to do with Toni?"

"I can explain that later. Right now, we must leave. The police will be here soon."

Toni placed her palm to my neck. "You're burning up." Her voice was full of the seriousness she displayed when she cared for me after the stabbing.

"Come," the Concierge beckoned, "my car is in the driveway."

"What about Sofia?" Toni asked.

"Sofia can handle the police."

With the help of Kip and Toni, I staggered to the Concierge's car. I felt disoriented, as if the space-time that I existed in was slightly off from the rest of reality. For a moment it looked as if the Concierge's movements had a tracer element to them, like part of him trailed behind as he walked. I stopped to puke, but nothing came up.

Kip and Toni poured me into the back of the late model Mercedes sedan and Toni slid next to me. The faint unique sound of Italian police sirens sing-songed in the distance. Kip got in front.

The Concierge swung the big car in a tight U-turn around the villa's grand driveway and sped between ornate wrought iron front gates.

"Take the low road," Kip urged.

The Concierge angled the car into a curve. Gravel kicked up as he powered through the turn.

There was a box of tissues on the floorboard. Toni grabbed several and wiped my nose. "He won't stop bleeding."

"Cameron," the Concierge said, "think of the blood pumping in your nose."

I felt the rhythmic pulse and focused.

"Do you feel it?" he asked.

"Yes," I said. "It's kind of like biofeedback."

"Good. Now, think of it slowing, but just a little. The implant will do the rest."

I did.

After a few minutes and another sharp curve, he asked, "Has it stopped?"

Toni inspected my nostrils. "For the most part."

"I've never seen a gravitational field so large." Kip twisted in the front passenger seat and faced me. "How did you do that?"

"I don't know," I said. "I just thought of it, and it formed.

Toni put her palm to the back of my neck. "You're still hot." She leaned over the front seat console. "I don't like this. He should be much cooler."

"I'll be okay."

The Concierge's cell phone rang. Its ringtone sounded like a famous opera theme, but I couldn't place it. He dug out the phone and deftly maneuvered through another curve.

"Yes? … No … We had to … I *know* that … I can explain … Sofia can handle it … She's well trained … Yes …. Yes … All right, we'll be there in twenty minutes. *Ciao.*"

"What's going on?" Kip asked.

We entered a straight stretch of road. The pastoral countryside was quickly giving way to an urban landscape. The Concierge sucked in a hesitant breath. He let it out slowly and drummed the top of the steering wheel with his fingers.

"We have been summoned," he said and gunned the engine.

11

WHAT DO WE DO?

The car fell into a tense uncharted silence as we drove through the outskirts of Rome. Toni, her eyes closed, rested her head against the window, while Kip stared out his window watching the Roman suburbs rise around us. I occasionally dabbed at my nose, but it had stopped bleeding about 10 minutes back. I felt a little better.

"So ..." I hadn't broached the subject yet, hoping that my alien "friends" would volunteer the information. "... anybody want to give me some details on what the hell all that was about?" Crickets. "Look, if you want me to protect Toni, I need to know what's going on."

"I am afraid," the Concierge said, "that the war I spoke of has come to Earth."

"No shit. But what does this have to do with Toni?"

"She's next in line," Kip said, still staring.

"No, I'm not." Toni sat up and ran a hand through her curls.

"I am afraid, my dear," the Concierge glanced at her in the rearview mirror, "that whatever *you* think does not matter, because the Mirage do not see it that way."

"Who're the Mirage?" I asked.

"An extremist group. Their members come out of the Ruling Elite's Black Guard," the old man replied.

"Like the Gestapo?"

"That analogy is not far off, except the Mirage are not officially recognized."

"What do they want from Toni?"

The Concierge shot me an annoyed glance over his shoulder. "Her life, Mr. Harrison. Or was that not evident back at the villa?"

"I get *that*. I'm asking why."

"Her father's House tried to overthrow the Calaian government." Kip turned from the window. "It failed."

"And the Mirage want to make sure that no other member of his House attempts another coup," the Concierge added.

"I could care less about Calaian politics." Toni folded her arms. "I wish they'd just leave me alone."

"Do you have brothers or sisters?" I asked her.

"She's an only child," Kip said.

"What are these Mirage?" I asked. "On Earth, I mean."

"I believe the correct title is pack," the Concierge said.

"The word is Mob," Kip corrected.

"Well, they are not organized crime. They hide behind a legitimate business."

"That's what the Mob *does*."

"Yes," the Concierge said, "but the Mirage are only here to hunt down Calaians who supported the coup. ... They have no other goals."

"Right," I said, "like flying a military grade drone over public space and launching a missile isn't illegal."

This drew a stern glance from the Concierge in the rearview mirror.

"Why are they here? I mean, your people are on vacation ... shouldn't they be hunting them on Cala?"

"Some Calaians do not come here for vacation," the Concierge said. "Many are here to evade the Mirage."

"Can they go back?"

"Not until the struggle is over," Kip said.

I turned to Toni. "Are you in exile?"

She laid her head back against the seat. "I just want to be on vacation. I've publicly stated I have no desire to run for a position or any of that. I just want to live my life peacefully. What my father did was his own business. It has nothing to do with me."

"How many of them are there?" I asked.

"On Earth ... maybe twenty or thirty," Kip said. "There are hundreds on Cala. Maybe more."

"That's not that many here on Earth. Why not just take them out?"

The Concierge hit me with another dour look.

"They're very well, um, *supported*," Kip said. "Here and on Cala."

As we came off the highway no one answered my question. We were now in a Roman suburb that was made up of large stretches of compressed residential areas, patchworked by light industrial parks. There were no mega malls with big box anchors here. These suburbs were a postcard blend of the rural countryside and Rome's urban sprawl. Many of the houses had small gardens and were roofed with red clay tiles. We passed an old woman, scarfed head and black nun's shoes, sweeping the street in front of her modest home.

The Concierge drove down several narrow tree-lined streets before turning into the parking area of a five-story, black-glass professional building whose nondescript architecture was a stark contrast to the neighborhood. He cautiously angled into a visitor space and turned the car off. His fingers drummed again as he stared out the windshield.

"How are we going to play this?" Kip asked.

The opera theme filled the cabin. The Concierge dug his phone out. "Yes? ... Yes, we're here ... *Yes*, they're with us ... *Yes*, we're coming in." He unbuckled his shoulder belt, turned in his seat and regarded us like children. "Speak only if you are spoken to," he said, "and follow my lead."

"Who are these people?" I asked.

The Concierge's eyes went to me, and for the first time I saw a hint of fear. "The Viceroys."

The lobby wasn't anything special. Utilitarian, by Italian standards. Black marble adorned the walls and a strong cleaning fluid odor filled the air. A couple of grey office-like vinyl club chairs and a matching sofa elbowed around a small glass oval coffee table. I picked up the lead of the fanned maga-zines. *Mortuary Sciences Monthly.*

"This is one of those funeral homes." I turned to Toni. "The ones you told me about ... that do the DNA harvesting?"

The Concierge put a finger to his lips.

Yes. Toni mouthed. *Their headquarters.*

The elevator across the lobby dinged. Its polished brass doors parted, and an Asian gentleman stepped out. He was dressed just as I would expect from an international mortician mogul: an expensive haute black suit, trendy patent leather Oxfords and a thin black tie. His hair was nearly military short, and the guy definitely worked out.

"Enzo," he said walking up to the Concierge.

Enzo?

Enzo extended a hand and they shook. "Yoichi, you are looking very smart." His tone was a bit kiss-ass.

Yoichi's attention settled on us.

Enzo gestured. "Let me intro–"

"We *know* who they are." The scorn in Yoichi's voice hit us like a winter cold front. "Come ... they're waiting."

The elevator's operatic music was similar to Enzo's ringtone. Maybe Enzo had been in the Calaian mortuary biz? The elevator jerked to a halt at the fifth floor and opened its doors to a large conference room. Floor-to-ceiling windows lined one whole side of the room, while dark cherry wood cabinets, each containing a vast number of nondescript books, framed a conference table made from the same polished black marble as the lobby. Seated around the table were twenty stern-faced older men, all dressed like Yoichi. A woman, her thin blonde hair pulled tightly into a short ponytail, headed the table. She wore a simple black dress with a neckline that revealed a hint of cleavage. She was about my age, maybe younger. Her expression was as grim as the others, but her bearing exuded authority. Yoichi herded us into the far corner of the room.

The boss lady gestured for Enzo to approach. He did so with confidence without overselling it. She addressed the group in Italian. About a heartbeat later I heard her voice in English in my mind.

"Gentlemen," she said, "we have a situation. The Mirage on Earth have escalated their push. Enzo will brief you on the details."

Enzo proceeded in Italian, while my tech translated. He began with a brief history of the war on Earth and how it had evolved. Then he went into my relationship with Toni, and that I was a decent and moral human. This got a few sympathetic nods from a couple of old-timers. He described the theater incident and how Toni had selflessly used her cerebral tech to save hundreds of human lives. He recounted the attempted abduction in Rome, of Toni's pleading to save my life, the combat tech that she had implanted, and the reasons why he chose to use such advanced bio-interlacement neuralware on a human. A few board members scoffed at this disclosure. He made it clear the Mirage had crossed a boundary and that Toni's life, along with other Calaians seeking asylum on Earth, was in grave danger, and that today's testing confirmed that my neuralware performance exceeded even the wildest projections.

"The Mirage have become recklessly militant," Enzo continued. "Today's incident indicates that they are becoming more brazen, and their actions will only lead to a level of unacceptable exposure, and quite possibly, a violent *public* confrontation. They *must* be stopped."

The room fell silent. The boss lady stared at Enzo, then her attention slid to me. "Approach," she said in English.

I pointed to myself. "Me?"

She nodded.

I stepped up to Enzo's side.

"Why are you here?" she asked.

"Well, ma'am, I, um ... well, I guess because I went on a date."

A few of the board members stifled their laughs.

The boss lady raised her hand and the room went silent. She leaned on the table and eyed me under her severely cut bangs. "No, Cameron Harrison, why are *you* here? Why did Enzo take a risk on you? Why did he choose our most advanced neural combatware? But more importantly, *why* should this council even *care* about you?"

The base of my neck was getting very warm. I looked back at Toni. She smiled and I thought of the *Lao-Tzu* passage.

"I guess, ma'am," I said, turning into the boss lady's scrutiny, "I'm here because I care about someone who is very important on Cala."

The boss lady settled back into her chair and regarded me. "We first landed on this rock when your ancestors were crawling out of the African plains." She casually pointed a finger to a few at the table. "Some of us have watched your civilization struggle through world wars, political upheavals and a whole host of natural and manmade disasters. Yet in spite of all the pain you inflict on yourselves, I find your species fascinating. I even root for you, although I think I'm a minority in that."

More chuckles.

"Thank you, ma'am," I said.

"Be quiet." Her tone suggested she could, with a wag of a finger, wipe humanity away.

My tech instantly heated up, and a grav sphere formed right above the middle of the table. It expanded to about five feet and held. The conference phone slowly rose to its center. Enzo's eyes went big. Several of the Viceroys pushed back from the table.

A faint smirk snaked across the boss lady's thin lips. She leaned forward and inspected the sphere. "You see this, gentlemen? *This* is what we have lost on Cala." She pointed to me. "A spirit so deep, it manifests without thinking." She stood and leaned onto the table. "The Mirage have become a liability. They're a virus that needs to be eradicated." She straightened and raised her hand, palm up. My grav sphere shrunk to the size of a baseball and floated to her outstretched palm. The boss lady closed her fingers around it, and it vanished.

The aftereffects from my fight with the drone were catching up. I wobbled and Enzo caught me by the shoulder.

"We're not an army," one of the older Viceroys objected.

"I will return to Cala and deal with this," she said. She motioned for Kip to approach. "Captain?"

Kip came to my side and stiffened. "Yes, ma'am?"

"You served the Northern House, did you not?"

"I did."

"With distinction?"

"Yes."

"And you have chosen to live as one of them?"

"I have."

She tilted an impassive glance at Yoichi. "Is his tech still usable?"

Yoichi removed a tablet like Toni's from his coat's inside breast pocket. "Yes," he said after a few finger swipes, "but it's older."

"Activate him."

Yoichi did a few more finger taps. Kip flinched like someone had smacked him against the back of the neck.

"Captain, are you up to the task of dealing with the Mirage?" she asked.

"Do I have a choice?" Kip asked, rubbing the back of his neck.

"Not if you wish to remain on Earth. Toni Morgan, approach."

Toni came and stood next to me. She took my hand.

The Viceroys stood like cadets at a spring formal and faced her. They bowed their heads in unison, even the boss lady. Toni returned the gesture, and I saw the depth of her heritage reflected in the prideful pull back of her shoulders and the diminutive tilt of her head. These Viceroys were below her and, if the moment was right, Toni wasn't averse to reminding them of that fact. She raised her head and her family's dignity remained on full display.

"You are of an age to make your own decisions," the boss lady said to her. "Do you wish to leave Earth or stay?"

"I'd like to stay." Toni squeezed my hand.

"We cannot guarantee your safety here. Do you understand the potential consequences?"

"I do."

"Do you understand that death, by natural or outside causes, could occur, and that it could be real and permanent?"

"I do."

The boss lady surveyed the table as if this might be the last time she would see any of them. "I will return as soon as I can," she said behind a long sigh.

"What should we do in the meantime?" I asked.

The look she granted me carried a lot of judgment. "I *suggest*, Cameron Harrison, that you focus on staying alive."

12

WHY US?

Yoichi ushered us out, but Enzo stayed behind. We waited in the lobby about 15 minutes before he finally emerged from the elevator. His demean-
or suggested the boss lady had given him the equivalent of an offer he couldn't
refuse. We all picked up on it and gave him some distance. If the ride from the
villa had been silent, the ride back to our hotel was downright morbid. The
silence was broken only when Enzo took a call from Sofia. She'd explained to
the *Polizia* that the drone had just blown up over the villa, but the only injury
was a cow burned by falling parts. This news tempered Enzo's edginess. Surprisingly, when we pulled up to the hotel, he valeted and joined us in the bar.

"What can I get for you all?" Our waiter's heavily accented voice bare-ly carried over the bar's deafening synth-infused house music.

"Bourbon with ice, please." Toni practically shouted the words.

"Double," I said. "Lots of ice ... and not a well ... bring something good."

"Are you sure you want to drink with the way you feel?" she asked.

"Maybe it'll help."

"Do you have a preference?" the waiter asked.

"Surprise me."

Kip ordered a vodka-tonic, indifferent about the brand. The waiter turned to Enzo. "And for you, sir?"

After a long contemplation, Enzo glanced up from his stare-down with the bowl of mixed nuts. "Negroni."

"Very good. I'll have these right out."

We had settled into thick, well-worn leather armchairs, the kind you might find in the cigar lounge of a posh Southern country club. They ringed a low marble coffee table whose style was about 10 seasons ago. The music ebbed a bit.

"Enzo?"

The old man looked up and regarded me as if he couldn't quite decide whether I was friend or foe.

"What did the Viceroys say after we left?"

Enzo's eyes dropped to the bowl again. "They want us to neutralize the Mirage on Earth."

"Take them all out?" The alarm in Kip's voice was unnerving.

"Yes. And we have to be *very* discreet."

Enzo went on to explain that the Viceroys' mandate wasn't up for debate, and there would be hell to pay if we didn't comply. We sat stunned and joined Enzo in his stare-down with the bowl of nuts, collectively contemplating the directive. The din of conversation shouted over music swirled around us.

Our drinks arrived, and I offered a half-hearted toast to our future success. We took healthy swigs. Enzo, though, took a pensive sip and slowly lowered his Negroni to the table.

"Why?" I posed, regarding my glass' delicious amber liquid. It had a vanilla edge.

"Why what?" Toni asked.

"Why *us*?"

"Enzo and I have military backgrounds," Kip said.

"I have medical knowledge," Toni offered. "Maybe there's something they think I can do?"

Drink in hand, Enzo shook his head and pointed a finger at me. "It is you." He knocked back most of his Negroni.

I sat up. "Why?"

"You are the most powerful now."

Kip nodded. "It makes sense."

"Yeah, but guys," I said, "I'm not trained for this kind of thing."

"I wouldn't say that." Toni gave me a sideways look. "Back at the villa, you did look like a bad-ass grav master."

"What are we up against with the *Mirage*?" I downed the rest of my drink. Surprisingly, the after-effects of my grav display had subsided considerably.

Enzo settled back into his chair. "The Mirage are highly trained opera-tives, and they are ruthless."

"They're zealots," Kip added.

"The good news is they cannot leverage their cortical offense against us," Enzo said.

"Why's that?" I asked.

"Because ours will neutralize it." Enzo eyed the remnants of his drink. "Our cortical technology has a built-in mutual deterrent. It ensures that there is no unauthorized usage between Calaians on Earth. It lessens the risk of ex-posing our presence here."

"So they go old-school, like using the drone?"

Enzo nodded. "They have to resort to Earth's crude technology."

"Is my tech useless too?" I asked.

"No, your tech will–"

Suddenly, the back of my neck heated up. "What the hell?" I put a hand to the scar.

"What is it, Cam?" Toni asked.

"My tech just engaged." A flu-like ache shot through my joints. "Shit, it's scorching." A stream of white data cascaded down the right side of my field of vision. It seemed to float about six inches in front of me. "Whoa, *shit*. I have a massive info-dump scrolling in front of my eyes." The effect was nauseating.

Enzo and Kip sat up and began surveying the room. Enzo urgently asked, "What is the data?"

"Parameters, uh, distances, trajectory data. All in English." The room's color spectrum shifted; bodies acquired a glow around them. Details and colors were more pronounced yet saturated in a green hue. It felt as if my senses were enhanced and my mind on overdrive. An intense heat spread from my cerebral

implant and surged into every part of my body. The music hitting my now

hyper-sensitive hearing was borderline painful.

"Can you give us details?" Enzo demanded.

The bar was packed, but at the edge of my periphery, equidistant from

each other and triangulated around us, I could make out three completely

black human figures. In my new perspective, their forms had an electric blue

shimmer of a silhouette. My tactical system flashed a bright yellow outline

inside each body indicating, I guess, what kind of hidden creature might be

using it. For a split-second, I thought I glimpsed what a Calaian might actually

look like. Data sprang from the form and ran across my vision. It scrolled too

fast, and I couldn't pick out the info.

"Mr. Harrison?!"

"I've got three black figures about forty feet from us," I said.

"*What* are they?" Kip asked harshly.

"The data is streaming too fast. One is a – wait, they're moving in."

"Be alert, people," Enzo said. "These are Calaians. Are they coordinat-

ed?"

"Yes," I said.

"It's the Mirage," Kip said. "They've tagged us."

"We have civilians around us," Enzo warned. "Nothing grand."

The black figures assumed staggered positions. I thought of the data

stream going away, and my normal vision washed over the tactical perspective.

The closest one was to my right, but I couldn't see through the forest of young

business-types getting their drink on. Everyone was dressed as if they worked

at the same high-powered law firm. Two guys in slim-tailored business suits walked away and I saw her leaning against the faux wood skin of one of the bar's six massive structural columns. A silver cocktail dress hugged her athletic body like foil on a chocolate bar. I caught her stare. A brutal smirk spread from one corner of her clenched mouth.

"You see any of them?" Kip asked.

"Three-o'clock," I said, "silver mini-dress."

Enzo and Kip jerked their heads in that direction. With a hyper focus, the female Mirage came off the column. Her stride was scarily raptorial. I innately sprang in front of Toni. Enzo and Kip rose and watched the flanks.

The Mirage's dress caught a hot LED spot and sent white sparkles dancing across a table of hipster creative types. She stopped about six feet away, and I could finally see her. She was beyond gorgeous. Athletic small breasts were squeezed into the top of her strapless club dress, and her white hair was cut short along the angle of her sharp jawline. The Mirage scrutinized me from a set of sunken jacked-up black eyes.

"You the human?" she hissed. A guy backed into her, and she brushed him off with some kind of Aikido move. Her bare, sinuous arms handled his excessive bulk as if the guy was made of cardboard.

A suspicious calm moved through me. "It was two days ago."

The Mirage made a move toward me. I thought of her collapsing into the vacant club chair just off her right hip. Her eyes went slack, and the taut assault tension receded from her body. She pooled into the club chair like an over-served sorority pledge. I swung around, thought of the data, and my tactical perspective came down over my vision like a shutter. Combat parameters appeared at the bottom. One black figure was about 15 feet to the right of Kip, the other 10 feet off Enzo's left. Both were holding their ground.

"I think I see one," Kip said, out of the side of his mouth.

"I do, as well," Enzo added.

I lifted the tactical perspective and eyed the other two Mirages. These guys were big. Each easily over six-three. Toni tucked her legs tight to her chest. She looked scared. I stepped between Enzo and Kip. Each shot me a perplexed glance.

"I have this," I said, my voice a bit monotone. I took another step forward and raised a hand to each of the two Mirages as they stormed in.

For the blonde tatted one on my right, I thought of him fainting. Instantly he passed out across the legs of two guys who were settled into a narrow post-modern couch unit. They stood up and dumped him onto the glass coffee table they shared with the sister couch across from them. The blonde Mirage hit the glass hard, face down, and it shattered under his weight. Drinks went flying, and some of the people shrieked and jumped back onto their couch.

I spun and pinned my gaze on the last Mirage. He stopped, mid-step, a few feet from Enzo, a handgun partially drawn from under his coat. His sudden action dislodged long stringy black bangs that spilled down his forehead. His eyes darted to his comrade, now laying in a pool of shattered glass and blood. I met the Mirage's anger and wrapped a grav field around him up to his neck. He stiffened with his arms tight to his body. I glanced at the gun and thought of it compressing. It vanished. His eyes flared. I stepped closer. Enzo grabbed my arm, but I jerked out of his grip.

"This is *impossible*," the Mirage declared in an accent I couldn't place. "How are you doing this?"

"I'm from Krypton."

I thought of the field tightening a little. The Mirage coughed and struggled in the field's grip. Luckily, the crowd was focused on the blonde Mirage's aftermath. Two waiters were gingerly rolling him over.

I mentally pulled the Mirage closer. He slid the distance left between us. "If you or any of your fucking douchebag comrades comes near me or my friends *ever* again, I will crush them down to the size of a fucking proton. Are we *clear*?"

The Mirage managed a tight nod, despite the field's grip.

"Now, be a good boy, and go back and tell your asshole friends there's a new sheriff in town."

I released him and he stumbled back into two suits on their way to gawk at the blonde Mirage's mess. The guy straightened and eyed me like I had just killed his god. He started to advance, but I created two pinpoint grav fields the shape of fingers and dug in on either side of his windpipe. He fought against my hold. I squeezed harder.

"Don't make me," I said.

He gripped his throat and nodded again.

I released him. He gasped out a cough and stumbled back.

"Go," I snapped. "*Now!*"

The Mirage straightened and gave a slight recognitional nod, then turned and pressed through the crowd and out the bar's street entrance. Consumed by the moment's intensity, the hand at my shoulder snapped me back.

"Stand down," Enzo ordered.

I hadn't realized how on point I was. The cerebral implant's combat protocols released their grip. Various parts of my body relaxed as the flood of tactical influencers receded. My normal vision returned. I shook off the last of the implant's presence. My forehead was slick with sweat.

Disappointment was stretched tight across Enzo's face. "Why did you not *kill* them?" he demanded.

"I, um … well …"

"He's never done it before," Kip said. "It's not in his makeup."

Enzo grabbed my arm and leaned in. "We are at *war*." His anger was palpable. "We may not get an opportunity like this again."

I thought about his hand letting go and Enzo's arm jerked straight out to his side. My grav field's shimmer was barely visible in the club's torrent of lighting. He almost smacked a waitress in the face. She sidestepped his motion without spilling anything on her tray. He looked at his hand in dismay and tried his other, but that arm went straight out and barely missed Kip.

Enzo started to choke.

"Cameron, stop!" Kip demanded.

"I'm not thinking this," I replied.

"Think *not* choking him."

"I'm *am*!"

Enzo went to one knee. His face was becoming ashen.

Toni grabbed my arm. "Cam, stop, please. You're killing him."

"I don't know *how*. Usually I just think it and it happens."

Kip spun me around and frantically inspected the back of my neck. "There's no glow. His tech must be malfunctioning." He pulled out a tablet similar to Toni's and swiped its screen.

"What the fuck is *happening*?" Deep electrical impulses jolted through my body.

Toni grabbed the front of my shirt and pulled me to her lips. Her kiss was intense. I went with it and took her into my arms. After a long passionate moment, the impulses subsided. Enzo coughed and sucked in a huge breath. Kip helped him stand.

"Smart … thinking … Ms. Morgan," Enzo managed between gulps of air. "Diverting his … neural … protocols."

"I'm really sorry," I pleaded, "I didn't know how to stop it."

Enzo doubled over with a coughing fit.

"Is everything all right here?" our waiter asked, coming up.

"He just swallowed funny," Kip said. "He'll be okay." He patted Enzo's back. Enzo, still doubled over, gave a thumbs-up. "Bring us the check."

Our waiter nodded and hurried off.

Enzo straightened, regaining his breath. "It is not your fault." He cleared his throat. "We need to do a compete diagnostic. The tech is deploying on emotional signals. It might kill you. Something is terribly wrong."

"Let's get out of here." Kip's eyes scanned the bar. "There may be more of them."

"Check these two," Enzo said.

Kip pulled out a device similar to Toni's and swiped its screen. He nodded to the female Mirage. "She's out. Asphyxiation."

"Her tech?"

"Still active and engaged." A couple of glammed-up club girls had noticed the female Mirage seemingly passed out. The taller girl patted her face and looked like she actually gave a shit.

"What about his tech?" Enzo asked.

The blonde Mirage, who was now sitting up in the bed of shattered glass and mopping the blood from a nasty wound across the bridge of his nose with a napkin, shot us one of the meanest death-stares I had ever seen.

Kip looked up from his pad, stunned. "He's *not* engaged in the system."

Enzo regarded him dispassionately, then the Mirage clutched his chest and convulsed. The two waiters at his side tried to help, but he was having what looked like a heart attack. He collapsed back into the shards of glass sprawled across the floor. Someone called for a defibrillator. As the bar's deep dance bass thumped, I watched one of the waiters frantically begin CPR.

13

A POWERFUL CATALYST.

We were now in a sordid part of Rome, far from its touristy areas. Warehouses and row homes were heavily tagged with guerrilla paintings and Banksy wannabes. Corners were littered with thuggish teens and street musicians. A tall, ragged gutter poet stood on a fruit box and shouted angst-filled stanzas to three mangy dogs.

Enzo steered the Mercedes cautiously down a narrow alley, and we approached two large graffiti-covered doors. He clicked a button in his visor, and they parted slowly. Four rows of shop lights flickered on, revealing a cavernous garage. He pulled in and came to a stop just shy of a well-used metal utility cart and a large wooden workbench. He clicked the visor button again and the garage doors squeaked angrily closed. Even in the cocoon of the Mercedes's cabin, smells of oil and grease and fuel seeped in. We stepped out and the clunks of our car doors echoed around the garage. Enzo went to a wall panel and disarmed the security.

The ambush at our hotel bar put Kip and Enzo on a tactical edge. Even though Kip didn't know how the Mirage had gotten through our tech's cloaking protocols, he assured us his new encryptions would protect us. The real question was for how long. I didn't even know we had cloaking, but Enzo assured me we did, and it should have prevented the Mirage from discovering our whereabouts.

Parked in the shadows against one side of the huge space was a row of restored cars. Most were partially covered with worn green tarps, but two uncovered Bugatti roadsters stood out as testaments to an era when driving was a pleasure.

"How are you feeling?" Toni asked, walking up to my side.

"A little better, actually." I leaned against the Mercedes. "Is this your man cave?" I asked Enzo.

The old man walked over to one of the covered treasures and yanked its tarp back. Dust rose through slivers of light to the wooden rafters above. I let out a long low whistle.

"What is that?" Toni asked.

Enzo gestured to the car's magnificently polished silver body. "This, my dear, is a—"

"Maserati Berlinetta." I met Enzo's astonishment. "It was produced from nineteen fifty-three to nineteen fifty-five. It was designed by Pininfarina, and is considered the best-designed Maserati of all-time. There were only *four* made."

Enzo gave me a mockingly demure golf clap.

"My dad was into cars," I explained. "It bonded us when I was a teen-ager. I assume this is an original?"

"It is. Would you like to sit in it?"

"Hell to the yes."

Still not a hundred percent, I shuffled to the driver's side door as Enzo opened it. Spartan by today's standards, the Berlinetta's interior was a lesson in classic 1950s Italian design. Its over-sized lacquered wooden steering wheel and tall chrome shifter were things of beauty, but the ergonomics paled in comparison to the cockpit of even the cheapest modern car. I slid into the roadster's surprisingly contemporary bucket seats and gripped the wheel.

"What do you think?" Enzo's grin was all pride.

As I passed my attention over the interior, I thought of my dad and how he would have loved to be where I was now. A faint melancholy rose.

"Something wrong?" Enzo asked.

"No, no … still feeling just a little off." I ran my fingers across the car's leather headliner.

"Gentlemen," Kip said. "We have to get to work."

Enzo peered down through the window. "After all this is put to rest, we will take this out for a spin, eh?"

Kip pulled out his Calaian tablet and motioned me over to the utility cart. "Turn around," he ordered. I did, and he passed the device's leading edge down my spine.

"Well?" Enzo asked.

"There's definitely areas of major malfunction," he said.

"Can they be corrected?" Enzo asked.

"This tech is beyond anything I ever worked on. And even if I could, I would need the proper equipment to fully diagnose the specifics. I'm sorry, Enzo."

"There has to be something we can do," Toni said.

Kip shook his head. "I don't know what."

Toni frowned. "If Cam engages the tech again, it might kill him, or somebody else."

"I *know*. But this is prototype tech. Military level." Kip gestured to Enzo. "You did this. You need to fix it."

My head began to ache again. "This is *fucked* up," I blurted.

"Mr. Harrison," Enzo said. "You must control your emotional–"

I raised a hand and the old man visibly flinched. I fought to keep the tech from engaging. "Shut ... *up*."

"Cameron," Kip said, "listen, we–"

I raised my other hand, and Kip, too, drew back.

Somewhere near the edge of my perception, I experienced the same strange feeling I had back at the villa, like my reality was skirting normal time and space. I fell against the Berlinetta and grabbed its ornate side mirror for support.

Toni started for me, but I hit her with a hard glare.

The reality of my situation was boiling over. Just two weeks ago I was a nobody web designer, making a decent living doing sites for start-ups. My biggest concern had been where to have dinner. Now, I was up to my *ass* in an intergalactic political war with alien tech shoehorned into my skull.

"Cam," Toni said, "what's the matter?"

"Look," I rubbed my face and let out a frustrated sigh, "I'm trying to be a *team* player here, but come on. ... You all did this to me, remember?" I stabbed a thumb at the back of my neck. "I didn't ask to be made into some fucking Calaian *RoboCop*. Don't get me wrong, I *love* being alive, but when this is done you get to hang up your human bodies and cruise back to Cala ... I've got to deal with this for the rest of my life." I leaned against the driver's side door. "Shit, I feel like crap again."

Enzo didn't hide his disappointment. He folded his arms. "Maybe I have misjudged you."

"You're goddamn right you misjudged me. I'm not a killer. I didn't come out of the military. I'm a suburban kid, for fuck's sake."

"He needs training," Kip said to Enzo, "especially if he's going to be an asset."

"We do not know if his tech can be fixed, much less if he is trainable," the old man replied.

"What he needs is *rest*," Toni countered. "We all do, and you're–"

I let out a whistle like my old high-school track coach did when he wanted the team's full attention. The Calaians went silent.

"You know, I, ah, didn't plan on ... this." The emotion of it all was rising. My attention went to the shop floor and the dark center of an old oil stain. "I just wanted to go on a date." I looked up into their stares. "You say I don't know how to kill ... that I don't know death? I lost the love of my life. I *know* what death is. I had a conversation with it in the middle of the *fucking morgue!*" I pointed an angry finger at Enzo. "So don't lecture me." I took a step closer and pounded my chest. "I know all *about* it." I looked up into the room's old wooden beams, and the pain of that night poured over me like liquid despair. "I wanted to *kill* that *fucking* drunk driver!" I leveled my agony across all of them. "But you'll never know what that's like, will you? No, Cala is a *civilized* world." I sucked back the rage. "You want to make me the ultimate weapon? Sure, *no problem*." I held my glare on Enzo and outstretched my left hand. One of the Bugattis slid into the open area between us, its tires screeching across the cement. I snapped my fingers and within six seconds it crushed to the size of a candy bar. As the sounds of its destruction dispersed into the rafters, I got into the old man's face. "Anger," I said tightly, "is *also* a powerful catalyst."

Enzo regarded me with compassion. He patted the side of my face like an Italian father consoling a child.

"You are correct," he said. "We will never truly understand what you went through. That part of us ... that emotional fragility, well ... we have slowly lost that over millennia. And I *am* sorry that you got caught up in all of this. But," he clapped his hands onto my shoulders, "you *are* in this, Mr. Harrison, and we need you."

I wiped sweat off my forehead and stared at the tiny lump of compressed metals that had been the magnificent roadster. I took in a deep breath, and let my hate and anger slip away. "Sorry about the car."

Enzo put an arm around my shoulder and gave me a side-hug. "Nothing to worry about." He whispered, "It was a replica."

14

IT'S A START.

I was raw, and the last thing I wanted was to talk with anyone. The Calaians had ordered pizza and salads for dinner, but I didn't eat much. Afterward, Enzo settled into a duct-taped ratty shop chair, and Kip and Toni on grease-infused hard mechanic mats. I curled up on the bare cement floor with my back to them and tried to find comfort in a severely cracked cinder block corner wall. I think I fell asleep around midnight. When I woke, the smell of fresh brewed coffee made me roll over and face my reality.

"Hi." Toni was sitting cross-legged about four feet from me.

"Morning." I sat up and my lower back immediately spasmed. I pressed the heels of my palms into my eyes and tried to rub away my sleep-deprived bleariness. "Did you sit there all night?"

"Cam, I had no idea that–"

"Please ... I don't want to talk about it."

Toni's eyes went to the floor.

We sat there a moment, then she crawled over and wrapped her arms around my neck and bear-hugged me. She almost knocked me back. *I'm here for you.*

Her voice came into my mind like the sun cracking over a mountain. There was an intimacy about it that I hadn't felt in a long time ... an utterance meant just for me.

I hugged her back. *I know you are–*

"Would you two like some coffee?" Enzo stood by the wooden shop table, cup raised.

Toni twisted around. "Yes, please." She turned back. "Cam ... I–"

"I need to say something." I collected what I could of any mental fortitude I had left. "I've had, um, trouble ... you know ... dealing."

"She was the love of your life. It's understandable."

"I've also been afraid."

"Of what?"

I thought about meeting her gaze but couldn't. "Moving on."

"I think I know what you're feeling ... kind of. When you died, back in the alley, in those immediate moments, between all the pain and sadness, I felt really lost. I've never felt that before. I was so ..."

Behind her human eyes I could almost see Toni's Calaian mind trying to process the litany of strange emotions. "Scared?" I offered.

She nodded.

"It's weird," I said. "Unless you've been through a loss, it's hard to really understand the feeling of being adrift."

"You were lucky."

"How's that?"

"You got to experience a deep and wonderful relationship, even if short. From what I can tell, most people on your world don't even get close to that."

For being new to planet Earth, Toni had summed up the human condition pretty accurately. I had been so consumed by grief that I lost perspective for what I'd had with Karen. In that heartbeat I felt something leave my presence. Not like a weight being lifted. More like a loss, as if some deeply veiled part of me had separated and floated away.

Goodbye, Karen. I sat there a moment, then let out a long, cathartic breath. "Maybe it's time," I said more to myself.

"For what?" Toni asked.

"To move on."

We were standing around the big shop table, quietly sipping Enzo's god-awful coffee. It had the consistency of motor oil, and as I swirled what was left in my cup I wondered if it actually was. Kip was engrossed in his Calaian tablet. He hadn't looked up or even said good morning when Toni and I had walked over.

"I'm starving," I said after another bitter sip.

"Me, too," Toni said.

"Are you done?" Enzo asked Kip.

Kip set his tablet down. "It won't last, but it buys us some time."

"What's going on?" I asked.

"We believe the Mirage hacked our neural footprints," Enzo said. "That is why we were attacked back at the hotel. Our tech immediately compensated, and we were cloaked again after we left. But it will not last. I asked Kip to try and enhance the cloaking counter measures in all of our implants."

"Do the Mirage know we're here?" I asked.

"No," Kip said. "As far as I can tell, we've been securely cloaked since we left the bar. No intrusions."

"And no one knows about this garage," Enzo added.

"Are we stuck here?" Toni asked.

"No, but we should limit our movement."

"Great, so can we go get something to eat?" I asked. "It's almost noon."

Enzo shot Kip a questioning glance.

"I don't see why not," Kip said.

*   *   *   *

During the day, the area around Enzo's man cave didn't appear as ghetto as it did at night. Gone were the gritty street kids bent on jacking wayward tourists. The corner where the street poet had been riffing had a charming local trattoria anchored to it. The sun was high. Its glare stung my fluorescent fatigued eyes.

"I would kill for a pair of sunglasses," I mused, sidestepping an over-turned trash can. Its contents and smell were a putrid mess of diapers, rotten food and cat litter.

We emerged from the alley onto a boulevard that had been deserted last night. Now it was busy with cyclists, cars, and Euro minivans. A guy wearing short-shorts, Converse All-Stars and a sleeveless tank-top rode by on one of those old-time circus unicycles. That and the full daylight burn on all the building tags made the whole scene look like a Cirque du Soleil backdrop. We waited for the crosswalk signal to change.

"You don't need sunglasses," Kip said, looking each way down the boulevard.

"Just think of your vision getting darker," Enzo said. "The tech will do the rest."

"Really?" I asked.

"Wishing for something and directing the tech to *do* something are two different things. The tech is intuitive, Mr. Harrison. It takes time for it to understand your mental directives and, conversely, you must learn how it will react. It is a symbiotic relationship."

"Okay, darker. Right." I thought of my vision getting darker and it did, as if a full eclipse was occurring. "Oh, man ... this is *so* cool. Can I vary the—" But the dimming kept getting inkier. Suddenly, everything was black. "Oh shit! Guys, *guys!*" My world had been kicked out from under me. I felt hands, stopping my panicked movement. "Oh, shit, I'm blind!"

"Relax, Cam." Toni's soft sympathetic hand was at my cheek. "You went too far." I could hear the stifled laugh in her voice. "Just think of it going away."

"I *am*, but it's not working."

"Say to yourself something like, *I want my vision without any darkness*," Enzo suggested.

I did, and the lights of the world came back on.

"Oh, man." I put a hand to my chest and tried to catch my breath. "That scared the *shit* out of me."

"We have all done it, Mr. Harrison. There is nothing to be embarrassed about."

"My first time?" Kip said. "I stumbled right into a parked car. Nearly broke my kneecap."

"Try it again," Toni urged, "but just think of a little darkening."

I pictured a slight tinting across my vison and the world dimmed. I thought just a little darker, and it dimmed more. The crosswalk signal flashed two international figure icons walking hand-in-hand, rather briskly by the way they were leaning forward.

"Better?" Enzo asked as we did our own brisk walk through the crosswalk.

"Is this biotech like my smart phone," I asked, "where there's all these hidden aspects they don't tell you about in the manual?"

"I'll give you a lesson when we get back to—" Kip reached into his pocket and answered his vibrating cell phone. "Hey there, you still in New York? … Your flight was canceled? Too bad … No, in fact, remember that uncle I have … Yes … He's not doing well and I'm going to go stay with him for maybe a week … No, no that would be okay. Yes … Stay and visit your friends. Perfect. No take all the time you want … ok … ok … No, I'll get Nicole to take care of her, no she *loves* cats … ok … Love you, too … *Ciao*."

"Well done, Captain," Enzo said, stepping onto the curb.

"But can't the Mirage still get to Paul in New York?" I asked.

"Did you set up the intrusive cloaking protocols on Paul's cellular phone?" Enzo asked.

"Yes, but it's only a matter of time until they hack in." Trepidation was stretched taut across Kip's words. "Probably a couple of weeks. Maybe a month."

"That should hopefully be enough time for us to complete our mission," Enzo said. "Ah, here we are."

L'Osteria was the quintessential Italian trattoria. As we walked in, I spotted the street poet's fruit crate abandoned against the side of a local newspaper dispenser. It was early for lunch, so the place was practically empty. Each table had white tablecloths and several half-round red vinyl booths ringed the center dining area. As we waited for the hostess, Toni tugged my hand.

"Ca*m*." Her voice rose markedly on the M.

It occurred to me *L'Osteria* looked eerily similar to the restaurant where Marco and his gang of sex merchants had worked.

"I ... I can't–" She shook her head and backed away.

"It's okay," I said, "we don't have to eat here."

Kip picked up on Toni's trepidation. His attention jumped from us to the dining area.

"We can't eat here," I said.

Enzo was baffled.

Kip angled a serious look to the old man. "This looks like the restaurant where–" He bit off the rest.

"Ah, yes. Of course," Enzo said. "The red booths and such. Come," he gestured for us to leave, "I know another place."

I have a love/hate relationship with McDonald's and the Italian version didn't change my mind much, but Toni's nerves dissipated the minute we left *L'Osteria*.

"How's the pasta bar?" Kip asked.

"Not bad," I said around a forkful of overly parmesaned rigatoni. "A little garlicky."

"Thank you all," Toni said, munching on a fry.

"It is alright, my dear," Enzo assured. "The human mind's ability to retain and harbor severe trauma is remarkable."

This Mickey D's was vacuum squeezed into a shotgun space off of a charming *piazza*. It was crowded with what looked like the street kids from the night before, who now appeared rather pedestrian and harmless in the unforgiving brightness of daylight. We managed to find a booth near the back.

"What are we going to do about my tech?" I asked.

Enzo tapped the side of his shake cup and tried to suck out the last bits of goodness.

"It is almost impossible to alter the technology," he said, setting his cup down. "It has very complex encryption protocols and it is wet-wired into your brain and nervous system. It would be too dangerous."

"What would happen if we tried?" Toni asked.

"There's a seventy-three percent chance the host body would die." The way Kip answered suggested he wasn't totally convinced that this outcome was absolute.

"What are you thinking, Captain?" Enzo asked.

Kip hesitated. "There is a Calaian who could alter the tech."

"Surely you are not suggesting–"

"I am."

"Who is it?" Toni asked.

"Tucker Winston," Kip answered.

Toni let out a restrained under-the-breath gasp.

"Is he here ... on Earth?" I asked.

"He is," Enzo said.

"That's great. Where is he?"

Enzo placed his shake cup onto his tray and tilted an irritated look. "Prison."

*   *   *   *

The Viceroy hadn't left the planet yet, and Enzo managed to set up an audience. Only the boss lady had the power to spring Winston from jail. How was anybody's guess, but come on. If she truly had been around since Australopithecus used stone tools, surely she could have a five-year felon back on the street after breakfast.

While Enzo was gone, Kip and Toni gave me the backstory on Tucker Winston (or at least the Calaian inside the ride). Apparently, he was a legend on their home world. He had been instrumental in developing the core technology that formed the omnipresent, long-range cortical path enhancer. The CPPE and its family of deep neuro-particle, biological wave processors had become the technological foundation for their society. He was as close to a god as Calaians would countenance.

"Why is he in jail?" I kicked my feet up onto the shop table and leaned back in Enzo's ratty chair.

"Seems Mr. Winston likes the …" Kip's hesitancy didn't bode well for the answer, "young men."

"How young?"

"Doesn't matter in the Middle East."

"What kind of deal is Enzo going to cut to get this guy out?"

Kip shrugged.

It appeared that, when vacationing on planet Earth, you were subject to its laws, especially the laws of the country you were in at the time of your offense. Winston had been rounded up in a governmental sting of underground gay bath houses somewhere in the Middle East (Kip thought it had been Qatar). Five years in a Qatar prison. Nice vacation.

The massive garage doors squeaked to life and Enzo guided the big Mercedes in.

"Well?" Kip asked as Enzo emerged.

"He will be here the day after tomorrow." Enzo looked pretty good for a guy who had just sold his soul.

"How hard was it?" Toni asked.

"Surprisingly not that difficult. Carina –

"Who?" I asked.

"The *boss* lady – she has quite the reach within several governments."

"Did you have to cut a deal?" I asked.

Enzo regarded me curiously.

"Did you have to negotiate with the Viceroys … give up something of value?"

"Oh, no, not at all. She understood the concept and its importance. Now, if you all will excuse me, I have to make some arrangements." Enzo retreated to the garage's back room. We stood there, a little perplexed.

"Should I be nervous?" I said, breaking the silence.

Kip regarded me like a doctor would a terminally ill patient. "Prepare yourself."

15

BEING. HUMAN.

The Calaian tech god emerged from the Mercedes and took stock.

"Enzo," he bellowed assessing his new surroundings, "what the *hell* is this?"

The old man eased the car door shut. "The best that you can do." He regarded Winston coolly over the top of the Mercedes. "Or would you like to go back to your *previous* situation?" Even though he was dealing with a Calaian legend, Enzo was obviously in no mood to be jacked with.

The ride Winston occupied wasn't even close to the ideal masculine form, and it looked like Enzo had gotten him some clothes from an IperCoop. Disheveled brown hair that barely covered a large bald spot hung down around a pudgy unshaven face like a misplaced mop head. *Rode hard and put up wet* came to my mind. Maybe two years in a Qatari prison had taken its toll. Winston leaned heavily onto the roof of the Mercedes, seemingly resigned to his new situation. "Where's this human you've altered?"

Everyone turned in my direction. I gave the Great One a sarcastic two-finger salute.

He gestured as if I was a bad filet the butcher had presented. "*Him?*"

"Mr. Harrison is not your typical recipient," Enzo said.

Winston grunted his disapproval and shut the car door. He turned a wary eye on Enzo. "Did you get my list?"

"I believe you will be very pleased at what I could procure on such short notice."

Winston walked his middle-aged paunch into the center of the garage.

"We'll need to clean all this up," he said, rubbing his prison stubble. "There can be no contamination during the operation."

The Great One cast me a glance from under hooded eyes and something raw shivered through me. Having alien technology integrated into my nervous system without my consent was life changing enough, but something in Winston's demeanor pressed home the fact that he was the alien master and I was his lab rat. He flashed a wicked grin.

*   *   *   *

It took us the better part of the day and some of the night to set up the surgical bay. The unit looked like something ground forces would set up near a pandemic zone. I don't know where Enzo had scraped it together, but the rental truck the equipment came in was the size of a semi. Around eight o'clock one of his man-cave neighbors called and bitched about it blocking the alley.

Winston didn't lift a finger to help. He kicked back in the shop chair with a Calaian tablet like my 12-year-old nephew playing the latest *Halo*. In the six hours it took us, Winston left the screen only twice; I assume to relieve his ride's base needs.

I leaned sideways, groaned, and desperately tried stretching the tightness out of my lower back. Toni came up and rubbed the heel of her palm into the knot.

"How's that feel?" she asked, pressing harder.

"I'll give you an hour to cut that out."

Toni playfully slapped my butt.

The lid to one of the high-tech cargo boxes hissed shut. "Kip, what's all that equipment you've been helping Enzo with?" I nodded to the makeshift prep station just outside of the sealed surgical bay.

Kip passed his hand down the side of another cargo box and its lid began to close. "This is Calaian. Enzo got it through Carina. It was all on Tucker's list."

"How did you get it to Earth?"

"It came in from the moon facility."

"How? By spaceship?"

"Something like that." The box hissed shut and Kip stacked it onto another one.

"Mr. Harrison?"

I turned to the Great One's discerning glower.

"Yeah?"

Winston walked up, a Calaian tablet held loosely in one hand. He made a stirring motion with a downward finger. "Turn around, I want to see Ms. Morgan's handiwork."

I turned and he shoved my head forward. I shot him an annoyed glare over my shoulder. "You've got to work on that bedside manner."

Winston pushed harder. "Keep your chin *down*," he ordered.

I buried my chin into my chest and folded my arms. Winston's fingers probed the area of the scar. His ragged breath was hot on the back of my neck. Expected from an overweight asshole.

"Not bad, Ms. Morgan," he said as he inspected the area.

"Thank you," Toni replied.

I felt the cool edge of the Calaian device touch my skin. My tech heated up.

"Interesting," Winston mumbled, dragging the device slowly down my skin.

I cocked my head to one side. "What are you–?"

Winston slapped the back of my head. "Quiet, human."

I pulled out of his grip and faced him. "Let's set the ground rules *right* now. You may think you're the superior species here, but you're on *my* planet, so how about you cool it with the *human this* and *human that* bullshit."

Winston, his hands loosely raised in conciliation, shrugged. "Okay, Cameron. Chin forward, *please*."

I turned away, and Winston passed the device up and down my neck.

"So you're the wayward daughter of the North," Winston said coarsely under his breath.

"Ex*cuse* me?" Toni's inflection was drenched in birthright and defiance.

"Oh … nothing." Winston didn't hide his patronizing tone.

"No," she said, stepping closer, "finish your thought."

This was all happening behind me, but I got the distinct impression Toni was *beyond* pissed.

"Well," Winston replied, the word coated in deep, generational loathing, "only the bitch daughter of the Northern House would fall for a human."

Something primal seized me. I spun on the Great One. "What the *hell* did you just say?"

Winston stepped back, his Calaian tablet held out like a weapon. "You heard me, Earthman. … Your girlfriend is a *bitch*."

The back of my neck exploded in a heat I thought would set my hair on fire. I wrapped the Great One in a grav field large enough to swallow the Mercedes. He floated ten feet off the garage floor twisting and flailing like a trout fighting an angler's line.

I pointed. "Fuck *you*, asshole."

Winston started laughing and tried pointing at me as he slowly twisted upside down in the sphere. "Quite the weapon you have here, Enzo."

The old man shook his head like a father whose child had done something idiotic but endearing. "Let him down, Mr. Harrison."

I reduced the grav field and dangled Winston about a foot off the garage floor, then collapsed it. Like a discarded marionette he landed in a heap just off the Mercedes's left rear bumper. Enzo walked over and extended a hand but the Great One brushed it away.

"You owe her an apology," I said.

Winston went to one knee and raised a hand in a gesture of truce. "I meant no offense. I had to find out if your tech could distinguish a real threat using your base cognitive platform. I had to elicit a strong emotional response." He struggled to stand, but his girth fought against his will.

"Apologize," I demanded.

The Great One lowered his head in submission, just like the Viceroys. Kneeling on one knee, he looked like any other Calaian subject. Toni walked over, knelt and put a hand on his shoulder.

"Stand," she said softly.

Winston did, and Toni rose with him, her eyes never leaving his.

"I'm sorry," he said.

Toni bowed her head in some sort of Calaian acknowledgement. "Please help us."

*   *   *   *

Morning came too soon. The Great One wanted to get an early start to finish the surgery before 10 a.m., which would leave time for testing in the afternoon.

Winston held up an impossibly thin scalpel. "Do you remember when we used instruments like these?"

Enzo glanced up from what looked like a cross between a laptop and a piece of futuristic audio gear. He sketched a smile that suggested those weren't the best of times and went back to his screen of multi-colored, multi-dimensional shapes.

"Is that your language?" I asked, unbuttoning my shirt.

"Language," the old man didn't look up, "is a relative term."

Winston picked up something with the industrial form of a lime green Braun shaver.

I tossed my shirt onto a two-shelfed metal cart. "How are surgeries done on Cala? Robotics?"

"The word robotics doesn't really apply." Winston pressed his thumb on the device's surface and a bright blue electric-looking stylus projected from one end.

"You're like programmers more than surgeons?"

"Um, yes." Winston leaned over to Enzo. "Not very bright, is he?" he whispered.

"I heard that." I pulled my undershirt over my head and tossed it onto the cart. "Is this going to hurt?"

"No," Enzo said. "I am telling your tech to begin numbing certain parts of your spine and neck. If you would climb onto the bed, face down please."

"That's a massage table."

"Yes, well ... we *were* rushed for time."

I got on the table and nestled my face into the cradle and tried to relax. I could feel my neck going numb. Warm tingling ran down the length of my spine.

"Can you feel my fingers?" Enzo asked.

"You're touching me?"

"I take that as a no."

The face cradle gave me a limited view of the surgical tent's white vinyl floor. Toni scooted into my field of vision, wriggling along the floor on her back.

"What are you doing down there?" I asked.

"Seeing how my guy's doing."

"Are you going to stay there the whole time?"

"How long will this take, Tucker?" she asked.

"About sixty minutes," he replied.

Toni laid the back of her head onto the floor and tried to get comfortable.

"You don't have to do this." My cheeks were smooshed by the face cradle and the words came out a little muddled.

"I know." She folded her hands onto her stomach.

"Suit yourself." I felt a finger touch the tip of my right ear.

"Cameron," Enzo said, "we are ready."

Toni grinned and mouthed *Be strong.*

"Why don't you just ... say ... it?" But I suddenly realized I couldn't hear my voice. In fact, I couldn't hear a damn thing. Like the time I tried acid, Toni's face began to morph. I laid there for probably 15 minutes, fascinated, and watched her different facial aspects slowly congeal like a rain-soaked watercolor.

Mr. Harrison, can you hear me? Enzo's voice washed in from somewhere at the edge of my mind.

What's happening to me? Toni's face has been –

Sensory distortion is a side-effect of the surgery. I am sorry if it brings you discomfort.

It's not that bad, just weird. How's it going?

Mr. Winston is quite the genius.

A jagged sting knifed through the middle of my brain. *Oh, shit!*

What is the matter?

The pain intensified. *Something is tearing through my skull.*

Hold on. The old man's voice, which had brought me some comfort as I floated in the Great One's hallucinatory purgatory, vanished. *Enzo?* The pain struck again, but this time with a savagery that was beyond what I could endure. *ENZO!*

I am here.

Please, this is really killing– Before I could finish, the pain exited my brain. I let out a relieved gasp. Toni's face was back to normal, but now it was filled with irate concern. She scooted out of view.

Better, Mr. Harrison?

I sucked in a tattered breath. *Yes.*

I am so sorry. Tucker had to make some adjustments to the procedure.

How ya doing, Earthman? It was Winston.

I tried to swallow, but the muscles of my throat didn't seem to respond. Spittle formed in the center of my lips. *Are we almost done?* A large drool drop left my mouth and splatted right where Toni's face had been.

About another fifteen minutes.

Is it going well?

The Great One let out a restrained, ominous snicker. *Remember how angry you got when I called you a human?*

Yes? I answered, cautiously.

Well ... after my brilliance today, calling you human won't be quite accurate anymore.

16

WHATEVER I WANT.

"The Mirage are extremely hard to detect," Enzo said.

"Hence, their name?" I asked.

"Winston corrected the malfunctions in your tech, Mr. Harrison, and added some ... oh, what is the word?"

"Upgrades?"

"Yes. These will allow you to sense the Mirage faster and, hopefully, defend against anything they throw at us."

"So ... I'm more powerful than they are?"

"We are about to find out."

Lunch arrived from a deli around the corner. My nerves were on edge, and I picked at it. Afterwards, we assembled in the open space in front of the large shop table. Enzo dug around in an old satchel and produced a device that looked like a chrome golf ball. He lobbed it into the air between us and it dropped about a foot, hovered, and rose to eye level, where it stopped. A faint hum seemed to emanate from nowhere in particular.

"What's that?" I asked.

"A tactical reactive combat training sphere," Enzo said. "I have modified it to give off the same kind of signature a Mirage would on this planet. Engage your defense system."

I thought of my cerebral implant's combat protocol and the wash of data appeared in my vision. The garage's color scheme shifted like it had at the hotel bar. The chrome golf ball now had an eerie black humanoid form. My tech tried to ascertain the Calaian hidden inside, but every time it drew a figure the graphic collapsed. I fought the reflex to step back.

"What do you see?" Winston asked.

"A black figure," I answered.

"Good. Now wear this."

I thought of the protocols lifting and they did. The Great One was holding red shop rag.

"What, do you want me to go all *Karate Kid* on this thing?"

"Just blindfold yourself."

I walked over and took the rag.

"Make it as tight as you can," he said.

"Why don't I just darken my vision?"

"It won't be the same."

I wrapped the rag around my head, tied it in the back and pulled it down over my eyes. "Okay, I can't see anything. Now what?" The rag felt damp and smelled like dirty oil.

"Engage your tech."

What appeared in my vision was a detailed real-time active wireframe of the entire space, including parts of the sidewalk and the empty building next door. It was kind of like that new video game they had made a movie about, *Demon*-something. I turned my head in Toni's direction, and her partially rendered wireframe waved girlishly.

"What do you see, now?" Enzo's avatar asked, walking up. His eyes lacked pupils and the whole scene creeped me out a little.

"A wireframe of my surroundings," I said.

"Give it a moment." The teeth of Enzo's avatar were forming behind his lips. "The first time it engages, it takes a minute to map out the space and build an accurate model."

Seconds later, the wireframe morphed into a strangely realistic rendition of the garage. It couldn't quite execute human vision, but it far exceeded the video game version. Skin tones were brighter, shadows more transparent.

"I think it's done rendering," I said.

The simulated Enzo walked through the black figure to the utility cart. He picked up a tablet and tapped. The figure straightened and flexed its appendages.

"The Mirage simulation came to life," I said.

"Good," Enzo replied. "Let us see how your tech interacts."

The black form rushed me, arms flailing. I stepped aside at the last second and it lumbered past me through one of the tarp-covered cars.

"Your reaction time is too slow, Mr. Harrison. Again."

The black form rushed faster this time. I thought of jumping over it and flew 15 feet into the air. It ran under me into the corner where I had slept. I spun awkwardly and settled to the cement. The Calaians were staring at me as if I defied some sacred law of their physics.

Kip came off the Mercedes, his attention darting from the rafters to me. "What did you just *do?*"

"I don't know," I said. "I just thought of jumping."

Winston chuckled.

"Not normal?" I asked.

"Do it again," Enzo said.

I thought of jumping the distance to him and launched off. I soared like a slow-motion long jumper and landed three feet from him. The touchdown was a bit rough. I straightened and lifted the rag off one eye. "Like that?"

Enzo's eyes went to the device and back. "Your implant formed a gravitational field and you used it to …" he shook his head in disbelief, "… *propel* over to me."

I pulled the rag off. "Isn't that what you wanted? I figured forming a grav tunnel–"

"Tunnel?" Kip asked.

"Yeah, something to fly down … or through. Why, is that wrong?"

Enzo shook his head again. "I have never seen that done before. I just wanted to test if your tech would sync with your reaction time. This," he gestured to my grav path, "is *amazing.*"

"Cam?"

I jumped to Toni but overshot the mark. She playfully shrieked as I sailed past. The concrete was slick, and I skidded into one of the covered cars and rolled onto its hood. I would've expected pain or a bruise, but no. The grav field must have dampened the impact.

"Are you okay?" Enzo asked.

I thought of lifting off the hood, and damned if I didn't float over to Toni.

"I'm fricking Superman!" I exclaimed as I settled down next to her.

"Don't get carried away with yourself," Winston said.

"He is correct. I doubt you can stop a bullet." Enzo turned to the Great One. "Can he?"

I folded my arms across my chest and struck a sarcastically defiant stance. "I stopped a drone."

"A military drone travels less than 300 miles-per-hour," Enzo said. "A bullet travels at 1800. Nevertheless, this *is* a remarkably unexpected aspect of the alteration to your cerebral implant."

"What are his vitals?" Winston asked.

Toni glanced at her tablet. "Normal."

I touched the back of my neck. "I don't feel as hot as I have been. Is that good?"

"The tech has fully integrated into your nervous system," Winston said.

"Can you hover?" Kip had his tablet out and was scanning me.

I thought of slowly rising. As my feet came off the ground, I felt co-cooned in an invisible cushion of air. There wasn't a feeling of gravity lifting me under my feet, I just … rose. The upgrades seemed to have adjusted everything. Even the distortion field was barely visible now.

"What do you feel?" Kip asked.

I shrugged, which sent me down a little. "Weightless, I guess? I also feel a little light-headed and slightly nauseous."

"That might be because of the gravity change," Toni said.

"Please come down," Enzo said.

I thought of lowering slowly. The field disappeared just off the ground and I lost my balance. Kip caught me.

"I'm going to have to practice my landings," I remarked.

"You will not be doing this in public," Enzo said.

"Too much exposure?"

"We cannot take that chance, especially with social media's 24-hour eye."

"Figured that. Okay, what's next?"

"We need to determine your reaction threshold." Enzo grabbed a large wrench off the utility cart, weighted it in his hand, then flung it at me like a hatchet. My defense protocol engaged instantly, and the wrench froze about a foot from my extended hand. It floated the rest of the way. I closed my fingers around the handle.

"Nice try, but I'm too fast." I hefted the tool in my hand, reared back and flung it down a tight grav field that ended inches from Enzo's face. The old man reflexively jumped back but was pinned against the utility cart by the hovering tool.

"You could have hurt him!" Kip exclaimed.

"No way," I replied.

"Do not get *cocky*, young man." Enzo tried to snatch the wrench from the air, but it held in place. He shot me an impatient look.

"Hey, you threw first. What if my tech hadn't engaged fast enough, huh? I'd be getting stitches now." I released the grav field. Enzo caught the wrench and tossed it onto the cart, where it clattered to a stop.

For the rest of the morning, Enzo, Winston and Kip put me through my paces. They tested multiple objects from multiple directions, and every time they threw, my tech sensed the incoming danger and engaged various sized grav fields. Winston finally tried a large pocketknife, which made Toni so mad she chewed him out.

"Guys," I said, folding the knife closed, "I think we've established that I can sense and stop most incoming objects. I'm starving. Let's grab some lunch."

"I have one more test." Enzo, his back to us, was digging something out of the satchel. He turned and my attention zeroed in on the Glock.

"*Easy*," I said, hands cautiously raised, "I need to build up to this one."

Toni stepped between Enzo and me. "You are *not* going to fire that at him!"

I hadn't seen Enzo cow to Toni since the Viceroy meeting. He lowered the weapon and bowed his head. "I will not shoot it *at* him. We just need to see how fast his tech is."

"Well…" Toni hesitated. "Okay then. But if anything happens—"

Winston folded his arms. "It won't."

"Where do you want me?" I asked.

"By the far wall, near where you slept," Enzo said.

As I walked over, Enzo motioned for Toni, Winston and Kip to stand behind him.

"Where are you aiming?" I asked.

Enzo pointed the Glock towards another smaller utility cart off to my right.

"Really? You're going to put a hole in it."

"No, I will not, Mr. Harrison, because you are going to stop the bullet."

"You're that confident?" Kip asked.

"I am," Enzo replied. "Ready?"

"Fire away," I said.

"The rest of you might want to cover your ears."

Winston, Kip and Toni complied. Enzo raised the Glock and fired. The gunshot's crack reverberated across every hard surface with excruciating clarity. The utility cart jerked back about a foot. The hole the bullet made in its top drawer was about the size of a penny. Enzo stared at the cart, his jaw grinding.

"Sorry about that," I called out. "Let's try–"

Enzo leveled the gun and shot off four rounds in quick succession. The cart jumped back. The acrid smell of gun powder hung in the air.

"He didn't stop them." There was real disappointment in Kip's voice.

Enzo's attention remained seared on the cart. He tilted his head as if something had caught his eye. He lowered the Glock and walked halfway to the cart. Suspended about four feet from the floor, I could barely make out three of the four bullets he had gotten off. They floated aimlessly like little armored bees, side-by-side. Enzo plucked the closest one out the air.

"*What* did you do different, Mr. Harrison?" he asked, inspecting it.

"I thought of a grav field shaped like a catcher's mitt."

"Amazing." Enzo scanned the area around the bullets. "I can barely see the field."

"It made sense."

Winston shook his head and snickered again. "To a fourteen-year-old."

"Okay Mr. Tech God, let's see *you* do that."

"*Gentlemen.*" Enzo raised his hands, the Glock's muzzle pointing up. "All that matters is that he stopped them."

"Was that harder to do?" Toni asked.

"Not really," I said. "I do feel a little headachy, though. Any more tests?"

Enzo waved me over. "That will be enough for today."

"I don't like this headache," Toni said as I walked up.

"It's barely there," I replied.

She pulled her Calaian tablet from her back pocket and ran it down the side of my head.

"Those devices you have do more than just enhance your interface beam, right?" I asked.

"Uh-huh." Toni's attention was locked onto to her screen.

"They help amplify the *beam*, as you call it," Kip said, "but each one is also modified to complement our skillsets. Mine is set up for military use and Toni's is medical."

"What's yours set up for?" I asked Enzo.

The old man considered me like a professor asked a dumb question by a student. "Whatever I want it to be."

17

IT'S FUNNY. YOU KNEW, DIDN'T YOU?

Along with the Great One's otherworldly surgical equipment, Enzo had bought five queen-sized inflatable air mattresses, linens, toiletries, towels and fresh clothes. The take-away was, we weren't leaving the man cave anytime soon. Dinner was Chinese takeout and sodas. I was jittery after the testing and had collapsed onto the bed Toni made for us near my previous sleeping corner. Despite two layers of sheets, every time I moved the cheap plastic underneath made a noise that sounded like farting.

"Can't sleep?" Toni whispered, spooning into me from behind.

"Still a little wired from the testing. My thoughts won't turn off."

Winston and Enzo sat at the shop table, perched on two metal grey stools. A bottle of Dalmore 25 stood between them. I could barely see them around the edge of the surgical tent. After dinner we had discussed taking the tent down, but Winston advised to leave it. If something went wrong, he wanted to be able to quickly "address it," whatever the hell *that* meant.

"How are you feeling ... besides wired?" Toni asked.

"A little cold, actually."

She snuggled closer, pressing herself against me from shoulders to toes. "That better?"

I nodded. "Those two ever going to go to bed?"

"Calaians don't sleep as much as humans," she whispered. "The tech alters the ride's circadian rhythms. On Cala, a day lasts seventy-four of your hours. They could be up awhile."

"Tell them to at least turn off the overheads. They're keeping me awake."

She gestured and the boys from Cala clicked off everything but the lone desk lamp. A soft, warm glow descended over the space. Kip, on the opposite side of the garage, stirred on his mattress. More plastic farts.

"We gotta get some real beds if we're going to stay here," I whispered.

"Enzo is doing his best."

"If we're cloaked and walled up, why don't we just check into a fancy hotel?"

"I can ask in the morning."

We laid there stubbornly still trying to fall asleep with Enzo and Winston's conversation murmured in the background. Occasionally, one of them would let out a laugh or a restrained belch.

"Toni, can I ask you something?"

"Sure."

"Back at the hotel bar, when my defense system engaged, I think it tried to display the creature inhabiting the human bodies the Mirage were using."

"Oh?" The surprise in her voice was unconvincing. "What did you see?"

I tried to remember the graphic outline, but it had only flashed for a second before disappearing. "It looked like a cross between a dog on its hind legs – a skinny dog – and an upside-down pear with four arms. And the arms were shaped like bird legs ... at least that's what the outline suggested."

Toni spit out a restrained laugh. "*What?*"

"That's what it drew."

"Cam, we are *not* upside-down pears with dog legs."

I twisted around to face her and scooted up onto one elbow. "Okay, so what are you?"

"Do you really need to know?"

I could tell I was treading into a touchy subject.

Toni moved closer. "I understand how weird this must be to you, but it's weird for me, too." She thought for a moment, and I wondered what she was doing, in her pod, on the dark side of the moon. Her eyes fell to what little space remained between us. "Cam?"

"Yes?"

"I'm scared."

"Of the Mirage?"

"Well, yeah." She looked into my eyes. "But there's something else."

"What?"

"It's us, I mean … it's … it's what might happen to *us*."

"You're scared of falling in love?"

She nodded.

"That makes two of us."

"Really?"

"Well, sure. I mean, come on … We're not even the same species, much less from the same planet. And think about it … what would our kid look like?"

For a split-second Toni didn't get the joke, then she burst out laughing.

"I know you've been thinking about it," I said playfully.

"Oh yes," Toni said, laughing, "our half-Calaian, half-human pear-child."

"With four bird arms."

She laid her head back and cackled.

Winston edged his head around the side of the surgical tent and shot us a look.

I waved him off. "Go back to your Scotch," I said through a chuckle.

He nodded and his head disappeared.

As our laughter waned, something wonderful moved through me. Although I'd been through a lot, this alien, from a planet trillions of miles away, was seriously making me think of falling in love again.

"Look," I said, "I know this is crazy. I don't even know you. Hell, I'll never know the *real* you. And this," I motioned between us, "whatever *this* is … I haven't felt for a long, long time. I don't want to–"

Toni halted me with a finger to my lips.

"What I'm scared of," she said slowly, "is that what I'm feeling ... isn't *real*. That it's some kind of processed emotion the tech has created."

"It does that?"

"It's programmed to give us the best experience while vacationing. I've heard rumors it will manufacture false emotions."

"Do you think what you're feeling is manufactured?"

"I don't think so. It feels so ... genuine."

"Have you posed this idea to Kip?"

This caught Toni. "Why would I do that?"

"To see if what he feels for Paul might be fake. He fell in love when his tech was active, then, when he decided to stay, part of his tech was turned off. You could find out if there was a difference ... before and after."

"I don't know, Cam. That's very personal. Besides, how would he know the difference?"

"You're overthink–" I got the finger to the lips again.

"Cam, *you* know what love is ... *human* love. I don't, and I may never know."

"Believe me," I said, "you'll know it when you feel it."

Toni twisted away from me. "Hold me," she said, pulling the blanket over her shoulder.

I settled in next to her. Enzo and Winston clicked off the task lamp and headed to their mattresses.

"It's funny," I whispered after a few quiet moments.

"What?" she replied.

"I'm becoming more Calaian, and you're becoming more human."

18

THANKS FOR NOT KILLING ME.

Someone's mattress fart dragged me out of a perfectly fine dream. I was on a beach, Toni in a lounger beside me. Her white bikini top clung to her body in a wet t-shirt sort of way. Waves lapped on the shore and the bronze sun dipped into the sea in a godlike, spectacular fashion. Throaty macaw screams competed for attention with the sound of the surf, the feel of the dense humidity, and the taste of sea salt in the air.

In the morning I'm going out and getting five regular mattresses, I thought, still half asleep. *I'll use my own money if I have to–* Out of the corner of my eye, I caught a figure moving through the shadows of the garage's cavernous darkness, behind the row of roadsters. I peered over my shoulder to–

ward Kip and Winston. Sleeping soundly. Toni was likewise sound asleep. Enzo was snoring loudly out of view behind the surgical tent. I started to call his name but thought better of it. I engaged my combat tech.

Night vision washed down, and strategic data started scrolling in an electric green ticker across the bottom of my vision. Every surface took on a quivering green cast to its edges, and heat signatures were rendered in various shades of yellow and red. An indistinct black humanoid form suddenly stepped from behind the surgical tent. My heart jumped. I leaned forward to get a better look.

"Don't even *think* about it," a male voice whispered into my left ear from behind. His accent was vaguely familiar.

Something hard and cold pressed against the soft spot where my neck and skull met. A gun barrel. I instinctively raised my hands.

"Good boy." The accent was thicker now.

I tracked the figure in front of me as it slinked from Winston's mattress to Kip's, where it stooped and put something to Kip's head. The thing stood, looked at whatever it was holding, and moved to my mattress. In the enhanced reality rendered by my combat tech, the dark figure showed faint bits of static dancing inside its form. It knelt on one knee and leaned onto a forearm casually draped across it. Its faceless head regarded me.

So you're the altered human? The voice sounded feminine as it poured into my mind like liquid glass. The figure reached toward my face and strong, thin human fingers grabbed my chin and pivoted my head to regard the left side of my face, then the right. The gun pressed more firmly into the back of my skull. *You're kind of cute this close.*

You look like a dark piece of shit, I thought back.

Its raspy laugh, similar to a heavy smoker's, reverberated through my mind. *You're funny.* It let go and motioned for me to stand.

"Up," said the man behind me holding the gun.

I slowly stood. The cold cement sent a shock up through the soles of my bare feet. I was a few inches taller than the female figure.

The gun against the back of my head vanished, only to tap the side of my shoulder twice.

"Move," the male voice ordered.

I took the hint and stepped forward.

The figure raised its hand again and spread its fingers. The overheads flickered on.

"Turn off your tech," the male voice ordered.

I disengaged my combat tech and its night vision shuttered down. My normal vision returned, and the humanoid form morphed into the female Mirage I had collapsed into the club chair at the hotel bar. Now she was dressed in a black turtleneck with vinyl patched shoulder pads, black leggings and black Nike running shoes. Their grey swooshes were the only glitz to the entire getup. Her hair was pulled back to accentuate an angular jawline. In her left hand she held a Calaian tablet.

"Thanks for not killing me," she said.

Kip sat up and put a hand to his forehead to shade his eyes from the fluorescent lights' glare. The Great One sat up and threw off his blanket.

"What the hell is–?" Kip abruptly cut off as soon as he saw the Mirage. He sprung to his feet, but his right foot caught in the blanket and he stumbled to his knees onto the cement.

The female Mirage, eyes firmly on me, pressed a blue organic shape on the tablet with her thumb. Kip's scream echoed throughout the garage. She sneered. Behind me, Toni sat up.

"Stay," the male Mirage ordered.

"Okay," Toni said timidly.

Again, he jammed the gun against the soft spot at my neck. "*Don't* engage."

I raised my hands higher. "Yes sir."

Winston started to get up and his mattress protested. The female Mirage cut him a severe look over her shoulder.

"If you like living, Tucker, I wouldn't *do* that."

Winston sat back down and angrily folded his arms across his barrel chest.

"Ennnn*zzzo*?" the female Mirage called out. "Come out, come out wherever you are."

The crack of the Glock firing cut the air. The bullet whizzed between me and the female Mirage and impacted the wall six feet away. Fragments of cinder block sprayed around us. Her steely blue eyes slid in the direction of the shot.

Enzo fired again. The female Mirage jerked her head away, her wince suggesting the old man hit his target. Then I saw the bullet floating about ten inches from her temple. She cautiously opened one eye and plucked the projectile from the air. Astonishment registered across her face.

Another shot rang out and the female Mirage jumped away so fast her movement looked like a video in fast forward. She landed on her back foot and spun into a tight combat stance. The gun in her right hand had appeared out of nowhere, aimed in Enzo's direction. A bullet hit the wall again. More cinder block sprayed.

"You have three seconds to show yourself," the male Mirage called out, "or the daughter of the Northern House *dies*." His accent finally registered like a nail to the head. It was the tall Mirage from the hotel bar … the one I had spared.

I spun on him, and he pressed the barrel of the gun against my forehead. His other hand held another gun aimed at Toni.

"Oh, *please*," he urged, "do something stupid."

I froze, eyes locked on the gun aimed at Toni.

"Stop!" Enzo yelled, stepping from behind the tall metal roller cabinet. "I am coming out." With raised hands, he cautiously walked into the open space in front of Kip – who was now crouched on one knee and poised to go feral on the Mirage. The old man held the Glock loosely in his left hand.

The female Mirage straightened and pocketed her weapon. She extended her right hand. "The gun … slowly."

Enzo walked over and gingerly placed the Glock onto her outstretched palm. She gestured with her head for him to step back. The female Mirage lobbed the Glock back at Enzo, but the weapon stopped in midair and quickly imploded, folding and crunching down until it was a lump of dark grey metal about the size and shape of a charcoal briquette. It fell to the floor and clattered toward the old man's feet.

"Now," the female Mirage said loudly, gesturing, "will you all join Enzo?"

I extended a hand to Toni, helped her off the mattress, and we walked over to Enzo. Kip slowly stood and fell in behind the Great One, who was angrily pulling his t-shirt down over his girth. He glared at the female Mirage as he shuffled beside us next to Enzo. Tension prowled around us like a lion sizing up its trapped prey.

The male Mirage came up to his associate's side, guns still leveled. The female Mirage stuffed her Calaian tablet into a large back pocket on her warmup top. She calmly removed a pack of cigarettes from a front pocket, drew one and sparked it with a slim chrome lighter. She sucked in a deliberate drag, savored, and exhaled the smoke up towards the rafters. Her eyes moved to each of us and lingered, as if scheming our individual demises.

The hum of the overheads filled the void. Time seemed to stop.

The piercing sound of the garage doors scraping along their rusted metal floor tracks snapped our attentions around. As the doors rolled to the sides, three high-end matte black BMW touring motorcycles slipped in one after another through the slowly widening maw. Engines revving, each took up a strategic position in a semi-circle around us. Their ominous riders, faceless behind black visors and perched on their bikes like futurist executioners, regarded us dispassionately.

As the doors clunked to a stop, a fourth bike roared in and stopped in front of our two captors. Its rider, dressed in the same sinister fashion as the others, raised a fist. All four shut their bikes down and drew large handguns out of hidden jacket pockets. They didn't aim. Instead, they just held them casually at rest on their gas tanks in a scarily blasé show of force. A black Eurovan pulled up quietly in the alley and blocked the garage entrance. The fourth rider remained seated and stared at us. I tried to imagine who or what was studying us behind that blackout visor.

"Took you long enough," the female Mirage said, exhaling her last drag. She flicked the cigarette away and it vanished.

The fourth rider's helmet canted in her direction and moved slowly back to us.

"We have a bonus." The female Mirage gestured to Winston. "The man himself, fresh from prison."

The fourth rider nodded in agreement.

"It looks like we're late to the party." The female Mirage pointed to the surgical tent. "They've already augmented the human."

The fourth rider bent forward, reached up with both gloved hands and pulled the helmet off. A tangle of blonde hair spilled onto the padded shoulders of the black leather biker jacket.

Toni's gasp sent an acrid chill through me.

The Viceroy boss lady rested her helmet on her lap and flashed us a relaxed smile.

19

REMEMBER ME

"Hello, Enzo."

The old man squared his shoulders and faced the boss lady's gaze. "Carina," he said as if the name left a bad taste.

"It's nice to see you made such good use of the money we gave you. How did the procedure go?"

"Better than expected."

Carina nodded. "Tucker, do you concur?"

The Great One snorted and snubbed her question. He folded his arms in defiance.

The female Mirage pulled a tablet from her warmup top's back pocket and stormed up to Winston. She jammed the device under his nose. He pulled his head back, but she kept it pressed.

"Answer her motherfucker," she said, "or I'll deactivate your ride."

Carina shook her head almost imperceptibly. "Wren, dial back the theatrics, *please.*"

Wren slowly withdrew the tablet and stuffed it back into the pocket.

Winston glared down at her. He cleared his throat. "It went very well."

"So glad to hear that." Carina beckoned me with her index finger.

I walked toward her but about halfway she motioned for me to stop. I was in my boxers and undershirt.

"Take off your shirt," she said offhandedly.

"Why?" I asked.

"Just do it."

I did and dropped the shirt by my feet.

Carina scrutinized me for a moment. "What do you think?" she asked Wren.

"I'd definitely do him," she replied.

"No, Wren, take some readings. Find out what's changed since you encountered him at the hotel."

The female Mirage pulled her Calaian tablet out again and positioned herself behind me. She slowly scanned the entire length of my body, starting at the back of my ankles and ending at the top of my head. She poked around on the device's screen, waited, then nodded to herself.

"Well?" Carina was getting impatient.

"Nine percent more muscle mass, sixteen percent cognitive gain and his tech has grown by six percent." Wren lowered the tablet, gave me a seductive grin and licked her top lip. She walked back to her spot next to the tall male Mirage with the guns, which hadn't wavered since he first leveled them.

"How do you feel after the procedure, Mr. Harrison?" Carina asked with faux concern.

"I was feeling good until you guys showed up. Can I put my shirt on now?"

She nodded.

I picked up my undershirt and pulled it over my head.

"No headaches?" Carina asked.

"No," I answered.

"Any issues with sleeping?"

"Other than having a gun jammed to my head?"

Carina sucked in a tired breath. "Okay, Enzo ... we'll take it from here." She started to put her helmet back on.

"Take *what*?" I demanded.

Carina stopped, the helmet poised above her head. "You, of course."

"No way!" Toni said behind me.

Carina pulled the helmet on, flipped her visor up and outstretched her hand.

Toni clutched her chest and gasped loudly. She collapsed to the floor in an articulated slow-motion. My augmented tech went into full response mode and sent a brutal electrical pulse coursing through my body. I spun back and extended my hands. A greenish-blue distortion field rippled across my fingers. The boss lady's eyes widened. She snapped the visor down. She motioned to the riders. They raised their weapons and aimed. I made two fists and an enormous semi-circular grav wave erupted.

The tall male Mirage squeezed off two rounds and two of the riders got off one each, but the wave engulfed them, bullets and all, and sent them flying throughout garage.

The boss lady took a direct hit. She and her bike flipped end-over-end and impacted the far wall. The trailing end of the wave went out the garage doors and broadsided the Eurovan, crumpling it almost in half. The truck flew across the alley and against the heavily tagged brick wall of the adjacent building. Anything not tied down was caught up in the wave and smashed against the garage's inner walls and support columns.

The wave dissipated about as fast as it had appeared. Stray scraps of paper and trash fluttered to the floor around me. I stood alone in a fighting stance in the center of the garage's open space, arms outstretched, fists clenched tight. My spinal column felt like it was on fire. One of the Mirage riders had been impaled on some exposed rebar. He hung part way up one of the building's support columns, sideways, four rusty steel rods protruding from his stomach. Skewered entrails dripped from the tips. Another Mirage rider, who had been thrown across the garage and into the east wall, was tangled up with his bike and old car parts.

I didn't see Wren or her associate, but to my far left, the third Mirage rider was remarkably still upright on his bike. The hand holding the gun was visibly shaking. I pivoted toward him, fists aimed. He threw the gun at my feet and raised his hands. I made a sweeping motion to my right and he and his bike flew out the garage entrance and crashed into the crushed-in side of the

Euro-van. He crumpled to the ground helmet first. The bike landed on top of him.

I lowered my arms, took a deep breath and tried to shake off the residual effects of the electrical surge. The fire in my spine receded. Through the eerie quiet, a soft moaning rose from behind one of Enzo's classic cars. It was smashed against one of the building's support columns. I peered over its mangled hood. Wren was pinned between the car's ornate grillwork and the concrete column. I stepped back, built a grav field around the car's rear end and dragged it off her. Wren's scream was sickening.

"Cameron?" Kip yelled.

"Don't any of you come out!" I yelled back. "It's not safe!"

Wren looked up, her face sculpted in deep pain. Dark, thick blood leaked over the corner of her bottom lip and trickled down the side of her neck. The top of her warmup was drenched in blood. She had a hand on a massive gash in her abdomen. I caught a glimpse of her guts through the gore. Her other arm lay limp at her side. She tried to say something, but the blood drowned the words.

"Don't try." I knelt next to her. "Engage your cerebral interface."

Wren gave a feeble nod. *Pretty ... impressive.* Her voice came into my mind ragged and slightly garbled. Before me was a broken shell of the highly trained operative I had seen in the hotel bar. Her cheek had a deep gash, exposing teeth and gums. Guilt washed over me. My heart went out to her.

What can I do? I asked.

She coughed out a shallow, bloody laugh. *Get me ... a new ... ride?*

I feigned a weak smile.

She started to speak but a wave of pain rippled through her. Her back arched and her face contorted. Tears streamed down her cheeks. The wave abated and she sucked in a frayed breath.

I took her limp hand. *Can you feel my hand?*

A … little. She coughed again. More blood washed over her bottom lip.

I'll stay here with you.

No need … Calaians are … tough.

Even though Wren the Calaian was probably somewhere on the moon alive and unharmed, she had to be in immense pain. They all suffered death at my hands. I had … murdered them.

I want to, I said.

A ghost of a smile appeared, then vanished. *You're … very … kind.*

I held her hand and watched her life drain away. Her breathing became more ragged. After a few seconds, her eyes got heavy.

Hu … man?

Yes?

Please … re … member … me.

20

ADVANCED THINKING.

"Cam?"

"Toni, don't come out!"

"Why?"

"It's pretty gruesome."

I placed Wren's hand on the blood-stained concrete floor and closed her eyelids with the tips of my fingers. I stood and looked back toward the surgical tent and the row of tarp-covered exotic cars, all of which had been behind the wave and hadn't been damaged. Enzo was in the center of the open space, surveying the aftermath, fists on his hips. His attention went to the Mirage rider impaled on the rebar. Wren was blocked from Enzo's view by the car's front end.

I put a hand to the back of my neck. It was still very warm. "I guess I just reacted."

"At least we are alive," he said.

"I … uh–"

"You did the right thing, Mr. Harrison, albeit a little over the top." Enzo surveyed the scene. "We are going to have to work on controlling your emotional interface."

The Great One emerged from behind the Berlinetta. His attention also was transfixed by the impaled Mirage rider. Kip and Toni stepped from behind a tarp-covered roadster.

Enzo turned and raised a hand. "Do *not* bring her out here, Captain."

"I've seen worse," Toni said.

Toni, Kip and Winston joined Enzo.

I looked down at Wren's body. The spreading pool of blood beneath her was about to reach my shoe.

Kip and Enzo walked around the front of the car. They regarded Wren, their expressions impassive.

"I stayed with her," I said, "until … you know."

"Noble of you," Enzo remarked.

"Is she really dead," I asked, "or alive on the dark side of the moon?"

Kip knelt and passed his tablet the length of her body. "She's really dead." He turned his attention to the old man. "What's our next move?"

"The real question is what side are the Viceroys on?" There was worry in Enzo's voice.

"The Viceroys may not be aware of Carina's actions," Kip said, standing.

"Quite the contrary; they probably sanctioned it."

"What's the gain?" I asked.

"You, Mr. Harrison."

"How are we going to clean this up?" Winston asked.

"I will take care of the bodies," Enzo said.

"How?"

"Grav them down," I said.

"A crude way to put it, Mr. Harrison, but nonetheless accurate." Enzo turned to Kip. "Captain, can you take care of the van?"

"I can try," Kip replied.

"I got it." I thought of the van being crushing and we watched it disappear. I didn't pinpoint the field. The third Mirage rider and his bike went with the van. It was too dark in the alley to see clearly. For a fleeting second, I felt a pang of remorse.

"You engaged almost instantly this time," Kip remarked.

"He should have sensed the threat and engaged faster." Winston pulled out a tablet and studied something on its screen.

"Nice work, Winston," I said, not hiding my contempt. "I'm now the ultimate alien weapon."

He eyed me and frowned. The creases of his thick cheeks deepened.

"Don't give me that look. It's what the four of you planned all along, *right?*"

Enzo regarded me disapprovingly. Kip dropped his eyes to the floor.

I drew near and cast a hateful glance across all of them, including Toni. "I'm not a dumb human." I let the last word rest on the Great One. "You probably weren't in a Qatari jail, were you?" I moved my disdain to Kip. "Do you even *have* a partner?" I glanced at Toni and met her pained expression. "Are your feelings real or are they created by your implant's AI, or maybe you're a part of this, too?" Finally, I stared at the old man. He had that same look from the hotel club, when I wasn't sure if he thought of me as friend or foe. I didn't bother saying anything.

I looked into their faces and thought of the dead humans who could have never imagined that one day their bodies would be a *ride* for an alien.

Their play was utterly clear.

"Well?" I demanded.

Their collective silence spoke volumes.

"That's what I *thought*."

I kept my scowl on them as I brought each one of the Mirage bodies out. I started with the one against the front wall. The grav field held his body stiffly, carrying him on his back, appendages sticking out at sickening broken angles. Next came Carina. The distortion field was more noticeable against her all-black body suit, and her helmet was crushed in on its right side. She probably died instantly. The impaled Mirage rider slid free of the rebar, tipping into the field's cocoon head-first. His entrails floated in front of his head like a grotesque parade balloon. I laid him next to Carina's body, in a pile just off Enzo's feet. With their helmets still on, the only way to tell them apart was by their injuries.

I looked where Wren had fallen and lifted her body tucked in a fetal position, her arms folded across the gash in her abdomen. Blood oozed from her wounds and floated as thick globules in the grav field's bubble. I stepped out of the way as it floated past and presented it to Enzo. I came behind Wren as she hovered a few inches from the old man and pushed her into his chest. He extended his arms and I lowered her reverently onto them. I dropped the grav field and Enzo struggled with the weight of her lifeless body. Her blood, free of the gravitational force, splattered to the floor.

"I want her taken care of … properly." I glanced around at the horror. The guilt swelled again. My attention settled on the pile of bodies. "Take care of *all* of them."

Shock registered on Enzo's face. He slowly nodded.

Suddenly, as if time and space had shifted, the universal constants changed, the Calaians in front of me were now no longer the superior species. They were just another civilization. One that didn't scare me anymore. I stepped away and looked back toward Toni, who had been watching all of this with her arms folded tightly against her chest. I let my sorrow linger, then headed for the alley.

"Cam!" Toni called out. "Please … don't *leave–*"

"Don't!" I said, raising a hand to her plea. Remorse and shame overwhelmed me. I turned away.

"Where're you going?" Kip asked.

"Home," I said, not looking back.

"What happens if the Mirage return?"

I looked over my shoulder into the hell I had just created. Enzo was still holding Wren's body, her head resting against his right shoulder, the hand I had held dangling from a limp arm. I couldn't help but think of Michelangelo's *Pieta*.

"By my count, there's forty-thousand collective years of advanced thinking standing in front of me." I watched a large drop of blood drip from Wren's fingers. "You figure it out."

21

TOP SHELF.

I woke to Roz staring at me. She reached out and batted the tip of my nose. The look on her face said, *Get up, asshole, I'm starving.*

My flight back from Italy had gotten in late and my jet lag was brutal. Having a shit-ton of alien tech now a permanent part of my body was weird enough, and I hadn't even considered the possible ramifications of airport security. But when I went through the scanner in Fiumicino Airport, nothing beeped or buzzed. The stern-faced Italian guards waved me through like any other tourist.

Roz squeaked a pitiful meow and hopped off the bed.

"Okay, girl … I'll feed you."

I swung my legs around, groggily sat up and checked my phone. *10:52 a.m.* I shuffled to the kitchen, poured some kibble into Roz's bowl and sat at the counter. It was raining, and the patter on the roof was soothing. I had been gone about three weeks, but it felt like a lifetime. My vacation auto-reply cut down on email, and most of the voicemails were trying to reach me before my car's warranty ran out.

Jesus. What*ever.*

I had made my mind up about the Northern House's real intentions, but a small part of me hoped to hear from Toni. Then again, what was her agenda?

My phone buzzed. Josh. "Hey, man."

"You back?" His voice was *way* too upbeat.

"Got in late last night."

"Dude, you sound like shit."

"Bad jet lag."

"You coming to the bar tonight?"

"When?"

"My shift starts at five-thirty."

"Save me a seat."

"Bam!" He clicked off.

I let the phone slip from my fingers onto the counter. I lifted my hands and inspected them. Remarkably, my new and deadly ability had left no trace after exploding from my fists. No burn marks, no broken skin, *nothing.* During the flight back, after too many bourbons, I had seriously considered that all of it – the Asshole Deluxe, meeting Toni, the trip, the drone, the Viceroys, Wren … my fucking *death* – had been a horrific dream. But the images on my phone said otherwise. I had almost deleted them, but that would only be running from reality.

My phone dinged. A text had come through. Didn't recognize the number.

How was Italy?

Who is this? I texted.

Get a lot of rest?

WHO THE HELL IS THIS?

Agent Davis.

Shit. I stared at my screen, a bit dazed and a bit freaked. It was a blast.

Wanna have lunch, tell me about it?

What are you now, my BFF?

About five seconds ticked by with no reply.

Cameron, he texted back, right now, I may be the only friend you've got.

*   *   *   *

Gloria's was one of my favorite restaurants. Not because of the margaritas or the street-side patio, but because it offered the best Salvadoran menu in the city. Agent Davis was seated in the farthest booth from the entrance. He stood as I approached.

"Thanks for coming," he said, extending a hand.

I didn't take it. "Where's the grey suit?" I replied flatly.

Davis looked down at his white Guayabera and tan cargo shorts and shrugged. "I'm off duty. Sit, I've ordered us a couple of top-shelfs."

As I sat, a waiter brought two margaritas on the rocks to the table.

"Two top-shelfs, *señors*," he said, ceremonially placing them down. "One with salt and one not." He set a basket of blue corn chips down along with a small bowl of black bean dip.

"How did you know I didn't want salt?" I raised the glass and took a drink.

Davis licked some salt off the rim, took a sip and eyed me for a long and excruciating moment.

I picked up a chip, thought about eating it, but instead put it back.

"Cameron," he said after another lick and a sip, "how's the new tech Winston put in you functioning?"

Oh, fucking hell. The tech heated up.

The agent lifted his eyes from his margarita. A faint buzz came from under the table. Davis reached into a cargo pocket and produced a tablet-like device similar to the Calaians', but this one was matte black and smaller. Its screen had a conventional human interface.

"Oh, *look*," he said, eyebrows raised, studying the screen, "I've struck a nerve."

Previosly, I would have been freaking, but the Great One's upgrades had given me a new sense of confidence. "Why am I not surprised?" I picked up the chip again and bit off half.

"Because you're a smart young man," Davis said, still glued to the tablet. "Damn, they have *really* improved you. ... I can't make out what some of this new tech does."

Davis needed a little demo. I thought of the basket of chips compressing down. It did.

Davis watched it vanish with detached amusement. "Not quite what you did in Vitale's garage." He set the tablet down. "I bet you're a hit at parties."

I took another sip. "Vitale?"

"Enzo."

I nodded. "You know, you don't look like Will Smith."

Davis let a smirk through. "I love those movies."

"Yeah ... they're hysterical." I pushed the tablet aside with the edge of my hand and leaned onto the table. "Since you know what I'm capable of, why don't you just get to the fucking point?"

"So *angry* now." Davis leaned back against the booth's tall vinyl seatback. "So full of loathing and contempt."

I formed a four-inch grav sphere in the center of the table. The bowl of dip was the first to be drawn in, then the drink menu, then the saltshaker. The pepper shaker started to slide in the direction of the mini black hole.

Davis's smarmy demeanor shifted. He leaned onto the table and stopped the shaker with the back of his hand. "You need to listen," he said gravely.

"Why?" I asked.

"Because ... you're not human anymore."

"Tell me something I don't already know." I thought of the sphere and it dissolved away.

The tension in Davis's jaw muscles relaxed. "Your Calaian girlfriend–"

"She's *not* my girlfriend."

Davis picked up the tablet. "You're right, she isn't–"

"What about her?"

"She's off the grid."

"What do you mean?"

"She's gone, Cameron."

"Back to Cala?"

"No."

"Why don't you ask Enzo or Kip where she is?"

Davis leaned into the space between us. "They're *all* gone."

22

YOU MISSED ONE.

A sharp, hot sensation shuddered through my nervous system.

Davis glanced at his tablet. "Now I have your attention."

"How do you know all this?" I asked. "What are you?"

"The only thing I can tell you is what we *aren't*."

"And that is?"

"The Men in Black, if that's what you're thinking."

"But you're like them, right?"

Davis mugged a *Maybe*.

"You can't tell me?"

"All I can say is we're loosely affiliated with one of the national security agencies and the military."

This was going nowhere. I was tired of being played, whether by Calaians or my own. "Fuck this." I started to scoot out of the booth.

"You're not worried about alien technology growing in you?" I stopped at the edge of the booth's seat cushion. "Or that they have Toni?"

I started to look over my shoulder but pulled it back.

"Come on, Cameron, what are you going to do," Davis said, "be a web designer the rest of your life?"

I turned. "How do you know she wasn't in on it ... that I wasn't just being played so they could implant the tech so I could be their experiment ... their *weapon*?"

Davis made a face like these were stupid assumptions. "We don't."

I stood and took a step away.

"What was the body count in the garage?" he asked.

I stopped cold. My mind flashed on the row of Mirage bodies I had laid at Enzo's feet. Carina, the three riders, Wren and ... oh *shit*.

"Yeah ... you missed one."

Wren's associate ... the tall Mirage with the handguns. My frustration leaked out.

"Don't beat yourself up. That was a fluid situation." Davis sat back and folded his arms. "I'm only going to offer you this chance once, Cameron. Come with us. The Mirage have to be shut down before they go public. You can help us do that."

I stood there, fighting with myself, but Agent Davis was right. What *was* I going to do? My life, or at least my former life, was over. My parents were gone, I only had a small handful of real friends, and I *was*, now, partially Calaian. Staring at the spot where the mini black hole had been, I slowly nodded.

"Smart move." Davis slid out of the booth and stood. "Come on, we don't have much time. My car's around back."

I followed him out a side entrance to the parking lot. The rain had stopped, and the sun was breaking through the clouds. The ground was wet and steamy, and the humidity hung in the air like a thick hangover.

"Can we stop at my loft so I can get some things?" I asked, walking up to his silver Ford Explorer. "I also gotta feed my cat."

Davis activated his key fob. The door locks clicked open. Suddenly, the high-pitched whine of sport bike down-shifting, which wasn't unusual for Greenville Avenue, came in from my right.

We both looked back just as the orange and black crotch-rocket angled into the row we were in. The helmeted rider lifted a hand from the handlebars and flicked out a long black baton. Before Davis could reach for his gun, the rider smacked the baton to the side of his head in a deftly simple yet violent movement. The impact launched Davis off his feet and onto his back. His head whiplashed against the steaming cement. Blood poured from the gash.

The motorcycle skidded to a stop at the end of the row. The rider looked back and motioned me to get on. I hesitated. The rider angrily slapped the empty seat.

An ominous black van veered into the parking lot's entrance. I swung my fists in the direction of it and engaged my combat tech. Nothing happened. I looked at my fists stunned.

"Don't!" The rider's voice sounded female. "Shut it down!"

My adrenaline-fueled attention darted between the van and the motorcycle. *Fuck it!* I ran to the bike, climbed on and wrapped my arms around the rider's waist. A woman. She gunned it down the back row, leaned into a tight turn and raced towards the rear exit. The black van was barreling toward us at a right angle. If we didn't gain speed, it would T-bone us before the exit. She leaned forward and opened the throttle. I matched the lean and buried my face into her back. The motorcycle's engine pitch was deafening.

Out of the corner of my eye I saw the front bumper of the black van miss the bike's rear wheel by inches. We caught some air exiting the parking lot and shot across Greenville to the sound of blaring horns and screeching tires. I snuck a glance back as we sped away down a side street. The van had crashed through a tall wood fence into a brightly painted Asian food truck parked in the alley.

We sped down several streets to a major intersection. The rider blew through the light as it turned red and headed west on Mockingbird Lane. We whined down to the speed limit, crossed Central Expressway and cruised through the posh and highly policed township of Highland Park. After we made it through HP, the rider finally sat up as we crossed the tollway back into Dallas proper. I tapped the top of her helmet and motioned to pull over. She edged out of traffic and into the parking lot of a boarded-up Church's Chicken. I hopped off and backed away.

The mirrored visor canted in my direction and she cut the engine.

"Who are you?" I yelled.

The rider pulled the helmet off. Her short black hair was pressed to one side. She ran a gloved hand through it and shook her hair out. Her smile looked strangely familiar.

"You're fucking welcome," she said, resting the helmet on a leather clad thigh.

I pointed back the way we had come. "You *killed* Davis!"

She waved off my declaration and pulled a Calaian tablet out of an inside pocket in her racing jacket. "I just grazed him. They're treating him right now." She pointed to the screen. "He'll be fine." She stuffed it back into the pocket and wiped some sweat from her brow. "Besides, Cameron, the group Davis works for doesn't have your best interest in mind, *believe* me."

"Is that why my tech couldn't engage. Something in the black van did that?"

She nodded.

"How do you know me?" I kept my distance.

She dropped her chin and produced a mischievous grin. "You don't remember?"

I slowly shook my head.

She swung a leg over the gas tank, slid off and approached, holding the helmet in her left hand and playfully bouncing it off her thigh.

I thought about backing up, but instead engaged the combat tech and held my ground. The tech rendered her as a black figure. Green static danced inside her form.

"Shut it down, Cameron," she said with a dismissive wave.

I did. She was a little shorter than me, with an angular face and an athletically lean body. Her hair was now spikey. It glistened from sweat in the midday sun. She got within three feet and stopped. Her green eyes studied me. "You really don't remember me, do you?"

"No ... I don't."

She stepped closer, and a smile slid onto her face. "You were holding my hand when I died."

A tremor shot down my spine, and it wasn't my tech. "*Wren?*"

23

BEING LEVERAGED.

Behind her eyes, I imagined the Mirage operative laughing. I took a step back and raised my fists.

Wren lifted her gloved hands in a gesture of calm. "Easy, I'm not a threat."

"Bullshit."

A faint grav field appeared across my knuckles. Her eyes went to it.

"I'm not with the Mirage, Cameron." Trepidation edged her words. "I was undercover."

"For who?"

She slowly lowered her hands and stepped closer. "People ... high up in the Calaian government."

"Why should I trust you?"

"You don't have to, but believe me, I'm your best hope for staying alive."

I relaxed my attack stance and the combat tech shuddered down. "Is that really you," I gestured at her body, "in *there?*"

The shyness in her nod was uncharacteristic of the old Wren. She motioned to herself. "In the flesh."

"How can you jump from ride to ride so easily?"

"I'm a DE."

"A what?"

"Digital Entity. I used to be a living being on Cala a few years ago, but I had an ... accident. There's a lot of risk in being a Liaison."

"You *died?*"

She shrugged. "Yeah, it sucked, but at least I'm here. Alive. Sort of."

"That's crazy."

"Is it? Our cerebral projection technology essentially does this already. A DE is the next logical step."

"Where do you reside, in some intergalactic mainframe?"

"Not that basic, but yes. I'm fully backed up on Cala, but I function from our base on your moon. They continuously run backup sequences ... just in case. And there're four spare rides available for each of us. This one is close to my old one, but I like it better." She punched the air between us, then examined her arm as if it were a power tool. "Sharper reflexes. I had it enhanced. What do you think?"

"Um … it's great. I mean you look good."

The warm smile reappeared. "I was hoping you'd like it." Wren reached out with her right hand and touched my forearm. It was an awkward gesture, but surprisingly I didn't mind. She left it a second and looked like she was going to say something, but then she grabbed her helmet with both hands. "Let's go," she said pulling it down over her head. She walked over to the motorcycle, adjusting the chin strap as she went.

"Where?" I asked.

"I want you to meet somebody," she said over her shoulder.

"What if I don't go with you?"

Wren climbed onto the motorcycle, started it and flipped the visor up. "You got a plan B?" she called out. She reached back and patted the passenger seat.

I reluctantly climbed on and wrapped my arms around her waist. I could feel her stomach muscles flexing under the thin leather jacket.

"Can you not drive so crazy?" I yelled into the side of her helmet.

"Sure, you bet." She revved the engine, clicked it into gear, and popped a small wheelie as we sped out of the parking lot.

*   *   *   *

It seemed this version of Wren didn't have the aggressiveness of the old model. Or maybe I was being suckered again, played by another Calaian organization that had its own agenda for me and my new *Power Ranger* abilities. As we raced in and out of I-35's eight lanes of insane traffic, it became obvious Wren was ignoring my request. She took us to the industrial district just south of DFW airport, where acre upon acre of nondescript warehouse campuses resided as testaments to the booming Metroplex economy.

We exited the highway, turned down a side road and cruised into the expansive empty parking lot of an un-logoed warehouse. Taller than most of its neighbors, the building looked practically new. Wren rode up one of the loading dock ramps and stopped in front of a huge rolling door. She beeped the bike's horn, which was a stark contrast to its throaty idle. The door rose halfway, squeaking almost exactly like the ones at Enzo's garage. We glided into a cavernous space.

About 50 feet in front of us was an open cubicle office setup. It was roughly 400 feet square and floated in a vast sea of blackness bathed in pools of track lighting. After the roll door slammed shut, the effect was enhanced. Four heads popped up from their workstations and regarded us as just part of the day's agenda. They were roughly my age, of various races and genders, and all of them were impossibly good looking.

Wren cut the engine and pulled her helmet off.

"You're late," a young girl's voice said out of the darkness.

"We had a complication," Wren answered.

I rubbed the road grime from my eyes and climbed off. Wren followed, leaving her helmet perched on the gas tank. An African-American teenage girl emerged from the shadows. She looked all of fifteen and wore tight Capri jeans, flat square-tipped shoes and a yellow hoodie with an old, faded Billie Eilish graphic.

Wren put her hands on her hips and looked down. "What the hell is *this*?"

The girl looked up, clearly annoyed. "My current ride is still in the tank. This was all I could get on short notice. Custom ride for someone who wanted an adolescent experience." She pointed at me. "This him?"

Wren jerked a glance toward me. "No, I picked this guy up at a Starbucks."

The girl didn't like Wren's humor. She came closer, and ran her scrutiny up and down me. "Glad you came, Mr. Harrison." Her voice was a little deeper than a typical kid her age, and her accent was pretty neutral. "I'm Commander Carlton Abbott, the leader of this unit." She glanced down at her body. "Usually, I'm not a fifteen-year-old girl."

"Why am I here?" I let my skepticism carry the words.

Wren walked to Abbott's side.

"We work for the Calaian high government," Abbott said.

"Which House?" I asked.

"None of them."

"Are you Viceroys?"

"The group we operate from oversees them." Abbott gestured to Wren. "Liaison Wren had been embedded into the Mirage. You first met her in your hotel's bar, then at Vitale's garage. Your *display* permanently damaged the ride she was using. We had to reinsert her into a new one. Unfortunately, she won't be able to go back to the Mirage."

I folded my arms. "What's this have to do with me?"

"As you've probably concluded, the Viceroys have been compromised."

"What I want to know is why?"

"Why what?"

"Why was *I* chosen?"

"Hard to say. Genetics. Personality traits. Malleability. The real question is what were you chosen *for*?"

"Who decided all this?"

"In the Northern House hierarchy, it's up to the discretion of the lead operative."

"Enzo?" I asked.

Abbott shook his head. "Kipling Bishop."

"Who?"

The Calaian commander regarded me like a puppy that didn't get it. "*Kip*, Mr. Harrison."

* * * *

Once my eyes adjusted to the warehouse's black expanse, I noticed several free-standing living units around the open workspace. Apartments, bathrooms, and a full kitchen flanked a common lounge area. This was the Calaian commander's base of operations. Abbott sent one of the team for pizza and joked that it and beer were the two main reasons Calaians vacationed on Earth. Wren was aloof, busying herself at one of the cubicle farm's workstations.

During dinner I learned the "war" was bigger and more serious than Enzo let on. The Mirage weren't just a band of rogue ex-military bent on eliminating Calaians who opposed them; they were an organized movement whose sole mission was the overthrow of the entire Calaian governmental structure. Abbott's unit was charged with shutting down the Mirage's efforts on Earth, and they'd been damn close to doing that until my display, as Abbott called it, killed the old Wren and dropped the curtain on their two-year infiltration effort.

"They sound like the Bolsheviks." I bit off the pointy end of a slice of margarita pizza.

Abbott looked questioningly around the rim of his Coronita and drank down what was left.

"Correct," one of his team remarked. He was the spitting image of James Dean, and hell, who knows, he might have been.

"But how do they operate here?" I asked. "You all have a base on the dark side of the moon to project yourselves. Where's their base?"

"They operate from an orbital in the Cala system," Abbott said, twisting off the cap of another Coronita. "They project in via a series of superluminal cerebral trans-link platforms."

"From *Cala?*"

He nodded taking a swig.

"One hundred and six of your light-years," the James Dean lookalike added.

"Why don't you sever the connection, or just take out the orbital?" I asked.

"Their cloaking is too advanced," Abbott said. "Besides, space *is* big. The platforms are always moving."

"But if we could take out the main receiving platform here on Earth," Dean said, "the whole system would collapse."

"Let me guess," I said. "The Liaison was just about to find out where it was, right?" I glanced over my shoulder to Wren. She gave a thumbs up without removing her attention from what she was doing.

"What's the Earth expression?" Abbott asked. "*Shit happens?*"

"How long have y'all been battling the Mirage? Here, I mean."

"Five Earth years," Dean replied.

"Every time we take one of them out," Abbott said, "a replacement arrives."

"Where do they source their rides?"

Abbott glanced uncertainly at Dean. Dean shrugged.

"They tap your, um, unwanted individuals," Abbott said.

"Homeless people?"

"That's one group," Dean said matter-of-factly.

"Do they ever attack your moon base?" I asked.

Abbott shook his head. "Too fortified. The fight is here."

I took a swig from my Corona. "I need some clarity."

"About what?" Abbott asked.

"I get the whole thing about the tech neutralizing other tech so you have to resort to our *primitive* methods to fight your war here." This got a few chuckles from some of the team. "But why is Wren the only one who can be brought back from the dead when her ride dies? Is it because she's a digital entity?"

The chuckling died. Abbott pushed his plate of pizza aside. "You're correct ... Liaison Wren is a digital entity, but she's chosen a different path." He picked up his Coronita and tipped it back.

"What path have you all chosen?"

"Death," he said, like it was the obvious answer.

"You *choose* to die?"

"It's our…" Abbott snapped his teenage ride's dainty fingers. The nails sported girlish pink polish. "Help me someone, what's the Earth term?"

"Religion?" an Asian woman with shoulder length black hair offered.

"Philosophy?" James Dean suggested.

"Some call it a belief," a red-bearded hipster said.

"Yes … a *belief*," Abbott agreed. "We choose to die an actual death because of our beliefs, Mr. Harrison."

"Do the Mirage share those beliefs?" I asked.

"Most do."

An awkward quiet established itself. I polished off the dregs of my beer.

"Well," Abbott said, pushing away from the table, "these bodies of yours require long periods of reduced environmental stimuli."

"Sleep?" I asked.

Abbott gave me a restrained if not polite smile. "Good night, all."

Everyone said their good nights, collected their trash and left almost in unison. I sat alone and contemplated what the hell I had gotten into … again. I twisted in my chair and draped an arm over its back. "I never got to ask the real question," I said to Wren.

"Isn't it obvious?" She didn't look up.

"It's my new augmented tech. … They need it, or me, really, to defeat the Mirage, right?"

Wren flashed another thumbs-up and picked up a tablet in the same motion and started interacting with it.

It had been a long day. The adrenaline rush I had been running on since Gloria's parking lot had run out hours ago, and my jet lag was tugging hard. "Where do I do *my* period of reduced environmental stimuli?"

Wren finally looked up and pointed to the last door on the line of apartments. "Use that one. It's got fresh sheets."

*　　　*　　　*　　　*

The unit was furnished like it had been lifted straight from an Ikea showroom. My bed was comfortable with brand new sheets, still sporting Ikea tags. With no windows, the space was pitch black, which suited me fine. I always slept better that way.

I finally checked my phone and found what I feared. Josh had blown it up with text messages, pissed I hadn't shown up at the bar. I texted that I was beat from the trip and I'd see him soon. He texted a whisky drink and thumbs up emojis.

I laid back against the mound of pillows and began to drift off. After a few minutes of slipping in and out of sleep, the creak of my unit's door snapped me awake. I engaged my combat tech and the night vision deployed. A figure entered the dark narrow hallway, but my tech rendered it differently. Instead of a green glow around its human ride, this being had no surface details. Just a solid green glowing human figure. No clothing detail or facial features. I cautiously sat up and formed a grav field at the end of the bed. It stepped closer and I saw the green static swim inside a female-shaped form.

I dropped the field and my combat tech. The room went pitch black again. "Liaison, what the hell are you *doing?*"

Wren emerged from the darkness and into the soft residual glow from my phone's screen. She pulled off her top, then wriggled her shorts down. The dim light edged the contours of her elegant naked body.

"Oh Jesus ... look, Liaison ... I'm not sure this is a—"

She pulled back the sheets and slid next to me. Like Toni, she was warm, but unlike Toni, her body was lean and toned. My phone winked out and she rucked a leg over my hip.

"I want you," she whispered.

I started to gently push her away, but she wrapped her foot against my thigh and pulled herself close. The girl was strong.

"Come on, Earthman," she laughed. "Let's have some fun."

"I'm not really sure we—"

"Shut up, Cameron, I don't want to get married, I just *want* you."

She pressed her lips against mine and I turned away.

"What's the matter?" she asked.

"This is weird."

"What you did, back in Italy ... that was really kind. I just want to say thank you."

"Yeah, but—"

"Cameron. It's no big deal. Besides, I've always found you kind of hot." She gave me a peck on the lips.

"I don't know—"

"You held my hand. You stayed with me. You made it a lot easier to let go." Her voice cracked on the word *go*. "I've done that so many times. You know how many of them I did alone?"

"All of them?"

"No one's ever done something like that for me, Cameron. *No* one." She kissed me again, this time with more desire. "Let me show how much that meant to me."

"Liaison–"

"Wren."

"Wren. I, um–"

"You don't find my ride desirable?"

"*No* ... no, it's not that."

"It's Toni, right?"

I shook my head a little. "No ... it's *not* her. It's me." Even in the darkness I could sense her puzzlement. "Wren, I appreciate you wanting to, you know ..."

"Fuck your brains out?"

I let a small laugh escape.

"I get it," she said.

"Get what?"

"You're one of those *sensitive* humans."

"It's not that. It's ... oh, come here." I put my arm around her. "Just let me hold you."

She went with it, and we laid there in the dark and held each other.

"Thank you," she whispered after a few moments.

"For what?"

"For being there ... back in Vitale's garage."

The scene of that carnage flashed into my mind's eye. Horrific. A twinge of guilt shuddered through me.

"I told Enzo to take care of you … properly. I guess that was kind of a stupid thing to ask, since you didn't really die, and your ride … well–"

"It was a nice thought," she said, "but this ritual your species has of burning the body is weird."

"Saves space."

She slapped my chest in mock disgust.

I went to stroke the top of her head. My hand passed over the back of her neck. A faint red glow flashed for a millisecond.

She looked up and our lips met awkwardly in the darkness.

"Another time," she whispered.

"Is that an order, *Liaison*?"

"Damn, right, soldier."

24

WHAT THE DATA SUGGESTS.

"Coffee?"

I looked up from my phone at one of Abbott's crew standing across from the kitchen table. It was the pretty Asian woman. Her hair was pulled back into a tiny bun.

"Um, no … thank you."

"French roast." She raised her cup. "It's *awes*ome."

"I can't have caffeine. Sparks my migraines."

She frowned. "Your tech should neutralize that effect."

She had a point. I hadn't tried coffee since the implant. "Okay, I'll take a cup. Thanks."

She walked to a slick chrome device that looked like a high-tech es-
presso machine had mated with an industrial microwave. She removed its glass
drip decanter and poured a generous portion into a large black mug. As it heated up, a bright green, smiling cartoon alien head appeared along with the
words, *Take me to your sugar,* in Comic Sans font.

"Sugar?" she asked.

"I know you guys do."

She looked back with a wry grin. "It's like crack to us." She tore the
tops off four sugar packs and dumped them in. "Here you go," she said stirring
as she walked. She handed me the mug; the alien's big black eyes stared at me.

I took it with both hands, blew off the heat and sipped. Man, I missed
coffee.

"You look like you didn't sleep well." She took a sip from her mug.
"Was the bed uncomfortable?"

I shook my head. "No, it was fine. Just having a hard time waking up."

Another frown. "But you *are* awake."

"It's an expression—"

"Morning," Wren said through a yawn as she walked into the kitchen.
Her bare feet slapped against the tile floor. Her baggy plaid pajamas were adorable.

"How'd you sleep?" the Asian girl asked.

Wren shot me a half-grin side glance as she poured a cup. "Amazingly." She crossed behind me, ran a discreet finger across my shoulders, and circled the table and choose a seat opposite me.

"Good morning, everyone," a sturdy older man said. I hadn't met him yet. He acted as if his day had started hours ago. His salt-and-pepper hair had a West Texas preacher quality.

The Asian straightened, pulling back her shoulders not quite to full attention. "Good morning, sir."

"Morning, Abbott," Wren said through another yawn.

"What happened to your little girl ride?" I asked.

"Back in the tank," he said, pouring a cup.

"This ride suits you better, sir," the Asian said.

"Thank you, Sato."

"Sugar," I blurted.

Sato turned and smiled. "You know Japanese?"

"I dated a girl from Tokyo once," I said. "She taught me a few things."

Wren took a rather noisy slurp and cut me an impish side eye.

"How did you get all this here?" I motioned to the office area. "Your Calaian equipment, that is?"

Abbott pointed with his cup to a huge open area just behind the living units.

I looked over to the empty dark expanse. It was probably 400-by-600 feet and six stories tall. "What?"

Sato snickered into her mug.

"Come." Abbott walked to the edge of the darkness. I followed.

"Walk in." He motioned with his cup again.

"Okay," I said skeptically. Four steps into the murkiness, something invisible hit my forehead, or more accurately, I head-bumped something. I stumbled back and straightened with a hand in front of my face. I reached up and a warm, solid surface greeted my fingertips, but I couldn't see anything.

"Engage your combat tech," Abbott said.

Out of the darkness something coalesced. Looming over me was a gigantic insectlike spacecraft magically rendered in various shades of deep greys and browns as it emerged from the background. I had bumped into a section of its underbelly that dipped closest to the ground. There were four of these circular sections, each about 20 feet in diameter. The craft had no landing gear and was floating roughly 10 feet off the cement floor. My tech adjusted my visual range and more came into detail. I reached up again. Its surface felt and looked like a turtle shell, but the patterns seemed vaguely African. The plating (if that's what it was) undulated at my touch. I lightly punched the surface and ripples spread out in concentric waves.

"It's *alive*," Wren teased in a lame Dr. Frankenstein voice. Both she and Sato chuckled.

"Bizarre," I said, returning to Abbott's side.

"From your perspective," he replied.

I dropped my combat tech, and the craft faded back into shadows and darkness.

"That's how you move around our planet, cloaked and undetected?"

"Most of the time," Abbott replied.

"What do you mean?"

"Sometimes the cloaking, um, uncloaks. It's an issue with your planet's weather. There's a lot of energy in thunderstorms and tropical depressions."

"What happens when you decloak?"

"We make the front page of the tabloids," Wren said, joining us. "Let me see your forehead." She raised on her toes and inspected. "That's what I thought."

"What?" I leaned down to give her a better view.

"It attached to your skin."

"What did? I don't feel anything." I raised my hand, but she batted it away.

Wren looked over her shoulder. "Sato, can you bring me my intra-pad?"

The Asian trotted over with a tablet in her hand. "Here you go, ma'am."

All three Calaians curiously examined my forehead. Wren pointed the tablet toward where I had smacked into the craft. "There," she said.

Something fluttered past the corner of my eye and fell to the floor. I looked down at the tiny shell-like material. Sato picked it up and approached the invisible craft. She raised the material into the air and it vanished from her fingers.

"Now that," I said, rubbing my temple, "is some creepy shit."

"Defense protocol," Abbott said.

"What would it have done if it had stayed on my head?"

"Knocked you out, then erased your recent memories," Wren replied. "Let me see your hand."

I held my hand out. Wren passed the tablet over it. More invisible bits of shell reformed, dislodged from my knuckles and fingertips and fell to the floor. Sato scooped the pieces and they did their vanishing act, returning to the collective that was the craft's biological skin.

Wren gently rubbed my knuckles with her thumb. "All better?" I nodded and she walked back to the kitchen area and leaned against the counter.

"While you were asleep," Abbott said, "we think we found where the Mirage are keeping your friends."

"Let's get something straight," I said loudly enough for everyone to hear. "I'm not friends with them or with you or with any other Calaians."

Beyond Abbott's shoulder I caught Wren smiling. She pressed her tongue against the side of her open mouth, luridly stroked the air with a closed hand and raised an eyebrow mischievously.

Abbott nodded as if my declaration made some sort of sense.

"So where are they?" I asked.

Abbott walked to a workstation in the offices. The hipster with the red beard was seated in front of a strange-looking computer console. Instead of a monitor, a blank flat screen faced straight up. The guy wore an interface that resembled VR headgear a sci-fi doctor might wear for some delicate, remote operation. It was as white as powdered sugar, had an organic quality and completely hugged his face. Only his beard stuck out from the bottom of its tendrilled webbing. A global rendering of Europe formed about six inches above the flat panel. It was more realistic than a typical hologram, and the detail suggested it was a real-time feed from space. The bearded guy reached out and rotated it a quarter turn to center on Paris. "Right in the heart of the City of Lights," he said.

"Hiding in plain sight," Abbott muttered.

The bearded guy turned as if he could see Abbott through the headgear, but then again, he probably could. "Might be their main base of operations." The hologram morphed into a cascading downward scroll of tiny colored splotches, probably Calaian technobabble. He pointed. "Look at these defensive stats."

Abbott leaned closer and studied the data stream.

"How did you find them?" I asked.

Abbott straightened but didn't answer.

"We've been trying to hack their superluminal stream's cloaking protocols for over a year," the bearded guy said. The data stream morphed into a three-dimensional celestial map. "We finally broke through earlier this week." He pointed to an area three-quarters the distance from what I guessed was Cala. "Here."

"Why do you need a permanent base on our moon if this kind of technology exists?" I asked.

"It's a volume issue," Abbott said. "At any given time, up to ten-thousand Calaians are on Earth. An interstellar trans-link platform system can't handle that kind of cortical projection capacity."

"What *is* its capacity?"

"About a hundred individual projections." The bearded guy peeled off the headgear. When the last of it released from his forehead, he wadded it into a ball and placed it on the workstation's counter. Its color changed from sugar white to slate grey while it compressed into a sharp-angled cube about an inch square.

"Is that where they're holding them … in Paris?" I asked.

Abbott nodded. "You better get ready."

"Why's that?"

"We leave tomorrow."

25

ANYTHING BUT NORMAL.

Dude, where the hell are you?

It's complicated

It's Toni, right? Josh's text ended with a handcuff emoji of a penis that had a dog collar on it.

Fuck you.

Calling it like it is, bro. You r pw'd

Josh didn't know the half of it. Hell, he didn't know the millionth of it.

I'm going back to Europe tomorrow

Whoa. Really? U luv her?

Like I said, it's complicated

Two yellow smiley-faced emojis having sex popped up.

Where do you get these porn emojis?

This girl I met ... she's a freak!

A knock at my unit's door pulled me away from my texting.

I'll call ya when I get back. Might be gone a while. Nicole is taking care of

Roz

An airplane, glass of whiskey and more emojis having sex popped up on my phone. "It's open," I said, clicking my phone's screen off.

Wren peered around the edge of the door. "Hey."

"Hey, yourself."

"Can I come in?"

"It's a free planet."

Wren entered and sat on the edge of the bed. She wore a tight, dry-fit sleeveless top, black leggings and fluorescent pink running shoes. Sweat glistened on her arms.

"Keeping your ride in shape?" I asked.

"Abbott wants us tight and ready."

I took in the Calaian. "What is this?" I finally asked.

Wren straightened. "What's *what?*"

"You know ... *this*. The flirtation. Wanting to jump my bones. Is Abbott having you soften me up to go along with the program?" It was a fair question, especially after what I had been through.

Wren made a face.

"I'm a big boy. I learn from my mistakes. I may have gotten suckered once, but I'm not going to be suckered again. I *am* grateful to be alive, although the thought has occurred to me that the 'getting stabbed' (I gestured for air quotes) thing in Rome was just a setup to implant me."

"Listen, Cameron." Wren took my hand. "I won't lie, we *do* need your help. Abbott is determined to end this conflict."

"But ...?"

"He won't force you to do anything you don't want to do. He's a by-the-book kind of guy."

"Then what's in it for me?"

"Abbott will help you."

My turn to make a face. "With what?"

Wren squeezed my hand. "Getting the tech out ... but only if you want that."

"What if I don't?"

"As long as you have our tech inside you," she raised a hand and crossed two fingers, "then we're like this ... Calaians and you, I mean."

"Is that what you were sent here to deliver ... my terms of employment?"

She shrugged, then nodded. "Sorry." She let go and sat back.

"Don't worry about it," I said through a sigh. "I don't have a choice, really."

The uncertainty of my situation sat between us like an unwanted guest.

"Will you?" she asked finally.

"Take the tech out?"

She nodded.

"I don't know. Is the procedure dangerous?"

The question caught her off guard. "I'm not sure. I don't think it's ever been done."

"Which one? The tech being put in a human or being taken out?"

"From what I know – which *is* limited – neither has happened."

I shook my head.

"What?" she asked.

"Six weeks ago, I was a normal guy. Now ... I don't know what the hell I am."

Wren scooted closer. "You're anything but normal."

"Thanks, I guess."

She put her palm to my cheek. "I don't know if Toni and Bishop played you. I don't know *shit*, really. I just know what Abbott and his unit tell me. I'm a tactical asset ... a hired gun. They like the fact that I can be repurposed again and again."

I took her hand from my cheek and held it. "How many times have you ... you know?" Her faint grimace told me she was counting back through the rides she'd occupied and deaths she'd experienced.

"Too many," she said flatly.

"But back in Vitale's garage, that was different?"

"Only because you were there, at my side."

"Is it weird?" I asked.

"It was at first, but you get used to it. Eventually you can't tell the difference. Hell, I've forgotten what it was like to be alive ... really alive."

"How long will you be a digital entity?"

"As long as they need me, I guess."

"What happens when Abbott doesn't *need* you anymore?"

Wren shrugged again. "I guess my time will be up, unless someone wants to buy me."

"*Buy* you?"

"On Cala, I'm what you would call a commodity. I've been processed to be what I am from birth. Once I came of age, I was sold to a House. There I worked security, honed my skills." She leaned in. "Became *damn* good at what I do."

"How did you get hooked up with Abbott?"

"I served out my tenure, then I got connected with the Calaian high command."

"Secret police?"

Wren thought for a moment. "I guess, but not with the sinister connotation of your world. It's our military."

"Are you old?"

A slow smile formed across Wren's lips. "I'm younger than Toni, if that's what you're asking."

"But probably a lot older than me."

The smile dimmed. "Does that bother you?"

"Are you kidding?" I pointed to the back of my neck. "Thanks to this shit, I now live in a continuous state of botheredness."

We sat quietly for a moment, the energy from the night before rising between us.

"Last night ... what was that?" I asked.

"I wasn't softening you up."

"Then what was it?"

The hard edge that always lingered around Wren fell away. "Pretty damn nice," she said.

I moved closer and gently kissed her. I began to pull back, but Wren took my hand and held my kiss. After a moment, she let go.

"I've got to go, um, pack," she said. "We leave after breakfast."

"Are we taking the stealth flyer?"

Her face went into question.

"The ship I hit my head on."

"Oh, right … yes, we are. You'll like it. It's a little *different* than what you're used to." Wren slid off the bed and walked to the door.

"Hey," I said.

She stopped and turned.

"I thought last night was pretty damn nice, too."

26

ONE OTHER THING.

After Wren left, I showered in the common bathroom. Shaving at one of the four sinks (wearing only a towel around my waist), I caught Sato checking me out as she brushed her hair at the farthest sink. It wasn't a sexual leer. More like she was studying me. She was in sports underwear that complimented her athletic body. Back in the apartment, I found a large open suitcase sitting on the bed. It was filled with new Calvin Klein and Michael Kors clothes. Everything was tasteful and the correct sizes. Even the three pairs of Nike shoes fit perfectly. I put on a pair of Klein black jeans, a putty-colored Kors button-down and a pair of black cross-trainers and headed for the kitchen for another cup that *awes*ome coffee.

At the edge of the area where the cloaked Calaian spacecraft hovered sat a dozen equipment cases, the same kind that had been off-loaded for my surgery. Abbott's unit milled about in the kitchen. Wren was leaning against the counter, near the coffeemaker. I walked up to her side. She playfully bumped my hip with hers.

"Nice clothes," she side-whispered.

"Funny," I side-whispered back, "they magically appeared in my room."

"You're welcome."

"What's going on?"

"Mission brief."

Abbott strode into the kitchen and put his hands on his hips. I flashed on his little girl ride doing the same thing. The pose he struck, especially the turned foot, was eerily similar. "Eyes forward, people."

Sato lobbed a chrome golf ball like the one Enzo had tossed into the center of the kitchen. It froze in midair about four feet off the floor and emitted a kind of holographic projection from its top. A dimensional map of Paris formed from the beam.

"We believe the Mirage enterprise is in this area." Sato pointed to the neighborhood around the Musée d'Orsay. "Intel suggests it might be within a few blocks of the museum. The background data will propagate now."

All the Calaians closed their eyes.

I elbowed Wren. "What's prop–?" As if my brain had been pried open, a dense info dump on the Musée d'Orsay and its *arrondissement* poured into my mind. What resembled a Wiki site rapidly scrolled through my vision. I stumbled forward from the surge. Wren grabbed my arm and steadied me. Her eyes were still closed. She pulled me back to her side. A second later, the pressure inside my skull and the data scroll vanished. I gasped.

Wren slowly opened her eyes. "Kind of like an orgasm, eh?"

I put a hand to my chest and caught my breath. "Uh ... no. *Not* like that at all."

She leaned into my ear. "You just haven't had the right data loaded."

Abbott approached the floating chrome ball. "We'll land just outside of Paris in roughly one hour."

"One *hour*?" I whispered.

Wren shushed me.

"There is a private gala at the museum tonight," Abbott continued. "According to our operatives, the top Mirage commander for Earth will be there. We land at 1 p.m., Paris time, so that will give us a few hours to prepare."

The hipster bearded guy raised a hand.

Abbott pointed. "Trent?"

"Why will he be there?"

Abbott folded his arms. "The front company the Mirage operates is associated with the museum—"

Sato opened her eyes. "It's a venture capital group. The Mirage commander is a large private donor. The company is called *Cala* Capital."

"That's lame," I whispered.

Wren shushed me again.

"Mr. Harrison and Liaison Wren will pose as patrons. It's a ..." Abbott hesitated.

"Fundraiser?" I offered.

"Yes. A *fundraiser.*" He pivoted back to the group. "They will take the Mirage commander captive. Our plan is to use the commander as a bargaining chip and negotiate a truce. The Mirage, as you already know, value their leaders. This should bring them to the table." The Paris map morphed into a split screen. The image of an athletically built bald man in his mid-50s materialized to the left of the map. His porn star moustache was trimmed just above the upper lip. The portrait looked like it had been lifted from a corporate website. "This is the last known image of the Mirage commander's ride. His Earth name is Philippe Baudin. The Liaison and Harrison will attend the party posing as a couple wanting to become patrons. Because Harrison's enhanced tech is unaffected by our cerebral implant's defense protocols, he'll use his CGFG to disable the Mirage commander. The Liaison will assist if the situ warrants it."

"This is your master plan?" I said.

Abbott regarded me harshly. "You have something to add?"

"How am I going to take this guy captive, and what's a CGFG?"

"Concentrated Gravity Field Generation. You'll use your tech to knock him out. We'll have operatives posing as paramedics. They'll come in and remove the commander."

I rolled my eyes. "Eff this." I pushed off the counter.

Wren grabbed my arm. "Easy, killer. I'll teach you how to do it."

I made a face and settled back against the counter.

"Why do you disapprove?" Sato asked.

Abbott eyed her and she shrugged off his glare.

I opened my mind to the catalog of data that had been dumped into my brain. Approaching the holoprojection, I gestured to the map. "Paris is the most densely populated city in Europe. There are over 10 million people in the metro area, almost three million in Paris alone. Twenty-thousand people per square kilometer live near the museum." I could barely keep up with the flow of data. "The last and only time I engaged this new tech, a lot of people died. I don't want any human collateral damage."

"Your *point?*" Abbott's irritation cut the air between us.

I got in the commander's face. I clenched my hands and engaged my tech. A grav field built around my fists and enveloped us. We slowly rose off the tile floor. Abbott struggled against the pressure of the field. His team came to attention and approached. Abbott gestured for them to stop.

"I don't want anyone killed unnecessarily. Are we clear, commander?"

Abbott's acknowledgement was a cold stare.

I lowered us to the floor and dissipated the field. I passed my best *don't fuck with me* glare over the Calaians. "Sato?"

"Yes?"

"Will Baudin have any people protecting him?"

"Unknown. It's a very exclusive guest list," she said. "Only he is named."

"Okay, then. Let's go do this." I returned to Wren's side.

The huge Calaian spacecraft decloaked and Abbott sternly motioned for his unit to load up. As they filed past, no one made eye contact. I stepped in behind the last one, but Wren yanked me around.

"Look at you, barking orders and kicking ass." She pressed against me. "Ever done it while going ten times the speed of sound?"

*   *   *   *

The inside of the craft was straight out of a Ridley Scott movie. While it had aspects of H. R. Giger's cold biomechanicalness, there was something quite beautiful about it. I couldn't put my designer's finger on it, but its surfaces and contours exuded an elegance, as if a feminine entity had birthed it. The lack of buttons or switches was a bit unnerving, and the only things that remotely resembled instrumentation were small panels peppered across the bulkhead. Each one contained the same Calaian color blobs that seemed to dominate their communication technology, and in these panels the color forms slowly undulated like a two-dimensional lava lamp.

The "cockpit" didn't have a view screen, and the two pilots were apparently flying the craft from the comfort of Calaian organic loungers that looked like they had grown out of the flooring. The pilots wore the same face-hugging gear that Trent used in the warehouse, and one of them, a muscular guy whom I hadn't met, tapped his fingers on an invisible panel only he could see. James Dean stood between them, his hands resting casually on the backs of their headrests.

Since I went grav-ass on Abbott, his team had kept their distance. Wren, though, was playing it cool, cutting only the occasional glance and ever-so-slight grin. Abbott kept his attention locked on his tablet. I think he was either embarrassed or very pissed. Probably both.

"How fast can this thing go?" I asked the group.

"Sub-light," Dean said matter-of-factly.

"You mean just under the speed of light?" I asked.

"*Yes.*"

"You want to experience it?" Wren turned to Abbott and girlishly clapped her hands together. "Oh, *please*, Daddy, can we go to Mars?"

"We're supposed to be in Paris by one o'clock." Dean turned to Abbott. "I would *not* advise this, sir."

The Calaian commander considered the request. "How long will it take?"

A small holoscreen, its color blobs swirling, formed in front of Dean.

"Mars, in its present position, is approximately one-hundred and forty-nine million kilometers," he said. "It will take about eleven minutes, one way." He turned back to Abbott, who had settled into a lounger that wasn't there a second ago. "Is this acceptable, sir?"

Abbott looked up from his tablet and eyed me with a good deal of loathing. "*Sure.* Indulge the human." Sarcasm dripped from the words.

Dean patted the muscular pilot on his shoulder.

"Wait," I said. Dean looked over. "I want to say something."

Wren shook her head. "Are you *serious?*"

"How do you know what I want to say?"

"I *read* your file."

"Come on then," I implored.

She rolled her eyes. "Go ahead, get it out of your system."

"Say *what?*" Dean demanded.

"*Engage.*" I motioned with my forefinger. Somebody snickered behind me.

Dean patted the muscular pilot again and the guy nodded.

Nothing happened. A few seconds ticked by.

"Uh, are we, you know … at sub-light?" I asked.

"Just passed your moon," Dean said. "About to go to sub-light."

"Is there a view screen?"

The pilots spun their loungers around, and a large free-floating screen materialized in front of them. Like the tablet, it pixelated from a center point out to its edges until the complete object was formed. The screen's surface was densely black, like thick velvet, then a white dot pattern emerged. The stars seemed to come out of the screen. The thing's resolution must have been a billion K.

After several moments, the star field didn't exhibit any motion. No light-streak warp tunnel. Nothing.

"So ... are we, you know, folding space?" I asked.

"You would *not* understand the concept," Dean said drolly, avoiding eye contact.

"This is a workhorse ship." The muscular pilot turned. "Is that the right word ... workhorse?"

"I guess," I said, "but you–"

A dirty brownish-orange blob appeared on the screen and stole my attention. It grew until it filled the screen's field and froze. There was no perceptible feeling the craft had stopped.

Abbott gestured apathetically. "There it is. Mars. God of War. The Red Planet. Big *fucking* deal."

I was speechless.

Wren came up to my side. "Pretty cool, eh?"

"The trip or the planet?" I asked.

"Okay!" Abbott clasped his hands together. "Back to Paris and let's hit the limit. We're cutting this close."

We approached Earth's atmosphere roughly eight minutes later. As with Mars, I had no sensation of movement at all, so with the view screen gone, there was little to do except, well, quietly stare at each other. The Calaians who were standing seemed to be caught in some kind of trance. Maybe they were upgrading their tech's software? Abbott's attention hadn't left his tablet, and the pilots just did their thing. Wren stood by my side and didn't say a word.

"Entering the exosphere," the muscular pilot said finally. "We'll be at the point in thirty-two seconds."

"Are we cloaked?" I asked Wren.

"We never were *un*cloaked," she replied.

"In position," the muscular pilot said. "Resting engaged."

"Let's hustle, people," Abbott said coming to his feet.

The bulkhead behind me morphed into an opening and something resembling a ramp built itself to the floor. I followed Dean down.

"Why does it take sixty minutes to get to Paris, but only eleven to get to Mars?" I asked him.

"We don't run at sub-light in your atmosphere," he said over his shoulder.

"What's the propulsion?"

"You wouldn't comprehend that either."

"It manipulates gravity, right?"

He didn't answer and stepped off the ramp. I looked back to the "door" we had just exited. The ramp and what I could see through the opening were the only evidence that anything was hovering there. After the last Calaian walked off, the ramp and the opening dissolved away.

We were now inside a huge warehouse, similar in square footage to the Calaians' Dallas base, but this looked more like an old Parisian train station. The open atrium we had "parked" in was six floors high. Dozens of ornate black wrought-iron columns rose from the cement floor to support the next floor above. Each floor appeared to have the same number of columns, and all of it supported an expansive weathered, iron-framed glass roof. A couple of ancient push carts parked in various dusty corners rounded out the building's Hogsmeade motif. How the craft navigated through crowded Parisian airspace undetected and landed *inside* this building was beyond me.

"Harrison, Wren," Abbott called out, motioning.

A finely boned, older man in a dark blue three-piece tailored suit was standing next to him. We both trotted over.

"Sir?" Wren asked.

"This is André," Abbott said. "He'll show you where you can prepare for tonight." He swung his attention to a large black Mercedes sedan about 50 feet away. The shine on it looked like it had been poured on. "He'll also be your chauffeur."

"*Bonjour!*" André said with a clipped nod. "This way, please."

He started to walk away, and Wren and I fell in behind.

"Harrison?" Abbott said to my back.

"Yeah?" I asked, turning.

"Listen, I know you're a little on edge, but Baudin … he's a …"

"Bad mother*fucker*?"

"Yes."

"What if he puts up a fight?" I asked. "What do we do then?"

Abbott looked at his boots and acted like this was the question he had been dreading. He raised his eyes. "Kill him."

"Won't that–?"

"It won't. The Mirage's hierarchy is fragile. They're a top-heavy organization. Take out the leader, they're in disarray. If we can't get leverage, then we need to send a message ... a *serious* one. Do you understand?"

"I do." I started to leave.

"There's, uh, one other thing. If the time comes ... will you be able to take out Toni Morgan, if needed?"

The question took me aback. It must have shown on my face.

Abbott stepped closer. "I can't make you to do anything you don't want to." He forced down a dry swallow. "But things could get a little ugly with this mission. I need to know ... can you *kill* her if needed?"

"Jesus, Abbott, I don't really know. I mean, I had feelings for Toni, *real* feelings. It would depend on the moment, what was going on, like if she was threatening my life or something."

"Harrison, I *need* you to acknowledge ... yes or no?"

"I don't think I can just ... kill her."

Abbott took in a long breath and let out an equally long frustrated sigh. "I've died more than a hundred times on shithole planets I can't even re-member." His attention went to his unit as they unpacked the gear. "Many of these people have too, at my side." Abbott stepped closer. "If any of *my* kind die a real death because of your petty human feelings, I *will* kill you."

I confronted the commander's threat. "I thought murder was forbid-den on your planet."

Abbott's eyes narrowed. "We're not *on* my planet."

27

YOU'RE FORGETTING SOMETHING.

André escorted me to some old offices, just off the atrium.

"You can change in here, Mr. Harrison." He opened a door whose upper half was frosted glass. A long crack ran diagonally from a lower corner to its center. Ornate worn black lettering edged in faded gold leaf spelled out COMPTABILITÉ. "A set of clothes is waiting for you inside. If you need anything, I will be right here."

The large room was empty except for a wooden chair, a standing full-length mirror and a rickety coat rack. Hanging on the rack was a tuxedo, and on the floor, neatly arranged at the rack's base, was a pair of black patent formal leather oxfords. On the chair were a pair of black socks, a tuxedo white shirt and grey boxers, all Armani.

I stripped naked in front of the mirror and studied my body. Typically, I work out two to three times a week, but I hadn't touched a weight for weeks. Somehow, my body looked like I had been pumping iron like a pro. My pecs had real definition, my traps stood out, and my quads were beginning to look like a sprinter's. When Wren ticked off the stats to the boss lady, I hadn't thought much of it, but now I could see the physical changes the new tech was making, and I wasn't sure if it scared me or gave me a sense of power. I guess whoever picked out my ensemble had taken into consideration my muscle mass gain. The tux fit perfectly. But the shoes, probably because they were new leather, dug a little into the sides of my ankles. I hadn't tied a formal bow-tie since my wedding, as far as I could remember, but after a few attempts I nailed it. A soft knock at a side door pulled my attention from the mirror.

"Yeah?" The door opened a fraction. I was expecting André.

"It's me," Wren said. "Can I come in?"

"Sure."

The door swung open and Liaison Wren stepped through. *Whoa.*

"How do I look?" she asked.

I folded my arms and admired her. "Stunning comes to mind."

I had only seen the Liaison crack a full-on grin once, but what emerged was the biggest and brightest. Whoever styled Wren's short hair had spiked it into shiny points, and her makeup was red carpet glam and made her green eyes appear brighter than usual. ... Maybe her tech was enhancing them. Her dress looked like a designer had wrapped her with a foot-wide roll of blood-red aluminum foil. It started from her right shoulder and spiraled down covering the parts that needed to be while exposing the rest of her perfectly. The spiral ended just below her sexy Venus dimples and poured to the floor like a delicate crimson waterfall. Two elegant slits exposed the edges of her toned legs. Her pumps were the same color as the dress and lifted her almost to my eye level.

"Your mouth is open, Mr. Harrison," she said walking up.

"With good reason." I took her by the waist with both hands. Her skin was warmer than usual.

"You look pretty yummy, yourself." She adjusted my bowtie. "Perfect."

We took each other in. I gently guided her close and kissed her. After a delicious moment, I pulled away. Her eyes were still closed.

"Your mouth is open, Liaison Wren."

She closed it and slowly opened her eyes. Puzzlement washed over her. She put a hand to her chest.

"Something wrong?" I asked.

"I-I don't know. I felt an odd sensation … right here."

I let a knowing smile build. "Your *heart*, maybe?"

"Maybe, but–"

"Excuse me." André's head appeared around the doorframe. "May I come in?"

"Sure," I said.

"My, *my*," André said, walking up arms spread, "don't you two make a *hand*some couple."

Wren gave a curt smile and fidgeted with the upper part of her dress.

"Thanks, André," I replied.

He handed us each a sheet of paper. "Here are your identities for the evening. We chose to print these out rather than send them via your tech. I heard you had a little difficulty with our method of transfer, Mr. Harrison."

"I appreciate your concern." I took the sheet.

"Look, *dear*," Wren said, pointing to hers, "we're rich."

"We're also trying to attain the museum's patron status while being total unknowns in that scene," I added, scanning the text. "Not easy."

"And," André produced a dark blue velvet ring box, "you're married." He angled the top open. Nestled inside were two simple gold bands. "Our demographic intelligence suggests a sixty-three percent interface success rate as a married couple." He pulled the larger ring out. "Yours, Mr. Harrison."

I slipped it on and an echo of me doing the same thing, the morning of Karen's accident, washed in on the tide of conveniently forgotten memories.

André pulled the other ring out and pocketed the box. "And here's–"

"Wait, André … let me."

He hesitated and handed me the ring.

I turned to Wren. "Give me your left hand."

She cautiously raised it. "What are you doing?"

"It's an Earth custom, my dear," André said.

I gently took Wren's left hand and slid the band onto her ring finger. Her eyes became big with realization. "Oh, now, *wait* a minute–"

"It's all right," I said, "this isn't legal." I raised her hand to my lips and gently kissed the ring finger.

Wren gasped softly and pulled her hand away. "I, um … I have to finish getting ready."

André and I watched her scurry from the room.

"She makes a beautiful human woman," André remarked as the door shut behind her.

"She certainly does," I said.

André faced me. "Forgive me, Mr. Harrison, but I have been on your planet for quite a few years – I am a Concierge – and I have to say ..." He paused, seemingly unsure.

"It's okay, André, you can speak your mind."

"Yes, well ... I have witnessed quite a few of our people grapple with emotional attachment to your species, and ..."

"What sort of attachment do you mean?" I knew where he was going.

"*Love*, Mr. Harrison." He gestured to the side door. "Clearly Liaison Wren is in the beginning throes of it." He put a hand to his chest. "I've seen this happen *so* many times."

"And me, André ... am I in the beginning throes?"

"Not yet, but I sense you're a man who has previously dealt with that emotion's complexities. I think you'll let whatever you and Liaison Wren are experiencing run a more *natural* course. Would you agree?"

"I would."

"*Magnifique!* Now, if you're ready, I'll take you to the car."

André led me back to the atrium, past the cloaked Calaian craft to the glossy-beyond-mirror-sheen Mercedes. He opened a rear door and I slid into its cocoon of luxury.

"I'll bring Liaison Wren," he said and shut the door.

Soft classical music hung inside the cabin. Through the heavily tinted glass I watched Abbott's team finish laying their Calaian equipment onto three long folding tables. A few of the pieces looked like weapons. The opposite passenger door opened and Wrenn glided elegantly into the seat, now wearing a wrap of the same material as her dress. I caught a whiff of gardenia.

"Come here often?" I asked.

"What? No, I've never–"

"Wren, I'm kidding. It's an expression." I thought about taking her hand, but instead I kept mine in my lap. André climbed into the driver's seat and started the engine. "So how are we going to–"

A tapping at my window cut off my question. I lowered it. Abbott filled the window's frame. He put a hand to the car's roof and leaned in.

"You two ready?" he asked.

"Considering we're winging this," I said, "yes, I think we're as ready as we'll ever be."

"You'll have to improvise. Go with the action flow. With your new tech, I doubt you'll have any trouble with him. We're going to be close by. Just contact us with your cerebral interface. You've used that before?"

"A few times," I answered.

"Touch base with me now." I mentally said "hi," and he patted the top of the car. "Okay then. Good luck."

I raised the window as André pulled away and steered the car toward a large door at the far end of the atrium.

"How long will it take to get there?" Wren asked.

"About thirty minutes, depending on traffic conditions," André said through the open window that divided driver from passengers.

"You got a plan, Liaison Wren?" I asked.

"There are a lot of operational challenges and unknowns." Her voice had that military tenor I had heard before. "There'll be a lot of civilians. Basically, it'll be us against him. I can take out any event security, you'll have to deal with Baudin. If things get difficult, let me take the heat. I've done this a *lot* more times than you have."

"Is there going to be any support?"

"What do you mean?"

"You know, our guys posing as waiters and staff."

"You watch too many movies."

"Won't the Mirage have undercover people at the event?"

"Always a possibility."

The weight of the situation pressed down hard on me. Wren's own tension radiated from her in waves. We sat quietly as André maneuvered through the busy Parisian streets. We stopped at a red light, and in the cab next to us, a teenage girl talked animatedly on her cell phone in the backseat. Our eyes met, but I doubt she could see me through the window's dark tint. She flipped me off as the cab pulled forward.

"Abbott wants me to kill Baudin if I can't incapacitate him," I remarked.

Wren nodded and looked out the window. I took her hand and she turned back, dark eyebrows raised in pensive question. "Please don't do anything that will … um …" I let go. "Never mind." I moved my attention to my window.

She put a hand to my shoulder. "What?"

"Nothing. Something stupid. We need to focus on the job at hand."

"Cameron?"

I twisted around to gaze into Wren's green eyes. "Yes?"

"Don't do anything that will get yourself killed."

I let out a small laugh and nodded. "That's what I was going to say."

Wren scooted closer. "You're forgetting something, Earthman," she whispered.

Our lips were almost touching. "What's that, Calaian?"

"If something happens, I can always be brought back. You … can't."

28

NOT TONIGHT.

I had been to the Musée d'Orsay during my honeymoon. Karen had always wanted to go, so on our first day in Paris we strolled its halls and took in its magnificent collections. The memory always stood out, and tonight its grand hall was as breathtaking as the first time I saw it. A memory of Karen and me standing on the exact spot on the same stairs where I stood now dislodged from my memory and landed hard on my consciousness.

"Hey, soldier," Wren said, "where'd you go? I need you focused."

"Sorry." I straightened the lapels of my tux. "I'm here. Let's do this."

Wren stared forward for a fraction of a second, then snapped back. "Oh, Cameron, I'm so sorry. You were here, on your honeymoon." She put a hand to my arm. "Are you okay?"

"What else does your database say about me?"

"Sorry."

"Do you have a complete file?"

"I wouldn't say it's *complete*–"

A short, burly middle-aged man with a glass of champagne in hand waddled up. "*Bonsoir*." His eyes went to my name tag. "Ah, Mr. Robertson. Welcome. I am Pierre Lautrec – no relation to our famous artist. I am the Director of Donor Relations for the museum." He extended his hand.

"*Bonsoir*," I said, shaking it. "Please, call me Richard. And this is my wife, Terresa."

Wren extended her hand. With her movement the dress revealed a little side-boob that I caught Lautrec eyeing. "*Bonsoir*, madame." He raised Wren's hand for the classic French "kiss the hand" thing.

"Thank you, Mr. Lautrec," Wren said, a bit puzzled.

"Are all American women as striking as you?" he asked.

She pulled her hand away demurely. "Only the rich ones."

Lautrec acted like he wasn't sure if he should laugh or not. "Yes, um," he smiled politely, "I saw your names on our new donor list and I wanted to come over and personally welcome you to the Musée d'Orsay." The flourish he made to the grand hall looked a bit rehearsed.

"Thank you, Mr. Lautrec," I said. "We're honored to have been invited."

"I'm told you want to become Elite Members, yes?"

"*Oui!*"Wren exclaimed, her enthusiasm a bit over the top.

"Oh, that *is* grand," Lautrec replied. "There are some members I'd like you to meet, but for now, please, get a glass of Champagne, have some of our delicious *hors d'oeuvres* and take in our world-famous artwork. I'll find you later and introduce you around. If you need anything, just ask any of the staff to find me."

Lautrec gave a slight bow and hurried away to another couple admiring a Rodin sculpture.

"I think we've been officially welcomed," I remarked.

"Abbott's crew did a good job of implanting us on the invitee list." Wren slipped her arm around mine. "Come on, *Richard*, let's find the bar."

Wren? Harrison? Abbott's voice barely registered in my mind over the din of the guests. I pointed to my head and mouthed, "Do you hear that?"

Wren nodded.

What's the situ? Abbott asked.

People are still filing in, sir, Wren said. *It's getting crowded.*

Affirmative. Go mingle.

"Can he hear everything we're thinking?" I asked as we walked down the grand staircase.

"Probably, so we won't be having any married sex tonight," Wren said. *Did you get that, Abbott?*

Silence.

We found a popup wine and beer station behind the original bronze model for the Statue of Liberty. There was hardly a line.

"*Uh, deux Champagnes, s'il vous plait,*" I said, butchering the language.

The bartender poured two generous glasses.

"*Je vous remercie,*" Wren said, taking her glass.

"Your French sounds perfect," I said as we waded into the throng.

"I'm a DE ... you should hear my Mandarin. Let's see if the target's made it inside."

As Paris's rich and beautiful chatted and laughed, Wren and I surveyed the crowd for the Mirage commander. Predictably, a lot of middle-aged bald guys with good physiques milled about. I hoped for the porn star moustache to appear.

Wren? Harrison?

Yes sir? Wren replied.

Any sign of him?

Not yet.

Something's up. He should be there. The frustration in Abbott's voice came through.

He may be caught in the entrance line, I offered.

Doubtful, Abbott said. *Watch yourselves. I don't like the feel of this.*

Should I engage my tech? I asked.

Negative. The Mirage have encountered you already. They'll be on the alert. Let me know of anything out of the ordinary.

Will do, Wren said.

We walked back up the grand staircase, stopped about halfway and scanned the crowd.

"I don't see anyone who comes close to him," Wren said.

I let out a frustrated sign. "This crowd is too–"

"*Bonsoir,*" a male voice said firmly from behind us.

We turned, and I almost dropped my Champagne.

Toni, dressed in a stunning off-the-shoulder white gown, her curly hair spilling elegantly over her bare shoulders, stood behind us on the arm of a handsome Frenchman with a full head of dark wavy hair and no moustache. The two of them looked like they just walked off a couture runway.

"Liaison Wren and Cameron Harrison," the man said smugly. "Aren't you two the absolute *picture* of elegance." He leaned into Toni's ear. "Look, my dear, your lover has already discarded you for someone *younger*."

She didn't reply. Her frightened eyes fixed on me.

"You two look surprised," Baudin said dryly. "I suppose you were expecting a bald man with a pencil moustache. ... I got tired of that ride. Oh, Cameron, if you're thinking of engaging that technology Winston put in you, I wouldn't." He gripped Toni's upper arm and yanked her closer. She clumsily tried to make his action seem natural. "Ms. Morgan will die a *real* death." He skinned a tight smile across his perfect teeth. "Do we have an understanding?"

"Yes," I said, the word catching in my throat.

Baudin focused on Wren. "My god, Liaison, that ride you're wearing is absolutely stunning." He let go of Toni and she stumbled from the sudden release. He clasped his hands together. "What shall we do? See who's the fastest at engaging their combat tech? Or maybe see if Abbott's team really *knows* what they're doing?"

I took an instinctual angry step forward, but Wren planted a firm hand to my chest.

"Don't *stop* him, Liaison. This is what I came here to see." He gestured down my body. "The love-struck human now with the *soul* of a Calaian."

I pushed against Wren's hand, but her grip was surprisingly strong.

Baudin stepped close. "Cameron, if you even try to do what you did to my people back at Vitale's garage, Toni's head will explode all over that expensive Armani tux you're wearing." He caressed the fabric of my lapel between his fingers. "We wouldn't want that–"

"I *will* find a way," I growled.

"To what? Kill me?" Baudin shrugged. "Maybe. Someday. But not tonight. Now ..." He grabbed Toni's arm again and pulled her forward. "All four of us are going to walk out of this event like the best of friends."

"Abbott will track us," Wren said, coolly.

"I don't think so," he said. "Winston provided us with excellent insight into how to sever the cortical tracking link."

"Then he must have also told you how to disarm my tech," I said.

Baudin pulled a clownish pout. "Sadly, the great Calaian legend died before we could get the full information from him. Doesn't matter. Now that we have you, we can pry the technology out of your fragile human body." He flashed a contrived smile. "*Shall* we?"

As we followed Toni and Baudin up the Musée d'Orsay's grand staircase, off to my left I caught glimpses of a man moving through the crowd. He matched our pace but hung back. I couldn't make out his face. At the top of the stairs a line for another bar station impeded our exit. Baudin craned this way and that, looking to find a way around the bottleneck. After a frustrated second, he pushed his way through the drink line tugging Toni along. Wren grabbed my hand and pulled me forward. Just before being swallowed in the line for drinks, I glanced over my left shoulder in time to see a tuxedoed Agent Davis emerge from the crowd.

29

PLAYTIME IS OVER.

We stepped outside into the golden hue of the setting sun. Limos and town cars were still stacked up waiting to disgorge Parisian glitterati. The red carpet we had strolled moments ago was now crowded with such people. Baudin's stride quickened. He led us past the red-carpet melee, down the curved driveway, to a waiting jet-black stretch limo. As we approached, both its front doors swung open and two large dark suits emerged. I recognized the driver as the Mirage from the hotel bar and Vitale's garage. We locked eyes and he flashed a recognizing smirk.

"Is the cloaking engaged?" Baudin asked. The guy nodded. "You two in first."

Wren and I climbed in and sat back against the cool black leather seats. Toni and Baudin settled into two seats facing us, a walnut-topped center console between them. The guy from Vitale's garage squeezed his bulk behind the steering wheel; the other Mirage took the front passenger seat. Our limo merged into the line of exiting town cars, crept down the driveway and slipped into the evening traffic.

Baudin opened a drawer in the console and removed a cut crystal whiskey glass already filled with a two finger pour. He regarded it curiously before taking a measured sip. The limo made a slow right turn. He pointed with the glass. "Would you like one, Cameron? Bourbon, isn't it?" He winked at Wren and said to her, "I know you won't. Always on point." He patted Toni's exposed knee. "And I know the High Sovereign won't partake." He leaned forward like he was about to divulge a dark family secret. "Poor dear, she's so scared I don't think drinking has even crossed her mind." He patted her knee again, settled back and moved his gaze across Wren and me. "Liaison, that death back in Vitale's garage sounded excruciating," he said finally. "How many have you gone through, now?"

"Too many." Wren's voice was tight with anger.

Baudin leaned forward, forearms on his knees, the glass cupped with both hands. He effortlessly kept his balance as the limo took a sharp corner. "I have to say, Liaison, the way you infiltrated us was *very* well done." He tilted his attention to me. "Did she not tell you?" He tipped a nod to her. "This one is a *real* professional. Eats men like candy. She cozied up to mine. Got close to one." His eyes went back to her. "What was it that made Toren fall for you?" He leaned back and swirled his drink. "Ah, yes … anal." He shook his head.

"You humans and your body's immeasurable desire for provocative sex. Well, it sure got Toren to vouch for you–"

"Shut up," I growled.

Baudin cracked a faint smile and leaned onto the console. "You see that, Toni? The Liaison has already worked her magic on your lover. Or should I say *ex*-lover?" He pointed again with his drink and a bit of its contents sloshed over the rim. "He's defending his turf. What was it, Cameron ... did she lick your –?"

Wren launched at Baudin like a tiger but froze mid-lunge, splayed finger just inches from his face. His grav field shimmered across her body.

He made a pushing motion with his hand and Wren was pressed into the seat. He wagged his forefinger in a "No-No" gesture and the grav field vanished. Wren sucked in a panicked breath.

"Well," he mused swirling what was left in his glass, "that looked like a true emotional reaction." He leaned into Toni's ear. "Liaison Wren has actual *feelings* for Mr. Harrison." His eyes bulged with feigned realization. He let out a loud guffaw. "Oh, I should have recognized this! It's *love*, isn't it?"

Toni stared at me like I had just killed her first born. Her lower lip started to quiver. Baudin raised a finger to her cheek and waited for a tear to roll onto it.

"The human body *is* a wonder," he said. He examined the tear, rubbed it between his thumb and forefinger and inhaled deeply. "It actually secretes fluids in response to certain emotional states." He focused his attention on me with a vague frown. "Cameron ... I think you *broke* her heart."

Something cold and primeval erupted inside me. My combat tech detonated across my vision. Without a thought, a deadly grav field pulsed around my right fist. Baudin's eyes flared with amusement.

"*That*," he said, pointing, "is what killed my team?"

Wren's glare registered fear and anger and something even more unsettling ... awe. She cautiously put hand to my forearm. "Stand down, Cameron," she said. "He controls Toni."

"Don't worry," Baudin said, "she'll be fine. I give you my word. Now go ahead, unleash hell. I *dare* you."

I raised my fist to the asshole's face. He leaned into it, his nose stopping just shy of the undulating grav field.

"Come on," he taunted, "*do* it."

I did.

A second ticked by like an eternity. He raised an eyebrow. "What's the matter, slugger? ... Something wrong?"

I thrust my fist again. Nothing.

Baudin settled back, crossed his legs and downed his drink.

I stared at my fist. "What the *hell*?"

Baudin's snarkiness and bravado drained away. He carefully placed his empty glass onto the console's walnut top and folded his arms.

"Playtime," he said gravely, "is over."

Toni convulsed slightly and slumped against the console. I glanced to my right in time to see Wren's head flop forward. Baudin reached for the decanter and–

30

I'M SORRY.

"Camy, can you hear me?"

I opened my eyes to an endless black void. Was I floating? Standing? The female voice came from in front of me yet inside me at the same time. It was vaguely familiar, but too distant to recognize.

"Camy, it's me."

Then the realization hit. *Oh, my God.* "Karen?"

My voice felt separated from my being. I had formed my late wife's name but didn't feel my lips move. I tried reaching out. My arms wouldn't respond.

The love of my life emerged from the blackness as if stepping through a tear in the fabric of time. She wore the same clothes as she had the morning I last saw her. That afternoon she had driven to her death. A soft light followed Ka-ren as she approached, her sandals stepping on top of what looked like thick black oil. She stopped a few feet away.

And smiled.

My heart, suspended in all the memories of her, ruptured. I fought back the tears.

"Is it really *you*?" I asked, my voice cracking.

She nodded.

"W-what's happening to–"

Karen stepped close and put a finger to my lips. I could see her face in detail, as if she had stepped into a bright dawn light. Her body was translucent.

"Everything will be okay." The calm in her voice was as welcoming as a warm spring rain. Her hand caressed my cheek. "I have *so* missed you, my darling."

"Oh, Karen ... I've missed–" As soon as I mouthed the words, a thought intruded from the deep. *Darling?* Karen hated that word. She said it sounded like something her elderly fundamentalist aunt would say.

Karen's hand along with her gentle smile froze like a video. She became more transparent until she vanished like a foggy breath on a cold morning. The infinite depth around me digitally fractured, starting somewhere behind me, then silently tore across my field of vision. It washed down each side of my periphery in a cascade of pixeled brilliance and revealed that I was suspended in a grav field about fifteen feet above the cement floor of a large modern warehouse. The lighting was dim, but it appeared the walls rose at least four stories. The ceiling was barely visible. Thin multi-colored tubes ran from both my forearms down to organic shaped equipment on the floor. I was upright, but my arms and legs felt limp and useless.

Below me, I watched Baudin enter through the vast room's only door with Toni at his side. Both were dressed casually. He looked up.

"That was meant to comfort you while you wait." His voice reverberated off the metal walls and dissipated when it reached the ceiling.

I remained silent.

"You know we aren't the bad guys, Cameron."

"What are you then?" I asked.

"*Very* determined."

"What am I waiting for that requires comforting?"

"Death. Cala is sending a specialist to perform the operation. It will take a few days for his core to arrive and be transferred into a ride." He gestured up. "Sorry for the holding field. I can't take any chances with Winston's technology and your unpredictable human emotions. It's a lethal combination."

"I'm sure you're *really* sorry."

Baudin put his hands on his hips, looked to the floor and shook his head. "Your judgment of us is based on what *others* have told you." He looked up. "You've never been to Cala. You haven't lived under the Viceroy's oppression. You've never died over and over and *over* again serving a ruling elite that has absolutely zero interest in your sufferings."

"I've died before," I said.

"And how did it feel?"

I thought back to waking up in Kip's apartment after the knife attack, to discovering the Calaian tech and the recovery's intense pain.

Baudin took a few steps toward me, reached up and made a pulling motion. The field that held me suspended slowly lowered until we were eye-to-eye.

"You, of all humans, should have some empathy," he said. "You *know* what it's like. Just think of doing that a dozen times, no, a *hundred* times over!"

"This isn't *my* war!"

"It isn't. But what's inside you could change the course of it."

Even if my tech could prevent their war from bleeding into humanity, they'd still have to rip it out of me.

"Fuck you," I said.

Baudin considered me, turned and walked back to Toni. "Your ex is really quite noble," he said to her. "Don't be too long." He strode briskly out the door.

Toni, dressed in a simple grey knit sweater and black jeans, looked up for the first time.

As I saw her face, my mind flashed through several moments we shared. "You okay?" I asked, unable to think of anything else.

She shrugged nervously and folded her arms across her chest.

"I won't do anything that will put you in jeopardy," I said.

She nodded.

An awkward moment lingered.

"I thought you were in on it," I finally blurted. "That you were one of them."

She shrugged again. "Humans are naturally skeptical. It's in your evolution. I don't blame you for thinking the way you did." Her eyes returned to the floor.

"Did we ever have *anything*?" I asked.

By the time Toni looked up, her eyes were rimmed with tears. "I fell in love with you." She winced and rubbed her temples. My grav holding cell began to rise.

"What's going on?" I asked.

Toni forced a painful nod. "He's telling me to come back. I have to go." She turned and headed to the door.

"Toni?" I called out, as the grav cell found its position high above the floor.

She stopped but didn't turn back.

"I ..."

Toni stood there a moment and let the pain of what I couldn't say shudder through her. She slapped the light switch, plunging the room into a semi-darkness, and hurried out the door. The clank of it closing echoed through the cavernous space.

31

WAY BEYOND.

I floated above the floor for what seemed forever but was probably an hour or so.

"Hello?" I yelled for the dozenth time.

They had to be monitoring me. Probably not with a camera but with some Calaian device working through my tech.

"Heee*lllllo*?"

The AC kicked in somewhere above me.

"Hey, douche bags, I know you're watching. I have to take a monu-mental piss. How're we going to work this?"

Silence. Again.

"Jesus," I muttered. "I really *have* to–"

The creak of the door opening filled the emptiness. It was in the shadow of a protruding support column, cast by an especially bright EXIT sign. *Finally.* "Hey, um, I don't feel like having my piss floating around me. I really have to go."

A lone figure walked into the room but stayed in the column's shadow. "How bad do you have to go?" the guy asked.

I engaged my combat tech. Its vision pierced the shadow. "Pretty bad, Agent Davis."

Davis stepped into the ambient light of the EXIT sign. He was still wearing his tux. A smug half-smile spread across his face.

"It's not funny," I said. "Gimme a break."

Davis reached into his inside breast pocket and came out with a black tablet. He thumbed its screen. My grav cage began to lower.

"How the hell did you get in here?" I asked, touching down.

"I'm cloaked." Davis thumbed the screen again and my grav cage vanished. The sudden weight of full gravity caught me off guard and I stumbled forward. He pocketed the tablet and came to my side.

I gestured to the tubes. "What should I do with these?"

"Pull 'em out. They should be self-healing."

I yanked out all four tubes and watched my skin heal in a matter of seconds. The tubes fell to the floor and dissolved into long, multi-colored lines of powder that snaked back to their respective machines.

"Thank you," I said, rubbing my forearms.

"There's a bucket over there, near that mop." Davis pointed to the corner near the EXIT sign. "Make it quick."

I did, as best I could.

"How are you cloaked?" I asked, zipping up. "And how did you get rid of my holding cell?"

Davis patted his coat where he had pocketed the tablet.

"You have better technology?" I asked.

"*Way* better." He motioned to the door. "Let's go, we don't have much time."

"Where's Baudin and Toni?"

"As best as we know they're gone."

Beyond the door was a dark carpeted hallway. A man lay crumpled in a heap off to my right.

"This way," Davis whispered, heading to the left.

My combat tech cast the wide hallway in dull shades of green and black. "They're bringing a specialist in from Cala to yank out my tech," I whispered back.

"Not anymore."

Two more bodies greeted us at a T intersection. A male and a female.

"Are they dead?" I asked.

"Let's just say they're not coming back," Davis said. He peered around the corner into another dark hallway. He gestured for me to follow and his gait quickened.

"How's your head?" I asked.

He shot me a questioning look over his shoulder. "My head?"

"The motorcyclist with the baton ... back in Gloria's parking lot?"

"How *is* Liaison Wren?"

"She has a new ride."

Davis nodded like he understood.

"Did Baudin take Wren?" I dreaded the answer.

"Yes. Kip's probably with them."

A pang of fear cut through me. "Where'd they go?"

"Still working on that."

"Why'd they leave?"

"They might have detected my cloaked presence. Hard to say."

"Baudin can stop my tech."

"I know. Just learned that like you did."

"And you're not concerned?"

Agent Davis didn't answer.

The hallway ended at two double glass doors. Outside, I glimpsed a large empty parking lot. The sun was barely approaching the horizon. I could smell rain in the air, and pools of standing water peppered the gloomy lot.

Davis did something on his tablet and we pushed the doors open and stepped outside. I half-expected an alarm to go off, but nothing. The air was cool and damp from the storm. Distant thunder rumbled across the urban landscape. I noticed several cars in handicapped spaces parked next to the building on my left.

Davis referenced his tablet and motioned to the left. "My car's over–"

The headlights of all the vehicles erupted across my combat tech's night vison. The glare was painfully blinding, but my tech quickly compensated. Car doors swung open and imposing figures swiftly took positions, handguns drawn. Baudin was the last to emerge. He opened the back passenger door and ceremonially helped Toni out.

She remained motionless while he stepped to the front of the car. He drew in a long, measured breath and regarded the reddening clouds. "I love how your atmosphere smells after a thunderstorm."

I tried to engage my grav wave, but nothing happened.

Baudin leveled his attention on Davis. "Who the hell are *you*, and how did you get past my team?"

Davis opened his stance. "You're not the only ones with advanced tech," he said coolly.

The sneer on Baudin's lips would've killed a normal human. "I don't give a shit what kind of tech you—" His face filled with shock. He sank to a knee, then he along with the other Mirage muscle guys crumpled to the asphalt. Only one to the far right remained standing. He hesitantly aimed his handgun, but the look on his face was on the far side of dumbfounded. He cocked a glance down the row of fallen operatives.

Davis casually thumbed his tablet and the Mirage goon dropped as if his skeletal system had vanished. Toni looked to her left and right and finally settled on us.

" *Way* better?" I let my skepticism play between us.

"Okay, it's not infallible." Davis pocketed the tablet. "Sorry about your tech. Had to keep it off-line. Don't want another public mess like at Vitale's garage."

I gestured to the row of bodies. "Are they also not coming back?"

"Not anytime soon." Davis motioned Toni over.

She stepped around Baudin's body and proceeded a few steps before she stopped. She spun around, walked back and planted a fierce kick to the side of the asshole's head. As she joined us, the trees that ringed the far side of the parking lot began to sway. I didn't feel any wind, and the trees and shrubs near us didn't move. A light pole about 50 yards out buckled and crashed to the ground. A distant paper cup whipped into the air and rode a vortex toward us, picking up trash and leaves in its path. Before I thought to react, the roofs of the four Mirage cars compressed as if an invisible giant stepped on them. A blast of hot air hit all three of us.

A circular opening, like the one I had seen in Abbott's cloaked craft, appeared 20 feet above the crushed cars. Sato stood in its maw.

"One of you call for an Uber?" she yelled down.

32

THAT WAS PRETTY GREAT.

No one said a word as we traveled to what I assumed would be the warehouse where we had departed 18 hours earlier. Sato wore the face-hugger and appeared to be piloting. James Dean stood behind her, also wearing head-gear. Toni sat in a lounger on the other side of the bridge (if that's what it was). She made eye contact once by accident. I asked Davis how he could have tech that was more powerful than mine and whatever the Mirage commander had. He just shrugged.

"Sequencing," Sato said, breaking the silence. "We're in."

Dean patted her right shoulder. "Excellent navigation."

He gestured to the bulkhead behind us and a circular opening formed. We were back in the ornate 19th century warehouse. A ramp formed to the floor. It ended at the feet of Abbott, who stood with arms folded like God Almighty. His team was lined up behind him as if greeting a visiting dignitary. Davis followed me down.

"*That* didn't go as planned," Abbott said as I approached.

"No shit," I answered.

"We didn't know about Baudin's disruption tech."

"Obviously." I motioned to Davis. "Commander, this is–"

"Carlton," Davis said, extending a hand.

"Quinn," Abbott said, taking it. "Thanks for the help on this one."

"Our pleasure." Davis glanced up at the opening, which was the only visible aspect of the cloaked ship. "When did you start keeping this on Earth?"

"About a year ago."

"We *had* an agreement."

"The stakes escalated."

"That's one way to put it."

"Quinn, the time for playing by the rules is over. You saw what they did in Rio."

"And Milan."

"*Exactly.* You understand our need–"

"Excuse me," I interrupted. "How long have you known each other?"

"Eight years," Davis said.

Abbott gestured. "This man is one of your best."

"Best, *what?*" I asked.

"Best–" Abbott's attention was drawn to the top of the ramp.

I turned and saw Toni standing there. Just like the Viceroys, all the Calaians, including Abbott, bowed their heads in unison.

Toni raised her hand slightly and they looked up.

"Welcome, your High Sovereign," Abbott said.

"I don't recognize that title," she said as she descended the ramp. "Please, call me Toni."

It was weird, just as it had been with Enzo, to see Abbott and his team submit to Toni's Calaian status. The scared little girl held hostage at the Mirage commander's side was gone. The regal Toni, whom I'd seen for a fleeting instant at the Viceroy's conference room, now held court.

"Did they hurt you?" Abbott asked.

"No, but I can't speak for the others." She turned to Davis. "Thank you, Mr.–?"

"Davis, ma'am," he said.

"Quinn is one of our human envoys," Abbott said.

"The equivalent of Wren?" I asked.

"In a sense, although I don't think he has the combat training Wren has." Abbott turned to Davis. "No offense, Quinn."

"None taken," Davis said.

"Toni, we'd like to do a debrief," Abbott said, "but only if you're up to it."

She nodded.

"Thank you. This way, please."

As the rest walked off, I grabbed Davis's arm. "Why didn't you tell me about you and Abbott?"

"What fun would that be?" he replied.

"No, seriously. What the *hell?*"

"Look, we don't advertise our relationship with the Calaians. That would be too dangerous."

"And what, exactly, *is* your relationship?"

Davis hesitated. "We've known about their visitations since the nineteen-thirties."

"And you're okay with it?"

"It's a fair trade off."

"For what?"

"Where do I start? Radar, integrated chips, stealth technology? Once in a while, when they think we can handle it, they dole out an aspect of their knowledge. For them it's ancient tech, but the arrangement works for us, and humanity benefits."

"That's effed up."

"Cameron, *think*. It's like an apprenticeship for our civilization. We can't advance that quickly on our own. They're just offering us a chance."

"So their citizens can *vacation?*"

"Have you been to Cala?"

"Have you?"

"No. But from what I've been told, you'd understand why Earth is heaven for them."

"But if it's heaven, aren't we afraid they'll just take over?"

Davis shook his head. "It's not allowed."

"What do you mean it's *not* allowed?"

"Just that. Their moral code is wet-wired into their biology. Conquest is not important to them anymore."

"Bullshit."

Davis started to say something but held back.

"It's the Mirage, right? They're not just hunting down Calaians they don't like. What's going on, Davis?" I stepped closer and lowered my voice. "Tell me the *truth*."

Another hesitation. "The Mirage want Earth for themselves."

A jagged ancient tremor rose through me. My tech instinctually engaged. Davis's tablet vibrated inside his jacket pocket.

"Shut it down, Cameron. It's not an invasion."

I took a deep breath to calm down. "What is it, then?"

"They just want to live among us."

"And how's *that* going to work?"

"It's not. Calaian high command won't allow it."

"I thought the Viceroys were the rulers."

"The Viceroys are the political rulers of Cala. The Guardium is the military. Abbott works for the Guardium. The two don't always see eye-to-eye."

"I don't get it. If the Guardium is so powerful, why don't they just take out the Mirage?"

"It's not that simple. Their culture is complicated. Killing is forbidden, and death ... well ... with their digital entity technology it's an option. Also, the Viceroys have their own agenda."

"Humans are caught in the crossfire?"

Davis nodded.

"And let me guess, the tech inside me is the key that everybody wants. It's the game changer, right?"

"That about sums it up."

"Why?"

"Whatever Winston put in you, the effect is new even to Calaians. Something in *our* biology allows you to produce such a powerful CGFG. Everyone wants to know why."

"To duplicate it, right?"

Davis nodded.

"I knew I shouldn't have swiped right," I muttered.

Davis put a hand to my shoulder. "What's done is done. You have to deal with it."

"I'm tired of *dealing* with it."

He took my shoulders in both hands. "Cameron, you're not the first to have greatness thrust upon them. History is full of such people. They rose to the occasion. You can, too."

"Davis, this is different. This is intergalactic. I'm a web designer. I cry at movies."

"What you did back in Vitale's garage? I'd say *that* was pretty great."

"I just reacted. I wasn't thinking."

"And the drone? Just *reacting*?"

"Yeah, well–"

Davis's fingers dug in. "You have it *in* you, Cameron. It's what drives you to react. Just like the drone and Vitale's garage."

I sucked in an unsure breath. "Look, I don't have *the force*. I have an advanced bio tech that we now know can be shut down."

"True, but ..." Davis removed the tablet, "we have a little help."

"Yeah, how *did* you drop all those Mirage goons back in the parking lot?"

Davis's hesitation didn't bode well. "Cameron, there's something else I haven't told you."

Oh, crap. "What's that?"

"Calaians aren't the only aliens visiting Earth."

33

NOT THIS TIME.

Davis's words seeped through me like emotional acid.

"There're *others?*" I asked.

"Afraid so," Davis said.

"Where're they from?"

"We're not sure. All we know is they're from an area of space that's a lot farther away than Cala, and they're a *lot* more advanced."

I glanced about as if they might actually be standing next to us. "What do they look like?"

"We're not sure about that, either."

What the–? "Then how do we know they're even here?"

Davis put a finger to his temple. "They come to us … in our minds."

I was dumbstruck. I shook my head.

Davis picked up my confusion. "We believe they're called Natierians. Their language is a mixture of implanted image projection and a kind of neurological cuneiform. One scientist believes they can speak any language."

"It's like symbols?"

"Of a sort. It's hard to explain unless you've experienced them, um, *talking* to you."

"Have you? What's it like?"

"Lucid dreaming, but you're not asleep."

"What do the Calaians think? … Are they threatened?"

"Not that we can tell. They had a run-in hundreds of years ago, but we don't have any details except the Natierians withdrew contact. The Natierians don't seem interested in conquest. … They just want to, um, help, but in a very measured way."

"Measured, like the Calaians drop technology on us?"

"They don't exactly intervene, but they don't sit idly by, either."

I pointed to his coat. "The tech that dropped the Mirage … that's theirs, isn't it?"

"They make it available."

"What's their planet like?"

"We're not even sure they inhabit a planet."

"So what are they? Omnipotent beings, like Q in Star Trek?"

"Your guess is as good as ours. We don't think they're godlike, just beyond our understanding."

"How often do they connect?"

"There doesn't seem to be a pattern, but since they made themselves known to humanity about eight years ago, there've been roughly a hundred conversations. The dialogue is done through ten prominent scientists around the globe."

"Not playing favorites, are they?"

"Doesn't appear so."

"What the hell? This just keeps getting crazier and crazier."

Davis put his hand to my shoulder again. "Come on, let's see what the High Sovereign is telling Abbott."

We walked over to the area near the offices where Wren and I had changed. The first few were empty, and the two in the middle contained some of Abbott's team at Calaian workstations, wearing face-huggers. In the last office Abbott and Dean were seated in metal folding chairs at an old wooden table. Toni sat across from them. The energy in the cramped room was all business. Toni looked up expressionlessly.

Abbott gave us a nod.

"What do we have so far?" Davis asked.

"Toni was just about to tell us where she thinks the Northern House hostages are being held."

"The Mirage have been somewhat courteous to them," Dean said, "except for their treatment of Tucker Winston."

"They were brutal," Toni offered. "They used a forbidden technique."

"What's that?" I asked.

"It involves using the implanted tech in a way that devastates the Calaian brain." Toni didn't hide her disgust.

"Is that why he died?" I asked.

She dropped her eyes to the middle of the table. "Yes."

"Was it a real death?" Davis asked.

Abbott twisted in his chair and regarded the agent. "You think it wasn't?"

"If he backed himself up, he could be useful."

Abbott considered the idea. "Link to Trent and contact the moon," he ordered Dean. "See if Winston parked himself in any of their cores."

Dean nodded and sat motionless while he contacted Trent via cerebral link.

"If he's not there, contact the Guardium. He might be stored somewhere on the home world." Abbott gave Davis a wary look. "Winston's brilliant. It would be like him to back himself up somewhere." He turned back to Toni. "I'm sorry, please, go on."

"I was kept separated from the others," Toni said, "except at meals. That's when I overheard Philippe tell his team to pack up because they were going to the mountains. The next day the two of us ate alone."

"When was that?"

"Two days ago."

"In that timeframe they could be anywhere," I said. "Can we track them via their tech?"

"Normally yes," Abbott said, "but the Mirage are using a cerebral veil. It's similar to what the Mirage commander used on you. Some type of bio-interface masking. We've never encountered it before. We've been trying to hack their ride's implants, but the Mirage tech is too evolved."

"Maybe I can help." Davis reached into his coat pocket for his tablet.

Abbott shook his head.

"It's worth a try," Davis said.

"Not this time, Quinn."

"Why?"

Abbott regarded his old human friend, faint dejection visible in his knotted brow. "The tech they're using … it's Natierian."

34

DIFFERENT DATA.

They gave me the office where I had dressed previously. The mirror and chair were now in a corner. A cheap bed of the sort you'd buy from a discount mattress place dominated the room. Dinner was pizza and sports drinks, and most of the Calaians retired early. I hung around and tried to pry more out of Davis about the Natierians and their connection with the Mirage, but he was close-mouthed. Said he'd explain later. He and Abbott had disappeared shortly after dinner, maybe to plan our next moves, but more likely they withdrew to some nearby bar to drink and exchange war stories. Toni hadn't joined us either. I presumed she spent the night on the ship. Trent was the only Calaian still awake. He was stationed in the office two down from mine, wearing a face-hugger and waiting, I was told, for information whether the Great One was backed up on the home world. As for rescuing Kip, Wren and Enzo, everything seemed contingent on finding Winston. Toni's "insight" had been limited. A knock snapped me out of my depressive thoughts. I swung my legs off the bed and nearly tripped over my open suitcase.

"Who is it?" I asked.

"It's André, sir."

I opened the door. "I wondered what happened to you."

"How are you holding up?" he asked from a polite distance.

"I've been better." I took a seat on the edge of the bed. André followed.

"Are you worried about her?" he asked.

"Which one?"

"Liaison Wren."

I hesitated before nodding.

"What's the matter?"

"André, I know she's just a DE–"

"*Just?*"

"Well, yeah, I mean … She doesn't exist, as a living being. She's an illusion. A computer-generated representation riding along in a cloned human body."

André grabbed the chair from the corner and set it next to the bed, facing backwards. He straddled the seat and rested his arms across the top rail. "Yet, you're still worried for her … as a *representation*."

"I know. Weird, right?"

"What defines life, Mr. Harrison?"

"I don't know, André. A kind of condition, I guess, that separates us from inanimate things?"

An enlightened smile appeared on André's face. "In this galaxy alone, there are beings that would challenge that definition of life," he said. "Liaison Wren is as alive as you and me. Her life essence is backed up and stored digitally, just like yours is physically stored as memories in the brain … She is *not* a representation."

The Calaians apparently had the technology, however it worked, to capture the life force of a being, store it, and project it into any other species' cloned body, but I was still struggling with the idea of emotional attachment to a technologically generated human.

André picked up on my pensiveness. The smile reappeared. "Mr. Harrison, I have been on your planet since the early 18th century, and I have seen countless people meet and instantly fall deeply into this condition you call love. It also happens to our people when they spend a long time here. It truly is a remarkable thing to witness."

"André, come on … how could I have that kind of feeling for Liaison Wren? I barely know her."

André looked to the floor as if he'd find his next words etched in the ancient, cracked floorboards. "I … I took a liberty." The old Calaian looked up. "The implanted cerebral technology sends a continuous flow of physical and mental data back to our central cores on your moon. I took the liberty to review yours and Liaison Wren's at the moment you discovered her in Vitale's garage. Her human ride was mortally damaged."

"Yeah, so?"

"Mr. Harrison ... when humans are attracted to one another, their bodies, including their brains, go through a series of biological changes."

"Sure, dopamine and stuff. Everybody knows that."

"Yes, and ... I reviewed the Liaison's data when you comforted her. She ... well, she became emotionally attached ... as did you."

I flashed on Wren sprawled on the garage floor, her previous ride torn apart, her life literally seeping out. "Really? I don't remember feeling that."

"Your emotional response was not as ... Oh, how can I put this ... deeply *felt* as the Liaison's, but it registered, nonetheless. She not only connected with you viscerally, she connected on a subconscious level too. You see, Mr. Harrison, you reached out and offered comfort to – from your perspective and hers – an enemy. Your compassion affected Liaison Wren deeply and formed the basis for her emotional bond with you."

"Your data indicated all *that?*"

"Fascinating, isn't it?"

"So you're saying she and I just clicked. Is that why when I saw her again, in her new ride, I *knew* it was her?"

"More than likely."

"You know I was married once."

"It's in your profile. Karen, I believe. I'm sorry for your loss."

"I appreciate that, André."

"If you don't mind, what was your initial connection to your wife?"

"What do you mean?"

"Was it sexual, spiritual, or possibly just a friendship?"

I thought back to the afternoon I met Karen, at one of my old boss's pool parties. I was just hanging in the shallow end, and she brought a date who got shitfaced and passed out on the master bed. We knew each other by reputation from the business, but our paths hadn't crossed. She walked up, looking fantastic in a lime green bikini, spinning her date's BMW fob on her finger. We chatted for a long time when she surprised me by asking if I was free for lunch the following week. That's all it took. We met and I fell for her before dessert.

"All of them," I answered.

"Mr. Harrison, many humans believe they have fallen in love, when in reality, they're just in lust."

"Different dataset?"

André nodded.

"Think we'll find her?"

"I don't really know, but … What's the Terran expression? … If I were a betting man?"

"Yeah?"

"I would bet all I have that we will find her."

Even though he mangled the phrase, his sentiment was comforting. "Thank you, André."

"For what, Mr. Harrison?"

"I don't know … for putting things into perspective?"

André stood and regarded me with an almost godlike benevolence. "My pleasure, Mr. Harris–"

"They found Winston," Davis blurted loudly from the doorway. "He's backed up at the moon base. Got some intel from sources high up in the Guardium."

"Great," I said. "When will he, you know … *be* here?"

"Abbott says ten minutes. Want to see it happen?"

"See *what* happen?"

"The transference," André said. "Come, I'll take you."

35

PUPPET MASTERS.

We were in part of the Calaian ship I hadn't seen before. The bridge was near what I assumed was the front (although it was hard to know what *was* the front), and we had always entered through that "forward" entrance. This time we entered somewhere midship and made our way through several corridors to a room that looked like a medical bay. The walls, like the bridge, had several small screens with the familiar undulating color blobs, and a large operating table dominated the center of the space. Oddly, four extensions protruded at right angles from its upper half. The table was maybe nine feet long and four feet wide, and like the loungers on the bridge, it seemed to sprout from the turtle shell-like flooring. Was it a reflection of what a Calaian body looked like? Did they have four arms? Or maybe two arms and wings?

Winston's new ride/clone, a human male in his mid-40s with a medium build, lay on its back in the middle of the table. It looked small compared to the size of the apparatus and was already dressed in a simple black t-shirt, grey jeans and a pair of black nondescript cross-trainers, all of which looked like they came from a Walmart clearance table. Its hands were folded neatly across its abdomen, and what looked like an artificial breathing unit covered its mouth and nose. The unit had the distinct clean lines and smooth metal of other Calaian tech. Hovering above the table was a chrome ball like the one Sato had tossed out in the mission briefing, but this one was about the size of a basketball. It loomed over the table like a watchful sentry. Toni and Dean flanked one side of the table with Abbott opposite. Davis and I stood in the shadows against a bulkhead, and Trent and Sato were on the other side of the room, just outside the wash of down-lighting that ringed the table.

"Have you ever seen this before?" I side-whispered to Davis.

"Once," he replied.

"Is it cool?"

Davis made a *meh* gesture.

Dean glanced at the nearest wall display. Its colors were swirling. "In four, three, two" he announced.

The chrome ball lowered until its bottom edge touched the ride's forehead. At the touchpoint, a yellow glow emanated from under the ride's skin. A few seconds later, the ball returned to its position above the table and the ride opened its eyes.

Abbott folded his arms. "Winston," he asked gruffly, "are you in there?"

The ride tilted a confused look at Abbott and jerked to a sitting position. It looked about the room and examined its hands suspiciously. It pulled the breathing unit off and tossed it to the floor. Like the face-huggers, the gear collapsed into a tiny dark grey box. Sato retrieved it from the floor and pocketed it in a pouch on the front of her sweater.

"Mirror," the ride said in a rough baritone.

Abbott had a short-handled one at the ready. He handed it over.

The ride examined its face, especially its chin and nose.

"To your liking?" Abbott asked curtly.

"I've been handsomer," Winston replied, passing a finger down his jawline.

Abbott snatched the mirror and passed it to Sato. "You should be grateful you're in a ride at all."

"Why have you brought me here, Abbott?" The Great One's tone was indignant.

Abbott slammed his palms onto the table. He leaned into Winston's new face and jabbed an angry finger at me. "You're going to clean up the shit-mess you've made with this human."

Winston zeroed his attention on me like a howitzer. "Are you *enjoying* your upgrades?" he asked.

"Every damn day," I said.

Winston slid off the table, wobbled a bit while he gained his footing, and approached me. He extended his right hand and clicked his fingers, never taking his eyes off me. Sato hurried over and handed him a tablet.

His eyes narrowed. "Turn around—"

Before he could finish, I wrapped him in a tight grav field and threw him into the middle of the room, floating on his stomach. Dean reacted first, but my combat tech's field was too fast for any of them. I pressed the Calaians, Toni included, against different bulkheads in full-body grav cocoons. Dean was seething, his arms pressed against his sides.

I strode close enough to Winston to smell his stale breath huffed in and out. "New rules. One. I'm not your pet. Two. I'm not your experiment. Three. This is about finding the others, period. And four … if anyone tries to mess with me or my tech or Agent Davis or *any* other human … they'll regret it." I let that linger.

The edge of Winston's lip curled into a snarl. I tightened the field around him, and he winced from the pressure. I stepped closer, tightened the field a little more and sent the message home.

"Are we clear?" I asked.

Winston stared me down. "We're *clear.*"

I released everyone except Winston. They all stumbled from the sudden gravity. Abbott dropped to a prone position on the floor.

"All of you, get out." I glanced at Abbott. "Except you."

Abbott's team trudged solemnly toward an opening that formed behind me. Dean shot Abbott a questioning glance as he went past. Abbott motioned with his head to keep moving. The opening disappeared behind them. I rotated the Great One into an upright position and hovered him a foot off the floor.

I folded my arms. "Y'all have jerked me around since day one. You can't blame me for being a little *reactionary.* I'm in defensive mode right now, and just a little sleep deprived, so let's cut the shit." I pointed to Winston. "You're here to find Kip, Wren and Enzo. And you're going to figure out a way to block the Mirage's ability to shut me down."

"What if I don't?" Winston said grudgingly.

"I've done a lot of killing lately, thanks to you, and I'm getting pretty good at it. I wouldn't hesitate to make you suffer, even if it's for a few seconds, before you jacked out into some storage bank."

"Cameron, calm the *hell* down." Abbott's voice was low and stretched with restraint. "You've made your point." He glanced at Winston. "Can you believe this? Give these humans a little power and they go all Western House on you."

I got in the Great One's face. "Why was this done to me?" I demanded.

Winston fought to hold the answer down. "They needed the leverage," he said reluctantly.

"Who did?" Davis asked, coming out of the shadows from the bulkhead.

"The Mirage."

"Are you one of them?"

"They can make some issues go away."

"And how was that supposed to work?" I asked.

"Kipling mapped it out," Winston said. "You would fall for Toni–"

"Which I did."

"Then you would have an ... accident."

"The stabbing." My anger carried the words. "Was Marco a Mirage?"

"No. He was a hireling. To keep you alive, Toni would demand the implant of the cerebral tech."

"Was Toni in on all this?" I pressed.

"I-I don't know," Winston said.

"Go on."

"Originally, the Mirage wanted to bring you around gradually ... to their cause. Then I would implant my new tech."

"But the first tech malfunctioned," I said.

"Yes. The plan shifted."

"Sounds like a classic turning program," Davis said as he joined us in the circle of downlight. "Are the Viceroys part of the Mirage?"

"No," Winston said, "but many are sympathetic."

Davis walked closer and studied Winston like a piece of art. "Do you know the Natierians are helping the Mirage?"

The Great One's expression immediately changed, as if he harbored grave knowledge about the seemingly omnipotent aliens. "Release me," he demanded.

I did. Winston dropped to the floor and stumbled into Abbott.

"Tucker," Davis said, "you know something. What is it?"

Winston straightened and adjusted his t-shirt. "The Natierians don't take risks. Their decisions are calculated, based on extreme long-range quantum projections ... scenario variations into the trillions."

"Okay," I said, "they're the market analysts of the galaxy, so what?"

Maybe I *was* stupid because I wasn't getting the drift. Davis stepped to my side.

"Cameron," he said in a fatherly tone, "the Natierians are puppet masters. They, um, *nudge* civilizations in the direction they feel is best."

"And? Davis, just bottom line it for me."

Davis seemed lost for words. Abbott drilled his *stupid human* look into me. "What he's saying is the Natierians have chosen sides."

36

BE CAREFUL, HUMANS.

The idea the Natierians went about the galaxy course-correcting civilizations was hard to comprehend.

"It's obvious." Disdain rimmed Winston's words. "The Natierians gave the Mirage their tech because they will win and be allowed to live among you. This will be a turning point in human evolution."

"By giving them their tech, they're *guaranteeing* they'll win," I countered. "What's in it for them?"

"They're not *in it* for anything," Abbott said. "Davis is right, they're puppet masters. They do it because they can. We're like pets to them. They interfered with Calaian evolution about five-hundred years ago."

"What happened?" I asked.

Abbott stared as if caught in a time warp of memory. "We fought against them." His focus returned to the present. "We went our own way."

"Were they pissed?"

Abbott's training in pop culture clearly hadn't given him knowledge of this phrase. The face he made suggested urination was something he found disgusting.

"Did they get *angry*?" Davis offered.

"Natierians don't get angry," Abbott said. "They just move on."

"What was the cost?" I asked.

Abbott hesitated, then let out a weary sigh. "About five-hundred years of evolutionary growth."

"We were like you once." Winston planted his attention on Davis and me. "Young as a race. Full of spirit and fight. Be careful, humans."

"Of what?" Davis asked a little too defiantly.

"Taking the easier path."

*   *   *   *

Wren ... can you hear me?

A light evening rain blanketed Paris. The echo of its patter on the building's glass roof four stories up filled the empty space like white noise. I felt foolish trying to cerebrally link to her, but what the hell. It was worth a try.

Wren, if you can hear me, it means you're alive. We're going to find you and bring you back. I just wanted you to know that I care for you ... and ... I –

"Cameron?"

I opened my eyes to Agent Davis's quizzical stare. I was sitting on the edge of my bed, and he was standing over me.

"What are you doing?" he asked, more than a bit concerned.

"Something stupid."

"You're trying to link to Liaison Wren, aren't you?"

"Pathetic, isn't it?"

The pity in Davis's smile kind of hurt. He sat next to me. "I know you'll find this hard to believe, but I have someone I care about too." Davis pulled his phone out, gave it several swipes and handed it over. A beautiful African-American woman, mid-30s, smiled from the screen. It was one of those cheesy portrait shots of her leaning against a tree in a park. The fill light was a bit harsh.

"She's pretty," I said, handing the phone back.

"Her name is Nala," Davis said, stuffing it into his coat's breast pocket. "It means Loved One."

"And is she?"

"Very much."

"Are you married?"

Davis shook his head, the emotions raw and exposed. "You care for Wren?" His question hit like a gut punch.

"The data says I do."

Davis chuckled. "Goddamn Calaians with their data-this and data-that. Who told you?"

"André."

"Figures. That old Concierge has been on this planet a long time. He's seen it all."

"He said my compassion is the foundation for our bond, whatever *that* means."

Davis stood. "Well come on, Mr. Compassionate, while you were trying to make a love connection, Winston's been working his magic. I swear, that Calaian is a pain in the ass, but he's a goddamn genius."

I rose to my feet. "He found Wren and the others?"

"Better than that. He figured out a way to beat the Natierian tech."

"Wren and Enzo?"

"He's still working on that. But once he hacks the cloaking, which *is* Calaian, then we'll be able to zero in on their location."

"Like finding an IP address."

Davis hesitated. "Kind of."

"What are you not telling me?"

"To block the Natierian tech, Winston needs to operate on you again."

*   *   *   *

I was alone, face down on the same table Winston's ride had occupied. The chrome disco ball that transferred Winston's digital essence into the lifeless clone loomed over me like a giant all-knowing third eye. Moments earlier, the Great One had been at my side trying to reassure me that this operation was going to be a *lot* smoother than the first. He was terrible at empathy. I didn't buy any of it. Someone touched my up-turned right palm.

"Winston," I said, "quit fucking–"

"It's me."

"*Toni?*" I went to one elbow and twisted around. "Hey," I said, taking her hand. I'd forgotten how warm she was and how good her hands felt.

She started to say something but cut it off.

I sat up and swung my legs over the side of the table.

Toni stepped close and took both of my hands into hers. We didn't say a word, just looked down at our hands and let the connection that felt so natural just weeks before wash over us.

"I'm sorry," I finally said.

"Me too," she whispered.

She tenderly rubbed my fingers.

"Do you love her?" Her eyes still hadn't lifted from our hands.

"The data says I might."

A faint smile appeared and vanished just as quickly. "What does your heart say?"

I let out a long sigh. "That I loved you ... before the shit hit the fan and I learned too much."

She stopped rubbing and squeezed my hands, her attention still fixed.

"Toni, look ... I'm–"

"You'll be different ... after this operation."

"Winston seems to think I'll be unstoppable."

Toni raised her eyes to mine. "Not if *I* can help it."

Her right hand clamped around both my wrists and slammed them to the table with the blunt force of an industrial press. Her left hand grasped my throat. As her fingers closed around my windpipe, her eyes turned predatory.

I tried to engage my tech. Nothing. Her grip tightened. I struggled, but she held me with an inhuman strength. Light streaks shot through my vision. I could feel consciousness slipping away. She yanked me close. Dark edges appeared and formed a tunnel around her face.

"When I'm done killing you," she snarled, "I'll kill the Sovereign–"

A loud crack like lightning erupted above me, as if reality had split open. A thin, jagged bolt of silver light struck Toni in the middle of her forehead. Her shoulders contorted against her neck and her eyes rolled back. She clenched her teeth so hard blood started to seep from her mouth. She spasmed backward, arms flailing. The chrome ball followed her to the floor and discharged another spark of light. It hit Toni's chest and flung her backward across the deck. She came to rest against the bulkhead in a tangle of contorted limbs.

"Stop!" I screamed, my voice cracking.

The chrome ball spun around as if to look at who had yelled. It hovered where it was, probably assessing the situation, and silently floated back to its previous position.

Gasping, I crawled off the table, but I couldn't take in enough oxygen. I crumpled to the floor. Darkness descended.

37

EVERYBODY STARTS SOMEWHERE.

I sucked in a ragged stale breath and awoke from a dreamless sleep. Agent Davis was at my bedside.

My mind rushed to the sick bay, the chrome ball, the silver lightning bolt. I grabbed his arm. "What *happened*?!" I tried to sit up.

Davis put a firm hand to my shoulder. His smile seemed sincere, but there was something behind it, like he was holding back a terrible truth. "Easy there, Cameron."

I settled against the pillows. Swallowing hurt, and Toni's fingers had left tender bruises on my neck.

"How's Toni?" I managed.

Davis's smile faded. "She's stable. Winston and one of Abbott's crew are with her. Her ride suffered some frontal lobe damage."

"Why did she do that?"

"She didn't. She had what the Calaians call an anterior intrusion. A Mirage commando breached her implant's main cerebral pathway and took over. The implant's defense protocols were compromised somehow."

"Natierian tech, probably."

Davis nodded reluctantly.

"Will she be the same?" I asked.

"Calaian technology isn't my expertise. I do know there's a huge amount of cerebral engagement between the ride and the Calaian occupant. ... They function essentially as one. The implants make the duality seamless. I've been told the ride is preset to be able to walk, talk, you know, have basic functionality. ... The Calaian occupant brings the, um, *personality*. But to answer your question, only time will tell."

"Yeah, but that bolt of energy struck Toni in the *head*."

"Brain injuries, from what my sources say, are a lot trickier. Because of the extreme integration, a kind of feedback can happen and the Calaian occupant can be injured. They have an auto-disengagement system to prevent it, but if the ride is injured and the Calaian occupant doesn't jack out in time, well..."

"Did she?"

Davis shook his head.

"Shit."

"Don't go jumping to conclusions. The trauma to the Calaian typically is a fraction of the trauma sustained by the ride. Until her ride heals, she's essentially a slave to it. … She has to function at whatever capacity her ride is at. It's kind of like having a stroke. Afterwards, you might feel okay, but you can't form words because of motor damage, or you can visualize what you want to say, but your brain can't bring the words forward. Make sense?"

"Kind of."

"We won't know the extent of the interface damage until she regains consciousness. Right now, Sato has her, and that includes Toni the Calaian, in an induced coma. There's some swelling on her ride's brain."

"Was her tech damaged?" I asked.

"Cameron, it takes a lot more than what a service drone can discharge to damage Calaian tech."

Cold comfort. The idea of Toni trapped in a damaged ride made me sick to my stomach.

"What happened to the Mirage commando?" I asked.

"Jacked out."

I leaned back and closed my eyes. The sight of Toni's crumpled body haunted my mind.

"How are you holding up?" Davis asked.

"Better. Hopefully, Toni the Calaian will be okay."

Davis patted my arm. "Get some rest."

"Right, I still have to be operated on."

"Already been done."

"*What?*"

"You were out, and Toni was in good hands with Abbott's crew, so Winston went ahead and did the dirty deed. He also worked on your throat while you were under."

"Was it bad?"

"No, just some deep bruising. She hadn't crushed your trachea, yet."

I gingerly rubbed my throat. "I meant the operation. ... How did that turn out?"

"According to Winston, a complete success. You are now cloaked, guarded, and armed to the teeth. The Mirage won't know what hit them."

I raised my hands and looked at them as if they were exotic weapons I might buy. "Does it really matter, since the Natierians have decided the outcome?"

Davis shrugged. "I know I said they're the puppet masters, but just because they're pulling the strings doesn't mean the outcome is sealed."

"*That's* comforting ... I guess."

"Okay, now get some rest. You're going to need it. Testing starts this afternoon."

*   *   *   *

Lunch consisted of crappy Chinese takeout and more warm sports drinks, the orange flavor, which I hate. The French Calaians, ironically, didn't seem to care much about taste. Flavor was superfluous to them. Eating was a mechanical event solely to replenish their ride's biological need for fuel. At least that's how it struck me. Although, like Abbott's Dallas crew, they did like their beer.

We assembled in the warehouse atrium, except for Sato who, I assume, was monitoring Toni. She'd been moved from the Calaian craft's sick bay to a room four down from mine. The large Calaian spacecraft was cloaked, but its presence loomed at the far side of the atrium like a phantom Zeppelin. Abbott and his team were milling together off to one side. I was standing to the right of them. Winston stood in the middle of the immense atrium, his attention buried in his tablet.

"How do you feel, Mr. Harrison?" he asked.

"I guess okay, considering," I said.

He glanced up. "She'll be okay. The damage is repairable." He pointed to the floor just to his right. "Stand here."

I took my position.

"Engage your combat tech." He was focused on his screen.

The tech fell across my vision and a strange hot, electric prickling shot through my nervous system and tingled my skin. This was new. I raised my clenched fists, and the grav fields hovered around them in a chilling display of raw gravitational power. Whether I liked it or not, I was becoming a real damn superhero.

"Cover the rest of your body, except your head," he ordered.

"You want me to just think it?" I asked.

He slowly looked up, frustration carved deep into his scrutiny. "*Yes.*"

I don't know why – probably the graphic designer in me – but I thought of the Michelin Man logo and its bulbous tire character. Instantly a thick grav field built across my body. It rippled down from my neck to underneath my feet. When it fully formed, I levitated slightly a few inches off the dusty cement floor.

"Does that feel stable?" Winston questioned.

I lifted my right knee and the action sent me up about 10 feet. "Sort of."

"Move backward."

"How?"

"Try releasing a small gravity burst from your fists."

I remembered the rage I felt in Vitale's garage, and the carnage that resulted. This time around, emotion and adrenaline couldn't be in control. I had to learn to handle whatever power had been installed in my head. I raised my fists and thought of a burst ...

"Harrison! Wait!"

A savage gravitational force ejected from my fists and threw me backwards. I was gliding through the open space, my outstretched arms and legs trailing. I barely managed to get my fists behind me and thought of a gentle micro-burst. I stopped inches from slamming into the old building's thick brick wall. I hovered a story off the ground and tried to steady myself in mid-air.

Agent Davis had joined Winston. Both looked up at me as if I were a kid whose first bike ride without training wheels had gone completely wrong. Davis had his hands on his hips and was shaking his head.

"*What?*" I yelled.

Winston let out a disgusted grumble. "Can you come down without hurting yourself?"

Oh, hell. I thought of releasing a tiny grav ejection from the middle of my back and damned if it didn't work. I floated toward Davis and Winston just a little too fast. Davis raised his arms and caught me as I skidded in.

"Don't say a damn thing," I said straightening.

"Everybody starts somewhere," Davis remarked.

"Winston, what have you done to my tech?" I demanded.

"Greatly enhanced it," he answered.

"No shit." I cleared the combat tech from my vision and looked down at my body. The field's faint shimmer was still present. "Why is this still around me?" I asked, inspecting the back of my arms. "I just shut off my tech."

"It's an autonomic defense module. You need to shut it down separately. Just think of it, uh, turning off."

I did, and the heat and prickliness faded.

"Once it merges with your original tech you won't need to do that."

"The tech's power is off the scale," I said. "I have to rethink all my mental cues."

"Yes," Winston said, "about a thousand-fold."

"Can this upgrade make me fly?" I asked.

The Great One looked up, puzzled. "You now have greater distribution and control of your CGFG. If you call that *flying*, I guess you can."

"Can I go fast?"

"In theory, but I advise you not to try. Even though you're cushioned by the CGFG, violent impact at high velocity can still damage your internal organs. Don't assume you're Superman."

"I was thinking more Ironman. I've always been more of a Marvel guy–"

"Tucker," Davis said, "let's show him what the new tech can *really* do."

Winston referenced his Calaian pad. "Over there," he commanded, pointing toward the wall I'd almost slammed into.

I reluctantly walked over, turned back and found myself in gunslinger position with the Calaian spacecraft, although because of its cloaking, it looked more like I was at the far end of a vast empty area almost the length of a football field.

"Here?" I yelled.

"More," Winston said.

I glanced over my shoulder. The wall was about 10 yards behind me. I took a few backward steps.

"How's this?" I yelled.

"That will be fine," Winston bellowed.

"Fine, my ass," I muttered under my breath. "What the hell is he doing?"

Abbott walked away from his crew and approached Winston. His gait suggested more than sparks were going to fly. He got into Winston's face, and they started arguing. Distance and echoes left me trying to piece together what they were saying. Abbott gestured towards the cloaked craft several times. Davis just stood there like the passive referee. After a few super-heated exchanges, Winston leaned into Abbott's anger with all the conviction of a granite mountainside. Abbott finally made an animated *whatever* gesture and stormed back to his team. The Calaian spacecraft decloaked, revealing itself from the background it had so perfectly blended into.

Before the craft fully formed, my newly enhanced tech auto-engaged. The hot electric tingles felt now more like jolts.

Winston and Davis trotted to Abbott's team. Then it struck me ... the Great One had set up a showdown: me and my enhanced Power Ranger ability against the Calaian craft and its sub-light capacity to magically move through solid buildings.

The ship raised from its hover position about 10 feet, the top of its living hull just shy of the atrium's support beams, four stories up. Then, like a bull about to charge, its nose angled down.

A few weeks ago, I would have crapped my pants at the prospect of dying by alien spacecraft impalement. Now?

Bring it fucking *on.*

I engaged my CGFG and felt the bizarre surface-shocks ripple as the grav field enveloped me. This time I included my head. I lunged forward, hands raised, and struck a determined combat stance against the prow of the menacing ship not 50 yards away.

Without any warning, an atomic-like flash soundlessly emanated from the craft's skin and drenched the entire space in a white-hot, retina-destroying glare. My combat tech shielded my vision, but in that micro-second the ship had vanished and reappeared a foot in front of my outstretched hands. My grav field shimmered across its living surface. The pulsing energy of the discharge rushed through my entire body. I spread my fingers and the craft's "nose" crumpled like cardboard.

Abbott broke from the group and rushed toward me. "Stop! *Stop!*"

I hit him with my best *back off* scowl, then forced one foot in front of the other and arduously walked the massive hovering craft back to the center of the atrium. Abbott froze, mid-yell, and watched, mouth agape.

About halfway back to the ship's original position, I stopped and gestured down with my hands. The huge craft settled onto the cement floor. Dust wafted up as it listed to one side and came to a rest. I kept my scowl on Abbott the whole way.

38

LOVE HURTS.

Sato stepped away from a hovering color-blob screen in the remote medical bay and came to Toni's bedside. She slept peacefully in what I can only guess was a Calaian hospital bed. It resembled a giant oyster shell floating above a shallow square tub filled with a fluid that looked like maple syrup. Like the ship's medical bay table, the bed was larger than her body, but Toni's ride was petite.

"How's she doing?" I asked.

"She's stable." Sato answered carefully. "The swelling is gone."

Toni's forehead showed no signs that a lightning bolt had struck it. Her skin looked flawless, as if they had given her a facelift during the repair operation.

"Will she be okay?" I asked.

Sato looked up. "She may need a new ride. The human body is so fragile. We're not sure if this ride will fully heal."

"But Toni the Calaian will be okay, right?"

"The High Sovereign should be mentally intact once she can fully return to her own body. Any damage to her Calaian brain should be repairable. It's her psychological state that concerns me. Duality is difficult for some Calaians to get accustomed to, especially the first time. Rides developed for recreational usage are supposed to be aseptic. That is, free of any residual personality."

"From the original *owner*?"

"Owner?" Sato asked.

"The human … when they were alive. But these are clones … copies. They've never *been* alive, so how can there be any leftover personality?"

"Clones, as you call them, are exact copies, made from DNA harvested from the original body. But we have discovered that deep within human DNA, certain markers can reside."

"What do you mean?"

Sato stared for a second, probably accessing the massive Calaian database. She blinked her dark eyes. "Traits, Mr. Harrison."

"Amazing."

"There are five basic personality traits that are defined in human DNA. Extroversion, neuroticism, agreeableness, conscientiousness, and openness to experience. If the human DNA was harvested from, say, an extrovert, there's an eighty-seven percent chance the clone will exhibit that tendency. If a Calaian who is an introvert occupies an extrovert ride, a conflict can occur within the Calaian mind. For some, it can be difficult to process."

I looked down at Toni and thought of our blind date, and how wonderfully quirky she had been. *God, she's beautiful.*

"You care for her," Sato remarked offhandedly, her attention riveted on her tablet.

"Is that what the *data* is showing?"

"Yes. There are also traces of elevated–"

"Sato?"

The pretty Asian looked up, her finger poised above the swirls of color. "Yes?"

"I loved the High Sovereign for a time. I still do in a certain sense."

Sato's eyes went to the screen. "The data suggests you are … confused."

"That's one word for it."

Sato balanced the tablet on the lip of the shell/bed's frame. "You are one of the most fascinating humans I've met." She began to reach for the tablet but resisted. "You have an unusually large capacity for this emotion."

"Which emotion? Confusion?"

"Confusion is a mental state. I'm referring to love."

"Yeah, well … I went without it for a long time."

"The death of your wife?"

"What, does everyone know my backstory?"

"Abbott believes we should know everything we can about the humans we interact with, especially their emotional states."

"Why? Because we're ruled by our emotions?"

Sato did the blank stare thing again. "One of your scientists termed it *the emotional elephant and the rational rider.* The rider sees the road ahead and steers the elephant. The elephant provides the strength and energy for the journey, but if the elephant takes off, the rider is powerless to stop it."

"Do y'all ever think for yourselves, or is interfacing with the mother mainframe just a necessity when living among us?"

"It makes it easier."

Toni's eyes moved rapidly under their lids. For a second, I thought they were going to open.

"The High Sovereign is lucky," Sato said, breaking the silence. "She was able to experience being with you."

"Oh, I don't know. I'm not that special."

Sato looked up with borderline anger. "You are *very* special, Cameron Harrison." She walked around the shell/bed to within a few feet. "Your bio-enhanced gravitational field capacity has never been attempted on a human *or* Calaian. The tech that's been implanted is revolutionary. What you did today … with our ship … that was unbelievable!"

"I didn't do much. The tech auto-engages."

"Yes, but you still have to *want* it to. The tech requires a clear communication path. You have to be open and willing for it to fully engage."

"Good to know."

Sato stared at me, then reached for the side of my face.

"What are you doing?" I asked, flinching.

"May I touch you?"

"Uh ... okay. Sure."

She gingerly put her palm against the side of my cheek. Her hand was almost as warm as Wren's. She studied my eyes. "You *are* special."

"Sato, what are you–?"

"Please," she said. "Be still."

She took my face in both hands. Before I could stop her, she pressed her lips to mine. I took her by her slim waist and gently pushed her away. She went with it, eyes closed and lips slightly parted.

"What the hell was *that?*" I asked.

"I've never kissed before. I wanted to know what the sensation was like."

"Sato, that wasn't cool."

She ran her tongue across her upper lip. "It was warm and salty."

"No, I mean that wasn't appropriate. ... Kissing me without my consent. Humans have boundaries."

"The data clearly indicates you're attracted to me."

"Just because I have a random thought–" I stopped. "Look, Sato, you can't force yourself on someone. It's a line you don't cross. A relationship takes time to develop – years even. Sometimes it just happens spontaneously. And there's different kinds."

"I know," she said, "we study this. But how do you know when to share the romantic version of this emotional attration between two people?"

"Sato, if you stay on my planet long enough, you'll find romantic love is a complicated emotion. You can, not often though, be in love with two different people ... at the same time ... for different reasons."

She made a face. "Odd. I want to try this kissing ritual again–"

"*Wait*, Sato ... it's not polite to just kiss someone. You have to get to know them."

"I know you."

"No, you don't."

"But I want–"

"You just need to find someone you're attracted to."

"I'm attracted to you."

"I'm flattered ... but I'm not attracted to you ... I mean, you're very pretty and sexy and smart in a mainframe sort of way, but I have someone. Hell, I have *two* someones."

"You find me sexy?"

"Well, yeah, but–"

"Let's have sex!"

"Sato, *no*! Look ... as tempting as that is, you just don't go around having random sex. I mean, I know guys who do that, but they're just horn dogs–"

"*Horn* dogs?"

I waved the question off. "Never mind. What I'm trying to say is love, when it's true and right, is about loyalty and commitment ... and, um, I'm committed–"

"Would you two please shut up."

"*Toni?*" I looked down. Her eyes were half open.

Sato rushed to the other side of the shell/bed and grabbed her tablet.

Toni lifted her hand and reached toward me. I took her hand in both mine.

"What happened?" she asked, drowsily. "Why am I here?" Her grip was weak and tentative.

"There was an accident, High Sovereign," Sato answered. "You were injured." From the darkness above the bed, a chrome drone ball lowered. Toni's eyes grew wide.

"Get that thing outa here," I snapped.

Sato gestured and the ball retreated.

I squeezed Toni's hand. "How do you feel?"

"I can't focus my thoughts," she said above a hoarse whisper. "I feel really weird."

"What do you remember?" Sato asked.

"I was with Tucker in the control bay. I asked if Cameron's procedure would take long. He said no and … um … I … I don't remember anything after that."

"Are you in any pain?"

"Not that I can … that I can … I can't think of the word. What's going on?"

"Be calm," Sato said. "You need rest. I'll give you something."

Sato touched her tablet a few times and Toni's eyes fluttered.

"Oh," she whispered and closed her eyes, "that's nice."

As I watched Toni fall back to sleep, something raw and deeply emotional moved through me.

"What's the matter?" Sato asked, referencing her pad. "Are you in pain?"

I sniffed back the start of some tears. "I'm okay."

"Why are you about to cry then?"

"Sato ... love can also hurt ... a *lot*."

Puzzlement filled the Calaian's face. "I'll never understand this emotion."

"Well, if it's any comfort," I said, regaining my composure, "I feel the same way."

39

UNDERDOG.

Morning came too soon. I woke around three to the thick blackness of my windowless room. I shuffled to the common bathroom area, pissed, shuffled back to the room and fell asleep. I woke up again in an REM-infused bleariness around five. I vaguely remembered bits of a dream about Wren. Giving up, I padded barefoot to the makeshift kitchen area hoping that some Calaian early-bird had made coffee. The Parisian sunrise was leaking through the building's angled glass roof, while the atrium was still cast in large, fragmented shadows. I found Trent standing below the nose of the hovering decloaked Calaian ship. The tablet he held underlit his beard and face in a muted, multicolored glow.

"Morning, Trent," I said.

"Good morning, Mr. Harrison." There was a distinct *I don't want to talk with you, but protocol demands I do* edge to his tone. He didn't look over.

I pointed to the crumpled fuselage above us. "Is it repairable?"

"Yes." Trent swiped and tapped his screen a few times, and the ship slowly began to regain its shape.

"Sorry I did that."

He lowered his tablet to his side. "Why is it so important for humans to display their insecurities?" The question came out like a teacher scolding me for fighting on the playground.

"What do you mean?" I knew exactly what he meant.

He gestured at the damage reforming itself. "The fact that your new biotechnologics have given you the ability to discharge your CGFG at near sub-light *and* control something the size and weight of our craft wasn't enough. You had to demonstrate to Commander Abbott and everyone that you are now the superior being."

I hadn't really thought what I had done was that bad, but now that Trent pointed it out, maybe I had reacted like a dick. It was amazing enough I could stop the huge spaceship, much less walk it back to its position … my new tech and its CGFG did that. That was sufficient, but Trent was right. Abbott rubbed me the wrong way from the start, and when he yelled at me, I wanted to shut his ass down.

"Trent, you have a point, but I think you're overgeneralizing. Not all humans are as insecure as me. Your commander and I have been, uh, at odds with each other, and … I'm a little tired of being treated like an inferior being."

The Calaian nodded, but I sensed my answer didn't work for him. He went back to his tablet and did another swipe. I started for the kitchen.

"You disrespected him," Trent said.

I stopped and turned.

Trent looked up again. "We've been through a lot … the team and Abbott."

"I know," I said. "He told me."

"Respect is important in Calaian culture."

"It is here too."

"Then why did you do it?"

I put my hands in the pockets of my Klein pajamas and pondered the question. I stepped closer and spoke in a low tone. "I'll let you in on a little secret about the human race … we love an underdog."

Trent didn't react immediately, probably while he accessed the great Calaian database of human slang.

"Under*dog?*"

I took another step. "Your people have been here for millennia, enjoying all that our planet has to offer. Taking advantage of our resources *and* our cultural riches."

"Your point?"

I got up into the Calaian's face. He didn't flinch.

"You didn't ask permission," I said.

Trent was a little taller. He leaned down. "We didn't *need* to."

I engaged the tech and a field built around my fist. Trent's eyes went to it.

"Maybe," I said, "it's time all of you rethought that."

Trent held my stare.

"There's a fresh pot of coffee, if you're interested," he said finally.

*   *   *   *

If the Calaians had been cool toward me before my little superhero demo in the atrium, they were now frigid. Before breakfast, I was shaving in the refurbished men's room when Dean walked in. It had four sinks. Three sinks were open. He caught my glance in the mirror and immediately about-faced and left. Before the "incident," I could have sat with any of them to share a meal, but this morning I was the outcast all the kids in the cafeteria shunned.

I was at one end on the longest folding table, eating some kind of French cornflakes knock-off, resigned to my new status when Abbott walked up, tray in hand.

"Mind if I join you?" he asked.

I paused with spoon halfway to my mouth. "Sure you want to do that, Commander? Might send a bad message to the team."

Abbott ceremonially plunked his plate and alien-eyed mug on the table, put aside his tray and sat across from me. The only sound for a minute was both of us chewing. I spoke first.

"Where's Winston?" I asked. "I haven't seen him since my test."

"Gone," Abbott replied brusquely.

"From here or from his ride?"

"We discovered his unoccupied ride last night."

"Back into the core he goes, I guess."

"Doubtful."

I dropped my spoon into the bowl. A bit of milk splashed over the side. "How exactly does that work? You're all sequestered in pods on your moon base, meanwhile living a second life here. If someone breaks the law – you know, does something really bad – do you arrest them at the moon base too?"

"They have to abide by the laws of the country where they committed the offense," Abbott said, not looking up from his plate.

"What if they get away with whatever they did?"

"Concierges make sure they don't."

"And if they're tried and found guilty and sentenced to death, what happens?"

Abbott finally stopped eating and looked up. "They die."

"A real death?"

"Yes." He took a swig of coffee.

"Wow. Kind of ensures you don't do something terrible while vacationing."

"That's the idea." Abbott's attention went back to his plate.

We ate in silence some more.

Abbott paused again and took a swig of coffee. "You saw the High Sovereign last night?"

"Yes. Sato's worried about her mental state, Toni the Calaian that is."

"She's strong. I don't think there's anything to worry about." Abbott scooped up some scrambled eggs onto a wedge of burnt toast. This was getting painful.

"Look, Carlton–"

Abbott glanced up.

"Trent said I disrespected you … crumpling the nose of your ship."

Abbott listened, chewing.

"I, uh, just wanted you to know I didn't mean to … disrespect you, in front of your team."

Abbott swallowed, stared dispassionately, then took another swig of coffee. Its smiling green alien's black eyes found me.

Davis walked up. "Have you two kissed and made up yet?"

"Abbott's asked me to be godfather to his firstborn son," I deadpanned.

"Good, because they've finally hacked in and might have pinged a location for Kip, Wren and Enzo."

"Where?" Abbott asked, his demeanor grave.

"Toni was correct about the mountains," Davis said. "It looks like they're in the French Alps."

"Have they pinpointed a location?"

"Not yet, but they're zeroing in."

Abbott abruptly stood. His fork clattered across his plate. He stared for a second, then the others around us stood in unison.

"Start getting ready," he barked.

"Where are we going?" one of the pilots from our Mars/Paris trip asked.

"Somewhere cold."

*　　　*　　　*　　　*

We assembled at the base of the ship, near some equipment cases like the ones I'd seen in Vitale's garage. Some members of Abbott's team were decked out in what looked like a cross between an Olympic high-tech running suit and something the North Face company might have designed if it had a lab at Area 51.

I was handed one of the suits and held it up by the shoulders at arm's length. "How does this work?" I asked no one in particular.

Up close it resembled the hull of the ship but felt more like what I imagined the shedded skin of a giant python might feel like. I swear it moved when I held it out in front of me. None of the team looked over.

Davis walked over wearing a darker version. He had two small backpacks slung over his shoulder. "Can't figure it out?"

"What was your first clue?"

He took the suit by the shoulders and popped it like he was shaking sand off a beach towel. It stiffened and magically peeled open, separating down the arms, back and legs. Even its footies opened.

"Step into it," he said.

Davis held it while I slid my arms and legs inside. It conformed itself to my clothed body, vacuum sealing around me like one of those food wrapping machines my mom used to have. The fit was snug but not uncomfortable.

"What is this thing?" I asked.

"It's Calaian thermal combat skin," Davis said. "It interfaces with your cerebral implant. If you get cold, it'll keep you warm. If you want to disappear into a snowbank, it can camouflage you in a second."

"What about my head?" I looked down my arms. "It's not covered."

"Just think of the skin covering it," Davis said wryly.

I did and a hood sprouted from the upper shoulders. It went up the back of my neck, slithered over my head, quickly enveloped my face, down my neck and merged with the collar. It grew to the edges of my eyelids, nostrils and lips but didn't intrude into any of them. A shiver went through me.

"Shit, this is freakish," I said, touching my face. "How do I, um, *un-*grow it?"

"Think of that."

It receded off my face and retreated into wherever it had come at the base of my neck.

"What's it rated for, temperature-wise?" I asked.

"You can comfortably exist in a climate of minus one hundred and thirty degrees Celsius. And it can function both in and out of water."

I'd seen a documentary once on Antarctica that said it got down to minus 93.

"Isn't this a bit overkill?" I regretted the words as soon as they left my mouth.

"For the French Alps. But Earth isn't the only planet Calaians visit." Davis handed me one of the backpacks. "This is yours. It has some basic supplies like food bars and water."

The backpack was made of the same material as the combat skin. It opened from the top, but there was no Velcro band or zipper. I reached and an opening appeared. I dug around the contents. A few food bars and two bottled waters on top. Three small potato-shaped objects were at the bottom. I pulled one out and inspected it.

"What're these?"

"Thought mines."

"They look like a frickin' potato." I gingerly placed it back at the bottom of the pack.

Abbott, who had been standing near the cases with his attention buried in his tablet, abruptly looked up and addressed his team. "Eyes on me!"

Dean lobbed a chrome golf ball thing into the open area between the cases and Abbott. It hung in the air and projected a 3D map of the French Alps into the room. Abbott pointed to a region just south of Geneva.

"We're headed to an area in the French Alps, about four hundred and twelve kilometers from our present position. The airspace around Paris is heavily trafficked, so we'll proceed under radar below the sound barrier for the conditions today. Keaton, you're piloting."

The husky Mars pilot gave a crisp affirmative nod.

"We don't know exactly what sort of defenses we'll encounter," he went on, "but we do know the Mirage have received assistance from the Natierians."

A few groans came out.

"I know," Abbott said, "we can't seem to escape them."

"Sir, what are we supposed to do with *him*?" Dean threw a *this piece of shit* head nod my way.

Abbott considered me with barely less scorn. "Mr. Harrison is our payload. We will be depositing him and Agent Davis at the drop zone."

"Bombs away," I side-whispered to Davis.

Abbott's eye narrowed on me. He let out a clipped sigh. "We will park in a holding position above the zone. If they need our help, we can be there in seconds."

"How should we defend against the Natierian tech?" Trent asked.

Davis stepped forward. "Fight fire with fire. We've been on the receiving end of Natierian technology for a few years." He pulled out his black tablet from a hidden side pocket. "I'll download new defense protocols into your implants. In two."

All the Calaians closed their eyes.

"Better brace yourself, Cameron, this is gonna hurt," Davis whispered before he tapped something on his screen.

Two of the Calaians flinched. The tall blonde I hadn't spoken to yet clutched the side of her head.

"You don't feel anything?" Davis asked.

I shook my head. "Not really. A slight warmth at the base of my skull." I tapped the back of my neck. "Right here."

The Calaians opened their eyes. Some shook off the download.

"What does it do?" Keaton asked.

"It gives you greater range to detect anything Mirage," Davis said. "Bio readings, energy sigs, their tech, even if they engage Natierian tech."

"We'll have an advantage," remarked the tall blonde. She was imposing in her combat skin, like a dystopic military character out of a Manga film.

"Do we know anything about the facility where they're holding Wren and Enzo?" I asked.

Davis eyed Abbott, who hesitated.

"Not exactly," Abbott said. "Their cloaking is multilayered. We have an idea of *where*, but not so much *what*." He turned to the projection, which morphed into a fuzzy aerial close-up of a snow-covered mountainside. "We got this off a DARPA Blackjack satellite."

I stepped closer. "There's nothing there, just trees and rocks." The alarm in my voice came out a little more defined than I intended.

A thin smile crept across Abbott's lips. "Load up."

40

FUCKING HELL.

The Calaian team Abbott assembled consisted of Dean, Trent, the tall Manga blonde, Keaton, and himself. Together, in our combat skins, we looked straight from a dark, futuristic Marvel comic.

Dean said we would take about 20 minutes to get to the drop zone at 600 miles per hour. Like the trip to Paris via Mars, I felt no aspect of flight. For all I knew we never left the atrium.

Davis and I were sitting in two bulkhead seats that literally grew out of the bridge's wall when we approached. They formed like a sped up time-lapse of two plants growing, in unison, three feet apart. They were perfectly proportioned to our bodies. It was simultaneously the creepiest and coolest thing I'd ever seen. This ship truly *was* alive.

"They're not much into planning things out, are they?" I whispered to Davis.

Davis shrugged. "I wouldn't say they wing it. They just let the dynamics of the action line dictate their moves."

"Do *we* have a plan?"

Another shrug.

"Great."

"One minute from the drop zone," Dean announced.

"Where are you putting us down, relative to the Mirage base?" I asked Abbott.

The commander, stone faced, looked up from his tablet. "As close as we can without incurring detection."

It felt like Abbott and his team weren't really on a mission. More like they were on a run to throw out the garbage.

"In position," Keaton said.

Abbott walked to the middle of the bridge and an opening formed below his feet. Snow and a bitter cold wind swirled up from the aperture.

He gestured to it. "Showtime, gentlemen."

Davis and I stepped closer and looked down. About 10 feet below was a bright white snowbank. Having grown up in the Midwest, snow and cold didn't bother me much, but the sight of this sent a chill through me even my combat skin couldn't warm. The wind gusted and a wave of icy powder blew across the snowbank's surface.

A hood grew over Davis's head and down his face. Two glass slits formed over his eyes. He looked like a hi-tech scuba diver minus the air tank. I thought of the same thing and a hood and facemask formed. As the lens propagated over my eyes, my combat tech engaged. Strategic data began scrolling just below my vision field.

Davis put a hand to Abbott's shoulder.

"Thanks for everything, Carlton," he said through another gust.

Abbott squinted through crystalline snow that blew into the opening. He wiped some of it off his face. "Make good use of your new weapon."

"I will."

The commander nodded. "Okay, then. Bring them back. If you need us, just use Cameron's cerebral link."

Abbott and Davis shook hands. Davis sat on one side of the opening and pushed off.

I walked to the edge, formed a grav field and floated over the opening.

"Thanks, Abbott," I said extending my hand.

The commander regarded me coolly. He placed his hand on top of my head and shoved me down. I floated out and watched the opening vanish into a bright blue sky. I sank until my feet grazed the surface of the snowbank. Davis was waist-deep in powder, desperately trying to dig himself out.

"Hold still," I yelled through the howl of the wind. "I'll make a field around you and lift you out."

Davis stopped flailing and the grav field enveloped him, along with some of the snowbank. The field made the snow dance as I lifted him out. Davis slowly twisted in the gravitational cocoon. The whole scene looked like a life-size snow globe.

I engaged a cerebral link to Abbott. *Abbott, have you moved the ship?*

Affirmative, answered Keaton.

Where's Abbott? I opened a link to him.

We've moved you to a secure cerebral com. We're in position about thirteen klicks above the drop zone.

I looked around to get my bearings and spotted a rocky outcropping 30 yards away. I moved Davis to it and settled down on the flattest part. I waited until he had twisted into a more upright position and dissipated the field. He and the snow floating around him dropped to the rock face. Davis landed on his hands and knees. Some of the snow fell onto him.

"Are you okay?" We were somewhat sheltered from the wind so I didn't have to yell.

Davis gave a thumbs up and stood. I brushed the snow off his back.

"Thanks," he said, brushing the last of it off his shoulders. "Got a little stuck back there."

"No worries." I looked around. "What do we think?"

It was about noon and the glare from the snow's reflection was painfully bright. Before I could think about dimming my vision, the suit's tech compensated and darkened the lenses over my eyes.

"What's your combat vision show?" Davis asked.

I engaged it and the visual spectrum shifted. Certain color fields deepened, and details that before had been washed out because of the snow's glare were now defined in vivid clarity. We were on the side of a foothill. Behind us a large mountaintop rose into the sky, its craggy summit skirted by fast-moving wispy clouds. The foothill's incline was gentle and in front of us was a small ridge. The snow that rimmed it resembled a long dollop of frosting. The tech made the snow slightly transparent. I could make out the rockface underneath.

"All I see is the mountainside," I said. "There's no sign of a cloaked structure anywhere."

Davis pointed and said, "Let's see what's on the other side of that ridge. Can you get us over there?"

I built a grav field around us, took Davis by the shoulders and pushed off. We floated across the wide ravine. The wind had kicked up and I had to make course corrections with little bursts from the grav field's surface, like an astronaut on an untethered spacewalk. We sailed over the ridge, passing its top by about five feet. Beyond the ridge was a deeper ravine. Its sunny side was void of the deep snowpack. The exposed rockface looked unforgiving.

"See anything?" Davis asked.

"Negative—"

My combat tech suddenly zeroed in on a huge, jagged rock formation. It drew a green circle around it and scrolled through a short list of what it detected: alloys, plastics, steel, titanium, and a few unfamiliar substances with details in outlined boxes. I asked for a visual zoom, but the structure was hard to discern even with maximum magnification.

"Got a hit." I pointed in the direction.

Davis shook his head. "Don't see it."

"I do."

"Put us down."

I lowered to the only flat spot in sight. Just as our feet touched the rockface I dissipated the field. Gravity took hold and brought us to our knees. The wind was fierce on this side of the slope.

"Why'd we land?" I shouted. "According to Abbott, my new tech's cloaking should allow us to walk right up and ring the doorbell."

"Not taking any chances," Davis yelled into the gale. "I want to see what's waiting for us before we make our next move. Besides, if they could really see us, we'd be dead already." He gestured. "Lead on."

I looked over the landscape to plot the easiest path and my tech supplied a brightly dotted green line. It snaked its way up the rockface to the top of the ridge, highlighting various slope angles and footholds along the path. Davis and I inched our way, sometimes crawling and sometimes sidestepping. Because of the grav field I could generate, I wasn't scared of falling. I urged Davis to move faster.

"The path leads just over the ridge," I said, maneuvering around a large boulder. "The hit should be on the other side."

Davis hand signaled *okay*.

We clawed to the lip of the ridge on our bellies and peered over. The wind ebbed a little. My combat tech focused on the sliver of exposed structure behind the rock formation and drew a green outline around it. Within seconds the rest of the hidden structure appeared as a detailed technical drawing. Nestled behind the rocks was a building that mimicked the massive granite formations around it. The dimensions translated to about two football fields long and 18 stories high, but the shape was irregular. A solid white line extended from the building outline, and a data block appeared.

"My tech has identified it," I said.

"What kind of building is it?" Davis asked.

"It's not a building. ... It's a ship. Calaian scout vessel. Northern House. Deep Space Intrusion Class. That mean anything to you?"

Davis slowly shook his head. "Fucking hell," he grumbled.

"What's the matter?" I asked.

"DSI Class are heavy with tech. Really advanced shit."

"Isn't anything Calaian really advanced shit?"

Davis tilted a look. "This mission," he shook his head again, "just got a whole lot harder."

41

BAIT.

I had never really seen Agent Davis rattled. Not even when Wren had raced down Gloria's parking lot on a 600cc sport bike brandishing a blackjack. He had smoothly spun around and pulled out his sidearm in one motion like being mowed down was all in a day's work.

"Do we need to call in the cavalry?" I asked.

"Not yet," Davis said. "Besides, I'm not sure what they could do. Abbott's ship is no match for a DSI Class."

"Even cloaked?"

Davis gave me an incredulous side-eye. "A DSI can, if challenged, take out a small planet. Our only chance is that Winston's tech can evade their security."

"How did the Mirage get one of these?"

"Good question. The Guardium are the only ones who have them."

"Think they're collaborating with the Mirage?"

"Maybe not the whole organization. Just one faction."

"Or one person."

Davis nodded pensively.

"What now?" I asked.

Davis shifted onto his side and folded his arms tightly to his chest. A hard, cold gust raked over us. "We wait."

"For *what?*"

"For the—"

Cam?

I made a slicing motion across my throat and pointed to my temple. Davis's eyes widened.

Wren, is this really you? Are you all right?

Yes, it's me. And I'm okay, I guess. Not hurt. They have my body sedated but since I'm a DE they can't really knock me out.

Won't the Mirage pick this up?

Not that I can tell. I'm masking the com.

Good. Hey ... I have to ask you something. What did I say to you in the limo ... before we went to the museum?

What? Oh, a test. Smart. My man's learning. You said don't do anything that will get yourself killed. And technically, I said it first.

Oh, Wren, I ... I thought I had lost you.

Not a chance.

Where are you?

*In a ship, but I don't know where we are. I can't get into any nav sys-
tems, but I've gained access to some platforms. Right now I've hacked the
ship's emergency cerebral com link. I'm burying my signal deep in the stream.*

What kind of ship are you on?

A big one. This thing is tricked out.

Is it a DSI Class?

How'd you know that?

I'm looking at it right now.

You are?! Where am I?

*You're in a ravine, nine thousand feet high in the French Alps. Davis
and I are about a mile away. How's Enzo?*

*I don't know, they've separated us. I think they're going to use me to
get to you.*

Bait.

Don't fall for it.

I don't care. We're coming to get you.

Where's Abbott?

He and his team are about eight miles above us.

Chickenshits.

Wren, you need to know something. ... I've changed.

The pause was telling. *What do you mean?* Even with the fuzziness of
the cerebral link, her anxiety came through.

My tech has been altered again by Winston. I'm ... different. I have abilities that you wouldn't believe.

Great, because we're going to need all the advanced tech we can get. Let me see what I can do from in here to get you access. I'll try and reconnect as soon as I can.

Hey Wren?

Yeah?

Please don't do anything that will get you killed.

* * * *

The Calaian thermal combat skins were amazing technology. I don't know how they did it, but as we huddled on the side of the slope for close to an hour, I never felt cold. Sure, there was the occasional gust that bit around the edges of my eyelids and lips, but somehow the skin maintained a perfect warmth around my body. I didn't sweat, or at least I didn't feel any.

"Has she reconnected yet?" Davis asked for the third time.

"I'll let you know as soon as she does, I promise."

My sarcasm was wasted. He was already buried in the readout panel on the wrist area of his combat skin. He looked up and said, "I don't want to wait too long." He took a water bottle, took a swig and returned it to his back-pack.

"Maybe she's waiting for it to get dark," I offered.

Cam?

"It's her," I said. *What've you got?*

From what I can tell they can't see you. I managed to hack into low-level internal coms, and there's no mention of you or Abbott. No alerts or defense protocols engaged. Nothing. Business as usual, whatever that means around here.

Good. So how do we get inside ... what's your plan?

What can your new tech do?

What do you want it to do?

Create an opening in the ship's hull about halfway up.

I don't know. We didn't test for something like that. We do have these potato bombs.

What are you talking about?

Davis calls them thought bombs. They're the size and shape of a potato.

Potato ... Oh shit, you mean a judgment mine. That's better!

Hang on. "Davis, are these judgment mines?" I asked, pointing to my backpack.

"Yes," he said.

I asked Wren, *What do these mines do?*

Her soft laugh felt good as it splashed against my mind. *Whatever you want them to do.*

Wren explained that judgment mines interacted with your cerebral tech. You thought of what you wanted it to do, and it did it. In our case, we could command it to interact with the ship's hull and force the hull's biologics to form an opening. It was no different than creating any other entrance or exit into a ship, but this would bypass the ship's central core. Essentially, it was a technological hacking weapon, but that barely scratched the surface of what a judgment mine could do. If we needed to destroy the ship, it could use the ship's own tech against it to accomplish the mission. Need to overthrow a city? A judgment mine could hack into a city's networks and take over the essential systems.

When do you want us to make our move? I asked.

Give me a second to find Enzo and figure out his situation … if I can.

Roger that.

Ooo, military speak. Sexy.

Really? You're thinking of sex at a time like this?

What can I say? Danger makes me horny.

"Do you think your digital girlfriend can hack in and cover for us," Davis asked after about five minutes.

"Hell if I know," I replied. "You don't like her, do you?"

"The girl clipped me upside the head. … What do you think?"

"Look, she's a badass, and if there was anyone we needed to trust right now, it's her."

Cam?

I motioned to my head. Davis sat up.

What do you have, Wren?

I think I can make this work. I've hacked into their primary sensor system. They still don't see you. When you're in position, place the judgment mine against the hull and ask it to create an opening. Aft section, level five, section twenty-three-b, midway up the hull.

I repeated the position to Davis. He tapped it in on his screen.

How long will it take you to get there? she asked.

Can I grav in?

Negative. Come by foot.

Okay. Hang on.

I ran my eyes from our position to the Calaian vessel and my tech drew another path along with data on distance, arrival time, obstacles and footholds.

"Forty minutes to get there?" I asked Davis.

"Sounds about right." He glanced at his screen. "It's two-eleven. Sunset is around five-thirty, but since we're in this ravine we'll be in shadows around four. That should give us time to get in and get out."

Wren, we can be there in forty minutes.

Good. I'm going to make it appear in their systems like nothing weird is going on in the section. Hopefully with your cloaking and my hacking, you should be able to get in undetected.

How many Mirage are on board?

I haven't been able to find that out. Based on the data I've seen, I'm thinking not that many, at least not typical for a ship this size. Twelve? Fourteen at the most?

Better than a hundred. Can you hack into their life support and ... I don't know ... take 'em all out at once?

Already tried. Those systems are waaaay walled up.

What about Enzo?

Negative. Still working it.

Okay. We'll head out now.

Be ready for anything, Cam. The ship's tech is really advanced, even by Calaian standards.

*   *   *   *

The 40 minutes my combat tech predicted turned into 60. The sun dipped behind the ridgeline and the temperature plunged. The path was easy to navigate and downhill, but going that direction is more treacherous, which applies exponentially in the dark. If one of us mis-stepped and sent a cascade of loose rock rolling downhill, it would set off alarms. The closer we came to the massive ship, the more my stomach drew into a tight, uneasy ball.

"See it yet?" Davis asked.

"No. The path leads around these rock walls."

Ahead of us jagged fin-like formations jutted from the ravine's floor and towered at least 16 stories into the Alpine air. The tops of them still basked in sunlight. As we neared the leading edge of the formation, I saw the nose of the Calaian ship.

"I see it," I said.

We rounded the lead formation and found the ship hovering about six feet off the ground, wedged into a narrow and deeply shadowed area between two of the vertical fins of rock. It was a perfect parking spot to hide from the world.

"What's it look like?" Davis asked over a rush of wind.

"Similar to Abbott's ship, but a *lot* bigger."

"Can we make it to the position Wren gave you?"

I scanned the length of the hull. "Depends on where the aft is."

Davis glanced at his screen. He pointed up. "I can't see it, but according to this schematic it should be right above us."

I swung off my backpack and dug out one of the three judgment mines.

"How do you arm it?" I asked.

"She didn't tell you?"

"No."

"Damn it, Harrison–"

"Hey, I'm not a soldier! I don't think of this shit like you do."

"*Okay.* Just … I don't know … Mind fucking meld with it and tell it to make an opening at the location Wren told us. Then place it against the hull."

Hey judgment mine, I thought, *please create an opening two six-foot humans can walk through from outside the ship on level five, section twenty-three-b.*

"Did you think it?" Davis asked.

"*Yes.* I even said pretty-please. How does it know English?"

"It's Calaian. It knows everything."

I handled the judgment mine like a live hand grenade and gingerly placed it against the hull. As soon as it made contact the thing began to merge like butter melting into hot toast.

"That was weird," I said, still staring at the spot where it disappeared. "Now what?"

"I guess we let it do its thing."

I gestured to the ship. "What do you see?"

"Nothing. Just a giant open space between two huge granite outcrop-pings." He pointed to the screen on his wrist. "I have the tech specs, but I don't see it live as you do."

"Not even a distortion field?"

He shook his head.

After a few minutes, we both glanced up, me to an area midway up the face of the hull, and Davis I guess to where he thought the opening would appear. The area around us slipped into twilight. The wind ebbed.

"Sun's going down," Davis remarked, looking at his screen.

"I don't want to do this in the … whoa, check it out!" I pointed to the large opening that formed exactly halfway up the side of the ship. At our low angle I could barely see inside, but it appeared the same as every entry/exit I'd encountered with Abbott's ship.

"I'll be damned," Davis remarked. "I can see the opening."

"Let's do this." I pulled my backpack over my shoulder and stepped up to Davis's side. "Going up?" He grinned and nodded. I formed a grav field and we slowly ascended.

Because of the ship's bulbous shape, the opening was at the apex of the hull's curvature and dangerously close to the rockface.

"I hope there's enough room for us," I said as we approached. "We can go in one at a time if we need to." I slowed and we gently floated level with the opening. Its diameter was about nine feet wide. The rockface was just a few inches off our backs.

"No welcoming committee," Davis said. "My skin's night vision drops off just inside. What can you see with your tech?"

"It's a storage room. Really big." Beyond the opening stood rows and rows of containers, somewhat like the ones I had seen with Abbott's crew, but these were more organic. They had the same turtle shell covering as the skin of the ship, but they looked more like bladders than equipment cases. "I don't like the feel of this."

Davis glared at me. "Let's hope your e-girlfriend knows what she's doing."

I cautiously steered us inside. The opening closed behind us. We settled onto the floor and I dissipated the grav field.

"This *is* a big cargo bay," Davis said, straightening.

I caught the faint impression of a large circular door in a wall at the end of the aisle where we stood. "Is that an actual door?"

Davis followed my gaze. "I don't think I've ever seen one in a Calaian ship before."

We walked about 60 feet, passing intersecting rows of bladder cases stacked three high in biotic webbing.

"Do you know what Calaians really look like?" I asked as we approached.

"No. It's classified. Why?"

"This indentation looks about fifteen feet wide."

"It's a cargo door, so it's probably bigger than most."

"I know, but the table in the medical bay on Abbott's ship is about nine feet long and has four arm extensions on it. What's up with that?"

"Hell if I know. Above my pay grade. I've heard rumors that they're a tall species, but nothing about four arms."

"Maybe they have wings, along with arms?"

"Maybe."

Unlike human battleships, with their exposed ductwork, bolts and rivets, this door followed the same organic intention that most Calaian design did; smooth, seamlessly connected elements set within a mantra of no right angles. Its circular form was a barely visible *bas relief.*

"It's an orifice," I said.

"Do we know how to open this ... orifice?"

"Hang on." *Wren?*

You in?

Yes. We're in a cargo bay.

I know, that's where I wanted you to be. It's a low priority section. Minimal security.

We're standing at a kind of door. It faces the interior of the ship. Can you open it?

A tiny hole appeared in the door's center and apertured out to the edges like a living camera shutter. Because the door had no frame, its material just merged into the wall around it. Beyond was a high-ceiling hallway bathed in a low orange glow.

Step into the hallway and take a right, Wren said.

I feel like we're walking into a huge animal's intestines.

Calaian biologics. It permeates our culture. Things aren't really built. They're grown, or more accurately, they grow themselves.

Are you cloaking us?

Don't need to. From what I can tell, your new cloaking is working great.

Where's the crew?

They work and live in the forward sections, three decks up. Most of the ship is unused–

"What's she saying?" Davis whispered.

"The crew isn't in this area and my tech's cloaking is hiding both of us perfectly, just like Abbott predicted."

Are you talking to Davis? Wren asked.

Just keeping him in the loop. We've come to an intersection.

Take a left.

Where're we going?

To where I think they're keeping me. Be on your guard.

Wren directed us down two more lengthy intestinal hallways until we came to another seamless T intersection. I gave Davis a play-by-play of our thought conversation.

Hold up, she ordered.

We pressed ourselves against the wall. It was warm on my back.

Holding, I said.

Give me the lay.

I peeked around the corner. *Empty hallway left and right.*

Good. Come left hallway and proceed about halfway down the hall. I should be in a room on your right.

We came to another circular door impression that was the same size as the one in the cargo bay. So much for Davis's theory.

We're here.

The door opened like its cargo bay cousin. Davis and I stepped cautiously into the darkness.

Do you see me? Wren asked.

Not yet, my tech is still adjusting to the–

The room exploded into bright illumination. My suit's tech couldn't shift fast enough to compensate. I reflexively raised my hand to shield the painful glare.

I can't see anything. Okay, now it's shifting ... Oh shit.

Cam, what's the matter?

42

BIGGER THAN ALL OF US.

As my visual tech adjusted, Kip's backlit figure slowly came into detail. "Cameron," he said. "Agent Davis."

He was dressed in a kind of urban tactical gear, similar to what we wore but not as tightly fitted. I couldn't tell exactly what he held in his hand, but the thing was leveled at us. Two Mirage stepped from the shadows aiming the same weapon from the hip. My visual tech finished adjusting, and I could finally see the room's detail. Behind Kip, Wren lay unconscious on what looked like an operating table. Dozens of delicate microfilaments rose from all parts of her body and disappeared into the blackness above us. She was naked except for a small towel draped across her groin. My combat tech autoengaged.

"He's deploying!" the taller Mirage yelled, aiming his weapon.

Cam, Wren said, *what is going–?*

Hold on! We have a situation.

"Indeed, you do," Kip said.

"You can hear us?"

Yes. And I would disengage, or Liaison Wren will die a real death.

Kip's words chewed through my mind like a chainsaw.

Wren's anger was palpable. *Bishop, what have you done?*

Liaison, your actions were predictable. We needed Cameron to come aboard without incident. We knew you would find a way ... Oh, and brilliant hacking of our security net.

The Calaian combat skin on Davis's face receded off his head. I asked mine to do the same. The room's stale air felt warm on my face.

"Why isn't anybody talking?" Davis demanded.

"Kipling has the ability to listen in to what I'm thinking. It's a fucking cerebral party line." I pointed angrily at the table. "What are you doing to Wren?"

Kip glanced over his shoulder. The weapon remained aimed. "We can't have her ride active. She's too ... volatile." He raised an open hand and made a *give it to me* gesture. "The backpacks."

We pulled the packs off our shoulders and tossed them at Kip's feet. The taller Mirage picked Davis's up and rifled through it.

"Judgment mines," he said, pulling one out.

He returned it and tossed Davis's pack to the floor.

Kip stitched a tight smile. "Smart."

"Cut the shit," Davis said. "You got us here, so let's talk."

The polite, accommodating flight attendant I had met on the plane weeks ago was gone. The brutally clever person before me now was apparently a Mirage operative with laser focus.

Kip regarded Davis with a fair amount of loathing. "About *what*, Agent?"

"Screw this," Davis muttered and touched his screen.

The shorter Mirage aimed his weapon.

Kip put a firm hand on the guy's wrist.

The Mirage glared. "*Sir?*"

Kip tossed a chrome ball into the space between us. It projected a ground view of Abbott's uncloaked ship. The craft was silhouetted by the setting sun, highlighted above by a darkening blue sky. Thin, wispy clouds in pink, yellow and rust slowly moved around it.

"What was the colloquialism you used on the ridge?" Kip asked sarcastically. "Send in the cavalry?"

A flash whited out the image. It flared and returned to normal in a second or two. A tremor passed through the DSI ship as the distant shockwave washed over it. In the projection, a bird flew through the now empty sky. The image winked out and the chrome ball floated back to Kip's outstretched hand. He pocketed it and shook his head slightly as if destroying Abbott, his crew and the ship disturbed even him. Nausea rippled through me. Kip lowered the weapon to his side.

"All ... we ... want," he said as if each word pained him, "is asylum on your god ... damn ... *planet.*"

"We can't allow it," Davis replied sternly. "You *know* that."

Kip looked up and let out a fatigued sigh. He turned to the taller Mirage and gestured apathetically. "Take them–"

I instinctually raised my fists and discharged three tightly compressed grav waves. They hit all three Mirage before Kip could finish. One wave came close to Wren's table and shoved it askew. The microfilaments remained attached.

What's going on? she asked.

Kip tried to take us. I've got them held in a field.

SHIT! Her inner yell sent a sharp pressure through my skull. *I should have recognized the play.*

Kip and the two Mirage floated in splayed positions as if freeze-framed in the middle of an action movie. Each soldier was about two feet off the floor. Their weapons were suspended away from their outstretched hands. Fields shimmered across their bodies.

Davis inspected each of them. "The impact of the wave must have knocked them out." He looked back. "Or maybe your tech knocked them out. Can you hold them?"

"The tech's doing it. I don't have to think about it."

Davis pointed to where the opening had been. "Mirage will be coming … ask Wren if she can see the crew."

Wren, we need an exit strategy. Can you see what the rest of the crew is doing?

Negative. They're all running cloaked. Can you see me?

Yes. You're on a table with a bunch of wires attached. They're all over your body. You're, um, naked. They do have a towel over your crotch.

The growl Wren made sounded like a very pissed-off tiger. *I'm going to kill every last one of these Mira—*

Wren, focus!

You got any judgment mines left?

Five.

Put one on my forehead.

Are you serious?

Just do—

"What the hell is she saying?" Davis's impatience was stretched taut over the question.

"The crew is cloaked. She wants us to put a judgment mine on her forehead."

"Um ... okay." Davis lifted a mine out of his pack and walked to the table. He held it over her forehead and hesitated. "You're sure about this?"

"Fuck if I know. Just do it."

He gingerly placed the mine on her skin and stepped back, hands raised. It teetered for a second, then began to sink into her skin.

Wren, it's, um ... merging with you.

Good. I'll take it from here.

It took the judgment mine about five seconds to disappear completely.

Davis lowered his hands. "So ... aren't you supposed to *think* something for it to do?"

"She said she'd handle it."

Davis reacted like that made sense, but he didn't like it.

Tense seconds ticked by.

"How are you doing with them?" Davis gave a nod to Kip and his men.

I shrugged. "I'm not really doing any–"

"Cam?" Wren lifted her head from the table.

"Wren!" I rushed over and took her hand. "Are you okay?"

She nodded and the wires began to detach. One-by-one they retracted into the darkness overhead. She tried to sit up as they released. Davis and I helped her.

"How do you feel?" Davis asked.

"What's the phrase … like hammered dog shit?" Her eyes went to the Mirage. "They looked knocked out." Her voice was incredulous.

"This new tech seems to act on its own," I said. "I've instructed it to hold them, but I don't have to keep my attention on them anymore."

Wren swung her legs off the side of the table. The towel fell away. Davis averted his eyes. "You want my combat skin?"

Wren gave a slow nod and hugged herself. "Yes, thank you."

Davis reached behind his head and fiddled with something. The skin unpeeled down his spine, arms and legs. He took it by its shoulders and wriggled out.

Wren slid off the table and stumbled into me. I put an arm around her and pulled her close. Even through my combat skin she felt good. I kissed the top of her head.

Underneath his combat skin, Davis had on a black t-shirt, dark grey running leggings and a pair of black cross-trainers. He held the skin out while still looking away. "It'll reshape to your size."

Wren stepped in and it sealed around her. "Oh, this feels good." She let out a long sigh like the skin gave her a measure of comfort. "I didn't realize how cold I was. It's okay, Agent, you can turn around."

"We have to figure out our next move." Davis's tone suggested the Mirage might storm the room any second.

"Where's Abbott?" Wren asked.

"Gone," I said. "Kip destroyed their ship."

Shock registered in Wren's eyes, but it didn't last.

"Can you breach their systems again and see what the crew is doing?" Davis asked.

Wren tilted a tough, steely-eyed look and nodded. She pulled her shoulders back and closed her eyes.

My mind went back to the destruction of Abbott's ship.

Davis picked up on it. "You okay?"

"Just thinking of Abbott." I swallowed the pain. "Assuming this goes right, how are we getting back to Paris?"

"Think the Liaison can pilot one of these?"

"She's a DE. I'm sure she can download that ability."

"I got partially through," Wren said, opening her eyes. "I can't see all of them, but from what I can tell, most of Kip's crew is just going about their business. No alarms. No cerebral chatter. Nothing. It's like they don't know anything about what's going on down here."

"Maybe Kip went rogue," I offered.

"Unlikely," Davis said. "You're the reason the Mirage took Vitale and the Liaison." He stared at the floor. After a moment, he glanced at Kip. "Release him."

I reluctantly dissipated the field and Kip landed in a heap on his side. His weapon fell and clattered to a stop not far from Davis's feet.

Davis kicked it aside. He put a couple of toe jabs into Kip's ribs. "Hey, asshole, wake up." Davis kicked again, but Kip blocked it.

"What the hell is going on," Davis demanded.

Kip went to one elbow and made eye contact. "You wouldn't understand."

Davis knelt and seized Kip's throat like a cobra. "I'm tired of dealing with your fucking kind." He yanked the Calaian close to his face. "Your war is getting *old.* Now ..." he tightened his grip, "you're going to tell us what's *really* going on or you're going to die a real fucking death."

Kip grabbed Davis's wrists. "It's ... bigger ... than ... all of us," he managed between gasps for breath.

"What *is?*"

Kip pointed behind us. "Them."

43

THAT IS UNFORTUNATE.

My tech instantly deployed and the grav field shimmered across my clenched fists. Wren and I turned. Davis shoved Kip to the floor and slowly stood.

In the center of the room hovered a translucent orange-blue vapor about the size and mass of a large person, but its appendages and head weren't fully formed. Within the mist, electrical discharges flashed like lightning inside a colorful storm cloud. The vapor brightened when they fired, but I couldn't discern a pattern.

"What is *that*?" Wren asked.

"A Natierian." Davis spun on Kip. "Is that your master?"

"Fuck you," Kip said hoarsely, rubbing his throat.

As we stared at the being, a collective awe filled the room.

Cameron … Harrison.

The voice in my mind had a melodic quality. Its androgynously human tone phased in and out, as if it traversed a vast distance.

"It's speaking to me," I said.

Wren and Davis shot me anxious glances.

Yes? I asked.

We are concerned.

About what?

The fusion of Calaian biotechnogistics and human biology.

Because it doesn't jibe with your prediction models for humanity?

Stillness filled my mind.

Yes, it said finally.

That ship has sailed.

Another stretch of silence.

Are you happy? it asked.

What a weird-ass question. *Define happy.*

Satisfied with your life. Content. Feeling … hopeful.

I don't know … Maybe.

That is unfortunate.

One of the discharges inside the Natierian exploded from the creature's form and surged toward me. My fists came up and released a grav wave that collided with the discharge in a tightly formed field five feet in front of me. A protective grav field had automatically enveloped me, but it was dangerously clear the Natierian energy wave was making ground. The shockwave from the fields' clash had knocked Wren and Davis to the floor. In my peripheral vision, the two Mirage goons remained suspended in their fields. The Natierian beam edged closer.

You cannot sustain your defense, the alien entity said calmly.

The sheer amount of energy being emitted warped the grav field around me and started to constrain my movement. I struggled to push back.

Suddenly, Kip lunged for his weapon. He landed on his side, grabbed it, twisted, and aimed at me.

Wren came off the floor with the prowess of a dancer and vaulted between us.

Whatever Kip's weapon discharged, its needle-thin beam sliced through Wren's body like a scalpel. The white-hot edge hit her just below the ribcage, and her momentum did the rest. I don't know if it was the tech or my mind's inability to process what was happening, but the scene played out in grisly slow motion as her two halves slid apart and landed on the floor.

A primordial hate consumed me like flash fire. I aimed my right fist and struck Kip before he could fire again. I watched with enhanced clarity as his head caved in on itself as if a black hole had magically formed in the middle of his face. The vortex grotesquely sucked in his cheeks and the rest of his head. Shoulders, upper body, torso and legs followed. He vanished in a matter of seconds.

I swung my right arm around and leveled both fists at the puppet master. Its beam was almost touching my skin.

This action, the Natierian said, *will not—*

With a scream I unleashed all my fury into a tightly focused grav wave. It surged straight through the Natierian's beam and engulfed its vaporous form. The beam broke off, but I kept up the pressure. The Natierian began to shrink down into a ball and it let out a sickening shriek. A final burst of lightning, and the creature was gone.

I cut off my field and my knees instantly buckled. I sank to all fours and tried to catch my breath. I hesitantly moved my gaze to the upper half of Wren's body. It had come to rest in a twisted heap of blood, entrails, and singed flesh. Her face was turned away. One of her arms was outstretched toward me, its fingers open as if beckoning me to save her.

My head fell and I tried to shove down the horror, but it was overwhelming. My anguish gushed out in convulsive sobs.

"Oh shit," I heard Davis say.

I twisted and saw the other two Mirage getting to their feet. Raising a shaky fist, I hit them both as I had Kip. Within seconds their bodies collapsed into nothingness.

Davis retrieved their weapons and knelt beside me.

"Why did she *do* it?" I barely choked out the words.

"She was a soldier."

"Do you think she's ... *gone?*"

Davis hesitated. "Yeah."

The hell of what had happened swelled again. My grief and anger shifted to a deep, animalistic hate. My combat tech tried to engage, but I fought the urge to destroy the ship, to destroy the Mirage. But most of all ... to destroy the Natierians.

"Fight it," Davis urged.

I did and the tech's power receded. Davis helped me to my feet.

"They will *pay,*" I uttered.

"I know … but not right now. We still have to get–"

The area in the wall that we had come through started to aperture open.

Davis pivoted and aimed both weapons. I raised my fists to the wave of Mirage that were about to rush in.

A narrow beam of light probed the darkness. Another joined it. A backlit figure cautiously eased into the room, one leg at a time. Its hands held a sinuous, black Calaian weapon.

"Stop," I yelled. "I'll destroy all of you!"

The figure pulled up and angled its head in our direction.

"Harrison, don't! It's Commander Abbott."

The combat skin on Abbott's head retreated. He stepped out of the shadows and Dean appeared in the aperture behind him.

Davis lowered his weapons. "We thought you were dead."

"Misdirection ploy," Abbott said, walking up.

Dean and the tall Manga blonde followed. Each carried the same long black weapon.

"How did you get in?" Davis asked.

"Used one of the–" Abbott's attention zeroed in on Wren's upper half, then darted to the lower half a few feet away. Dean saw it too and sucked in a gasp. The Manga blonde saw the gore and put a hand over her gaping mouth.

Abbott lowered his weapon to his side. "What happened?" he asked, his anger tempered.

"Kipling and two of his team were waiting," Davis replied. "Cameron gravved them, but a Natierian showed up. Things got a little … tense. Kipling went for his weapon to kill Cameron, and the Liaison played the hero. Any chance she's still in the core?"

"What kind of weapon was it?"

Davis held out the device. "This."

Abbott slowly shook his head. "Stylus caster. Its beam carries disruptor protocols that trace to the core and wipe out the source." The glance he gave me was full of compassion. "She's gone. What happened to Kipling and his team?"

"I killed them." Saying the words gave me a cold sense of satisfaction.

"What's the situ?" Abbott asked Davis.

"The Liaison was our connection to the ship," Davis said. "She'd hacked in. Said there was a small Mirage contingent, forward section, three decks up."

"They probably have us tagged." Abbott looked up into the darkness above us. "I hate these DSIs. This is an old one." He turned to Dean. "Can you get us an approach?"

Dean nodded and did the blank stare thing. "Have it," he said after a couple of seconds. He tossed a chrome ball. A side-view diagram of the ship projected. "We're here." He pointed to a section near the aft. "The Mirage are probably somewhere in this area." He moved his finger to the top of the ship on the other end. A bright orange dashed line snaked through the schematic and ended at his fingertip. "This approach is ninety-six percent efficient, if the Liaison's intel was correct, sir."

"Can you pilot one of these?" Abbott asked him.

"Yes, sir."

Abbott swung his weapon up. It started to hum. He glanced to the ceiling again. "All right. Let's finish this and get the hell out of here."

44

IT'S THERE, BELIEVE ME.

I felt dead inside as I followed the team down the corridor, putting one foot in front of the other in a plodding mechanical reflex that was torturous with every step. Abbott was on point. Dean and the Manga blonde flanked him abreast, Keaton and Trent followed, then me with Davis pulling up the rear.

The hollowness in my mind without Wren's voice there was tearing me up inside. I had come to love her snarky jabs at my stupid humanity. It was like a part of me had been gutted. I looked at my hands, considered the power that they could unleash, and knew I had failed to protect her.

We came to a wall at the end of a hallway. Another large circular impression loomed. Abbott raised a fist and the team held up.

"What's on the other side of this opening?" he asked Dean.

Dean referenced his wrist screen. "Weapons bay."

Abbott pondered the answer.

"What are you thinking?" Davis asked.

Abbott ran his fingers along the impression in the wall. "Something doesn't feel right."

"As a Calian or as a human?" I asked.

"Both," he said.

"What does your gut say?" Davis asked.

Abbott grinned. "Of all the human expressions I know, I like that one the most. This room is big, filled with equipment and lots of places to hide. It's a trap."

"Any other way?" I asked.

"Negative," Dean answered.

Abbott motioned for Dean to place a judgment mine to the wall. He did and it sank in. A second later the opening appeared. It was pitch black on the other side.

"Activate vision," Abbott ordered.

The team's combat skins formed over their faces. The skin was better than Kevlar at stopping small weaponry. My tech could compensate for my vison, so I left my head exposed. Funny, this give-a-shit attitude I now had. With Wren gone, part of me didn't care about what could happen next. There was even a small part that welcomed death, as if it were just another door, no different than the one we were about to step through.

We entered the cavernous space and began creeping along a pathway defined by rows of bizarrely shaped equipment and tall stacks of bladder containers. The team, in total combat posture, moved bent-legged, weapons raised. Abbott swung his attention and weapon from side to side at every intersecting aisle. The others followed suit.

A third of the way through, Dean said over the cerebral com.

Be sharp, Abbott warned.

My combat vision caught something in the blackness about 20 yards away, poised in the middle of the pathway. It looked like a human figure. My tech tried to cut through the darkness, but it didn't have the clarity it usually produced.

Got something ahead, just standing there, I said.

I don't see it, Abbott replied.

It's not on scans, Dean said.

It's there, I insisted, *believe me.*

What is it? Trent questioned.

Can't tell yet. Looks human.

Break out, Abbott ordered.

The team scattered and took positions behind cargo bladders. I followed Abbott to a forward position behind a large container. We crouched and peered around its edge.

Can you tell what it is yet? Abbott asked.

I can't make it out. It's definitely not a Natierian–

Cameron?

Wren's voice broke against my mind like a rogue wave.

I mouthed "Wren" to Abbott and pointed to my head. *Is that you in front of us?*

Just a digital projection, she said. *Backed myself up on the ship's core. Not the best platform, but better than the alternative.*

I'm coming.

I broke from Abbott, formed a grav tunnel and launched myself forward.

"Harrison!" Abbott yelled. "What the hell are you–?!" *Do any of you see anything?* he asked over the open com.

Negatives and *No sirs* came back from everyone else. I didn't care … *I* heard her. She was alive.

As I approached, Wren's digital projection raised its arms and smiled. She was dressed in Davis's combat skin.

"Wren!" I shouted.

Her smile grew wider. *Hey babe.*

"Harrison, stop!" Abbott and the team were running after me.

All I could hear was what my heart wanted me to. I came out of the grav tunnel too fast and stumbled into Wren's projection. Something about the size of a pool cue tip punched me in the chest and abruptly stopped me. I heard the faint sound of meat sizzling. Wren's smiling image dispersed, and the figure of Enzo Vitale appeared from behind the pixels.

"Hello, Cameron." Regret filled his voice.

I looked down at a glowing shaft of pure white light plunged into my chest. The smell of burnt flesh filled my nostrils. With that realization came excruciating pain. It erupted from the impact point and surged through my body. Blood splashed against the back of my throat and seeped into my mouth. I gagged on it and coughed blood across the lined features of Enzo's face.

"It's time," he said, my blood dripping down his cheeks and lips.

I started to collapse. Enzo let go of the light knife's handle, its pulsating beam almost completely buried. He took my shoulders in both hands and regarded me as a father might a dying child. I fleetingly remembered the garage.

"For ... what?" More blood filled my throat. I gagged again and began to choke.

"To die," Enzo said sadly.

45

PRETTY CRAZY.

Contrary to popular belief, when you die you don't see your life flash before your eyes. At least I hadn't on the sidewalk in Rome, nor in Vitale's arms. Your vision fades out and like falling asleep, you just drift off.

You'd think that coming back from the dead would be old hat for me now, but it wasn't. One thing that was consistent was the pounding headache when you came to, like the one I had now.

It also takes a few moments for your vision to come back, so you're disoriented when you first open your eyes. That, coupled with the migraine, make for a shitty return to the land of the living.

I put a hand to my chest expecting to find a hole or something, but my fingers found only the snake texture of the combat skin. I sucked in a breath and exhaled my relief. Abbott and his team must have done some Calaian medical magic.

As my vision returned, I found myself on top of a large bed in a room that eerily resembled the one Bowman was in at the end of the movie *2001: A Space Odyssey.* The floor looked like bottom-lit plexiglass, and the furniture was awkwardly 18th century with Greco-Roman sculptures inset into semi-oval wall niches. Mercifully, no alien black monolith loomed over me.

I sat up and examined my chest again. There were no signs of damage or repair anywhere across the suit's surface. I closed my eyes, took another breath, and held it for a delicious second.

"Feeling better?"

I opened my eyes to find Davis standing at the foot of the bed. He was dressed in his grey business suit; the same cheap one he'd worn at Terilli's.

"If you mean better than dead, yes I'm feeling *a lot* better." I looked around. "What is all this? Where am I?"

Davis gestured to the room. "This is a biotechnologic cerebral regeneration construct. It allows for proper healing."

"Why the *2001* motif?"

"It was extracted from one of your recent memories. You went to a science-fiction film festival nine months ago. During the movie *2001: A Space Odyssey* you thought about what it would be like to wake up in this room. It seemed an appropriate setting."

"Davis, c'mon, I really enjoyed the movie, but I wouldn't want to *live* in it. How about something more comforting, like my own bedroom?"

The room morphed into my Dallas loft. I was now in my own bed.

"Better?" Davis asked.

"Yeah, thanks." I eyed the agent. "You're not Davis, are you?"

"I am a biotechnologic representation. We ascertained that you regarded Quinn Davis as a father figure, so we thought you would be more comfortable interfacing with his likeness."

"Why not just use my dad? I have tons of memories of him."

"We calculated that would be too difficult for you, given your estrangement with him during the last years of his life. With Quinn Davis, there is an acceptable amount of trust associated with him. Would this be better?"

The Davis avatar shifted into a likeness of Karen.

"Oh, God, no!" I covered my eyes.

Davis instantly returned.

"Thank you," I said rubbing my temples.

"Are you in discomfort?" it asked.

"Just a headache."

The pressure and pain vanished.

"Better?" the Davis avatar asked.

"Yes, thank—" Then it hit me with guttural raw clarity. I sucked in a fearful gasp. I frantically felt my chest and arms. Ran my fingers through my hair. Touched my face. I hesitated, dreading the answer. "Am I … *dead?*"

A merciful smile appeared on the avatar's face. "As a biological human male … yes."

A deep and primitive spike of shock carved through me. "W-what *am* I then?"

"You are now a biotechnologic digital entity cached in the Guardium Central Core on the terrestrial satellite called the moon."

Panic flooded my being. "What happened? Why am I a fucking *DE*?!"

"Your Calaian cerebral implant and its advanced biologic augmentations uploaded your life essence one point three milliseconds before your human functions terminated."

My mind flashed on Enzo's face. My blood dripping from his cheeks. The light knife in my chest.

"Yes, but I thought—"

A second Agent Davis formed in the middle of the room. He was dressed in a simple pair of khakis, a black polo, and a pair of black cross-trainers.

"There he is," the new avatar exclaimed, walking up with arms spread.

I climbed off and met it at the foot of the bed. The first Davis looked on with a very un-Davis-like grin.

"Is this the real you?" I asked, looking it over.

The new Davis glanced down at his body. "Well, not exactly." He jerked a thumb at the other Davis. "But I'm definitely not him … or it. I would've been here to greet you, but I got caught in traffic." He faced the avatar. "You can go now."

The first Davis disappeared in a falling curtain of translucent pixels.

The new one extended its hand. I tentatively shook it. It was warm, like a physical human.

"Did something happen? … Are you dead, too?" I asked.

"No, Cameron. I'm in the real world. I've entered your regeneration construct using an external cerebral link system."

"Quinn, what *happened?*"

"Well ... you died," he said rubbing the back of his neck. "Pretty brutally too. Vitale suckered you with a cerebrally generated image of Wren that only you could see. The Mirage hacked Winston's tech, which everyone thought was impossible. They also hacked the team's combat skins. That's why they didn't pick up the Wren image or Vitale."

"Natierian help?"

Davis shrugged. "Maybe."

"Why Enzo? I thought he was a good guy."

"The Mirage got to him."

I thought of the look on Enzo's face when he had stepped off the elevator in the Viceroy's building, after staying back to talk with Carina. Now it made sense.

"Through the Viceroys," I said.

"Definitely Carina. Some kind of blackmail, Calaian style. It's a cluster fuck, believe me. Abbott's starting to unravel it all."

"So what went down after I ... you know ... died?"

Davis explained that after Vitale had stabbed me, my cerebral tech went into auto-defense mode. It scanned the bay and took out every Mirage it could find, including Enzo. Davis and the team hunkered down until it was done wreaking its havoc. The only thing Dean could surmise was that with the eminent death of its host, the tech, which is essentially an AI, went a little crazy. It was probably because I was in revenge mode at the time of my death, so the AI followed that emotional path to the logical end. The few Mirage it didn't take out surrendered immediately, and they gave up a lot of intel on their Earth operations and the Viceroy moles. Abbott even got some insight into the whole Guardium connection.

"Pretty crazy, eh?" Davis said.

I nodded, but my mind was struggling with the whole being dead thing. I leaned against the bedpost.

"You okay, Cameron?"

"I don't know," I said. "I'm still trying to wrap my head around being reduced to a string of ones and zeros."

"Well, if it's any comfort, you're not a string of ones and zeros. Calaian technology is a whole different animal. But, yes, I can sympathize. ... You're not flesh and blood anymore."

I looked into his artificial face. "I know, right. How screwed up is *that?*"

"I guess it depends on your definition of life," a familiar voice answered from behind me.

I spun and saw Wren standing on the other side of the bed. She was dressed in the red gown she had worn to the Musée d'Orsay.

"Hi, babe," she said behind a timid smile.

"Wren!" I exclaimed. "But how?"

"I initiated an emergency disconnect from my ride just before I jumped in front of you."

"Smart move," Davis said. "Those stylus casters carry a contagion stream. ... It would've traced your cerebral signal back to the core and wiped you out. Now, I'll let you two get, ah, reacquainted. Nice to see you again, Liaison." He smiled and his avatar pixeled out.

I gazed at Wren, still not quite believing what I was seeing.

"You going to say anything," she asked, "or just stand there and undress me with your eyes?"

"I thought you were gone," I said, my voice catching.

"Don't get all mushy on me, soldier."

"You're the one with the tears."

Wren wiped her cheek with the back of her hand and opened her arms. "Come here, you."

I walked into her hug and put all my feelings into our kiss. Although we were just digital representations, she felt so real in my arms. I wanted her.

After an intense moment, we took each other in.

"Is this going to work?" It just came out.

"You mean us, as DEs?" she asked. "I have no idea."

"I know, but your people do this on Cala, right?"

"Only the elites. I've been transferred over a hundred times, but that's because I was property."

I kind of heard her, but part of me was still grappling with the fact that I had died back on the DSI ship. There was an emptiness growing deep inside me. My legs went weak. I sat on the edge of the bed.

"Cam, what's the matter?"

I glanced into Wren's beautifully rendered avatar eyes. I thought of my parents. Of the life I wouldn't have. Of never growing old. And lost it.

Wren sat and put an arm around me. "Oh, babe, it'll be okay."

"No, it won't! I'm dead, Wren … *dead*."

She took me by the shoulders and gently turned me to face her.

"Cam," she said, "you're not dead. You've just transferred to another state of being."

"I'm not flesh and blood." Tears trickled down my cheeks. "I'm a ... a fucking *game* character."

Wren took my face with both hands. "No you're *not*. You're still Cameron William Harrison. Your essence is alive, just as it was before."

I was teetering on the edge of a crumbling precipice. Behind me was my old life, anchored in history and a tangible reality. Over the edge was an unknown abyss of living without being alive.

"But where am I, Wren? ... Where's *me*?"

"Where were you before?"

"What?"

"Where was your life essence *before* you became a digital entity?"

"I-I don't know ... in my soul?"

"And where was your soul?"

"I ... um ... I don't know–"

Wren pulled me into a tight hug. "Feel my heart beating?" she whispered.

I nodded against her shoulder.

"How do you know it's mine?" she asked.

"I just do."

"Are you alive?"

"I guess so."

"How do you know *that*?"

"I just do," I whispered.

As we held each other, the loft shifted to an evening setting. Street noise wafted on a light breeze through the patio's open doors.

Wren pulled from our embrace and put a tender hand to my cheek.

"Do you love me?" she asked.

"I do."

"Show me."

*   *   *   *

We made love, but to be honest we spent most of the time just holding each other, letting our affection and desire play between us. I had never seen Wren so free. With her military tough-girl façade down, she laughed and cried and told me she loved me so many times I lost count. I did the same and we ended up in each other's arms, entangled in warm sheets and exhausted passion.

I made dinner and introduced Wren to expensive bourbon and grilled salmon and garlic mashed potatoes. My refrigerator was fully stocked, and I got the sense whatever I wanted would appear on its shelves if I just thought about it.

Wren explained that my regeneration construct built the environment utilizing only *my* memories. It couldn't create something I had never experienced firsthand, and the re-creation would be based on my recollection of it, not actual reality. But I couldn't fool the construct and think of my loft as a palatial suite. It knew better. Exactly how, Wren told me, was a Calaian trade secret, and if Wren's digital entity was in my construct, she had to obey its parameters.

"That's amazing," I said around a forkful of garlic mashed potatoes. "The old ten-thousand-year advantage, eh?"

"The what?" Wren asked.

Oh shit. "I shouldn't have said that."

"Why?"

"It's, um … something I used to say to Toni. I'm sorry."

Wren set her wineglass down. "It's okay. You've been with other people. So have I. Well, not people. Humans … You know what I mean."

We ate in silence for a while – Wren savoring every bite she took, me savoring her being alive.

"Do we grow old?" I asked finally.

Wren looked up, the last forkful of salmon poised halfway to her mouth.

"Technically no," she said. "I mean, I guess Cala's sun will eventually burn out and the planet and the Central Core will be destroyed, but that's billions of years away. We could program the construct to age us, but at what rate? And for how long? We could be in here for a thousand years and never realize it."

"So we can't really die?" I pressed.

"Oh yeah, we can die," she said matter-of-factly, chewing. "Elites do it all the time."

"How's that work?"

She swallowed. "Is this foreplay?"

"Ah, no," I laughed. "Just my paranoia."

"Okay, well, our rides do eventually age, even though the tech can slow the process down. But we can get a new ride, either the same body or a different one."

"What about *us* … our digital being. That doesn't age, right?"

"Correct."

"Then how do elites grow old?"

"When elites finally get tired of living for hundreds of years, they instigate what's referred to as the Death Decree. It's a program that initiates a countdown in the Central Core. Elites don't know how long they have, just that the end has been set and it's coming."

"Like life."

"Exactly."

"Do they age?"

"Uh-huh," she said around the rim of her wineglass.

"That's kind of poignant."

"Not really. It's not a sad thing. Don't forget, they've lived a long, *long* time."

I drank down what was left of my wine. "Are you ready for dessert?"

"Um, sure … yeah."

"What do you like?"

"I don't know. I've never had it."

"You're *kidding* me."

Wren leaned onto the table. "Babe, I've been working since I was born. Doing the nasty shit elites wanted done. I didn't have time or the luxury for *dessert*."

"That's all going to change." I stood and began gathering up our plates. "You're in for a real treat."

I walked to the kitchen and paused, pondering what a foolish thing I was doing. I wasn't real anymore. I was a digital recreation. I didn't need to wash dishes–

"Hey, Earthman."

I turned, plates still in hand.

Wren was standing near the table. She undid the sash and let her robe slip off her beautifully toned, naked body.

"I want *you* for dessert," she said, hitting me with sultry eyes.

I let go of the plates. They hit the floor, shattering into pieces around my feet. I stepped through the shards. Wren put her arms around my neck. I picked her up, carried her back to my bed and laid her gently onto the sheets. I pulled off my robe, slid up next to her and took her into my arms.

"Will it always be like this?" she asked, her lips close to mine.

"What?" I kissed her. "Our love?"

She pulled back. "Yeah."

"If we're lucky."

46

PROFOUND QUESTIONS.

With his ship destroyed, Abbott had assumed control of the DSI scout vessel. On one of his periodic visits, Davis mentioned they were still parked in the French Alps after three days, but to me and Wren, it felt like we had been in Dallas for several weeks. The discrepancy, according to Wren, was due in part to what was called declarative cognitive recollection. The construct's parameters were set by my DCR, and those were based on how I remembered Dallas. Since most of my memories were positive, it was rendered with a constant 72 degrees, sunshine and pleasant people. On top of that, we went to bed at night but didn't actually "sleep," so those hours weren't part of the linear timeline of our digital existence. Time moved quicker here. The Dallas representation wasn't accurate by any stretch, but it was perfect for now. Davis said our new rides would be ready in a few days, when we would leave our temporary paradise and rejoin the real world.

I sat at the kitchen counter and sliced bananas into my cereal. Wren came through the front door. She smelled of sweat and energy and her workout clothes clung to her in the best ways.

"How was your run?" I asked.

"Good." She grabbed a dishtowel off the counter and mopped her face. "Damn it's hot in Dallas."

"Really? I thought it was going to be in the low seventies today."

"Okay, I confess, I didn't run in Dallas."

"Where were you?"

"Buna. It's a Cala colony planet. I did a job there once. The construct was pretty accurate."

"Katy Trail not good enough?"

She chuckled. "It's okay, but Buna is awesome. My ride there was an arthropod. ... It had six legs ... pretty cool for running."

"Sorry, but on the *real* Earth you'll have to make do with two."

"That's okay." She walked around the island and fixed me in her sultry gaze. "The human form has a lot going for it." She playfully cupped my crotch. "Wanna have some fun?"

I flinched. "You're turning into a little sex machine?"

"I've been called worse." She snatched a banana slice from the bowl and popped it into her mouth. "Hmm, ripened ovary."

"It's called fruit."

"Fruit *is* ovaries. Or is it *are* ovaries? English is the stupidest of all Earth's languages."

"No argument here—"

A knock from the pantry door startled us. We exchanged questioning *that's weird* looks.

"You know it's unlocked," I called out.

Davis sheepishly stepped into the kitchen.

"Good morning, Agent Davis," Wren and I sing-songed before bursting into laughter.

Davis frowned. "Good morning, children."

"What are you doing coming in through the pantry?" I asked.

"I transposed two numbers putting in the front door coordinates," he said. "I've got good news, though. Your rides are ready."

Wren and I exchanged glances. A faint sense of sadness passed between us.

"Oh … that's great," Wren said unenthusiastically.

"What's the matter?" Davis asked. "I thought you'd be happy."

"We are, it's just…"

An impish smile crept across Davis's face. "You're having too much fun enjoying your virtual love nest, right?" His eyes went to the unmade bed. One of its king pillows was in the middle of the room.

Wren shrugged. "Well, *yeah.*"

"Quinn, we know this is all temporary," I said. "We're both happy our rides are ready."

"Better be," Davis said. "The Guardium bent the rules for you two. You know they're," he raised his fingers in air-quotes, "*eternally grateful* for what you did to bring down the Mirage threat on Earth." Davis pulled out one of the counter stools and sat. "Okay, so, there are a few final details they need to know before they bring your rides out of the tanks." He turned to Wren. "You're getting a copy of your old ride, the one *he* fell in love with. Do you want anything tweaked?"

"I had a lot done to the old one," she mused. "Will all that transfer to the new ride?"

Davis reached over and plucked a banana slice out of my bowl. "Yes, but you can enhance it again if you want."

"Can they enhance my vision? I noticed a little blurriness in the old ride."

"I'll find out." Davis threw his attention at me. "And for you?"

"How long will these rides live?" I asked.

"You're not getting a ride, you're getting your old body with Winston's tech intact. I assume it will age naturally. Liaison, you would know more about this."

"Most rides can be set up to live longer than a human," she said. "Since Cameron is getting his original body, it'll have the new tech still in it, so I assume it will be able to slow down the aging process."

"How long do we want to be together, babe?"

Something moved through Wren and washed away the happiness that had been radiating from her. She glanced at me, then Davis. Her bottom lip quivered as she fought the urge to cry.

"Whoa, babe, what's the matter?" I put an arm around her.

"It's nothing." Wren shook her head and fought the urge to cry. "Man, this feeling is an *ass*-kick." She closed her eyes and took in a breath. Her tough-girl front returned. "I just, um ... I've never been this happy before."

"That's good," Davis said. "Isn't it?"

"You don't understand. When you're a slave who can be repurposed again and again, you don't consider the idea of dying. ... You don't even fear it. You're just a possession, a tool. But now that I have you," she looked at me, "I don't want this to *end*."

Davis slid off the counter stool and put a hand to her shoulder.

"You don't have to make that decision right now," he said in a fatherly tone. "The Guardium has formally stated they will honor both your wishes, for as long as you want to live."

I kissed the top of her head. "My tough soldier girl," I whispered.

Wren grabbed her towel. "Thank you both for understanding," she said, dabbing her eyes. "These human emotions are really hard to manage sometimes."

"These are profound questions," Davis said. "They're not easy to answer."

"I do know one thing I want changed," I said. "I don't want us to get cancer or die from some horrible, drawn-out disease."

"I believe things like that can't happen with your new bodies." Davis studied his wrist screen. "I have to go." He started for the pantry, abruptly stopped, and headed for the front door.

"I have one more question," I said to his back.

The agent turned and raised an eyebrow.

"Can her new ride get pregnant?"

Davis's other eyebrow went up. He looked at Wren and back to me.

"Cameron," Wren said, her dismay showing, "are you *serious?*"

The feeling in my chest seemed to come from some untapped area deep in my soul.

"Yes ... I am."

47

BORN AGAIN.

I had friends who were "born again" Christians, and while I respected their beliefs, religion had never been important to me. Not that I didn't believe in a higher power; I just couldn't buy into the idea of an all-knowing intelligence controlling the universe. But considering what I'd experienced over the course of the last few months ... well, let's just say I was questioning *every-thing*.

We stood in the living area, just off the kitchen. I took Wren's hand.

"You ready?" I asked.

She rolled her eyes. "Newby."

"Okay, so it's my first time. Cut me some slack."

"It's no big deal. One second you're here in the loft construct, the next you're on a table with Davis looking down at you. In the physical world. You won't feel a thing, I promise."

"You two ready?"

Davis's baritone filled the construct like an omniscient god. Wren snapped to attention.

"Yes," I said.

"We'll count down from five," he said. "They've asked that you stand a little farther apart."

Wren let go and took a large step sideways.

"That's good." Davis cleared his throat. "Okay. On my mark ... mark. Five."

"See ya on the other side," Wren said.

"Four."

"I love you," I said.

"Three."

"I love you more," Wren replied.

"Two."

"I love you to infinity."

"*One*."

Wren glanced at me, stuck her tongue out impetuously, and dissolved away in a distortion of color and texture. I stood there for an awkward second.

"Hello?" I called out, looking around.

The loft was eerily quiet, as if the construct's sound had been cut off. No street noise, no birds chirping, not even the hum of the refrigerator.

"Davis, what's going on?"

Silence.

"Okay, guys, this isn't funny."

A translucent orange-blue vapor began to coalesce in the center of the space.

"Oh, *shit.*"

A Natierian took shape and hovered. Three lightning bolts shot off in rapid succession inside it.

"Cameron ... Harrison." It was the same voice as before, but it reverberated around the loft like an actual sound wave.

I thought of my tech engaging, but I didn't have any. ... I was in a damn construct.

"What do you *want* from me?!" I yelled.

The vapor moved forward. I took a few steps back and bumped into the kitchen island. The vapor stopped about ten feet away.

"I don't have the tech in me," I said. "I'm a digital entity, thanks to you. I'm not a threat."

"You were never a threat," it said.

"You tried to kill me."

"We tried to assimilate the technology. You attacked us."

"Well, yeah ... that lightning beam, ray-thing came out of you and my tech autoengaged. Besides, I thought my tech had screwed up your master plans for humanity."

"We are not concerned with humanity."

"Then what the hell do you *want?*"

"Your advanced biotechnologistics."

"Then go get it! It's in my old body. Commander Abbott probably has it."

"It has to be sentient. You have to be in the body."

"Why don't you just make it yourselves if you're so advanced."

"It is not for us," it said. "It is for the Calaians."

"The tech doesn't work in Calaians like it does in me."

"We have a solution for that."

"I bet you do." I ran my hands through my hair and paced the room. The vapor followed. I motioned for it to back off, and it retreated to the center of the kitchen. "You're not going away, are you?"

"We have infinite time."

"Great. Okay, you want the tech, but the tech will protect me and it-self." I spread my arms. "It's a standoff. What do we do?"

"We can extricate the advanced biotechologistics without damaging your body."

"The beam thing again?"

"We have a less invasive method planned."

"But then I'll be back to my old self, right?"

"You will have the biotechologistics that maintain your digital exist-ence."

"Same body?"

"Yes."

"Why can't you just duplicate the tech, so I can keep my Superman powers?"

"It is not possible."

"I figured you'd say that. You know, Davis isn't going to want to give up his new weapon."

"He will adjust. Are we in agreement?"

"Let's review. I let you take Winston's tech out of my body and give it to the Calaians. In exchange, you don't bother humanity and I go back to being … what? Not exactly what I was, but I'm still myself with the basic gravitational protection package?"

"Essentially."

"Bullshit. Y'all don't make simple moves. There's something else going on. What is it?"

"The technology will help the Calaian civilization. Nothing else should concern you. Are we in agreement?"

It still didn't feel right, but if this could keep the Natierians out of humanity's future then it seemed worth it. I was going to miss playing Superman. "Okay, you have a deal."

"We will place you into your body. Please prepare yourself."

I spread my feet and straightened my shoulders. "Hey, wait, when are you–?"

48

HAPPILY, EVER AFTER.

"Cam? Are you in there?"

I opened my eyes to one of the big chrome service drones, like the one that zapped Toni. It was a few inches from my face and seemed to be regarding me like I was its patient. It retreated into the darkness above me. Davis's face slid in from the edge of my peripheral vision.

"Welcome back." His smile looked a little forced as he came into focus. "There's someone here who wants to say hi." He stepped aside, and in the adjacent glass-walled room I saw Wren dressed in jeans and a white camisole, sitting on a metal table. She smiled and wiggled her fingers in a sarcastically cute *hello.*

I started to wave back but stopped. The childhood scar on the back of my hand from when I had been sledding as a kid and wiped out into Tommy Truedson caught my attention. I sat up, raised the black t-shirt they had me in and inspected my chest. A tiny, inch-long scar ran vertically down my sternum. I touched my face, then pinched the skin on my forearm.

"It's your original body," Davis said reassuringly.

I grabbed him. "Is Wren okay?" The panic in my voice surprised even me.

"She's perfectly fine, Cameron." His eyes went to the death grip I had on his forearm. "Is something wrong?"

I frantically motioned for Wren to come over. Alarm washed across her face. She hopped off her table and pushed through the door that connected the two glass rooms.

"What's going on?" she asked, coming up to the table's side.

I put a hand to her cheek just to feel if she was real.

"It's you, right?" I asked with the same anxiety. "This is all real?"

She nodded and took my shoulders. Her grip was strong. "Cam, what's the *matter?*"

"How long did mine take?" I asked both of them.

"Your transference?" Davis questioned. "Same as the Liaison's. Four seconds."

"No way," I said.

"What are you talking about?" Wren relaxed her hold.

"Babe, when you left the loft ... I didn't."

"*What?*" Davis frantically referenced his black tablet. "That's impossible. You and Wren transferred at exactly the same time. It's in the data logs."

"Cameron," Wren asked gravely, "what happened after I left the construct?"

I told them about the Natierian forming, about our conversation and the deal we struck. Davis was visibly pissed. Wren looked concerned, but not freaked.

"Are you okay with all this?" I asked Davis.

"I won't lie to you, Cameron, I thought you wanted to make a difference." He shrugged. "But it's your body, your life. I can't force you to do something you don't want to do."

"What about you, babe? ... You okay with me not being your superhero boyfriend?"

"It's up to you," Wren said. "You'll still have the ability to use the tech's basic gravity control for protection. But if you're worried about how I feel, don't. I'll love you even if you're not Superman."

"Did they give any indication *when* they would remove the tech?" Davis asked.

"No. They transferred me before I could ask. They said they couldn't do the extrication until I was conscious and in my body. Something about the tech had to be active and in a living host."

Davis backed away and referenced his tablet again.

"What are you doing?"

"Checking your tech," he said, tapping at the screen.

The chrome service drone lowered from the ceiling's darkness and stopped about a foot from my face. It took all my willpower not to jump off the table.

"Hold still," Davis ordered.

I did and the drone slowly approached until its leading edge barely touched my forehead.

After a few seconds Davis looked up from his tablet. "Everything's intact and functioning."

The drone backed away and floated up into the shadows.

"Any idea how the Natierians will take the tech?" Wren asked.

"Supposedly," I said, "the beam that came out of the other Natierian – the one I crushed – was trying to take the tech out of me. They claim they have a less invasive procedure planned. I'm not sure I believe that."

"Pretty violent methodology," Davis grumbled. "I don't like this. It's not so much that you're losing your special abilities … I'm concerned about them giving it to the Calaians."

I rubbed my face. It felt exactly like it had before I died, even down to the late morning stubble. "Why are you so concerned? So what if the Natierians give the Calaians the technology? It's not like they can't handle it. They already manipulate gravity and travel the stars." I glanced at Wren. "Right?"

"I'm not worried about the good Calaians getting it," Davis remarked. "I'm worried about the *bad* ones."

"The Northern House," Wren said, more to herself.

"Toni's," I said. "I thought it was a good House."

"It's not so black and white," Davis said.

He and Wren exchanged quick glances.

"Agent Davis," Wren said, "can you give us a few minutes?"

Davis nodded, but his eyes remained full of their shared concern. He passed through the door to Wren's glass-walled room and left by another on the opposite side.

I swung my legs off the side of the table and Wren stepped between them and took my hands.

"First," she said, "I want you to know … well … I love you very much."

I squeezed her hands. "I love you, too, very much."

"I know you had something with the High Sovereign. It's not my place to know the details. That's between you and her–"

"It's okay. I can handle whatever it is you're going to tell me."

Wren nodded like what she was about to divulge wouldn't be pretty. "What did Toni tell you about her House and her father?"

"He was a corporate tech titan, like Steve Jobs. He had a vision for Cala, a noble one, I guess. He tried to change the government or something and failed. And he was murdered for it. I got the impression he and the Northern House are still loved by the downtrodden of Cala?"

Wren patted my hands. "That is *part* of the story. Yes, Toni's father was a leader of, well, we don't call it business, it's more of a position in society, and he did have a vision, but it wasn't noble. He believed in the system that I grew up in – the stratification of the population. The separation of higher-level species."

"So you're a certain type of species, Toni's another, and so on?"

Wren nodded.

"How many different higher-level species are on Cala?"

"Five."

"I thought there were just four Houses. Northern, Southern, Eastern and Western?"

"That's what Toni wanted you to believe. There are four main Houses, but there is a fifth. It's considered the lowest and it's not referenced as a House, typically."

"This is the House you come from, right?"

She nodded again, almost apologetically.

The revelation that Wren came from the slums of Cala didn't surprise me. I affectionately rubbed her hands.

"Toni's father," she went on, "wanted to abolish the House that I come from. Something to do with balancing the economic strata."

"Jesus, you're talking genocide. That's why you're so tough, so street smart. You fought your way out."

Wren looked away and closed her eyes. "I did more than fight. ... I did other things, things I'm not proud of."

"Hey, I don't care what you've done."

Wren looked back into my eyes, her anguish visible. "Cam ... I ... I did disgusting things."

I drew her close. "Wren, you *survived*. You beat the odds. Yeah, you did some nasty shit, but it made you strong and tough." A lone tear rolled down her cheek. I gently wiped it away with my thumb. "Come on now. You've never showed any emotion except maybe kick-ass."

"Technically, that's not an emotion."

"Why the tears?"

"You make me happy," she said. "I don't know how to process that. It's, uh, it's hard for me to trust anyone."

"That's understandable, but you trust me, right?"

She nodded, albeit hesitantly.

"Hey, we got off track. What was your point about Toni's father?"

"The Northern House still harbors her father's ideology. If they get Winston's tech …"

"Are the Mirage from your House?"

"They mostly come from the Ruling Elite's Black Guard, but yes, they're from my House. They were slaves, just like I was."

"That's why they want asylum and the tech. To level the playing field."

"They're extremists, Cam. They don't care about rules. The Northern House can't be allowed to have Winston's tech. They'll wipe out my species."

"And the Mirage can't have the tech, because they would wipe out the Northern House?"

"Yes."

"Then we'll just have to tell the Natierians the deal's off."

"You don't tell Natierians what to do. They have some universe-changing reason why they want to give Cala the tech."

"Do they want to give it to Cala," I asked slowly, "or just the Northern House?"

The revelation moved across Wren's face. "Oh *no*."

"Well," I said as I brushed a stray lock of wavy hair off her forehead, "so much for living happily ever after."

49

SETTLE YOUR DEAL.

The glass rooms where we had "arrived" were in a warehouse adjoining Abbott's main operations in Dallas. Davis told him about my deal with the Natierians and my decision not to give them the tech. He relayed the commander's reaction – a stern grunt and a nod. Davis also pointed out that keeping the tech left me at the Guardium's mercy. It would be only a matter of time before they came calling.

Somewhere over the last several weeks I had lost my cell phone. Davis presented me with a new one after I transferred. It probably had some secret spy tracking app on it. While I waited for Wren to come back (she needed to have something tweaked with her new ride), I went through about a hundred unread emails and texts. Of the few clients I had left after last year's economic downturn, most of them had kicked me to the curb because I had gone MIA. Not too tragic, given that I was never going be a web designer again. But the texts from Josh were upsetting. Early on he playfully gave me shit for not replying, since he thought Toni and I had become an item. I'd sent him a text saying things had gotten complicated, because it wasn't like I was going to go into any sort of detail. But as the weeks passed and I didn't reply, his texts grew angrier until the penultimate one said he'd gone to my loft and spoken with my neighbor, who was also worried about me. His final text said he was tired of my bullshit and to go fuck myself. ... No silly emojis, just the text in all caps with exclamation points.

"May I come in?"

I looked up to find Dean standing in the glass room's doorway.

"Oh, hey there, sure ... what *is* your name?"

"Michael Tolbert."

"How do y'all get these names?"

"They're generated prior to deployment. I've been told they're supposed to be nondescript, so as not to draw attention."

"Do you know you look like–"

"The American actor James Dean? Yes, I get that all the time. Commander Abbott wanted me to see how you were feeling after your transfer."

"I won't lie to ya, Mike, it's really weird. I mean, it doesn't feel any different than when I was alive."

"It shouldn't," Tolbert said matter-of-factly. He glanced at my phone. "Catching up?"

"Seems my old life is going away."

"It will. Also, I thought you might want to know the condition of the High Sovereign."

"How is she?"

"Much better. I believe she'll be leaving Earth and returning to Cala soon. She was wondering if you could meet with her."

"Sure. When?"

Tolbert did the blank stare thing. "She's pleased you accepted," he said, blinking back into focus. "This morning, if possible. She's in the center, where the living quarters are."

"Let me check with Davis and Wren and get back to you."

Tolbert nodded and turned to leave.

"Hey, Mike?"

"Yes?" he asked, opening the glass door.

"Thanks for everything you and the team did. I wouldn't be here if it weren't for y'all."

"I'm sure we will be seeing you again. I wish you and the Liaison all the best." His tone was completely flat and insincere.

He left just as Wren entered the other glass room. They talked for a moment next to the table where she had arrived, shook hands, and Tolbert left.

"I'll tell you, that's the kind of soldier you want watching your back," Wren said walking in. She sensed my energy. "You look like you just got some bad news."

"Toni wants to see me. She's going back to Cala."

"Oh ... okay. That's cool. When?"

"This morning. Do you think it's a good idea?"

"I don't have a say. I know Davis wants to meet and discuss how we'll deal with the Natierians. Maybe you should go see her now and get it out of the way." Her military tough-girl tone bordered the words like an order.

I hopped off the table. "Yeah, I probably should."

I started to leave when she took my arm.

"There's something else." She stepped close. "What is it?"

"I was just going through my emails and texts. Kind of depressing."

"You can't go back to your old life."

"I know, it's just—"

"What, Cam?"

"I think I've lost my best friend."

Wren let go and patted my chest. "Go see Toni."

"What are you going to do?"

"Figure out a way to make your friend understand."

*   *   *   *

Since my so-called vacation had turned into an intergalactic shitstorm, it was now late summer in North Texas. I stepped out of the warehouse where rides were produced, and a blast of hot air hit me like the exhaust from a semi. I hustled across an exterior loading dock into the next warehouse. I recognized it as soon as I entered the main door. Wren brought me here after clocking Davis upside the head weeks ago.

Sato met me inside. "She's waiting for you. Follow me."

Sato led me past the workstation area and a few heads popped up: Trent and the other Mars pilot whose name I never caught, and two new folks wearing the face-hugger tech. They stared me down as I passed. Beyond the apartment modules was a free-standing temporary structure that reminded me of the surgical tent we built in Vitale's garage. Sato unzipped the door flap, held it back and gestured for me to enter.

I ducked through and found Toni seated in a low-tech wheelchair. At the sound of my entry, she grabbed the wheels and spun it around.

"Hi, Cameron." Her smile was soft but hesitant. Her hands went to her lap.

I stopped a few steps inside. "Hi, Toni."

"Your High Sovereign," Sato said from the door flap, "just link with me when you're done."

Toni's smile brightened. "Thank you."

We both watched Sato zip the flap shut.

"She's been such a trooper." Toni's attention moved to me. "Trooper's correct, isn't it?"

"Yeah."

She stretched her arms toward me. Her right hand had a slight tremor. "Give me a hug, please."

I crossed the space between us, knelt and slid my arms around her. She rested her head against my shoulder. We stayed like that for a minute, sharing whatever energy was left of our feelings for one another.

"This feels good," she said.

After another minute we pulled apart, but still held each other's hands. I stayed on one knee.

"How are you doing?" I asked.

"A lot better than the last time you saw me."

"What happened to your legs?"

"They haven't come back online." She rubbed the tops of her thighs. "It doesn't really matter now. I won't be using this ride after today. I'm able to transfer now that this ride's brain has healed."

"Why don't they just create you a new ride, like this one?"

"They did, but I wanted to experience this." She rubbed the top of her legs again. "This must be very difficult for humans." She looked up, her face framed in pity. "Abbott says you're a digital entity now. I'm so sorry, Cam. Was it painful?"

"The dying part was. But at least I'm here, sort of. Tolbert says you're going to Cala?"

"Not yet. The moon facility first. Before I'm back in my own body, I need to … um," she put a trembling hand to her forehead, "I can't think of the word."

"Recuperate?"

"Yes, recuperate. I need some me-time, as a Calaian."

"If I had a me, I'd go for some of that time myself."

"What's it like … being a DE?"

The reality of my situation had been weighing on the nape of my neck like a boulder ever since I'd transferred. "You know, Toni, I can't really tell the difference from being physically alive to this, uh, state. It's pretty seamless, but I'm having a hard time dealing with the idea of being dead."

"I'm so sorry, Cam. I never wanted any of this to happen. I just wanted to come to Earth and get away from the troubles on Cala."

"Then you met me."

The smile that appeared seemed built from pain. "Yes, I did."

"Do you regret that?"

"Cam, I'll always cherish our time together."

We hugged again, a little longer than our first. She felt good in my arms, and my heart went to the time we had when everything was fresh and new and intense. I pulled out of our embrace and took her hands. I could feel the tremor.

"Listen, Toni, there's something dangerous going down. It involves the Natierians and your House. Don't go back to Cala. Stay on Earth for a while. Your life could be in danger. *Serious* danger."

"Cam, you're scaring me. What's going on?"

"Winston augmented my tech again, and this time it's crazy powerful. I stopped Abbott's ship at sub-light."

Her look was a mixture of confusion and disbelief. "That's incredible."

"Yeah, and the Natierians want it."

She shook her head. "For some masterplan, probably."

"We think they want to give it to your House. We don't know why. Wren's afraid your father's followers will use it to wipe out her species. She's from the Fifth House."

Toni let out a disgusted sigh. "I hate what my father became. His ideology, those who rallied behind him. That's why I left."

"Why didn't you tell me about your father's agenda?"

"I didn't want you involved."

"Well, *that* didn't work." We shared a brief chuckle.

"Don't go back," I pleaded, "at least not until all this settles down. And please don't feel weird about reaching out. Wren knows what you meant to me. She's totally cool with it."

"I'll be safe at our moon facility. And I'll let you know when I return, I promise." She lifted my hands to her lips and kissed them.

"Toni?"

She raised her eyes. "Yes?"

"Back in the medical bay ... when you were in recovery ... did you hear what I said to you?"

A faint smile appeared. "I love you, too, Cam."

As I left, I couldn't help but feel I was leaving part of myself behind, a few brief moments lost somewhere in a wonderful past.

Sato was loitering in the kitchen area, impassively stirring her coffee with a plastic straw. "How did it go?" she asked.

"As good as it could have." I turned to leave.

"I'm going back to Cala in a few days."

I stopped and faced her.

"Being reassigned," she said, "as soon as the High Sovereign transfers."

"Well, Sato ... I've enjoyed getting to know you."

The pretty Asian nervously tucked a lock of dark hair behind an ear. "You're becoming known. Do you know that?"

"What do you mean?"

"Your ability ... to bend gravity. You stopped our ship at *sub-light.* You're quite possibly the most powerful being on either of our planets, and you haven't even reached your potential. Soon, everyone on Cala will know of you."

"Great, maybe I can do the late-night shows."

"This isn't funny, Cameron."

"Actually, it is." I stepped toward her. "In case you haven't heard, I'm dead. This," I gestured down my body, "is an illusion ... to you *and* me. I have no idea if my consciousness is even real, or if it will develop in the same way it did when I was flesh and blood. For all I know, all this," I looked to the space around us, "could be AI-generated to fool me into doing things I normally wouldn't do."

"Oh, it's real," Abbott said, approaching from behind.

"It damn well better be," I replied.

Abbott casually took a paring knife off the counter. "Give me your hand."

I offered my left hand. He grabbed it and twisted it palm up. He poised the tip of the blade above my skin. I flinched and tried to pull out of his grip. He pressed the blade down harder, just shy of drawing blood.

"Real enough?" he asked.

"What the *hell*, Abbott?"

"Do you feel the fear flush through your nervous system? The instinctual reflex to pull out of my grip? Are those fake or are those the reactions of Cameron Harrison?"

I jerked free and Abbott placed the knife back onto the counter.

"Sorry for the dramatics," he said. "Digital existence is often best demonstrated with a visceral experience. Did you feel exactly like you did when you were alive?"

"Pretty much."

"And you reacted like yourself ... your *real* self. Can you feel your digital being in the core? Do you have any sense your thoughts are coming from somewhere else?"

"No. It's seamless."

"Then what's the problem?"

"You wouldn't understand."

"Are you sure about that?" A faint smirk played around his mouth.

"Are *you* a DE?"

The commander nodded. "Your species isn't at a point to understand yet, but the definition of life will someday change for the human race. You're just ahead of the curve."

"Commander?" Tolbert said, trotting up.

Abbott turned, the smirk dying into a quizzical scowl. "What?"

"They're here, sir. Out by the pad."

The uneasy breath Abbott sucked in suggested this would be the worst part of his week.

"How many?" he asked.

"Four, so far. Others are still forming."

"What's going on?" I asked.

Abbott's attention swung on me like a wrecking ball.

"Time to settle up on your deal."

50

CRAM IT UP YOUR GALACTIC ASS.

The "pad" was the area where Abbott's ship used to park. As we rounded the front of the apartment modules, I could see the signature Natierian bluish-green light dance in large, animated swells across the warehouse's far walls. Sporadic flashes of intense white light punctuated the scene.

"Dramatic entrance," Sato remarked.

"I *hate* Natierians," Abbott countered through gritted teeth.

The light show intensified as we angled around the back of the apartments. Wren and Davis were already there, standing near the exterior wall of the last module. In the center of the huge pad area, seven Natierian vapor forms undulated just off the cement floor. They differed in mass and height, but all displayed the same internal lightning show as the others. These Natieri-ans, though, were enveloped in some sort of mist displaying the same mix of colors.

"Have they done anything yet?" I asked Wren.

"No, they've just been manifesting." She pointed to a smaller Natierian on the end. "That one was the last to form."

Trent, the Manga blonde and Tolbert trotted up behind us. All were carrying the same intimidating black Calaian rifle. They handed one to Abbott. Its design seemed to merge with his hand and arm when he took it. Keeping their weapons at their sides, they formed into a loose line in front of us.

Abbott stepped forward, put his hands on his hips and regarded the Natierians with contempt born of centuries of suspicion.

"Is he cerebrally linking with them?" I whispered to Wren.

"Doubt it," she whispered back.

"You don't engage Natierians first," Sato said over her shoulder.

"They engage you," Tolbert added.

Abbott, clearly frustrated, glanced back and shook his head.

"Have you tested your tech since you transferred?" Davis asked me.

"No ... why?"

"This'll be interesting."

Out of the corner of my eye, I caught Toni wheeling toward us. Sato ran over and knelt. The two exchanged words until Toni made an angry ges-ture that signaled the conversation was over. Sato begrudgingly began pushing the wheelchair toward us.

"Toni, what are you doing here?" I demanded.

"This directly concerns my House." Her voice had the same resonance she used with the Viceroys, a kind of weaponized regality. "As the highest-ranking living member of my House, I need to be here–"

The mist around the Natierians suddenly swirled into a tall arch above them. A curtain of light cascaded down, and a new form began to take shape about five feet in front of them. Abbott took a few cautionary steps back. The new Natierian manifested, but instead of a vaporous shape it coalesced into human form. After a few seconds, the original ride of Tucker Winston appeared.

"Son of a bitch," Davis said under his breath.

"Is that really *him*?" I asked. "Flesh and blood?"

Wren checked her tablet. "Looks like it."

The Great One smiled out from behind the residual haze. "Commander Abbott."

"Thought you were dead, Winston," Abbott replied. "What'd you do? Make a deal with the devil, or are the Natierians your new masters?"

"I'm not a slave to *anyone*, Commander."

"Why the hell are you here?"

"Human interaction can be challenging for the Natierians, so they've asked me to facilitate. And since I'm the creator of the technology, they felt I would be the best intermediary."

"Since you're alive, why do the Natierians need Cameron? You can create the tech for them. You're the genius that started all this crap."

"Commander, Natierians don't *do* anything. They have others do it for them, and the technology is adaptive. It integrates with the host's nervous system and much of its biologic structure–"

"Then how *the hell* do you get it out of me?" I knew where this was going. Might as well cut to the chase. I pushed between the Manga blonde and Trent and walked to Abbott's side.

Winston's scrutiny hit me with an almost incomprehensible weight, like he was connected into some vast knowledge base that stretched into the deepest reaches of time and space.

"Mr. Harrison. I see you've adapted to your new station in life." He shifted his attention to Abbott. "Commander, the Natierians want to limit who they deal with in this matter."

Abbott folded his arms defiantly across his chest. "Don't give me that–"

Before he could finish, Abbott collapsed into a heap next to me. I heard the others behind me likewise collapse. I quickly surveyed the damage. Wren was on top of Davis, and a small puddle of blood was spreading under the Manga blonde's head. Toni was the only one who hadn't succumbed. Our eyes met and I saw my own shock mirrored there. I turned on Winston, fists raised.

He put his hands up. "Easy, human. They're unharmed."

"So help me, motherfucker–"

"We've just taken them all off-line." He motioned to Toni. "You can approach."

Toni started to roll herself toward us.

"No, you can walk now."

She stopped and glared.

"Your legs will work." He gestured with both hands as if coaxing a toddler to take her first step.

Toni cautiously lifted herself out of the chair. She took a few wobbly steps and straightened. She gave Trent's body a wide berth and shuffled next to me.

"How does that feel?" Winston asked.

"Like I'm being bribed," she answered.

"Your *Highness*. Don't be so cynical–"

"Tucker, you know I can't allow this technology to be brought to Cala." The regal tone again.

"And I'm not going to let you have it," I added.

"Well then," Winston regarded us sternly, "we'll have to do this the hard way."

I was reaching the end of my digital entity rope. I raised my fists again. "Listen, asshole, you and your Natierian masters can take your omnipotence and cram it up your galactic asses. You're not getting the tech, so tell them to leave Cala *alone*."

"That attitude won't help you, Harrison," Winston said.

"Tucker," the tone in Toni's voice came out more like a plea, "my father's allies will use the tech to destroy the Fifth House. ... That's genocide. Surely the Natierians *know* this."

"There's a higher outcome to be attained. ... It has to do with evolutionary shifts and species-capital. I'm a genius and *I* don't understand it all, but I don't have to. Not my position."

"What *is* your position?" I asked.

The Great One leveled his all-powerful gaze again. "Surgeon."

I engaged my combat tech and the grav field rippled across my fists. The lightning inside the Natierians grew frantic.

"It doesn't have to go down like this," I said.

"Cameron, you're a DE," Winston implored. "Just let the Natierians take what they want. The Guardium will grow you a new ride. It'll be just like your original body. … Better."

"It's not about him," Toni said. "It's about *her*." She gestured back at Wren.

Winston shuttled a glance at Wren and back to us. Confusion swam behind his eyes. He gestured and Wren sat up with a loud gasp. She rolled off Davis. Her eyes went to me, then to Abbott's team. She sprang to her feet like a cat and stormed up to my side.

"Winston," Wren demanded, "what the *hell* are you doing?"

"What should have been done decades ago." Winston's frustration leaked out. "Harrison, the Natierians will take the tech, one way or another."

"The Northern House will use it to destroy my species!" Wren's words contained the rage of a lifetime of slavery.

"You don't know that, Liaison."

Toni took an angry step forward. "You have *no idea* what you're talking about. You come from privilege and level. Your species has never had anything to fear. Ever. But since you invented the cerebral technology her kind has been enslaved. Tell them, Tucker." She took another step forward. "Tell them why you're *really* on Earth."

"What's she talking about?" I asked Wren.

"Go on," Toni demanded. "Tell them."

Winston shook his head. "High Sovereign, this will not–"

"*Tell* them!"

The depth and authority in Toni's voice startled us all. Winston grabbed his head and sank to one knee.

Toni went and stood over him like the angel of death. "Tell them about the thousands of Fifth House children who were *slaughtered* and what you're planning for Earth!"

Clawing his head, the Calaian legend crumpled to his side. He curled into a fetal position and shrieked. The Natierian forms floated back about 20 feet, internal lightning firing wildly.

Toni's rage physically manifested in a grav field that shimmered across her body. She raised a fist. "My father–"

"Was a *fool.*" Winston forcibly raised his eyes and met her wrath. "He lost faith! He tried to stop us!"

"Is that why you *killed* him?!"

Winston's eyes rolled back as he fought Toni's cerebral invasion. "*Yes!*"

The scream that erupted from Toni carried all the hate and guilt and despair she had been suppressing for years. Her grav field enveloped Winston's body. He struggled to fight it off. He convulsed onto his back, screamed, and his head exploded. Trapped inside the field, the gore swirled around his upper body like it had with the Asshole Deluxe. Toni brought her hands together and her grav field gruesomely compressed Winston's body into nothingness. She sucked in a tattered gasp and her knees buckled. Wren and I rushed to her side.

I cradled her head in my lap. "Toni? *Toni?*"

Wren pulled out a tablet and held it to Toni's forehead. "She's flatlining."

Abbott and his team started to regain consciousness.

"Sato, help!" I called out.

"She's really dying!" Wren yelled.

Sato groggily sat up and forced herself to focus. Shock swept across her face. She stumbled over, went to her knees, and pulled a tablet from behind her back.

"Commander," she said, her fingers dancing across the screen. "I need you here, *now*!"

"What's *happening*?!" I pleaded.

Sato shook her head. "Her tech is failing. She should be able to disengage, but she hasn't." She shot a savage look over her shoulder. "Abbott!"

The commander staggered over, still grappling with the aftereffects of whatever knocked them offline.

"What do you have?" he asked kneeling.

"Her vitals are in freefall and her tech is in a cascade shutdown. ... I can't reverse it."

"Get her next door."

"I got it," I said.

I built a grav field around Toni's body, lifted her off the floor and hurried toward the main exit. Wren joined me.

Sato pointed to an internal hallway. "This way."

I adjusted the grav field in that direction when something stopped us both. It felt like an invisible hand grabbed hold and wouldn't let go. Sato, who was trotting behind, bumped into Toni's grav field and sent ripples across its surface.

"Why have you stopped?" Sato demanded.

"I haven't." I struggled to move forward. "Something's ... holding us."

Wren and I saw it at the same time. The Natierian mist had drifted under Toni's body and was beginning to envelope her.

"Commander!" Sato's attention was locked onto something behind me. "They're approaching."

I looked back and saw the Natierians floating toward us.

"Ready weapons!" Abbott ordered.

Trent, Tolbert and the Manga blonde, blood matted on the side of her head, stood and raised their black rifles. High-pitched whines filled the air.

I engaged my tech. The back of my shoulders and neck flushed with an intense internal heat. The grav field undulated in front of my fists. I felt like a lion poised to strike.

The Natierians were almost on us.

"Commander," Trent called out, "they're not stopping."

"Stop or I'll destroy you!" I yelled.

The silence back hit me in the gut like Marco's knife.

"Wait!" Abbott said.

"I'm not going to let them take her!"

"No! Cameron, *let* them!"

"Are you insane? They'll–"

"They might help. It could be her only chance."

I shot a quick glance at Wren.

"He's right," she said.

I reluctantly disengaged. Abbott's team lowered their weapons.

Toni's body remained suspended inside the mist. The Natierian forms surrounded and engulfed her. As they merged with the mist one by one, Toni's body slowly was obscured. The dense cloud silently drifted to the pad area, reformed into a sphere, and faded away.

51

OH, I THINK WE CAN.

After the cloud that held Toni disappeared, Wren and I crashed in the apartment module where I had stayed before. Abbott had nothing to offer beyond "Be patient" and "I'll let you know" when he heard from the moon base.

Wren sat next to me on the edge of the bed. She put a hand to the back of my neck and kneaded my tense muscles. I let a weary sigh drain out. "Do you think Abbott's right? … That the Natierians will help Toni?"

"Hard to say," she said. "Their motives operate on a different level than other species."

"How was she able to take out Winston? I thought Calaians couldn't use their tech against each other."

"I … I don't know. Maybe she had her tech altered."

"Maybe the Natierians helped her?"

Wren's pensive nod was interrupted by a knock at the door.

"Come in," I said.

Davis stuck his head around the door frame. "Am I interrupting?"

I waved him in.

"Feels like a damn wake in here," he said as he settled into a lounger.

"Just trying to regroup," I said.

"I've got good news. Toni the Calaian is alive and resting comfortably at the moon facility. Seems our gaseous friends are more benevolent than we thought."

A wave of relief splashed against my soul.

"I still don't trust them," Wren grumbled.

"Most Calaians don't," Davis countered.

"Think they'll be back?" I asked.

Davis paused. "Probably not."

"But they didn't get the tech."

"We don't think they ever really wanted it."

"Then why all that bullshit we just went through?"

"You know how they work, with their grand projections and civilization-changing nudges. There's probably something else in play, we just don't see it yet."

"Think we'll ever know why?"

"Hundred years from now. Maybe."

Davis's words lingered.

Wren cut the pregnant silence. "What's next?"

Davis rubbed his late-day stubble as he considered the question. "I guess you two are free to go. We don't have anything for you … right now."

"That sounds ominous," I said.

"Look, Cameron, I won't lie. We're going to lean on you occasionally. Tap into that cerebral gravity muscle of yours."

"To do what?"

"Little stuff … like saving the world."

"What about the Viceroys?" Wren asked.

She nailed it. The powerful Calaian entity had us in velvet handcuffs.

"You know as well as I do, they're *always* around. But I can't speak for them. We don't … *interface* that much." Davis leaned forward. "We're too low a life form."

"What do we do about money?" It was an awkwardly pedestrian question, especially after all that had happened. But we were headed back into the real world, and I needed to know. "Do we have to get jobs?"

A wry smile edged onto Davis's face. "Already taken care of. How's five million in a joint investment account sound?"

"*Quinn,*" I said, "are you *serious?*"

"That's just seed money … Let you settle into your new life."

"I–I don't know what to say."

"A thank you will do." Davis stood. "Okay, the Guardium made this happen, so you know they'll be expecting something in return."

"Let me guess," Wren said. "Help out you and Abbott anytime you need us?"

"Among other things."

Wren slapped my arm with the back of her hand. "Welcome to being a slave, *honey.*"

"Paybacks are a bitch," Davis said.

"Yeah, but you've never been–"

I stopped Wren with a hand to her shoulder. "Tell the Guardium we're *very* grateful, Quinn."

"Also," Davis looked at Wren, "you need a last name."

"How about Harrison?" she posed.

"Slow down," I said. "Let's live together first."

"The joint bank account is in your name, Cameron and …" Davis paused for effect, "Wren *Johnson.*" He pulled out his black tablet and tapped the screen. "I'm sending both of you Wren's new backstory."

While Wren did the blank stare thing, I felt the information pour in like a lucid dream. It was the first time I had information transferred as a DE. The feeling was weird beyond words.

Wren blinked and returned.

"You okay?" I asked.

Her face screwed up with puzzlement. "What's a trust fund kid?"

52

IS THIS FOR REAL?

"Does your phone have a rideshare app?" Wren asked.

The morning cloud cover mercifully kept the Texas heat from frying us on the concrete loading dock. I swiped twice and found Uber between Candy Crush Saga and OpenTable.

"Yep," I said. "And why do I have Candy Crush?"

"You do? That should be on mine."

"You play Candy Crush?" I tapped my loft's address into the Uber app. Remembering it felt like dredging up some long-forgotten memory.

"Yeah, so?" she asked.

"I don't know, you don't seem like the kind of person who would be into that sort of game."

"What *should* I be into?"

"First-person shooter?"

"I can embrace my inner kid."

"You mean your inner kid inside your digital self inside a humungous Calaian core a hundred light-years away?"

"Something like that."

"Five minutes."

"What?"

I looked up from my phone. "Uber. Fabian will be here in five minutes in his twenty-two black Escalade."

"How far is it to your loft?" There was faint trepidation in her voice.

"I'm in Uptown, so if traffic is remotely normal, probably forty minutes. Something bothering you?"

"No, it's just ... I've never cohabitated before, either as a Calaian or a human."

"I won't lie to you, it's different. But there are pluses."

"Like crazy porn-star sex anytime we want?"

I coughed out a small laugh. "Well, yes, there *is* that. But I was talking about the less lustful benefits ... like waking up every day next to someone you love."

"Security?"

"I was thinking contentment."

Wren nodded, but I could tell something was on her mind.

"Babe, you're fidgeting," I said.

"I have this, um, *idea* I want to discuss with you."

"Please don't tell me you want your mother to come live with us."

"What? No! I never knew my mother. It has to do with your friend."

"Josh? I don't know. I think our friendship is over."

"Just hear me out. What if we–"

A black Cadillac Escalade sped into the warehouse's empty parking lot and angled to a stop at the loading dock. Its gold rims, low profile tires and ground effects running boards made it look like a secret service car if Lynx The Rapper was president. Its dark tinted driver's side window slowly lowered. A bald stocky white dude with a gold bike chain around his thick neck and Gucci wrap-around sunglasses smiled out from the dark interior. He laid a heavily tattooed slab of a forearm onto the window frame and leaned out.

"Yo, boss, you Cameron?"

"Yeah. You Fabian?"

"The one and only."

The Uber driver piled out wearing a vintage black AC/DC t-shirt, black plaid cargo shorts and ankle-high combat boots. He opened the passenger door like a seasoned pro.

Wren and I slid inside his urban assault vehicle and settled back.

"How's the traffic?" I inquired as we pulled away.

"Nasty, boss. Big wreck on thirty-five." The wiseguy look Fabian tilted over his shoulder matched his Brooklyn accent. "We'll take the tollway, if you're cool with the add-ons."

"Not a problem."

"Hey, if ya don't mind me asking, what were you two doing way out in the warehouse district … There weren't any cars in that parking lot. Kind of a strange place for a pickup, if ya know what I mean."

"We're both digital entities," I said offhandedly. "I was a human until I was stabbed with a light saber, and my friend here is from another planet. Her alien team works out of that warehouse. They have a huge spaceship that hovers just above the roof. It's about the size of the Cotton Bowl."

"Bet it messes with DFW's runway approach," Fabian said without missing a beat.

"Nah, it's just below the glide path. Besides, her commander told me that if a plane did come in too low, it wouldn't even put a scratch on it. Its hull is *alive*."

A few awkward seconds filled the Escalade.

"Sorry, man," I said into the silence, "just effing with ya."

Fabian nodded as if he picked up passengers like us all the time.

"You know," he said after a few more stilted minutes, "a few years ago I picked up a couple in Oak Lawn, real late at night. They said they were from another planet, too. Cala-something. Said they were vacationing, wearing cloned human bodies. … Can you *believe* that? Aliens, vacationing on Earth." He shook his head. "Shit, it takes all kinds in this world, eh?"

*   *   *   *

"I still think this is a messed-up idea."

Wren glanced at me. Her face-hugger looked a little big for her head, which I didn't think was even possible.

"It'll work," she said through the tentacles.

"Does Abbott know you're stealing this?"

"I'm not *stealing* it. Just borrowing it. Besides, what's he going to do … *fire* us?"

"How many of these are on his ship?"

"Fourteen. He won't even know it's gone."

"It is pretty cool. Kind of like your own personal flying – SHIT, that was too close!"

"Are you kidding? We're fifteen feet off the deck."

"*That* was the top of a semi. I thought you said you could pilot one of these."

"I can, it's just been a while."

"How long?"

"In Earth years? Twelve. This thing can fly itself."

We were skimming cloaked just above the parking lot that was north-bound Central Expressway at rush hour. The craft Wren was piloting looked like a miniature version of Abbott's old ship that Kip blew out of the sky in the French Alps. It was about the size of my uncle's old twin inboard cabin cruiser, but unlike the big Calaian ships, every maneuver it made could be felt with your whole body. Wren had graciously materialized front and side view screens so I wouldn't throw-up.

"You're going to miss the exit," I said.

"Exit?" She laughed. "We're not taking an exit. I'll angle in from the west and put us down just above street level. Now, you're sure he's home? We only have one shot at this."

"His text said he'd be there. But he's so pissed off, he might ghost me."

"He better not."

I pointed to the front view screen. "Northwest Highway is coming up. Head east."

As the craft banked into the turn, I felt the Gs in my stomach and swallowed down the urge to puke.

"There's no chance of decloaking?" I asked.

"Not unless we get struck by lightning. Given that there isn't a storm within a three-state radius, I'd say those chances are zero. Okay, we're coming up to the landing zone. Hang on, I'm taking us in steep."

Wren pitched the front end down and it felt as if its organic floor had fallen out. I wondered if my death grip would leave permanent indentations in my seat's living skin.

"There, on the right," I said. "The old single-story Tudor."

We came in hot and dodged through the dense trees. At the last second, Wren angled back to level and hovered just above two parked cars on the street. Some of the bushes lining the neighbor's driveway swayed from the craft's downwash. Wren peeled off the face-hugger and placed it on her lap. It compressed into a tiny square box that she pocketed in a side pouch of her pants.

"Ready?" she asked, running a hand through her spiky hair. The face-hugger had left an impression on her skin.

"Rub your face. That thing left a mark."

Wren rubbed with both hands.

"Better?" she asked.

"Very sexy. Okay, are we clear?"

Wren studied her tablet. "There're no home surveillance devices on this block. No drones. No city cameras. No cops or utility workers. Nothing. The neighbor to the north is old and watching TV in her bedroom, and the guy to the south is at work. The couple across the street are gone too."

"What about the house behind him?"

"For lease. It's empty."

"Any yard crews?"

"One, way down the block. Come on."

A small opening formed in the bulkhead behind us along with a ramp. We trotted down to the front yard and everything vanished behind us.

"I hope he doesn't flip out," I said as we walked across the cracked cement path to the front door.

"From what you told me, I bet he'll find this pretty cool."

We side-stepped an overgrown holly tree that partially blocked the right side of the 1950s metal-roofed patio. Just as we got close the front door opened and Josh stepped out. His eyes went to Wren, then cut to me.

"Look who finally decided to come back," he said uninvitingly.

Although it was late afternoon, he looked like he just rolled out of bed.

"Hey to you too," I said.

"Where's Toni?"

Blunt and to the point. That was Josh.

"A lot's happened since I saw you–"

Wren broke from my grip and marched up the steps.

"Hi, I'm Wren Johnson," she said sticking her hand out. "I'm a good friend of Cameron."

Josh gave it a halfhearted shake.

"Thanks for making time to see us," she said. A little too perky.

"Anything for my *best* friend."

"Oh, will you cut the crap," I said. "I lost my phone for fuck's sake. I've had a lot of shit go down."

Josh folded his arms tightly across his worn Gold's Gym t-shirt. "Me and your cat sitter were worried sick, man. We almost called in the cops."

I raised my hands in conciliation. "I know. I should have contacted you sooner."

"How about an *email*, douche?"

"Josh," Wren put a hand to his arm. He eyed her move warily. "Please understand, Cameron and I ... well, it's a long story."

"I'm off work tonight. I have plenty of time." He opened his barefooted stance. "Tell it to me."

"I think it would be better to show you."

Josh scowled. "What do you have, some kind of PowerPoint?"

Wren stepped down the cracked cement stairs and reached back for his hand. "Come on, there's something we want to show you."

Josh hesitated, then took it.

"Where are we going?" he asked as Wren led him across the front yard. He looked back. "Dude, what is she *doing?*"

"Just go with it, man," I said.

In the middle of the burned-up summer grass, Wren stopped and took out her Calaian tablet.

"Keep your eyes focused there," she said, pointing to a spot about 12 feet above the black F-150 parked in the street.

"What am I supposed to be looking–"

The craft's opening formed in mid-air. Josh's eyes nearly popped out of his head.

"Wait for it," I said.

The ramp built itself down to Josh's toes. He watched it all the way and jumped back when it reached the grass. He frantically looked from me to Wren to the opening to Wren and back to me. He yanked out of her grip and stumbled back a few steps.

"What the *fuck?*" he demanded.

I put a reassuring hand to his back. "It's cool, man, don't be scared."

Wren scrambled up the ramp and gestured for Josh to follow. "Come on. We can't stay exposed like this for long."

Josh leveled a panicked gaze at me. "Dude, is this for *real?*"

"Hopefully this will help explain why I lost touch," I said.

"No fucking *shit.*"

Wren looked like she was floating above the street standing in the craft's opening. Josh swung his astonishment to her and back to me.

"Dude, wh-where are you taking me?"

I'd never seen Josh scared, but his question dripped fear.

"Don't worry, it's just a quick trip."

"Yeah, but *where?*"

"The moon."

53

TIME WILL TELL.

Before we dropped Josh off, Wren practically beat into him the importance of never disclosing what he'd seen and done to anyone. *Anyone.* She even punctuated the point by having me compress the new F-150 parked across the street into a microscopic cube. Although Josh cheered me on – the neighbor was a supreme dick – I could tell it scared him. It wasn't so much the act of crushing the truck, but more the fact I had such power. He understood I wasn't strictly human anymore, but he definitely wasn't ready for the news I was a digital entity.

Wren and I had been "cohabitating" for more than a week, and I had the sense she genuinely enjoyed the routine of living in an urban setting. Unfortunately, this wasn't the loft construct. Dishes had to be washed, floors swept and trash taken out. In the mornings, Wren liked to run the Katy Trail, which she still felt wasn't as cool as Buna, but it was growing on her. She also fell in love with long bubble baths. The hotter the better.

"Katy Trail again?" I asked, looking up from my cereal.

"Thinking about Turtle Creek today," she said, lacing up her shoes.

Karen used to run. It always worried me because muggings, especially against women running alone, had escalated in Dallas. With Wren, however, I was more concerned for the poor schmuck who might try and roll her. He wouldn't know what hit him. Literally.

"That's a nice run, especially if you go into Highland Park," I offered.

Wren tapped her Calaian tablet and set it on the counter.

"You input into that every time you run," I said. "What are you doing?"

"Monitoring my ride's vitals." She tapped the side of her head. "Cerebrally linking."

"How far can that thing track you?"

"A thousand kilometers. Okay, babe. I'll be back in forty minutes." She gave me a peck on the cheek and playfully licked a dribble of milk from the corner of my mouth. "Yum, liquid food created by the mammary glands of Terran cows."

"It's actually almond milk."

"I'll have to try it."

"You be safe."

Wren shot the *silly human* look from the front door.

"What are you going to do?" she asked, deflecting.

"Laundry."

"Double rinse the blacks this time."

I saluted.

She blew a kiss and left.

Roz whined for more food. I shooed her into the living room. The loft fell quiet.

Halfway through the second rinse cycle a burnt smell wafted through the loft. I checked the toaster, but it was cold and there was nothing in it. To my right at the edge of the kitchen space, a translucent orange-blue vapor began to form. I leaned against the island, and just like with Winston, the Natierian continued to take a human form. I could begin to make out Toni's figure. The lingering mist dispersed, and she smiled that smile.

"Hey you." She was dressed like she had been on our first date.

I took a couple of steps but kept my distance. "What a wonderful surprise."

She looked around. "Where's Roz-Boz?"

"On her tower. How're you feeling?"

"Much better. I'm sedated. Induced coma, so I can heal faster." She gestured to herself. "The Natierians made this possible."

"One last goodbye?" I asked, then immediately regretted it.

Her smile faded. "I've made a decision." Her tone was soft but determined. "I'm going back to Cala to lead my family's House."

"Taking it away from the Nazi wannabes?"

She did the blank stare thing, probably referencing what a Nazi was. "Yes." Her voice was restrained yet defiant. She straightened her shoulders. "To restore our House's true legacy."

I thought of the Asshole Deluxe and the look he shot me before he jumped onto the counter. Had the Natierians nudged him to go to the theater? Had they factored Toni's reaction into their grand plan? Did that start the cascade effect that led to her decision to go back to Cala?

"Was that the Natierians' masterplan all along?" I asked.

"I think so. I was angry at my father and his followers. I'd grown numb to it all. That's why I left. To find myself again, my *real* self. The Natierians want Cala to change, and my leadership seemed the best path forward."

"So why all the focus on getting my tech if all they wanted was for you to take over Cala? All this death and destruction just to get you to change your mind?"

"If you look back, you'll see inflection points that triggered certain outcomes that put into motion a series of events that lead to my decision. They wanted it to be genuine and absolute."

"Is it?"

"Yes."

"But why did they appear to me when I was transferring? ... Why the deal?"

"We believe they were testing you, to see if you would allow the tech to be taken or not."

"What would that reveal?"

"What kind of human you are." Toni came closer. "Cam, you chose to give up your tech to keep the Natierians out of humanity's future evolution."

"Did they put us together?" I asked.

"Does it matter?"

I shook my head a little.

"You were the key, you know. You made me happy again, Cam … and you made me realize what I needed to be."

"And that is?"

"A leader."

"Was my death also part of the masterplan?"

Toni stepped closer and gently took my hand. "That was probably an unfortunate byproduct."

My death, I thought. *A byproduct for the masters of the universe to muse.*

Her eyes went to our hands. "You taught me what love is," she whispered.

I rubbed the tops of her knuckles. "Oh, I don't know, Toni–"

She rested her forehead against mine and I went with it. We stood there and said nothing. After a moment, she pulled back and let go. A part of me broke off inside.

"When are you going back?" I asked.

"On the next transport."

I nodded like I was cool with that, but I wasn't.

"Do you love Liaison Wren?" she asked.

"I think so. Time will tell."

"Are you happy?"

"Very."

"As much as with me?"

I felt a weak smile on my lips. "It's different."

Toni took a few steps back. The smile returned. "Goodbye, Cam."

"Goodbye, Toni."

Her form started to fade away.

"I'll reach out to you again," she said, her image almost gone.

"I look forward to that."

Toni morphed into a delicate curtain of vapor. The front door opened, and Wren walked through the last remaining particles.

"Hey, sexy!" she declared, and put her arms around my neck.

I took her around the waist. "How was your run?"

"Brutally hot." She leaned in and kissed me. Her lips tasted of sweat. "What are we doing the rest of our lives?" she whispered.

PAUL BLACK always wanted to make movies, but a career in brand design and advertising sidetracked him. Born and raised outside of Chicago, he is the international award-winning author of *The Tels, Soulware, Nexus Point, The Presence, The Samsara Effect, Cool Brain* and *Dark Slide*. His trilogy series, *The Tels*, was optioned for television. Today, he lives in Santa Fe, New Mexico, where he is creative director of Paul Black Design. In his off hours he feeds his passion for tennis and dreams of seven-figure movie deals.

I would like to thank my writer's group for their assistance, inspiration and patience: Lisa Glasgow, Brian Moreland, Pat O'Connell, and Bridget Boland. You all were there for me when I needed you.

For future trends in technology: www.socialtechnologies.com and its wealth of future forecasts and models of global trends. To NASA News and the Langley Research Center website for its white papers on the future of technology.

Special thanks to my editor, Jay Johnson, who ediited this book through a turbulent time in his life, but still gave me his very best.

And to Trish, as always, with love.

Santa Fe - October, 2023

THE WORLD IS NOT WHAT IT SEEMS For Jonathan Kortel, his life has changed forever. He has a telekinetic gift that is faster than light, and he's now part of a secret new group of humans. They're called the Tels, and they live in the shadows of a future where the Biolution and its flood of technology have changed all the rules.

Having been thrust into a world he cannot control, Jonathan begins a quest to uncover what's really going on in the Tel world. Because he soon realizes that he's not only their star pupil; he's their most important experiment.

Here continues the journey of Jonathan Kortel, picking up where *The Tels* left off, following Jonathan as he discovers his true destiny. Deeply intriguing and powerfully suspenseful, Paul Black has created a vision of the future that is haunting and disturbingly real.

NOVEL INSTINCTS
www.paulblackbooks.com

Available at all online retailers including **Amazon.com** and **BN.com**.

DESTINY AWAITS Jonathan Kortel is the most powerful telekinetic ever. There are others like him, and they're called the Tels. Able to manipulate gravity, they exist out at the edge of the next century, where the Biolution and its wave of new technology have changed life forever.

Blamed for the deaths of the Tel leadership, Jonathan escapes to a life of anonymity. But there's something strange happening in space that threatens all life on earth, and only Jonathan Kortel has the ability to stop it.

Here ends the Tels trilogy, author Paul Black's fascinating near-future series, introduced in his award-winning 2003 novel *The Tels*. Nexus Point continues where *The Tels* and *Soulware* (2005) left off, following the saga of Jonathan Kortel as he fulfills his prophetic destiny.

NOVEL INSTINCTS
www.paulblackbooks.com

DEEP IN THE BASEMENT of the University of Chicago Biological Sciences Building, Dr. William Kanter is on the brink of developing a technology that will replace the MRI. Yet the images captured aren't of his brain, they're his memories. And they only take up only a small portion at the end of the scan. What Kanter discovers throughout the rest of the scan could rock the very foundation of humanity.

Across campus, child psychologist Dr. Trenna Anderson is reviewing a disturbing home video of a young Wisconsin farm boy who suffers from night terrors. After witnessing the boy become a Nazi prison guard, L.A. crack whore and Inuit native, Anderson suspects the eight-year-old may have multiple personality disorder. But when conventional psychotherapy fails, Anderson reluctantly meets with a maverick inventor named Kanter who's rumored to have created a revolutionary machine that might be the boy's only hope.

Kanter thinks his invention will help mankind, but there are forces at work that want to destroy a machine that threatens to expose the world's most precious beliefs. Soon Kanter and Anderson find themselves embroiled in a deadly and dangerous world of government espionage, corporate greed and religious fundamentalism. Is Kanter's invention capable of changing the world? And if so, at what cost?

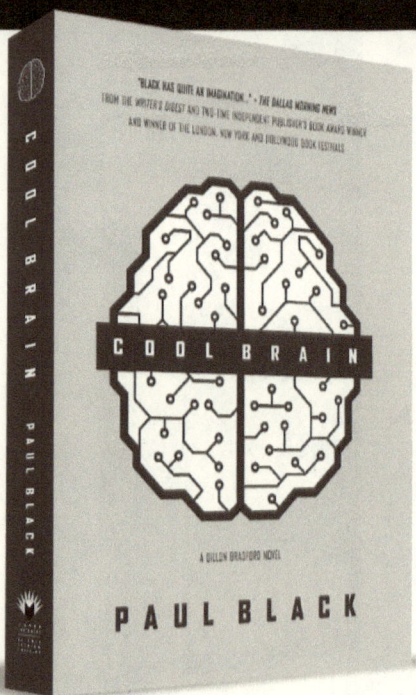

www.ingramcontent.com/pod-product-compliance
Lightning Source LLC
Chambersburg PA
CBHW031026030726
47497CB00004B/1031